1492

Admiral of the Ocean-Sea

MARY JOHNSTON
Edited by Paul Dennis Sporer

1492

Admiral of the Ocean-Sea

HAMBLEDON HILL PRESS

Anza Publishing, Chester, NY 10918
Hambledon Hill Press is an imprint of Anza Publishing

This work is a new, unabridged edition of *Admiral of the Ocean-Sea,* by Mary Johnston, originally published in 1923.

Library of Congress Cataloging-in-Publication Data
Johnston, Mary, 1870-1936.
1492 : Admiral of the Ocean-Sea / Mary Johnston;
editor, Paul Dennis Sporer.
p. cm.
ISBN 1–932490–16–7 (softcover : alk. paper)
1. Columbus, Christopher—Fiction.
2. America—Discovery and exploration—Fiction.
3. Jewish sailors—Fiction.
4. Explorers—Fiction.
5. Admirals—Fiction.
I. Title: Fourteen hundred ninety-two.
II. Sporer, Paul D.
III. Title.
PS2141.A15 2004
813'.52—dc22 2004015090

ISBN 1–932490–16–7 (hardcover)

∞ This book is printed on acid-free paper.

CHAPTER I

The morning was gray, and I sat by the sea near Palos in a gray mood. I was Jayme de Marchena, and that was indeed a good, *old Christian* name. But my grandmother was a Jewess, and in corners they said that she never truly recanted, and I had been much with her as a child. She was dead, but still they talked of her. Jayme de Marchena, looking back from the hillside of forty-six, saw some service done for the Queen and the folk. This thing and that thing. Not demanding trumpets, but serviceable. It would be neither counted nor weighed beside and against that which Don Pedro and the Dominican found to say. What they found to say they made, not found. They took clay of misrepresentation, and in the field of falsehood sat them down, and consulting the parchment of malice, proceeded to create. But false as was all they set up, the time would cry it true.

It was reasonable that I should find the day gray.

Study and study and study, year on year, and at last image a great thing, just under the rim of the mind's ocean, sending up for those who will look streamers above horizon, streamers of colored and wonderful light! Study and reason and with awe and delight take light from above. Dream of good news for one and all, of life given depth and brought into music, dream of giving the given, never holding it back, which would be avarice and betraying! Write, and give men and women to read what you have written, and believe—poor Deluded!—that they also feel inner warmth and light and rejoice.

Oh, gray the sea and gray the shore! But some did feel it.

The Dominican, when it fell into his hands, called it perdition. A Jewess for a grandmother, and Don Pedro for enemy. And now the Dominican—the Dominicans!

2
1492: ADMIRAL OF THE OCEAN-SEA

The Queen and the King made edict against the Jews, and there sat the Inquisition.

I was—I am—Christian. It is a wide and deep and high word. When you ask, “What is it—Christian?” then must each of us answer as it is given to him to answer. I and thou—and the True, the Universal Christ give us light!

Today all Andalusia, all Castile and all Spain to me seemed gray, and gray the utter Ocean that stretched no man knew where. The gray was the gray of fetters and of ashes.

The tide made, and as the waves came nearer, eating the sand before me, they uttered a low crying. *In danger—danger—in danger, Jayme de Marchena!*

I had been in danger before. Who is not often and always in danger, in life? But this was a danger to daunt.

Mine were no powerful friends. I had only that which was within me. I was only son of only son, and my parents and grandparents were dead, and my distant kindred cold, seeing naught of good in so much study and thinking of that old, dark, beautiful, questionable one, my grandmother. I had indeed a remote kinsman, head of a convent in this neighborhood, and he was a wise man and a kindly. But not he either could do aught here!

All the Jews to be banished, and Don Pedro with a steady forefinger, “That man—take him, too! Who does not know that his grandmother was Jewess, and that he lived with her and drank poison?” But the Dominican, “No! The Holy Office will take him. You have but to read—only you must not read—what he has written to see why!”

Gray Ocean, stretching endlessly and now coming close, were it not well if I drowned myself this gray morning while I can choose the death I shall die? Now the great murmur sang *Well*, and now it sang Not well.

Low cliff and heaped sand and a solitary bird wide-winging toward the mountains of Portugal, and the Ocean gray-blue and salt! The salt savor entered me, and an inner zest came forward and said No, to being craven. In banishment certainly, in the House of the Inquisition more doubtfully, the immortal man might yet find market from which to buy! If the mind could surmount, the eternal quest need not be interrupted—even there!

Blue Ocean sang to me.

A vision—it came to me at times, vision—set itself in air. I saw A People who persecuted neither Jew nor thinker. It rose one Figure, formed of an infinite number of small figures, but all their edges met in one glow. The figure stood upon the sea and held apart the clouds, and was free and fair and mighty, and was man and woman melted together, and it took all colors and made of them a sun for its brow. I did not know when it would live, but I knew that it should live. Perhaps it was the whole world.

It vanished, leaving sky and ocean and Andalusia. But great visions leave great peace. After it, for this day, it seemed not worth while to grieve and miserably to forebode. Through the hours that I lay there by the sea, airs from that land or that earth blew about me and faint songs visited my ears, and the gray day was only gray like a dove's breast.

Jayme de Marchena stayed by the lonely sea because that seemed the safest place to stay. At hand was the small port of Palos that might not know what was breeding in Seville, and going thither at nightfall I found lodging and supper in a still corner where all night I heard the Tinto flowing by.

I had wandered to Palos because of the Franciscan convent of Santa Maria de la Rabida and my very distant kinsman, Fray Juan Perez. The day after the gray day by the shore I walked half a league of sandy road and came to convent gate. The porter let me in, and I waited in a little court with doves about me and a swinging bell above until the brother whom he had called returned and took me to Prior's room. At first Fray Juan Perez was stiff and cold, but by little this changed and he became a good man, large-minded and with a sense for kindred. Clearly he thought that I should not have had a Jewish grandmother, nor have lived with her from my third to my tenth birthday, and most clearly that I should not have written that which I had written. But his God was an energetic, enterprising, kindly Prince, rather bold himself and tolerant of heathen. Fray Juan Perez even intimated a doubt if God wanted the Inquisition. "But that's going rather far!" he said hastily and sat drumming the table and pursing his lips. Presently he brought out, "But you know I can't do anything!"

I did know it. What could he do? I suppose I had had a half-hope of something. I knew not what. Without a hope I would not have come to La Rabida. But it was maimed from the first, and now it died. I made a gesture of relinquishment. "No, I suppose you cannot—"

He said after a moment that he was glad to see that I had let my beard grow and was very plainly dressed, though I had never been elaborate there, and especially was he glad that I was come to Palos not as Jayme de Marchena, but under a plain and simple name, Juan Lepe, to wit. His advice was to flee from the wrath to come. He would not say flee from the Holy Office—that would be heinous!—but he would say absent myself, abscond, be banished, Jayme de Marchena by Jayme de Marchena. There were barques in Palos and rude seamen who asked no question when gold just enough, and never more than enough, was shown. He hesitated a moment and then asked if I had funds. If not—

I thanked him and said that I had made provision.

"Then," said he, "go to Barbary, Don Jayme! An intelligent and prudent man may prosper at Ercilla or at Fez. If you must study, study there."

"You also study," I said.

"In fair trodden highways—never in thick forest and mere fog!" he answered. "Now if you were like one who has been here and is now before Granada, at Santa Fé, sent for thither by the Queen! That one hath indeed studied to benefit Spain—Spain, Christendom, and the world!"

I asked who was that great one, but before he could tell me came interruption. A visitor entered, a strong-lipped, bold-eyed man named Martin Pinzon. I was to meet him again and often, but at this time I did not know that. Fray Juan Perez evidently desiring that I should go, I thought it right to oblige him who would have done me kindness had he known how. I went without intimate word of parting and after only a casual stare from Martin Pinzon.

But without, my kinsman came after me. "I want to say, Don

Jayme, that if I am asked for testimony I shall hold to it that you are as good Christian as any—"

It was kinsman's part and all that truly I could have hoped for, and I told him so. About us was quiet, vacant cloister, and we parted more warmly than we had done within.

The white convent of La Rabida is set on a headland among vineyards and pine trees. It regards the ocean and, afar, the mountains of Portugal, and below it runs a small river, going out to sea through sands with the Tinto and the Odiel. Again the day was gray and the pine trees sighing. The porter let me out at gate.

I walked back toward Palos through the sandy ways. I did not wish to go to Africa.

It is my belief that that larger Self whom they will call protecting Saint or heavenly Guardian takes hand in affairs oftener than we think! Leaving the Palos road, I went to the sea as I had done yesterday and again sat under heaped sand with about me a sere grass through which the wind whined. At first it whined and then it sang in a thin, outlandish voice. Sitting thus, I might have looked toward Africa, but I knew now that I was not going to Africa. Often, perhaps, in the unremembered past I had been in Africa; often, doubtless, in ages to come its soil would be under my foot, but now I was not going there! Today I looked westward over River-Ocean, unknown to our fathers and unknown to ourselves. It was unknown as the future of the world.

Ocean piled before me. From where I lay it seemed to run uphill to one pale line, nor blue nor white, set beneath the solid gray. Over that hilltop, what? Only other hills and plains, water, endlessly water, until the waves, so much mightier than waves of that blue sea we knew best, should beat at last against Asia shore! So high, so deep, so vast, so real, yet so empty-seeming save for strange dangers! No sails over the hilltop; no sails in all that Vast save close at hand where mariners held to the skirts of Mother Europe. Ocean vast, Ocean black, Ocean unknown. Yet there, too, life and the knowing of life ran somehow continuous.

It wiled me from my smaller self. How had we all suffered, we the whole earth! But we were moving, we the world with none left out, moving toward That which held worlds, which was conscious above worlds. Long the journey, long the adventure, but it was not worth while fearing, it was not worth while whining! I was not alone Jayme de Marchena, nor Juan Lepe, nor this name nor that nor the other.

There was now a great space of quiet in my mind. Suddenly formed there the face and figure of Don Enrique de Cerda whose life I had had the good hap to save. He was far away with the Queen and King who beleaguered Granada. I had not seen him for ten years. A moment before he had rested among the host of figures in the unevenly lighted land of memory. Now he stood forth plainly and seemed to smile.

I took the leading. With the inner eye I have seen lines of light like subtle shining cords running between persons. Such a thread stretched now between me and Enrique de Cerda. I determined to make my way, as Juan Lepe, through the mountains and over the plain of Granada to Santa Fé.

CHAPTER II

I did not start for Granada from Palos but from Huelva, and I quitted Andalusia as a porter in a small merchant train carrying goods of sorts to Zarafa, that was a mountain town taken from the Moors five years back. I was to these folk Juan Lepe, a strong, middle-aged man used to ships but now for some reason tired of them. My merchants had only eyes for the safety of their persons and their bales, plunged the third day into mountainous wild country echoing and ghastly with long-lasting war. Their servants and muleteers walked and rode, lamented or were gay, raised faction, swore, laughed, traveled grimly or in a dull melancholy or mirthfully; quarreled and made peace, turn by turn, day by day, much alike.

One who was a bully fixed a quarrel upon me and another took my part. All leaped to sides. I was forgotten in the midst of them; they could hardly have told now what was the cause of battle. A young merchant rode back to chide and settle matters. At last someone remembered that Diego had struck Juan Lepe who had flung him off. Then Tomaso had sprung in and struck Diego. Then Miguel—"Let Juan Lepe alone!" said my merchant. "Fie! a poor Palos seafaring child, and you great Huelva men!" They laughed at that, and the storm vanished as it had come.

I liked the young man.

How wild and without law, save "Hold if you can!" were these mountains! "Hold if you can to life—hold if you can to knowledge—hold if you can to joy!" Black cliff overhung black glen and we knew there were dens of robbers. Far and near violence falls like black snow. This merchant band gathered to sleep under oaks with a great rock at our back. We had journeyers' supper and fire, for it was cold,

cold in these heights. A little wine was given and men fell to sleep by the heaped bales; horses, asses and mules being fastened close under the crag. Three men watched, to be relieved in middle night by other three who now slept. A muleteer named Rodrigo and Juan Lepe and the young merchant took the first turn. The first two sat on one side of the fire and the young merchant on the other.

The muleteer remained sunken in a great cloak, his chin on his arms folded upon his knees, and what he saw in the land within I cannot tell. But the young merchant was of a quick disposition and presently must talk. For some distance around us spread bare earth set only with shrubs and stones. Also the rising moon gave light, and with that and our own strength we did not truly look for any attack. We sat and talked at ease, though with lowered voices, Rodrigo somewhere away and the rest of the picture sleeping. The merchant asked what had been my last voyage.

I answered, after a moment, to England.

"You do not seem to me," he said, "a seaman. But I suppose there are all kinds of seamen."

I said yes, the sea was wide.

"England now, at the present moment?" he said, and questioned me as to Bristol, of which port he had trader's knowledge. I answered out of a book I had read. It was true that, living once by the sea, I knew how to handle a boat. I could find in memory sailors' terms. But still he said, "You are not a seaman such as we see at Palos and San Lucar."

It is often best not to halt denial. Let it pass by and wander among the wild grasses!

"I myself," he said presently, "have gone by sea to Vigo and to Bordeaux." He warmed his hands at the fire, then clasped them about his knees and gazed into the night. "What, Juan Lepe, is that Ocean we look upon when we look west? I mean, where does it go? What does it strike?"

"India, belike. And Cathay. Today all men believe the earth to be round."

"A long way!" he said. "O Sancta Maria! All that water!"

"We do not have to drink it."

He laughed. "No! Nor sail it. But after I had been on that voyage I could see us always like mice running close to a wall, forever and forever! Juan Lepe, we are little and timid!"

I liked his spirit. "One day we shall be lions and eagles and bold prophets! Then our tongue shall taste much beside India and Cathay!"

"Well, I hope it," he said. "Mice running under the headlands."

He fell silent, cherishing his knees and staring into the fire. It was not Juan Lepe's place to talk when master merchant talked not. I, too, regarded the fire, and the herded mountains robed in night, and the half-moon like a sail rising from an invisible boat.

The night went peacefully by. It was followed by a hard day's travel and the incident of the road. At evening we saw the walls of Zarafa in a sunset glory. The merchants and their train passed through the gate and found their customary inn. With others, Juan Lepe worked hard, unlading and storing. All done, he and the bully slept almost in each other's arms, under the arches of the court, dreamlessly.

The next day and the next were still days of labor. It was not until the third that Juan Lepe considered that he might now absent himself and there be raised no hue and cry after strong shoulders. He had earned his quittance, and in the nighttime, upon his hands and knees, he crept from the sleepers in the court. Just before dawn the inn gate swung open. He had been waiting close to it, and he passed out noiselessly.

In the two days, carrying goods through streets to market square and up to citadel and pausing at varying levels for breath and the prospect, I had learned this town well enough. I knew where went the ascending and descending ways. Now almost all lay asleep, antique, shaded, Moorish, still, under the stars. The soldiery and the hidalgos, their officers, slept; only the sentinels waked before the citadel entry and on the town walls and by the three gates. The town folk slept, all but the sick and the sorrowful and the careful and those who had work at dawn. Listen, and you might hear sound like the first moving of birds, or breath of dawn wind coming up at sea. The greater part now of the town folk were Christian, brought in since the five-year-gone siege that still resounded. Moors were here, but they had turned Christian, or were slaves, or both slave and Christian. I had seen monks of all habits and heard ring above the inn the bells of a nunnery. Now again they rang. The mosque was now a church. It rose at hand,—white, square, domed. I went by a ladder-like lane down toward Zarafa wall and the Gate of the Lion. At sunrise in would pour peasants from the vale below, bringing vegetables and poultry, and mountaineers with quails and conies, and others with divers affairs. Outgoing would be those who tilled a few steep gardens beyond the wall, messengers and errand folk, soldiers and traders for the army before Granada.

It was full early when I came to the wall. I could make out the heavy and tall archway of the gate, but as yet was no throng before it. I waited; the folk began to gather, the sun came up. Zarafa grew rosy. Now was clatter enough, voices of men and brutes, both sides the gate. The gate opened. Juan Lepe won out with a knot of brawny folk going to the mountain pastures. Well forth, he looked back and saw Zarafa gleaming rose and pearl in the blink of the sun, and sent young merchantward a wish for good. Then he took the eastward way down the mountain, toward lower mountains and at last the Vega of Granada.

CHAPTER III

The day passed. I had adventures of the road, but none of consequence. I slept well among the rocks, waked, ate the bit of bread I had with me, and fell again to walking.

Mountains were now withdrawing to the distant horizon where they stood around, a mighty and beautiful wall. I was coming down into the plain of Granada, that once had been a garden. Now, north, south, east, west, it lay war-trampled. Old owners were dead, men and women, or were *mudexares*, vassals, or were fled, men and women, all who could flee, to their kindred in Africa. Or they yet cowered, men and women, in the broken garden, awaiting individual disaster. The Kingdom of Granada had sins, and the Kingdom of Castile, and the Kingdom of Leon. The Moor was stained, and the Spaniard, the Moslem and the Christian and the Jew. Who had stains the least or the most God knew—and it was a poor inquiry. Seek the virtues and bind them with love, each in each!

If the mountain road had been largely solitary, it was not so of this road. There were folk enough in the wide Vega of Granada. Clearly, as though the one party had been dressed in black and the other in red, they divided into vanquished and victor. Bit by bit, now through years, all these towns and villages, all these fertile fields and bosky places, rich and singing, had left the hand of the Moor for the hand of the Spaniard.

In all this part of his old kingdom the Moor lay low in defeat. In had swarmed the Christian and with the Christian the Jew, though now the Jew must leave. The city of Granada was not yet surrendered, and the Queen and King held all soldiery that they might at Santa Fé, built as it were in a night before Granada walls. Yet there seemed large bands enough, licentious and loud, the scum of soldiery. Before I reached the village that I now saw before me I had met two such bands, I wondered, and then wondered at my own wonder.

The chief house of the village was become an inn. Two long tables stood in the patio where no fountain now flowed nor orange trees grew nor birds sang in corners nor fine awning kept away the glare. Twenty of these wild and base fighting men crowded one table, eating and drinking, clamorous and spouting oaths. At the other table sat together at an end three men whom by a number of tokens might be robbers of the mountains. They sat quiet, indifferent to the noise, talking low among themselves in a tongue of their own, kin enough to the soldiery not to fear them. The opposite end of the long table was given to a group to which I now joined myself. Here sat two Franciscan friars, and a man who seemed a lawyer; and one who had the air of the sea and turned out to be master of a Levantine; and a brisk, talkative, important person, a Catalan, and as it presently appeared alcalde once of a so-so village; and a young, unhealthy-looking man in black with an open book beside him; and a strange fellow whose Spanish was imperfect.

I sat down near the friars, crossed myself, and cut a piece of bread from the loaf before me. The innkeeper and his wife, a gaunt, extraordinarily tall woman, served, running from table to table. The place was all heat and noise. Presently the soldiers, ending their meal, got up with clamor and surged from the court to their waiting horses. After them ran the innkeeper, appealing for pay. Denials, expostulation, anger and beseeching reached the ears of the patio, then the sound of horses going down stony ways. "O God of the poor!" cried the gaunt woman. "How are we robbed!"

"Why are they not before Granada?" demanded the lawyer and alertly provided the answer to his own question. "Take locusts and give them leave to eat, being careful to say, 'This fellow's fields only!' But the locusts have wings and their nature is to eat!"

The mountain robbers, if robbers they were, dined quietly, the gaunt woman promptly and painstakingly serving them. They were going to pay, I was sure, though it might not be this noon.

The two friars seemed, quiet, simple men, dining as dumbly as if they sat in Saint Francis's refectory. The sometime alcalde and the shipmaster were the talkers, the student sitting as though he were in the desert, eating bread and cheese and onions and looking on his book. The lawyer watched all, talked to make them talk, then came in and settled matters. The alcalde was the politician, knowing the affairs of the world and speaking familiarly of the King and the Queen and the Marquis of Cadiz.

The shipmaster said, "This time last year I was in London, and I saw their King. His name is Henry. King Henry the Seventh, and a good carrier of his kingship!"

"That for him!" said the alcalde. "Let him stay in his foggy island! But Spain is too small for King Ferdinand."

"All kings find their lands too small," said the lawyer.

The shipmaster spoke again. "The King of Portugal's ship sails ahead of ours in that matter. He's stuck his banner in the new islands, Maderia and the Hawk Islands and where not! I was talking in Cadiz with one who was with Bartholomew Diaz when he turned Africa and named it Good Hope. Which is to say, King John has Good Hope of seeing Portugal swell. Portugal! Well, I say, 'Why not Spain'?"

The student looked up from his book. "It is a great Age!" he said and returned to his reading.

When we had finished dinner, we paid the tall, gaunt woman and leaving the robbers, if robbers they were, still at table, went out into the street. Here the friars, the alcalde and the lawyer moved in the direction of the small, staring white and ruined mosque that was to be transformed into the church of San Jago the Deliverer. That was the one thing of which the friars had spoken. A long bench ran by inn wall and here the shipmaster took his seat and began to discourse with those already there. Book under arm, the student moved dreamily down the opposite lane. Juan Lepe walked away alone.

Through the remainder of this day he had now company and adventure without, now solitude and adventure within. That night he spent in a ruined tower where young trees grew and an owl was his comrade and he read the face of a glorious moon. Dawn. He bathed in a stream that ran by the mound of the tower and ate a piece of bread from his wallet and took the road.

The sun mounted above the trees. A man upon a mule came up behind me and was passing. "There is a stone wedged in his shoe," I said. The rider drew rein and I lifted the creature's foreleg and took out the pebble. The rider made search for a bit of money. I said that the deed was short and easy and needed no payment, whereupon he put up the coin and regarded me out of his fine blue eyes. He was quite fair, a young man still, and dressed after a manner of his own in garments not at all new but with a beauty of fashioning and putting on. He and his mule looked a corner out of a great painting. And I had no sooner thought that than he said, "I see in you, friend, a face and figure for my 'Draught of Fishes.' And by Saint Christopher, there is water over yonder and just the landscape!" He leaned from the saddle and spoke persuasively, "Come from the road a bit down to the water and let me draw you! You are not dressed like the kin of Midas! I will give you the price of dinner." As he talked he drew out of a richly worked bag a book of paper and pencils. I thought, "This beard and the clothes of Juan Lepe. He can hardly make it so that any may recognize." It was resting time and the man attracted. I agreed, if he would take no more than an hour.

"The drawing, no!—Bent far over, gathering the net strongly—Andrew or Mark perhaps, since, traditionally, John must have youth."

He had continued to study me all this time, and now we left the road and moved over the plain to the stream that here widened into a pool fringed with rushes and a few twisted trees. An ancient, half-sunken boat drowsing under the bank he hailed again in the name of Saint Christopher. Dismounting, he fastened his mule to a willow and proceeded to place me, then himself found a root of a tree, and taking out his knife fell to sharpening pencil. This done, he rested book against knee and began to draw.

Having made his figure in one posture he rose and showed me another and drew his fisherman so. Then he demonstrated a third way and drew again. Now he was silent, working hard, and now he dropped his hand, threw back his head and talked. He himself made a picture, paly gold of locks, subtle and quick of face, plastered against a blue shield with a willow wreath going around.

I stood so or so, drawing hard upon the net with the fishes. Then at his command I approached more nearly, and he drew full face and three-quarter and profile. It was between these accomplishings that he talked more intimately.

"Seamen go to Italy," he said. "Were you ever in Milan? But that is inland."

I answered that I had been from Genoa to Milan.

"It is not likely that you saw a great painter there Messer Leonardo?"

It happened that I had done this, and moreover had seen him at work and heard him put right thought into most right words. I was so tired of lying that after a moment I said that I had seen and heard Messer Leonardo.

"Did you see the statue?"

"The first time I saw him he was at work upon it. The next time he was painting in the church of *Santa Maria*. The third time he sat in a garden, sipped wine and talked."

"I hold you," he said, "to be a fortunate fisherman! Just as this fisher I am painting, and whether it is Andrew or Mark, I do not yet know, was a most fortunate fisherman!" He ended meditatively, "Though whoever it is, probably he was crucified or beheaded or burned."

I felt a certain shiver of premonition. The day that had been warm and bright turned in a flash ashy and chill. Then it swung back to its first fair seeming, or not to its first, but to a deeper, brighter yet. The Fisherman by Galilee was fortunate. Whoever perceived truth and beauty was fortunate, fortunate now and forever!

We came back to Messer Leonardo. "I spent six months at the court in Milan," said the fair man. "I painted the Duke and the Duchess and two great courtiers. Messer Leonardo was away. He returned, and I visited him and found a master. Since that time I study light and shadow and small things and seek out inner action."

He worked in silence, then again began to speak of painters, Italian and Spanish. He asked me if I had seen such and such pictures in Seville.

"Yes. They are good."

"Do you know Monsalvat?"

I said that I had climbed there one day. "I dream a painting!" he said, "The Quest of the Grail. Now I see it running over the four walls of a church, and now I see it all packed into one man who rides. Then again it has seemed to me truer to have it in a man and woman who walk, or perhaps even are seated. What do you think?"

I was thinking of Isabel who died in my arms twenty years ago. "I would have it man and woman," I said. Unless, like Messer Leonardo, you can put both in one."

He sat still, his mind working, while in a fair inner land Isabel and I moved together; then in a meditative quiet he finished his drawing. He himself was admirable, fine gold and bronze, sapphire-eyed, with a face where streams of visions moved the muscles, and all against the blue and the willow tree.

At last he put away pencil, and at his gesture I came from the boat and the reeds. I looked at what he had drawn, and then he shut book and, the mule following us, we moved back to the road.

"My dear fisherman," he said, "you are trudging afoot and your dress exhibits poverty. Painters may paint Jove descending in showers of golden pesos and yet have few pesos in purse. I have at present ten. I should like to share them with you who have done me various good turns today."

I said that he was generous but that he had done me good turns. Moreover I was not utterly without coin, and certainly the hour had paid for itself. So he mounted his mule and wished me good fortune, and I wished him good fortune.

"Are you going to Santa Fé?"

"Yes. I have a friend in the camp."

"I go there to paint her Highness the Queen for his Highness the King. Perhaps we shall meet again. I am Manuel Rodriguez."

"I guessed that," I answered, "an hour ago! Be so good, great painter, as not to remember me. It will serve me better."

The light played again over his face. "*The Disguised Hidalgo*. Excellent pictures come to me like that, in a great warm light, and excellent names for pictures. Very good. In a way, so to speak, I shall completely forget you!"

Two on horseback, a churchman and a knight, with servants

following, came around a bend of the dusty road and recognizing Manuel Rodriguez, called to him by name. Away he rode upon his mule, keeping company with them. The dozen in their train followed, raising as they went by such a dust cloud that presently all became like figures upon worn arras. They rode toward Santa Fé, and I followed on foot.

CHAPTER IV

Santa Fé rose before me, a camp in wood, plaster and stone, a camp with a palace, a camp with churches. Built of a piece where no town had stood, built that Majesty and its Court and its Army might have roofs and walls, not tents, for so long a siege, it covered the plain, a city raised in a night. The siege had been long as the war had been long. Hidalgo Spain and simple Spain were gathered here in great squares and ribbons of valor, ambition, emulation, desire of excitement and of livelihood, and likewise, I say it, in pieces not small, herded and brought here without any "I say yes" of their own, and to their misery. There held full flavor of crusade, as all along the war had been preached as a crusade.

Holy Church had here her own grandees, cavaliers and footmen. They wore cope and they wore cowl, and on occasion many endued themselves with armor and hacked and hewed with an earthly sword. At times there seemed as many friars and priests as soldiers. Out and in went a great Queen and King. Their court was here. The churchmen pressed around the Queen. Famous leaders put on or took off armor in Santa Fé,—the Marquis of Cadiz and many others only less than he in estimation, and one Don Gonsalvo de Cordova, whose greater fame was yet to come. Military and shining youth came to train and fight under these. Old captains-at-arms, gaunt and scarred, made their way thither from afar. All were not Spaniard; many a soldier out at fortune or wishful of fame came from France and Italy, even from England and Germany. Women were in Santa Fé. The Queen had her ladies. Wives, sisters and daughters of hidalgos came to visit, and the common soldiery had their mates. Nor did there lack courtesans.

Petty merchants thronged the place. All manner of rich goods were bought by the flushed soldiers, the high and the low. And there dwelled here a host of those who sold entertainment,—mummers and jugglers and singers, dwarfs and giants. Dice rattled, now there were castanets and dancing, and now church bells seemed to rock the place. Wine flowed.

Out of the plain a league and more away sprang the two hills of Granada, and pricked against the sky, her walls and thousand towers and noble gates. Between them and Santa Fé stretched open and ruined ground, and here for many a day had shocked together the Spaniard and the Moor. But now there was no longer battle. Granada had asked and been granted seventy days in which to envisage and accept her fate. These were nearing the end. Lost and beaten, haggard with woe and hunger and pestilence, the city stood over against us, above the naked plain, all her outer gardens stripped away, bare light striking the red Alhambra and the Citadel. When the wind swept over her and on to Santa Fé it seemed to bring a sound of wailing and the faint and terrible odor of a long besieged place.

I came at eve into Santa Fé, found at last an inn of the poorer sort, ate scant supper and went to bed. Dawn came with a great ringing of church bells.

Out of the inn, in the throbbing street, I began my search for Don Enrique de Cerda. One told me one thing and one another, but at last I got true direction. At noon I found him in a goodly room where he made recovery from wounds. Now he walked and now he sat, his arm in a sling and a bandage like a turban around his head. A page took him the word I gave. "Juan Lepe. From the hermitage in the oak wood." It sufficed. When I entered he gazed, then coming to me, put his unbound hand over mine. "Why," he asked, " 'Juan Lepe'?"

I glanced toward the page and he dismissed him, whereupon I explained the circumstances.

We sat by the window, and again rose for us the hermitage in the oak wood at foot of a mountain, and the small tower that slew in ugly fashion. Again we were young men, together in strange dangers, learning there each other's mettle. He had not at all forgotten.

He offered to go to Seville, as soon as Granada should fall, and find and fight Don Pedro. I shook my head. I could have done that had I seen it as the way.

He agreed that Don Pedro was now the minor peril. It is evil to chain thought! In our day we think boldly of a number of things. But touch King or touch Church—the cord is around your neck!

I said that I supposed I had been rash.

He nodded. "Yes. You were rash that day in the oak wood. Less rash, and my bones would be lying there, under tree." He rose and walked the room, then came to me and put his unhurt arm about my shoulders. "Don Jayme, we swore that day comrade love and service—and that day is now; twilight has never come to it, the leaves of the oak wood have never fallen! The Holy Office shall not have thee!"

"Don Enrique—"

We sat down and drank each a little wine, and fell to ways and means.

I rested Juan Lepe in the household of Don Enrique de Cerda, one figure among many, involved in the swarm of fighting and serving men. There was a squire who had served him long. To this man, Diego Lopez, I was committed, with enough told to enlist his intelligence. He managed for me in the intricate life of the place with a skill to make god Mercury applaud. Don Enrique and I were rarely together, rarely were seen by men to speak one to the other. But in the inner world we were together.

Days passed. We found nothing yet to do while all listening and doing at Santa Fé were bound up in the crumbling of Granada into Spanish hands. It seemed best to wait, watching chances.

Meantime the show glittered, and man's strong stomach cried "Life! More life!" It glittered at Santa Fé before Granada, and it was a dying ember in Granada before Santa Fé. The one glittered and triumphed because the other glittered and triumphed not. And who above held the balances even and neither sorrowed nor was feverishly elated but went his own way could only be seen from the Vega like a dream or a line from a poet.

For the most part the nobles and cavaliers in Santa Fé spent as though hard gold were spiritual gold to be gathered endlessly. One might say, "They go into a garden and shake tree each morning, which tree puts forth again in the night." None seemed to see as on a map laid down Spain and the broken peasant and the digger of the gold. None seemed to feel that toil which or soon or late they must recognize for their own toil. Toil in Spain, toil in other and far lands whence came their rich things, toil in Europe, Arabia and India! Apparel at Santa Fé was a thing to marvel at. The steed no less than his rider went gorgeous. The King and Queen, it was said, did not like this peacocking, but might not help it.

They themselves were pouring gold into the lap of the Church. It was a capacious lap.

Wars were general enough, God knew! But not every year could one find a camp where the friar was as common as the archer or the pikeman, and the prelate as the plumed chieftain.

Santa Fé was court no less than camp, court almost as though it were Cordova. This Queen and King at least did not live at ease in palaces while others fought their wars. North, south, east and west, through the ten years, they had been the moving springs. It was an able King and Queen, a politic King and a sincere and godly Queen, even a loving Queen. If only—if only—

I had been a week and more in Santa Fé when King Boabdil surrendered Granada. He left forever the Alhambra. Granada gates opened; he rode out with a few of his emirs and servants to meet King Ferdinand and Queen Isabella. The day shone bright. Spain towered, a figure dressed in gold and red.

Santa Fé poured out to view the spectacle, and with the rest went Diego Lopez and Juan Lepe. So great festival, so vivid the color, so echoing the sound, so stately and various the movement! Looking at the great strength massing there on the plain I said aloud, as I thought, to Diego Lopez, "Now they might do some worthy great thing!"

The squire not answering, I became aware that a swirl in the throng had pushed him from me. Still there came an answer in a deep and peculiarly thrilling voice. "That is a true saying and a good augury!"

I learn much by voices and before I turned I knew that this was an enthusiast's voice, but not an enthusiast without knowledge.

Whoever spoke was strong enough, real enough. I liked the voice and felt a certain inner movement of friendship. Some shift among the great actors, some parting of banners, kept us suspended and staring for a moment, then the view closed against us who could only behold by snatches. Freed, I turned to see who had spoken and found a tall, strongly made, white-haired man. The silver hair was too soon; he could hardly have been ten years my elder. He had a long, fair face that might once have been tanned and hardened by great exposure. His skin had that look, but now the bronze was faded, and you could see that he had been born very fair in tint. Across the high nose and cheek bones went a powdering of freckles. His eyes were bluish-gray and I saw at once that he habitually looked at things afar off.

He was rather poorly dressed and pushed about as I was. When the surge again gave him footing, he spoke beside me. " 'Now that this is over, they might do some great, worthy thing!' Very true, friend, they might! I take your words for good omen." The throng shot out an arm and we were parted. The same action brought back to me Diego Lopez. Speaking to him later of the tall man, he said that he had noticed him, and that it was the Italian who would go to India by way of Ocean-Sea.

King Boabdil gave up his city to King Ferdinand and Queen Isabella. Over Granada, high against the bright sky, rose and floated the banners. Cannon, the big lombards, roared. Mars' music crashed out, then the trumpets ceased their crying and instead spread a mighty chanting. *Te Deum Laudamus!*

At last the massed brightness out in the plain quivered and parted. The pageantry broke, wide curving and returning with some freedom but with order too, into Santa Fé. I saw the Queen and the King with their children, and the Grand Cardinal, and prelates and prelates, and the Marquis of Cadiz, and many a grandee and famous knight. Don Enrique de Cerda and his troop came by.

Diego Lopez and I returned to the town. I saw again the man who would find India by a way unpassed, as far as one knew, since the world began! He was entering a house with a friar beside him. Something came into my mind of the convent of La Rabida.

CHAPTER V

Some days went by. The King and the Queen with the court and a great train of prelates and grandees and knights rode in state through Granada. Don Enrique, returning, told me of it in his room at night, of the Christian service in the mosque and the throning in the Alhambra.

"Now," he said, "after great affairs, our affairs! I have had speech with the Marchioness of Moya."

"That is the Queen's friend?"

"Yes. Dona Beatrix de Boabdilla. We stood together by a fountain, and when she said, 'What can I do for you?' I answered, 'There is something.' Then while all went in pageantry before us, I told her of the hermitage in the oak wood and of the unhappy small tower, and of you and me and those others, and what was done that day. Don Jayme, I told it like a minstrel who believes what he sings! And then I spoke of today. She is no puny soul, nor is she in priest's grip. She acts from her own vision, not from that of another. The Queen is no weak soul either! She also has vision, but too often she lets the churchmen take her vision from her. But Dona Beatrix is stronger there. Well, she promises help if we can show her how to help."

I said, "I have been thinking. It seems to me that it was wrong to come here and put my weight upon you."

"No!" he answered. "Did we not swear then, when we were young men? And we needed no oaths neither. Let such thoughts be. I am going to the palace tomorrow, and you with me. The King and the Queen ride with a great train into Granada. But Dona Beatrix will excuse herself from going. The palace will be almost empty, and we shall find her in the little gallery above the Queen's garden."

The next morning we went there, Don Enrique de Cerda and his squire, Juan Lepe. The palace rose great and goodly enough, with the church at hand. All had been built as by magic, silken pavilions flying away and stout houses settling themselves down. Sunk among the walls had been managed a small garden for the Queen and her ladies. A narrow, latticed and roofed gallery built without the Queen's rooms looked down upon orange and myrtle trees and a fountain. Here we found the Marchioness de Moya, with her two waiting damsels whom she set by the gallery door. Don Enrique kissed her hand and then motioned to me. Don Jayme de Marchena made his reverence.

She was a strong woman who would go directly to the heart of things. Always she would learn from the man himself. She asked me this and I answered; that and the other and I answered. "Don Pedro —?" I told the enmity there and the reason for it. "The Jewish rabbi, my great-grand father?" I avowed it, but by three Castilian and Christian great-grandfathers could not be counted as Jew! Practise Judaism? No. My grandmother Judith had been Christian.

She drove to the heart of it. "You yourself are Christian. What do you mean by that? What the Queen means? What the Grand Cardinal and the Archbishop of Granada means? What the Holy Office means?"

I kept silence for a moment, then I told her as well as I might, without fever and without melancholy, what I had written and of the Dominican.

"You have been," she said, "an imprudent cavalier."

The fountain flashed below us, a gray dove flew over garden. I said, "There is a text, 'With all thy getting, get understanding.' There is another, 'For God so loved the world'—that He wished to impart understanding."

She sat quiet, seeming to listen to the fountain. Then she said, "Are you ready to avow when they ask you that in every particular to which the Grand Inquisitor may point you are wrong, and that all that Holy Church through mouth of Holy Office says is right?"

I said, "No, Madam! Present Church is not as large as Truth, nor as fair as Beauty."

"You may think that, but will you say the other?"

"Say that church or kingdom exactly matches Truth and Beauty?"

"That is what I am sure you will have to say."

"Then, no!"

"I do not see," she said, "that I can do anything for you."

There was a chair beside her. She sat down, her chin on her hand and her eyes lowered. Silence held save for the fountain plashing. Don Enrique stood by the railing, and Jayme de Marchena felt his concern. But he himself walked just then—Don Jayme or Juan Lepe—into long patience, into greater steadfastness. Into the inner fields came translucence, gold light; came and faded, but left strength.

Dona Beatrix raised her eyes and let them dwell upon me. "Spain breeds bold knights," she said, "but not so many after all who are bold within! Not so many, I think, as are found in Italy or in France." She paused a moment, looking at the sky above the roofs, then came back to me. "It is hopeless, and you must see it, to talk in those terms to the only powers that can lead the Holy Office to forget that you live! It is hopeless to talk to the Queen, telling her that. She would hold that she had entertained heresy, and her imagination would not let her alone. I see naught in this world for you to do but to go out of it into another! There are other lands—"

A damsel hurried to her from the door. "There's a stir below, Madam! Something has brought the Queen home earlier than we thought—"

The Marchioness de Moya rose. Don Enrique kissed her hand, and Jayme de Marchena kissed it and thanked her. "I would help if I could!" she said. "But in Spain today it is deadly dangerous to talk or write as though there were freedom!"

She passed from the gallery, Don Enrique and I following. We came upon a landing with a great stair before us. Quick as had been her maidens, they were not quick enough. Many folk were coming up the broad steps. Dona Beatrix glanced, then opened a door giving into a great room, apparently empty. She pointed to an opposite door. "The little stair! Go that way!" Don Enrique nodded comprehension. We were in the room; the door closed.

At first it seemed an empty great chamber. Then from behind a square of stretched cloth came a man's head, followed by the figure pertaining to it. The full man was clad after a rich fancy and he held in his hand a brush and looked at us at first dreamily and then with keenness.

He knew me, differently arrayed though I was, and looked from me to Don Enrique. "Master Manuel Rodriguez," said the latter, "I would stop for good talk and to admire the Queen's likeness, but duty calls me out of palace! Adios!" He made toward the door across from that by which we had entered. The painter spoke after us. "That door is bolted, Don Enrique, on the other side. I do not know why! It is not usually so."

Don Enrique, turning, hurried to the first door and very slightly opened it. A humming entered the large, quiet room. He closed the door. "The Queen is coming up the great stair. The Archbishop of Granada is with her and a whole train beside!" He spoke to the painter. "I have no audience, and for reasons would not choose this moment as one in which to encounter the least disfavor! I will stay here before your picture and admire until landing and stairways are bare."

"If to be invisible is your desire," answered Manuel Rodriguez, "you have walked into trouble! The Queen is coming here."

Don Enrique exclaimed. Juan Lepe turned eyes to the painter. The blue eyes met mine—there rose the rushy pool, there dozed the broken boat. Manuel Rodriguez spoke in his voice that was at once cool and fine and dry and warm. "It is best to dare thoroughly! Perhaps I may help you—as thus! Wishing to speak with Don Enrique of an altar painting for the Church of Saint Dominic, I asked him here and he came. We talked, and he will give the picture. Then, hearing the Queen's approach, he would instantly have been gone, but alack, the small door is barred!—As for fisherman yonder, few look at squire when knight is in presence!"

No time to debate his offer, which indeed was both wise and kind! Chamberlains flung open the door. In came the Queen, with her the Princess Juana and several of her ladies. Beside her walked Fernando de Talavera, Her Highness's confessor, yesterday Bishop of Avila but now Archbishop of Granada. Behind him moved two lesser ecclesiastics, and with these Don Alonzo de Quintanella,

Comptroller-General of Castile. Others followed, nobles and cavaliers, two soberly clad men who looked like secretaries, a Franciscan friar, three or four pages. The room was large and had a table covered with a rich cloth, two great chairs and a few lesser ones.

The painter and Don Enrique bent low to the Majesty of Castile. In the background Juan Lepe made squire's obeisance. I was bearded and my face stained with a Moorish stain, and I was in shadow; it was idle to fear recognition that might never come. The Queen seated herself, and her daughter beside her, and with her good smile motioned the Archbishop to a chair. The two ecclesiastics, both venerable men, were given seats. The rest of the company stood. The Queen's blue eyes rested on Don Enrique. She spoke in a clear, mild voice, threaded with dignity. "Were you summoned thither, Don Enrique de Cerda?"

He answered, "No, Highness! I came to the palace to seek Master Manuel Rodriguez who is to paint for me an altarpiece for the Church of Saint Dominic. You and the King, Madam, I thought were in Granada. Not finding him in his own lodging, I made bold to come here. Then at once, before I could hasten away, you returned!"

The true nature of this Queen was to think no evil. Her countenance remained mild. He had done valiant service, and she was sisterly-minded toward the greater part of the world. Now she said with serenity, "There is no fault, Don Enrique. Stay with us now that you are here."

Bowing deeply, he joined a brother-in-arms, Don Miguel de Silva. His squire stood in the shadow behind him, but found a chance-left lane of vision down which much might be seen.

The Queen composed herself, in her chair. "This is the position, Master Manuel?" The fair man, so fine and quick that I loved to look at him, bowed and stepped back to his canvas, where he took up his brush and fell to work. The Queen and the Archbishop began to speak earnestly together. Words and sentences floated to Juan Lepe standing by the arras. The Queen made thoughtful pauses, looking before her with steady blue eyes and a somewhat lifted face. I noted that when she did this Manuel Rodriguez painted fast.

There fell a pause in their talk. Something differing from the subject of discourse, whatever in its fullness that might be, seemed to come into her mind. She sent her glance across the room.

"Don Enrique de Cerda—"

The tone summoned. When he was before her, "It was in my mind," said the Queen, "to send for you within a day or two. But now you are here, and this moment while we await the King is as good as another. We have had letters from the Bishop of Seville whom we reverence, and from Don Pedro Enriquez to whom we owe much. They have to do with Jayme de Marchena who has long been suspect by the Holy Office. He has fled Seville, gone none know where! Don Pedro informs us, Don Enrique, that years ago this man stood among your friends. He does not think it probable that this is yet so—nor do I, Don Enrique, knowing that you must hold in abhorrence the heretic!" She looked mildly upon him. "In youth we make chance friendships thick as May, but manhood weeds the garden! And yet we think it possible that this man may in his heart trade on old things and make his way to you or send you appeal." She paused, then said in a quiet voice, "Should that happen, Don Enrique, on your allegiance, and as a good Christian, you will do all that you can to put him in the hands of the Holy Office."

She waited with her blue eyes upon him. He said, and said quietly, "It was long ago, Madam, when I was a young man and careless. I will do all that lies in me to do. But Spain is wide and there are ships to Africa and other shores." She said, "Yes, I do not see such a one daring to come to Santa Fé! But they say that ten demons possess a heretic, and that he crosses streams upon a hair or walks edges of high walls."

With her ringed hand she made gesture of dismissal. He bowed low and stepped back to his former place. The sun flooded in at window. Manuel Rodriguez painted steadily. The Queen sat still, with lifted face and eyes strained into distance. She sighed and came back from wastes where she would be Christian, oh, where she would be Christian! and began with a tender, maternal look to talk with her daughter.

CHAPTER VI

The door giving upon the great corridor opened. One said, "The King, Madam!" King Ferdinand entered quietly, in the sober fashion of a sober and able man. He was cool and balanced, true always to his own conception of his own dues. The Queen rose and stepped to meet him. They spoke, standing together, after which he handed her to her chair and took beside her the other great chair which the pages had swiftly placed. After greeting his daughter and the Archbishop he looked across to the painter. "Master Manuel Rodriguez, good day!"

There fell a moment of sun-drenched quiet in which they all sat for their picture. Then said the King, "Madam, we are together, and here are those who have been our chief advisers in this affair of discoveries. Master Christopherus is below. We noted him in the court. Let us have him here and see this too-long-dragging matter finished! Once for all abate his demands, or once for all let him go!"

They sent a page. Again there was sunny silence, then in at the door came the tall, muscular, gray-eyed, silver-haired man whom I had met the day King Boabdil surrendered Granada.

He made reverence to the Queen and the King and to the Archbishop. It was the Queen who spoke to him and that gently.

"Master Christopherus, we have had a thousand businesses, and so our matter here has waited and waited. Today comes unaware this quiet hour and we will give it to you. Here with us are the Archbishop and others who have been our counsellors, and here is Don Alonzo de Quintantella who hath always stood your friend. In all the hurly-burly we yet took time, two days ago, to sit in council and come to conclusion. And now we give you our determination. In all reason it should give you joy!" She smiled upon him. "How many years since first you laid your plan before us?"

He answered her in a deep voice, thrilling and crowded with feeling. "Seven years, Madam your Highness! Like an infant laid at your feet. And winter has blown upon it, and sunshine carrying hope has walked around it, and then again the cold wind rises—"

The King spoke. "Master Christopherus, in war much else has to cease! In much we have had to find patience, and you have to find it."

"My lord King, yes!" replied the tall man. "It is eighteen years since in Lisbon, looking upon the sea one day, I said to myself, 'Is there a question that is not to be answered? This ocean is to be crossed. Then why do not I cross it? There is Cipango, Cathay and India! Gold and spices are there, and here lie ships, and between, when all is said, is only sea! God made the sea to be sailed! Yonder they worship idols, here we worship Christ. There are idols, here is Christ. Once a Christopherus carried Christ across water!' Eighteen years ago. I said, 'I can do it!' I say it today, my lord and my lady. I can do it!"

Of the seated great ones only the Queen's spirit appeared to answer his. He seemed to enchant her, to take her with him. But the King's cool face regarded him with something like dislike. He spoke in an edged voice. "Saint Christopher asked no great wage. That is the point, Master Christopherus, so let us to it! At last the Queen and I say 'We agree' to this enterprise, which may bring forth fruit or may not, or may mean mere empty loss of ships and men and of our monies! Yet we say 'yea.' But we do not say 'yea ', Master Christopherus, to the too great ferry fee which you ask! I say 'ask', but verily the tone is of command!"

The man whom they called Master Christopherus made a slow, wide gesture of deprecation. The Archbishop took the word. "Too much! You ask a hundred times too much! I must say to you that it is unchristianly arrogance. You talk like a soldan!" An assenting murmur came from the other ecclesiastics.

The Queen spoke. "Master Christopherus, if it be a great thing to do, is not the doing it and thereby blessing yourself no less than others—is not that reward? Not that Castile shall deny you reward, no! Trust me that if you bring us the key of India you shall not find us niggardly! But we and they who advise us stumble at your prescribing wealth, honors and gifts that they say truly are better fitting a great prince! Trust us for enrichment and for honor do you come back with the great thing done! Leave it all now to Time that brings to pass. So you will be clearer to go forth to the blessed carrying of Christ!"

She spoke earnestly, a Queen, but with much about her of womanly, motherly sweetness. I saw that she greatly liked the man and somewhere met his spirit. But the King was gathering hardness. He spoke to a secretary standing behind him. "Have you it there written down, the Italian's demand?"

The man produced a paper. "Read!" But before it could be unfolded, Master Christopherus spoke.

" 'Italian!' Seven years in Spain and ten in Portugal, and a good while in Porto Santo that belongs to Portugal, a little in England and in Ultima Thule or Iceland, and long, long years upon ships decked and undecked in all the seas that are known—fourteen years, childhood and boyhood, in Genoa and at Pavia where I went to school, and all my years of hope in Christ's Kingdom, and in the uplands of great doers-and your Highness says to me for a slighting word, 'Italian!' I was born in Italy, but today, for this turn, King Ferdinand, you should call me 'Spaniard'! As, if King John sends me forth he will call me Portuguese! Or King Henry will say, 'Christopher the Englishman' or King Charles, to whom verily I see that I may go, shall say, 'Frenchman, to whom all owe the marriage of East and West, but France owes Empire!' "

The King said, "It may be so, or it may not be so, Master Christopherus. Read!"

The secretary read: The Genoese, Cristoforo Colombo, called in Spain Cristobal Colon, and in the Latin Christopherus Columbus, states and demands in substance as follows: Sailing westward he will discover for the King and Queen of the Spains the Indies and Cathay and Cipango, to the great glory and enrichment of these Sovereigns and the passing thereby of Spain ahead of Portugal, and likewise and above all to the great glory of Christ and of Holy Church. He will do this, having seen it clear for many years that it is to be done, and he the instrument. And for the finding by going westward of the said India and all the gain of the world and the Kingdom of God and of our Sovereigns the King Don Ferdinand and the Queen Dona Isabella, he bargaineth thus:

"He shall be named Admiral of the Ocean-Sea, whereby he means the whole water west of the line drawn by the Holy Father for the King of Portugal. He shall be made Viceroy and Governor of all continents and islands that he may discover, claim and occupy for the Sovereigns. And the said Christopherus Columbus's eldest son shall hold these offices after him, and the heir of his son, and his heir, down time. He shall be granted one tenth of all gold, pearls, precious stones, spices, or other merchandise found or bought or exchanged within his admiralty and viceroyship, and this tithe is likewise to be taken by his heirs from generation to generation. He or one that he shall name shall be judge in all disputes that arise in these continents and islands, so be it that the honor of the Sovereigns of Spain is not touched. He shall have the salary that hath the High Admiral of Castile. He and his family shall be ennobled and henceforth be called Don and Dona. And for the immediate sailing of ships he may, if he so desire, be at an eighth of the expense of outfitting, for which he shall be returned an eighth of all the profit of this the first voyage."

The secretary did not make the terms less sounding by his reading. Wind in leaves, went a-stir through the room.

I heard a page near me whispering, "O Sancta Maria! The hanger-on, the needy one! Since the beginning of time I've seen him at doors, sunny and cloudy days, the big, droning bee!" Manuel Rodriguez painted on. I felt his thought. "I should like to paint *you*, Admiral of the Ocean-Sea!"

The room recomposed itself. Out of silence came the King's voice, chill and dry. "We abate so vast a claim for so vast reward! But we would be naught else but just, and in our ability lavish. Read now what we will do!"

The secretary read. It had a certain largeness and goodliness, as go rewards for adventure, even for great adventure, what the sovereigns would do. The room thought it should answer. The King spoke,

"We can promise no more nor other than this. It contents you, Master Christopherus?"

The long-faced, high-nosed, gray-eyed man answered, "No, my lord King."

"Your own terms or none?"

"Mine or none, your Highness."

The King's voice grew a cutting wind. "To that the Queen and I answer, 'Ours or none!' " Pushing back his chair, he glanced at sun out of window. "It is over. I incline to think that it was at best but an empty vision. You are dismissed, Master Christopherus!"

The Genoese, bowing, stepped backward from the table. In his face and carriage was nothing broken. He kept color.

The Queen's glance went after him, "What will you do now, Master Christopherus?"

He answered, "My lady, your Highness, I shall take horse tomorrow for France."

The King said, "France?—King Charles buys ever low, not high!"

The Sovereigns and the great churchmen and the less great went away together. After them flowed the high attendance. All went, Don Enrique among the last. Following him, I turned head, for I wished to observe again two persons, the painter Manuel Rodriguez and the Admiral of the Ocean-Sea. The former painted on. The latter walked forth quite alone, coming behind the grinning pages.

In the court below I saw him again. The archway to street sent toward us a deep wedge of shadow. He had a cloak which he wrapped around him and a large round hat which he drew low over his gray-blue eyes. With a firm step he crossed to the archway where the purple shadow took him.

Juan Lepe must turn to his own part which now must be decided. I walked behind Don Enrique de Cerda through Santa Fé. With him kept Don Miguel de Silva, who loved Don Enrique's sister and would still talk of *devoir* and of plans, now that the war was ended. When the house was reached he would enter with us and still adhere to Don Enrique.

But at the stair foot the latter spoke to the squire. "Find me in an hour, Juan Lepe. I have something to say to thee!" His tone carried, "Do you think the place there makes any difference? No, by the god of friends!"

I let him go thinking that I would come to him presently. But I, too, had to act under the god of friends. In Diego Lopez's room I found quill and ink and paper, and there I wrote a letter to Don Enrique, and finding Diego gave it to him to be given in two hours into Don Enrique's hand. Then Juan Lepe the squire changed in his own room, narrow and bare as a cell, to the clothing of Juan Lepe the sailor.

CHAPTER VII

Dusk was drawing down as I stole with little trouble out of the house into the street and thence into the maze of Santa Fé. That night I slept with minstrels and jugglers, and at sunrise slipped out of Cordova gate with muleteers. They were for Cordova and I meant to go to Malaga. I meant to find there a ship, maybe for Africa, maybe for Italy, though in Italy, too, sits the Inquisition. But who knows what it is that turns a man, unless we call it his Genius, unless we call it God? I let the muleteers pass me on the road to Cordova, let them dwindle in the distance. And still I walked and did not turn back and find the Malaga road. It was as though I were on the sea, and my bark was hanging in a calm, waiting for a wind to blow. A man mounted on a horse was coming toward me from Santa Fé. Watching the small figure grow larger, I said, "When he is even with me and has passed and is a little figure again in the distance, I will turn south."

He came nearer. Suddenly I knew him to be that Master Christopherus who had entered the wedge of shadow yesterday in the palace court. He was out of it now, in the broad light, on the white road—on the way to France. He approached. The ocean before Palos came and stood again before me, salt and powerful. The keen, far, sky line of it awoke and drew!

Christopherus Columbus came up with me. I said, "A Palos sailor gives you good morning!"

Checking the horse, he sat looking at me out of blue-gray eyes. I saw him recollecting. "Dress is different and poorer, but you are the squire in the crowd! 'Sailor Palos sailor'—There's some meaning there too!"

He seemed to ponder it, then asked if I was for Cordova.

"No. I am going to Malaga where I take ship."

"This is not the Malaga road."

"No. But I am in no hurry! I should like to walk a mile with you."

"Then do it," he answered. "Something tells me that we shall not be ill travelers together."

I felt that also and no more than he could explain it. But the reason, I know, stands in the forest behind the seedling.

He walked his horse, and I strode beside. He asked my name and I gave it. Juan Lepe. We traveled Cordova road together. Presently he said, "I leave Spain for France, and do you know why?"

Said Juan Lepe, "I have been told something, and I have gathered something with my own eyes and ears. You would reach Asia by going west."

He spoke in the measured tone of a recital often made alike to himself and to others. "I hold that the voyage from Palos, say, first south to the Canaries and then due west would not exceed three months. Yet I began to go west to India full eighteen years ago! I have voyaged eighteen years, with dead calms and head winds, with storms and back-puttings, with pirates and mutinies, with food and water lacking, with only God and my purpose for friend! I have touched at the court of Portugal and at the court of Spain, and, roundabout way, at the court of England, and at the houses of the Doges of Venice and of Genoa. They all kept me swinging long at anchor, but they have never given me a furthering wind. Eighteen years going to India! But why do I say eighteen? The Lord put me forth from landside the day I was born. Before I was fourteen, at the school in Pavia, He said, 'Go to sea. Sail under thy cousin Colombo and learn through long years all the inches of salt water.' Later He said, one day when we were swinging off Alexandria, 'Study! Teach thyself! Buy books, not wine nor fine clothes nor favor of women. Study on land and study at sea. Look at every map that comes before you. Learn to make maps. When a world map comes before you, look at the western side of it and think how to fill it out knowingly. Listen to seamen's tales. Learn to view the invisible and to feel under foot the roundness of my earth!'

"And He said that same year off Aleppo, 'Learn to command

ships. Learn in King Reinier's war and in what other war Genoa makes. Learn to direct men and patiently to hear them, winding in and out of their counsels, keeping thyself always wiser than they.' Well, I studied, and learned, and can command a ship or ships, and know navigation, and can make maps and charts with the best, and can rule seamen, loving them the while. Long ago, I went to that school which He set, and came forth *magister!* Long after His first speaking, I was at Porto Santo, well named, and there He said, 'Seek India, going westward.' " He turned his face to the sun. "I have been going to India fifty-six years."

Juan Lepe asked, "Why, on yesterday, were you not content with the King and Queen's terms? They granted honor and competence. It was the estate of a prince that you asked."

Some moments passed before he answered. The sun was shining, the road white and dusty, the mountains of Elvira purple to the tops and there splashed with silver. When he spoke, his voice was changed. Neither now nor hereafter did he discourse of money-gold and nobility flowing from earthly kings with that impersonal exaltation with which he talked of his errand from God to link together east and west. But he drew them somehow in train from the last, hiding here I thought, an earthly weakness from himself, and the weakness so intertwined with strength that it was hard to divide parasite from oak.

"Did you see," he asked, "a boy with me? That was my son Diego whom I have left with a friend in Santa Fé. Fernando, his half-brother, is but a child. I shall see him in Cordova. I have two brothers, dear to me both of them, Diego and Bartholomew. My old father, Dominico Colombo, still lives in Genoa. He lives in poverty, as I have lived in poverty these many years. And there is Pedro Correo, to whom I owe much, husband of my wife's sister. My wife is dead. The mother of Fernando is not my wife, but I love her, and she is poor though beautiful and good. I would have her less poor; I would give her beautiful things. I have love for my kindred,—love and yearning and care and desire to do them good, alike those who trust me and those who think that I had failed them. I do not fail them!"

We padded on upon the dusty road. I felt his inner warmth,

divined his life. But at last I said, "What the Queen and King promise would give rich care—"

"I have friends too, for all that I ride out of Spain and seem so poor and desolate! I would repay—ay, ten times over—their faith and their help."

"Stil—"

"There are moreover the poor, and those who study and need books and maps that they cannot purchase. There are convents—one convent especially—that befriended me when I was alone and nigh hopeless and furthered my cause. I would give that convent great gifts." Turning in the saddle he looked southwest. "Fray Juan Perez—"

Palos shore spread about me, and rose La Rabida, white among vineyards and pines. Doves flew over cloister. But I did not say all I knew.

"There are other things that I would do. I do not speak of them to many! They would say that I was mad. But great things that in this age none else seems inclined to do!"

"As what?" I asked. "I have been called mad myself. I am not apt to think you so."

He began to speak of a mighty crusade to recover the Holy Sepulchre.

The road to Cordova stretched sunny and dusty. Above the mountains of Elvira the sky stood keen blue. Juan Lepe said slowly, "Admiral of the Ocean-Sea and Viceroy and Governor of continents and islands in perpetuity, sons and sons' sons after you, and gilded deep with a tenth of all the wealth that flows forever from Asia over Ocean-Sea to Spain, and you and all after you made nobles, grandees and wealthy from generation to generation! Kings almost of the west, and donors to the east, arousers of crusades and freers of the Sepulchre! You build a high tower!"

Carters and carts going by pushed us to the edge of road and covered all with dust. He waited until the cloud sank, then he said, "Do you know—but you cannot know what it is to be sent from pillar to post and wait in antechambers where the air stifles, and doff cap —who have been captain of ships!—to chamberlain, page and lackey? To be called dreamer, adventurer, dicer! To hear the laugh and catch the sneer! To be the persuader, the beggar of good and bad, high and low—to beg year in and year out, cold and warmth, summer and winter, sunrise, noon and sunset, calm and storm, beg of galleon and beg of carrack, yea, beg of cockboat! To see your family go needy, to be doubted by wife and child and brethren and friends and acquaintance! To have them say, 'While you dream we go hungry!' and 'What good will it do us if there is India, while we famish in Spain?' and 'You love us not, or you would become a prosperous sea captain!'—Not one year but eighteen, eighteen, since I saw in vision the sun set not behind water but behind vale and hill and mountain and cities rich beyond counting, and smelled the spice draught from the land!"

I saw that he must count upon huge indemnity. We all dream indemnity. But still I thought and think that there was here a weakness in him. Far inward he may have known it himself, the outer self was so busy finding grounds!

After a short moment he spoke again, "Little things bring little reward. But to keep proportion and harmony, great things must bring great things! You do not know what it is to cross where no man hath crossed and to find what no man hath found!"

"Yes, it is a great thing!"

"Then," said he, "what is it, that which I ask, to the grandeur of time!"

He spoke with a lifted face, eyes upon the mountain crests and the blue they touched. They were nearer us than they had been; the Pass of Elvira was at hand. Yet on I walked, and before me still hung the far ocean west of Palos. I said, "I know something of the guesses, the chances and the dangers, but I have not spent there years of study—"

He kindled, having an auditor whom he chose to think intelligent. He checked his horse, that fell to grazing the bit of green by the way. "As though," he said, "I stood in Cipango beneath a golden roof, I know that it can be done! Twelve hundred leagues at the most. Look!" he said. "You are not an ignoramus like some I have met; nor if I read you right are you like others who not knowing that True Religion is

True Wonder up with hands and cry, 'Blasphemy, Sacrilege and Contradiction!' Earth and water make an orb. Place ant on apple and see that orbs may be gone around! Travel far enough and east and west change names! Straight through, beneath us, are other men."

"Feet against feet. Antipodes," I said. "All the life of man is taking Wonder in and making Her at home!"

"So!" he answered. "Now look! The largeness of our globe is at the equator. The great Ptolemy worked out our reckoning. Twenty-four hours, fifteen degrees to each, in all three hundred and sixty degrees. It is held that the Greeks and the Romans knew fifteen of these hours. They stretched their hand from Gibraltar and Tangier, calling them Pillars of Hercules, to mid-India. Now in our time we have the Canaries and the King of Portugal's new islands—another hour, mark you! Sixteen from twenty-four leaves eight hours empty. How much of that is water and how much is earth? Where ends Ocean-Sea and where begins India and Cathay, of which the ancients knew only a part? The Arabian Alfraganus thinks that Ptolemy's degrees should be less in size. If that be right, then the earth is smaller than is thought, and India nearer! I myself incline to hold with Alfraganus. It may be that less than two months' sailing, calm and wind, would bring us to Cipango. Give me the ships and I will do it!"

"You might have had them yesterday."

To a marked extent he could bring out and make visible his inner exaltation. Now, tall, strong, white-haired, he looked a figure of an older world. "The spheres and all are set to harmony!" he said. "I would have fitness. Great things throughout! Diamonds and rubies without flaw in the crown. We will talk no more about abating just demand!"

I agreed with a nod, and indeed there was never any shaking him here. Beneath his wide and lofty vision of a world filled out to the eternal benefit of all rested always this picture which I knew he savored like wine and warmth. His family, his sons, his brothers and kindred, the aged father in Genoa, all friends and backers—and he a warm sun in the midst of them, all their doubts of him dispelled, shining out upon them, making every field rich, repaying a thousand, thousandfold every trust shown him.

The day sang cool and high and bright, the mountains of Elvira had light snow atop. Master Christopherus began again to speak.

"There came ashore at Porto Santo some years ago a piece of wood long as a spar but thicker. Pedro Correo, who is my brother-in-law, saw it. It was graved all over, cut by something duller than our knives with beasts and leaves and a figure that Pedro thought was meant for an idol. He and another saw it and agree in their description. They left it on the beach at twilight, well out of water reach. But in the night came up a great storm that swept it away. It came from the west, the wind having blown for days from that quarter. I ask you will empty billows fell a tree and trim it and carve it? It is said that a Portuguese pilot picked up one like it off Cape Bojador when the wind was southwest. I have heard a man of the Azores tell of giant reeds pitched upon his shore *from the west.* There is a story of the finding on the beach of Flores the bodies of two men not like any that we know either in color or in feature. For days a west wind had driven in the seas. And I know of other findings. Whence do these things come?

"May there not be unknown islands west of Azores? They might come from there, and still to the west of them stream all Ocean-Sea, violent and unknown! The learned think the earth of such a size. Your Arabian holds it smaller. What then if it is larger than the largest calculation?"

He said with disdain, "All the wise men at Salamanca before whom the King set me six years ago thought it had no end! Large or small, they called it blasphemy for me, a poor, plain seaman, son of a wool-comber and not even a Spanish wool-comber, to try to stretch mind over it! Ocean-Sea had never been overpassed, and by that token could not be overpassed! None had met its dangers, so dangers there must be of a most strange and fearful nature! But if you were put to sea at fourteen and have lived there long, water becomes water! A speck on the horizon will turn out ship or land. Wave carries you on to wave, day to night and night to day. At last there is port!"

All this time his horse had been cropping the scanty herbage. Now he raised his head. In a moment we too heard the horsemen and looking back toward Santa Fé saw four approaching. As they came nearer we made out two cavaliers talking together, followed by serving men. When they were almost at hand one of the leaders said something, whereat his fellow laughed. It floated up Cordova road, a wide, deep, rich laugh. Master Christopherus started. "That is the laugh of Don Luis de St. Angel!"

Don Luis de St. Angel was, I knew, Receiver of the Ecclesiastical Revenues for Aragon, a man who stood well with the King. The horsemen were close upon us. Suddenly the laugher cried, "Saint Jago! Here he is!"

We were now five mounted men and a trudger afoot. The cavalier who had laughed, a portly, genial person with a bold and merry eye, laughed again. "Well met, Don Cristoval. Well met, Admiral! I looked to find you presently! You sailed out of port at sunrise and I two hours later with a swifter ship and more canvas—"

"'Don' and 'Admiral'!" answered Master Christopherus, and he spoke with anger. "You jest in Spain! But in France it shall be said soberly—"

"No, no! Don and Admiral here! Viceroy and Governor here—as soon as you find the lands! Wealthy here—as soon as you put hand on the gold!" Don Luis de St. Angel's laughter ceased. He became with portentous swiftness a downright, plain man of business. He talked, all of us clustered together on the Cordova road.

"The Archbishop kept me from that audience yesterday, leaving Don Alonso de Quintanella your only friend there! The Queen was tired, the King fretted. They thought they had come a long way, and there you stood, Master Christopherus, shaking your head! Don Alonso told me about it, and how hopeless it seemed! But I said, 'If you conquer a land don't you put in a viceroy? I don't see that Don Cristoval isn't as good as Don This One, or Don That One! I've a notion that the first might not oppress and flay the new subjects as might the last two! That is a point to be made to the Queen! As for perpetuity of office and privileges down the ages, most things get to be hereditary. If it grows to be a swollen serpent something in the future will fall across and cut it in two. Let time take care of it! As for wealth, in any land a man who will bear an eighth of the cost may fairly expect an eighth of the gain. This setting out is to cost little, after all. He says he can do it with three small ships and less than a hundred and fifty men. If the ships bring back no treasure, he will not be wealthy. If there is a little gain, the Spains need not grudge him his handful of doubloons. If there is huge gain, the King and Queen but for him would not have their seven eighths. The same reasoning applies to his tenth of all future gain from continents and islands. You will say that someone else will arise to do it for us on easier terms. Perhaps—and perhaps not for a century, and another Crown may thrust in tomorrow! France, probably. It is not impossible that England might do it. As for what is named overweening pride and presumption, at least it shows at once and for altogether. We are not left painfully to find it out. It goes with his character. Take it or leave it together with his patience, courage and long head. Leave it, and presently we may see France or England swallow him whole. He will find India and Cathay and Cipango, and France or England will be building ships, ships, ships! Blessed Virgin above us!' said I, 'If I could talk alone to the Sovereigns, I think I could clench it!' "

" 'Then let us go now to the palace,' says Don Alonso, 'and beg audience!'

"That did we, Don Cristoval, and so I hail you 'Don' and 'Admiral', and beg you to turn that mule and reenter Santa Fé! In a few days you and the King and Queen may sign capitulations."

"Was it the Queen?"

"Just. The King said the treasury was drained. She answered, 'I will pawn my jewels but he shall sail!' Luis de St. Angel says, 'It does not need. There is some gold left in the coffers of Aragon. After all, the man asks but three little ships and a few score seamen and offers himself to furnish one of the ships.' "

"With Martin Alonso Pinzon's help, I will!"

" 'Never,' said I to their majesties, 'was so huge a possible gain matched against so small a sending forth! And as for this Genoese who truly hath given and gives and will give his life for his vision, saith not Scripture that a laborer is worthy of his hire?' At which the Queen said with decision, 'We will do it, Don Luis! And now go and find Master Christopherus and comfort him, whose heart must be heavy, and indeed mine,' she saith, 'was heavy when he went forth today, and a voice seemed to say within me, "What have you done, Isabella? How may you have hindered!"'"

The Gatherer of Ecclesiastical Revenues laughed again with that compelling laughter. "So forth we go, and Don Alonso sends for you to his house. But you could not be found. Early this morning came one and informed us that the ship had put out of harbor, whereupon my nephew and I set sail after!"

The Admiral of the Ocean-Sea turned his face to the west. Not knowing, I think, what he did, he raised his arm, outstretched it, and the hand seemed to close in greeting. His face was the face of a man who sees the Beloved after long and sorrowful absence. So did thought and passion and vision charge his frame and his countenance, that for a moment truly there was effulgence. It startled. Don Luis held his speech suspended, in his eyes wonder. Master Christopherus let fall his arm. He sighed. The out-pushing light faltered, vanished. One might say, "A Genoese sea captain, willing to do an adventurous thing and make a purse thereby!"

CHAPTER VIII

Quitting the Vega of Granada, Juan Lepe recrossed the mountains. I was at wander. I did not go to Malaga. I did not then go to Palos. I went to San Lucar. I had adventures, but I will not draw them here. The ocean by Palos continued with me in sight and sound and movement. But I did not go to Palos. I went to the strand of San Lucar, and there I found a small bark trading not to Genoa but to Marseilles. Seamen lacked, and the master took me gladly. I freshened knowledge upon this voyage.

The master was a dour, quiet Catalan; his three sons favored him and their six sailors more or less took the note. The sea ran quiet and blue under a quiet blue heaven. At night all the stars shone, or only light clouds went overhead. It was a restful boat and Jayme de Marchena rested. Even while his body labored he rested. The sense of Danger in every room, walking on every road, took leave. Yet was there throughout that insistent sight of Palos beach and the gray and wild Atlantic. All the birds cried from the west; the salt, stinging wind flung itself upon me from the west. Once a voice, faint and silvery, made itself heard. "Were it not well to know those other, those mightier waters, and find the strange lands, the new lands?" I answered myself, "They are the old lands taken a new way." But still the voice said, "The new lands!"

We made Marseilles and unladed, and were held there a fortnight. I might have left the bark and found work and maybe safety in France, or I might have taken another ship for Italy. I did neither. I clung to this bark and my Catalans. We took our lading and quitted Marseilles, and came after a tranquil voyage to San Lucar. Again we unladed and laded, and again voyaged to Marseilles. Spring became summer; young summer, summer in prime. We left Marseilles and voyaged once more San Lucar-ward. There rushed up a fearful storm and we were wrecked off Almeria. One lad drowned. The rest of us somehow made shore. A boat took us to Algeciras, and thence we trudged it to San Lucar.

My Catalans were not wholly depressed. Behind their wrecked ship stood merchants who would furnish another bark. The master would have had me wait at San Lucar until he went forth again. But I was bound for the strand by Palos and the gray, piling Atlantic.

August was the month and the day warm. The first of August in the year 1492. Two leagues east of Palos I overtook three men trudging that way, and talking now loudly and angrily and now in a sullen, dragging fashion. I had seen between this road and ocean a fishing hamlet and I made out that they were from this place. They were men of small boats, men who fished, but who now and again were gathered in by some shipmaster, when they became sailors.

In me they saw only a poorly clad, sea-going person. When I gave greeting they greeted me in return. "For Palos?" I asked, and the one who talked the most and the loudest gave groaning assent. "Aye, for Palos. You too, brother, are flopping in the net?"

I did not understand and said as much. He gave an angry laugh and explained his figure. "Why, the Queen and the King and the law and Martin Pinzon, to whom we, are bound for a year, are pressing us! Which is to say they've cast a net and here we are, good fish, beating against the meshes and finding none big enough to slip through! Haven't you been pressed too, scooped in without a 'By your leave, Palos fish!' A hundred fish and more in this net and one by one the giant will take us out and broil us!"

The second man spoke with a whine. "I had rather a Barbary pirate were coming aboard! I had rather be took slave and row a galley!"

The third, a young man, had a whimsical, dark, fearless face. "But we be going to see strange things and serve the Queen! That's something!"

"The Queen is just a lady. She don't know anything about deep and fearful seas!"

"Where are you going," I asked, "and with whom?"

The angry man answered, "The last of that is the easiest, mate! With an Italian sorcerer who has bewitched the great! He ought to be burned, say I, with the Jews and heretics! We are going with him, and we are going with Captain Martin Pinzon, whom he hath bewitched with the rest! And we are going with three ships, the *Santa Maria*, the *Pinta* and the *Niña*."

The third said, "The *Santa Maria's* a good boat."

"There isn't any boat, good or bad," the first answered him, "that can hold together when you come to heat that'll melt pitch and set wood afire! There isn't any boat, good or bad, that can stand it when a lodestone as big as Gibraltar begins to draw iron!"

The second, whose element was melancholy, sighed, "I've been north of Ireland, Pedro, and that was bad enough! The lookout saw a siren and the *Infanta Isabella* was dashed on the rocks and something laughed at us all night!"

"Ireland's nothing at all to it!" answered the angry man, whose name was Pedro. "I've heard men that know talk! The Portuguese going down Africa coast got to Cape Bojador, but they've never truly gotten any further, though I hear them say they have! They sent a little carrack further down, and it had to come back because the water fell to boiling! There wasn't any land and there wasn't any true sea, but it was all melted up together in fervent heat! Like hot mud, so to speak. It's hell, that's what I say; it's hell down there! Moreover, there ain't any heaven stretched over it."

"What does it mean by that?" asked the second.

"It means, Fernando, that there wouldn't be any sky, blue nor gray nor black, nor clouds, nor air to breathe! There wouldn't be any thunder and lightning nor rain nor wind, and at night there wouldn't be stars, no north star, nor any! It would just be—I don't know what! Fray Ignatio told me, and he said the name was 'chaos'."

"That was south. That wasn't west."

"West is just as bad!"

Fernando also addressed the young man, the third, calling him Sancho. "If there were anything west for Christian men, wouldn't the Holy Father at Rome have sent long ago? We are all going to die!"

"But they didn't know it was round," said Sancho. "Now we do, and that's the difference! If you started a little manikin just here on an orange and told him to go straight ahead, he'd come around home, wouldn't he?"

"You weary me, Sancho!" cried the first. "And what if you did that and it took so long that you come back to Fishertown old and bald and driveling, and your wife is dead and all the neighbors! Much good you'd have from knowing it was round!"

"When you got right underfoot wouldn't you fall; that's what I want to know?"

"Fall! Fall where?"

"Into the sky! My God, it's deep! And there wouldn't be any boat to pick you up nor any floating oar to catch by—"

The vision seemed to appall them. Fernando drew back of hand across eyes.

I came in. "You wouldn't do that any more than the ant falls off the orange! Men have come back who have been almost underfoot, so far to the east had they traveled. They found there men and kingdoms and ways not so mightily unlike ours."

"They went that way," answered Pedro, jerking his hand eastward, "over good land! And maybe, whatever they said, they were lying to us! I'm thinking most of the learned do that all the time!"

"Well," said Sancho, "if we do come back, we'll have some rare good tales to tell!"

There fell a pause at that, a pause of dissent and exasperation, but also one of caught fancy. It would undoubtedly be a glory to tell those tales to a listening, fascinated Fishertown!

Juan Lepe said, "For months I've been with a trader running from San Lucar to Marseilles. I've had no news this long while! What's doing at Palos?"

They were ready for an audience, any audience, and forthwith I had the story of the Admiral fairly straight—or I could make it straight—from that day when we parted on the Cordova road. These men did not know what had happened in March or in April, but they knew something of May. In May he came to Palos and settled down with Fray Juan Perez in La Rabida, and to see him went Captain

Martin Pinzon who knew him already, and the physician Garcia Fernandez and others, and they all talked together for a day and a night. After that the alcalde of Palos and others in authority had letters and warrants from the Queen and the King, and they overbore everything, calling him Don and *El Almirante* and saying that he must be furnished forth. Then came a day when everybody was gathered in the square before the church of Saint George, and the alcalde that had a great voice read the letters.

"I was there!" said Fernando. "I brought in fish that morning."

"I, too!" quoth Sancho. "I had to buy sailcloth."

It was Pedro chiefly who talked. "They were from the King and Queen, and the moral was that Palos must furnish Don Cristoval Colon, Admiral of the Ocean-Sea—and we thought that was a curious thing to be admiral of!—two ships and all seamen needed and all supplies. A third ship could be enterprised, and any in and around Palos was to be encouraged to put in fortune and help. Ships and those who went in them were to obey the said Don Cristoval Colon or Columbus as though he were the Queen and the King, the Bishop of Seville and the Marquis of Cadiz! It didn't say it just that way but that was what it meant. We were to follow him and do as he told us, or it would be much the worse for us! We weren't to put in at St. George la Mina on the coast of Africa, nor touch at the King of Portugal's islands, and that was the whole of it!"

"All seamen were to be given good pay," said Sancho. "And if anybody going was in debt, or even if he had done a crime—so that it wasn't treason or anything the Holy Office handles—he couldn't be troubled or held back, seeing it was royal errand. That is very convenient for some."

Pedro lost patience. "You'd make the best of Hell itself!"

"He'd deny," put in Fernando, "Holy Writ that says there shall be sorrows!"

They embarked upon loud blame of Sancho, instance after instance. At last I cut them across. "What further happened at Palos?"

They put back to that port. "Oh, it didn't seem so bad that day! One and another thought, 'Perhaps I'll go!' Him they call The Admiral is a big figure of a man, and of course we that use the sea get to know how a good captain looks. We knew that he had sailed and sailed, and had had his own ship, maybe two or three of them! Then too the Pinzons and the Prior of La Rabida answered for him. A lot of us almost belong to the Pinzons, having signed to fish and voyage for them, and the Prior is a well-liked man. The alcalde folds up the letter as though he were in church, and they all come down the steps and go away to the alcalde's house which is around the corner. It wasn't until they were gone that Palos began to ask, 'Where were three ships and maybe a hundred and fifty men *going*?' "

"We found out next day," said Fernando. "The tide went out, but it came back bearing the sound of where we were going!"

"Then what happened in Palos?"

"What happened was that they couldn't get the ships and they couldn't get the men! Palos wouldn't listen. It was too wild, what they wanted to do! It wouldn't listen to the Prior and it wouldn't listen to Doctor Garcia Fernandez, and it wouldn't even listen to Captain Martin Alonso Pinzon. And when that happens—! So for a long time there was a kind of angry calm. And then, lo you! we find that they have written to the Queen and the King. There come letters to Palos, and they are harsh ones!"

"I never heard harsher from any King and Queen!" said Fernando.

"There weren't only the letters, but they'd sent also a great man, Señor Juan de Penelosa, to see that they got obedience. Upshot is we've got to go, ships and men, or else be laid by the heels! As for Palos, her old sea privileges would be taken from her, and she couldn't face that. Get those ships ready and stock them and pipe sailors aboard, or there'd be our kind Queen and King to deal with!"

"Wherever it is, we're going. Great folk are too tall and broad for us!"

"So there comes another crowd in the square, before the church. Out steps Captain Martin Pinzon, and he cries, 'Men of Palos, for all you doubt it, 'tis a glorious thing that's doing! Here is the *Niña* that my brothers and I own. She's going with Don Cristoval the Admiral, and the men who are bound to me for fishing and voyaging are going, and more than that, there is going Martin Alonso Pinzon, for I'll ask no man to go where I will not go!'

"Then up beside him starts his brothers Vicente and Francisco, and they say they are going too. Fray Ignatio stands on the church steps and cries that there are idolaters there, and he will go to tell them about our Lord Jesus Christ! Then the alcalde gets up and says that the Sovereigns must be obeyed, and that the *Santa Maria* and the *Pinta* shall be made ready. Then the pilots Sancho Ruiz and Pedro Nino and Bartolomeo Roldan push out together and say they'll go, and others follow, seeing they'll have to anyhow! So it went that day and the next and the next, until now they've pressed all they need. So I say, we are here, brother, flopping in the net!"

"When does he sail?"

"Day after tomorrow, 'tis said. But we who don't live in Palos have our orders to be there tonight. Aren't you going too, mate?"

I answered that I hadn't thought of it, and immediately, out of the whole, there rose and faced me, "You have thought of it all the time!"

Sancho spoke. "If you'll go with us to Captain Martin Pinzon, he'll enter you. He'd like to get another strong man."

I said, "I don't know. I'll have to think of it. Here is Palos, and yonder the headland with La Rabida."

We entered the town. They would have had me go with them wherever they must report themselves. But I said that I could not then, and at the mouth of their street managed to leave them. I passed through Palos and beyond its western limit came again to that house of the poorest where I had lodged six months before and waking all night had heard the Tinto flowing by like the life of a man. Long ago I had had some training in medicine, and in mind's medicine, and three years past I had brought a young working man living then in Marchena out of illness and melancholy. His parents dwelled here in this house by the Tinto and they gave me shelter.

CHAPTER IX

Rising at dawn, I walked to the sea and along it until I came at last to those dunes beneath which I had stretched myself that day of grayness. Now it was deep summer, blue and gold, and the air all balm and caressing. The evening before I had seen the three ships where they rode in river mouth. They were caravels, and only the *Santa Maria*, the largest, was fully decked. Small craft with which to find India, over a road of a thousand leagues—or no road, for road means that men have toiled there and traveled there—no road, but a wilderness plain, a water desert! The Arabians say that Jinn and Afrits live in the desert away from the caravans. If you go that way you meet fearful things and never come forth again. The *Santa Maria*, the *Pinta* and the *Niña*. The *Santa Maria* could be Master Christopherus's ship. Bright point that was his banner could be made out at the fore.

Palos waterside, in a red-filtered dusk, had been a noisy place, but the noise did not ring genially. I gathered that this small port was more largely in the mood of Pedro and Fernando than in that of Sancho. It looked frightened and it looked sullen and it looked angry.

The old woman by the Tinto talked garrulously. Thankful was she that her son Miguel dwelled ten leagues away! Else surely they would have taken him, as they were taking this one's son and that one's son! To hear her you would think of an ogre—of Polyphemus in the cave—reaching out fatal hand for this or that fattened body. Nothing then, she said, to do but to pinch and save so that one might pay the priest for masses! She told me with great eyes that a hundred leagues west of Canaries one came to a sea forest where all the trees were made of water growing up high and spreading out like branches and leaves, and that this forest was filled with sea wolves and serpents and strange beasts all made of sea water, but they could sting and rend a man very ghastly. After that you came to sirens that you could not help leaping to meet, but they put lips to men's breasts and sucked out the life. Then if the wind drove you south, you smelled smoke and at night saw flames, and if you could not get the ship about—

In mid-afternoon I left the sands and took the road to La Rabida. By the walled vineyard that climbs the hill I was met by three mounted men coming from the monastery. The first was Don Juan de Penelosa, the second was the Prior of La Rabida, the third was the Admiral of the Ocean-Sea.

Fray Juan Perez first saw me clearly, drawn up by wall. He had been quoting Latin and he broke at *Dominus et magister*. The Admiral turned gray eyes upon me. I saw his mind working. He said, "The road to Cordova—Welcome, Juan Lepe!"

"Welcome, Excellency!"

I gave him the name, seeing him for a moment somewhat whimsically as Viceroy of conquered great India of the elephants and the temples filled with bells. His face lighted. He looked at me, and I knew again that he liked me. I liked him.

My kinsman the Prior had started to speak to me, but then had shot a look at Juan de Penelosa and refrained. The Queen's officer spoke, "Why, here's another strong fellow, not so tall as some but powerfully knit! Are you used to the sea?"

I answered that I had been upon a Marseilles bark that was wrecked off Almeria, and that I had walked from San Lucar. He asked my name and I gave it. "Juan Lepe."

"I attach you then, Juan Lepe, for the service of the Queen! Behold your admiral, Don Cristoval Colon! His ships are the *Santa Maria*, the *Pinta* and the *Niña*, his destination the glorious finding of the Indies and Cipango where the poorest man drinks from a golden cup! Princes, I fancy, drink from hollowed emeralds! You will sail tomorrow at dawn. In which ship shall we put him, Señor?"

"In the *Santa Maria*," answered the Admiral.

So short as that was it done! And yet—and yet—it had been

doing for a long time, for how long a time I have no way of measuring!

Juan de Penelosa continued to speak: "Follow us into Palos where Sebastian Jaurez will give you wine and a piece of money. Thence you will go to church where indeed we are bound, all who sail being gathered there for general confession and absolution. This voyage begins Christianly!"

Said Fray Juan Perez, "Not to do that, Juan Lepe, were to cry aloud for another shipwreck!"

He used the tone of priest, thrusting in speech as priests often do, where there is no especial need of speech. But I understood that that was a mask, and could read kinsmanly anxiety in a good man's heart. I said, "I will find Sebastian Jaurez, and I will go to church, Señors. A ship is a ship, and a voyage a voyage!"

"This, Juan Lepe," said the Admiral in that peculiarly warm and thrilling voice of his, "is such a voyage as you have never been!"

I made reply, "So be it! I would have every voyage greater than the last." And as they put their steeds into motion, walked behind them downhill and over sandy ways into Palos. There I found Sebastian Jaurez who signed me in. I put into my pocket the coin he gave me and drank with him a stoup of wine, and then I went to church.

It was a great shadowy church and I found it full. Jaurez piloted me to where just under pulpit were ranged my fellow mariners, a hundred plain sailormen, no great number with which to widen the world! A score or so of better station were grouped at the head of these, and in front of all stood Christopherus Columbus. I saw again Martin Alonso Pinzon who had entered the Prior's room at La Rabida, and with him his two brothers Francisco and Vicente. Martin Pinzon would be captain of the *Pinta* and Vicente of the *Niña*. And there were Roderigo Sanchez of Segovia, Inspector-General of Armament, and Diego de Arana, chief alguazil of the expedition, and Roderigo de Escobedo, royal notary, and with these three or four young men of birth, adventuring for India now that the war with the Moor was done. And there were two physicians, Garcia Fernandez and Berardino Nuñez. And there was the Franciscan, Fray Ignatio, who would convert the heathen and preach before the Great Khan.

The Admiral of Ocean-Sea stood a taller man than any there, tall, muscular, a great figure. He was richly dressed, for as soon as he could he dressed richly. A shaft of light struck his brow and made his hair all glowing silver. His face was lifted. The air about him to my eyes swam and quivered and was faintly colored.

Fray Juan Perez preached the sermon and he used great earnestness and now and again his voice broke. He talked of God's gain that we went forth upon, reaping in a field set us. One thing came forth here that I had not before heard.

"And the unthinkable wealth that surely shall be found and gained, for these countries to which you sail have eight-tenths of the world's riches, shall put Castile and Leon where of old stood Pagan Rome, and shall make, God willing, of this very Palos a new Genoa or Venice! And this man, your Admiral, how hath he proposed to the Sovereigns to use first fruits? Why, friends, by taking finally and forever from Mahound, and for Holy Church and her servant the Spains, the Holy Sepulchre!"

In the end, we the going forth, kneeling, made general confession and the priest's hands in the dusk above absolved us. There was solemnity and there was tenderness. A hundred and twenty, we came forth from church, and around us flowed the hundreds of Palos, men and women and children. All was red under a red sunset, the boats waiting to take us out to the *Santa Maria*, the *Pinta* and the *Niña*.

We marched to waterside. Priests and friars moved with us, singing loudly the hymn to the Virgin, Lady of all seamen. Great tears ran down Fray Juan Perez's checks. It was a red sunset and the west into which we were going looked indeed blood-flecked. Don Juan de Penelosa, harking us on, had an inspiration. "You see the rubies of Cipango!"

It is not alone "great" men who bring about things in this world. All of us are in a measure great, as all are on the way to greater greatness. Sailors are brave and hardy men; that is said when it is said that they are sailors. In many hearts hung dread of this voyage and rebellion against being forced to it. But they had not to be lashed to the boats; they went with sailors' careless air and dignity. By far the most went thus. Even Fernando ceased his wailing and embarked.

The red light, or for danger or for rubies in which still might be danger, washed us all, washed the town, the folk and the sandy shore, and the boats that would take us out to the ships, small in themselves, and small by distance, riding there in the river-mouth like toys that have been made for children.

The hundred and twenty entered the boats. It was like a little fishing fleet going out together. The rowers bent to the oars, a strip of water widened between us and Spain. Loud chanted the friars, but over their voices rose the crying of farewell, now deep, now shrill. "Adios!" The sailors cried back, "Adios! Adios!" From the land it must have had a thin sound like ghosts wailing from the edge of the world. That, the sailors held and Palos held, was where the ships were going, over the edge of the world. It was the third day of August, in the year fourteen hundred and ninety-two.

Chapter X

We lost the headland of La Rabida, Palos vanished, a haze hid Spain. By nightfall all was behind us. We were set forth from native land, set forth from Europe, set forth from Christendom, set forth from sea company and sailors' cheer of other ships. That last would not be wholly true until we were gone from the Canaries, toward which islands, running south, we now were headed. We might hail some Spanish ship going to, coming from, Grand Canary. We might indeed, before we reached these islands, see other sails, for a rumor ran that the King of Portugal was sending ships to intercept us, sink us and none ever be the wiser, it not being to his interest that Spain should make discoveries! Pedro it was who put this into my ear as we hauled at the same rope. I laughed. "Here beginneth the marvelous tale of this voyage! If all happens that all say may happen, not the Pope's library can hold the books!"

The *Santa Maria* was a good enough ship, though fifty men crowded it. It was new and clean, a fair sailer, though not so swift as the *Pinta*. We mariners settled ourselves in waist and forecastle. The Admiral, Juan de la Cosa, the master, Roderigo Sanchez, Diego de Arana and Roderigo de Escobedo, Pedro Gutierrez, a private adventurer, the physician Bernardo Nuñez and Fray Ignatio had great cabin and certain small sleeping cabins and stern deck. In the forecastle almost all knew one another; all ran into kinships near or remote. But the turn of character made the real grouping. Pedro had his cluster and Sancho had his, and between swayed now to the one and now to the other a large group. Fernando, I feel gladness in saying, had with him but two or three. And aside stood variations, individuals. Beltran the cook was such a one, a bold, mirthful, likable man. We had several dry thinkers, and a braggart and two or three who proved miserably villainous. We had weathercocks and men who faced forward, no matter what the wind that blew.

The Admiral knew well that he must have, if he could, a ship patient, contented and hopeful. I bear him witness that he spared no pains. We had aboard trumpet and drum and viol, and he would have frequent music. Each day toward evening each man was given a cup of wine. And before sunset all were gathered for vesper service, and we sang *Salve Regina*. At night the great familiar stars shone out above us.

Second day passed much like first,—light fickle wind, flapping sails, smooth sea, cloudless sky. Today beheld sea life after shore grown habitual. We might have sailed from Marseilles or Genoa and been sailing for a month. If this were all, then no more terror from the Sea of Darkness than from our own so well-known sea! But Fernando said, "It is after the Canaries! We know well enough it is not so bad this side of them. Why do they call them Dog Islands?"

"Perhaps they found dogs there."

"No, but that they give warning like watchdogs! 'If you go any further it shall be to your woe!' "

"Aye, aye! Have you heard tell of the spouting mountain?"

This night the wind came up and by morning was blowing stiffly, urging us landward as though back to Spain. The sky became leaden, with a great stormy aspect. The waves mounted, the lookout cried that the *Pinta* was showing signals of distress. By now all had shortened sail, but the *Pinta* was taking in everything and presently lay under bare poles. The *Santa Maria* worked toward her until we were close by. They shouted and we back to them. It was her rudder that was unshipped and injured. Captain Martin Pinzon shouted that he would overcome it, binding it somehow in place, and would overtake us, the *Pinta* being faster sailer than the *Santa Maria* or the *Niña*. But the Admiral would not agree, and we took in all sail and lay tossed by a rough sea until afternoon when the *Pinta* signaled that the rudder was hung. But by now the sky stretched straight lead, and the water ran white-capped. We made no way till morning, when without a drop of rain all the cloud roof was driven landward and there sprang out a sky so blue that the heart laughed for joy. The violent wind sank, then veered and blowing moderately carried us again southward. All the white sails, white and new, were flung out, and we raced over a rich, green plain. That lasted through most of the day, but an hour before sunset the *Pinta* again signaled trouble. The rudder was once more worse than useless.

Again it was mended. But when the next morning it happened the third time and a kind of wailing grumble went through the *Santa Maria*, there came pronouncement from the Admiral. "The Canaries lie straight ahead. In two days we shall sight them. Very good! we shall rest there and make a new rudder for the *Pinta*. The *Niña* will do better with square sails and we can change these. Fresh meat and water and some rambling ashore!"

Beltran the cook had been to the Canaries, driven there by a perverse wind twenty years ago when he was boatswain upon a big carrack. He said it was no great way and one or two agreed with him, but others declined to believe the Admiral when he said that in two days we should behold the volcano. Some were found to clamor that the wind had driven us out of all reckoning! We might never find the Canaries and then what would the *Pinta* do? Whereas, if we all turned back to Palos—

"If—If!" answered Beltran the cook, who at first seemed strangely and humorously there as cook until one found that he had an injured leg and could not climb mast nor manage sail. "'If' is a seaman without a ship!—He's a famous navigator."

"Martin Pinzon?"

"Him too. But I meant our Admiral."

"He hasn't had a ship for years!"

"He was of the best when he had one! I've heard old Captain Ruy tell—"

"Maybe he wasn't crazy in those days, but he's crazy now!"

That was Fernando. I think it was from him that certain of the crew took the word "crazy." They used it until one would think that for pure variety's sake they would find another!

The sixth day from Palos there lifted from sea the peak of Teneriffe.

This day, passing on some errand the open door of the great cabin, I saw the Admiral seated at the table. Looking up, he saw me, gazed an instant, then lifted his voice. Come in here!"

He sat with a great chart spread upon the table before him. Beside it the log lay open, and he had under his hand a book in which he was writing. Door framed blue sky and sea, a pleasant wind was singing in a pleasant warmth, the great cabin which, with the rest of the ship, he made to be kept very clean, was awash with light and fineness of air. "Would you like to look at the chart?" he asked, and I came and looked over his shoulder.

"I made it," he said. "There is nothing in the world more useful than knowing how to make maps and charts! While I waited for Kings to make up their minds I earned my living so." I glanced at the log and he pushed it to me so that I might see. "Every day from Palos out." His strong fingers touched the other book. "My journal that I keep for myself and the Queen and King Ferdinand and indeed for the world." He turned the leaves. The bulk of them were blank, but in the front showed closely covered pages, the writing not large but clear and strong. "This voyage, you see, changeth our world! Once in Venice I heard a scholar learned in the Greek tell of an old voyage of a ship called *Argo*, whence its captain and crew were named Argonauts, and he said that it was of all voyages most famous with the ancients. This is like that, but probably greater." He turned the pages. "I shall do it in the manner of Cæsar his Commentaries."

He knew himself, I thought, for as great a man as Cæsar. All said, his book might be as prized in some unentered future. He did not move where time is as a film, but where time is deep, a thousand years as a day. He could not see there in detail any more than we could see tree and house in those Canaries upon which we were bearing down.

I said, "Now that printing is general, it may go into far lands and into multitude of hands and heads. Many a voyager to come may study it."

He drew deep breath. "It is the very truth! Prince Henry the Navigator. Christopherus Columbus the Navigator, and greater than the first—"

Sun shone, wind sang, blue sea danced beyond the door. Came from deck Roderigo Sanchez and Diego de Arana. The Admiral made me a gesture of dismissal.

The Canaries and we drew together. Great bands of cloud hid much of the higher land, but the volcano top came clear above cloud, standing bare and solemn against blue heaven. Leaving upon our right Grand Canary we stood for the island of Gomera. Here we found deep, clear water close to shore, a narrow strand, a small Spanish fort and beginnings of a village, and inland, up ravines clad with a strange, leafless bush, plentiful huts of the conquered Guanches. Our three ships came to anchor, and the Admiral went ashore, the captains of the *Pinta* and the *Niña* following. Juan Lepe was among the rowers.

The Spanish commandant came down to beach with an armed escort. The Admiral, walking alone, met him between sea and bright green trees, and here stood the two and conversed while we watched. The Admiral showed him letters of credence. The commandant took and read, handed them back with a bow, and coming to water edge had presented to him the two captains, Martin and Vicente Pinzon. He proved a cheery old veteran of old wars, relieved that we were not Portuguese nor pirates and happy to have late news from Spain. It seemed that he had learned from a supply ship in June that the expedition was afoot.

The *Santa Maria* and the *Niña* rode close in shore. Captain Martin Pinzon beached the *Pinta* and unshipped the hurt and useless rudder. Work upon a new one began at once. The Admiral, the two captains and those of rank upon the ships supped with the commandant at his quite goodly house, and the next day he and his officers dined aboard the *Santa Maria*. The Admiral liked him much for he was more than respectful toward this voyage. A year before, bathing one day in the surf, there had come floating to his hand a great gourd. None such grew anywhere in these islands, and the wind for days had come steadily from the west. The gourd had a kind of pattern cut around it. He showed it to the Admiral and afterwards gave it to him. The latter caused it to pass from hand to hand among the seamen. I had it in my hands and truly saw no reason why it might not have been cut by some native of the West, and, carried away by the tide or dropped perchance from a boat, have at last, after long time, come into hands not Indian. Asia tossing unthinkingly a ball which Europe caught.

The *Pinta* proved in worse plight than was at first thought. The *Niña* also found this or that to do besides squaring her Levant sails. We stayed in Gomera almost three weeks. The place was novel, the day's task not hard, the Admiral and his captains complaisant. We had leisure and island company. To many it was happiness enough. While we stopped at Gornera we were at least not drifting upon lodestone, equator fire and chaos!

Here on Gomera might be studied the three Pinzon brothers. Vicente was a good, courageous captain, Francisco a good pilot, and a courageous, seldom-speaking man. But Martin Alonso, the eldest, was the prime mover in all their affairs. He was skillful navigator like his brothers and courageous like them, but not silent like Francisco, and ambitious far above either. He would have said perhaps that had he not been so, been both ambitious and shrewd, the Pinzons would never have become principal ship-owning, trading and maritime family of Palos and three leagues around. He, too, had family fortunes and aggrandizement at heart, though hardly on the grand, imperial scale of the Admiral. He had much manly beauty, daring and strength. His two brothers worshipped him, and in most places and moments his crew would follow him with a cheer. The Admiral was bound to him, not only in that he had volunteered and made others to go willingly, but that he had put in his ship, the *Niña*, and had furnished Master Christopherus with monies. That eighth of the cost of the expedition, whence else could it come? If it tied Martin Pinzon to the Admiral, seeing that only through success could those monies be repaid, it likewise made him feel that he, too, had authority, was at liberty to advise, and at need to become critical.

But the Admiral had the great man's mark. He could acknowledge service and be quite simply and deeply grateful for it. He was grateful to Martin Pinzon who had aided him from his first coming to Palos, and also I think he loved the younger man's great blond strength and beauty. He had all of Italy's quickness to beauty, be it of land or sea, forest, flower, animal or man. But now and again, even so early as this, he must put out hand to check Pinzon's impetuous advice. His brows drew together above gray eyes and eagle nose. But for the most part, on Gomera, they were very friendly, and it was a sight to see Admiral and captains and all the privileged of the expedition sit at wine with the commandant.

Juan Lepe had no quarrel with any of them. Jayme de Marchena swept this voyage into the Great Voyage.

The *Pinta* was nearly ready when there arrived a small ship from Ferro bringing news that three large Portuguese ships had sailed by that island. Said the commandant, "Spain and Portugal are at peace. They would not dare to try to oust us!" He came to waterside to talk to the Admiral. "Not to fight you," said the Admiral, "but me! King John wishes to keep India, Cipango and Cathay still veiled. So he will get time in which to have from the Holy Father another bull that will place the Portuguese line west and west until he hath the whole!" He raised his hand and let it fall. "I cannot sail tomorrow, but I will sail the day after!"

We were put to hard labor for the rest of that day, and through much of the moonlit night. By early morning again we labored. At mid-afternoon all was done. The *Pinta*, right from stem to stern, rode the blue water; the *Niña* had her great square sails. The Guanches stored for us fresh provisions and rolled down and into ship our water casks. There was a great moon, and we would stand off in the night. Nothing more had been seen of the Portuguese ships, but we were ready to go and go we should. All being done, and the sun two hours high, we mariners had leave to rest ashore under trees who might not for very long again see land or trees.

There was a grove that led to a stream and the waterfall where we had filled the casks. I walked through this alone. The place lay utterly still save for the murmuring of the water and the singing of a small yellowish bird that abounds in these islands. At the end of an aisle of trees shone the sea, blue and calm as a sapphire of heaven. I lay down upon the earth by the water.

Finding of India and rounding the earth! We seemed poor, weak men, but the thing was great, and I suppose the doers of a great thing are great. East—west! Going west and yet east. The Jew in me had come from Palestine, and to Palestine perhaps from Arabia, and to Arabia—who knew?—perhaps from India! And much of the Spaniard had come from Carthage and from Phoenicia, old Tyre and Sidon, and Tyre and Sidon again from the east. From the east and to the east again. All our Age that with all lacks was yet a stirring one with a sense of dawn and sunrise and distant trumpets, now was going east, was going Home, going east by the west road. West is home and East is home, and North and South. Knowledge extendeth and the world above is fed.

The sun made a lane of scarlet and gold across Ocean-Sea. I wondered what temples, what towns, what spice ships at strange wharfs might lie under it afar. I wondered if there did dwell Prester John and if he would step down to give us welcome. The torrent of event strikes us day and night, all the hours, all the moments. Who can tell with distinctness color and shape in that descending stream?

CHAPTER XI

An hour after moonrise we were gone from Gomera. At first a light wind filled the sails, but when the round moon went down in the west and the sun rose, there was Teneriffe still at hand, and the sea glassy. It rested like a mirror all that day, and the sails hung empty and the banner at maintop but a moveless wisp of cloth. In the night arose a contrary wind, and another red dawn showed us Teneriffe still. The wind dropping like a shot, we hung off Ferro, fixed in blue glass. Watch was kept for the Portuguese, but they also would be rooted to sea bottom. The third morning up whistled the wind, blowing from Africa and filling every sail.

Palos to the Canaries, we had sailed south. Now for long, long days the sun rose right aft, and when it set dyed with red brow and eyes and cheek and breast of the carved woman at our prow. She wore a great crown, and she looked ever with wide eyes upon the west that we chased. Straight west over Ocean-Sea, the first men, the first ships! If ever there had been others, our world knew it not. The Canaries sank into the east. Turn on heel around one's self, and mark never a start of land to break the rim of the vast sea bowl! Never a sail save those above us of the *Santa Maria*, or starboard or larboard, the *Pinta* and the *Niña*.

The loneliness was vast and utter. We might fail here, sink here, die here, and indeed fail and sink and die alone!

Two seamen lay sick in their beds, and the third day from Gomera the *Santa Maria*'s physician, Bernardo Nuñez, was seized with the same malady. At first Fray Ignatio tried to take his place, but here the monk lacked knowledge. One of the sailors died, a ship boy sickened, and the physician's fever increased upon him. Diego de Arana began to fail. The ship's master came at supper time and looked us over. "Is there any here who has any leech craft?" Beltran the cook said, "I can set a bone and wash a wound; but it ends there!"

Cried Fernando from his corner. "Is the plague among us!" The master turned on him. "Here and now, I say five lashes for the man who says that word again! Has any man here sense about a plain fever?"

None else speaking, I said that long ago I had studied for a time with a leech, and that I was somewhat used to care of the sick. "Then you are my man!" quoth the master, and forthwith took me to the Admiral. I became Juan Lepe, the physician.

It was, I held, a fever received while wandering through the ravines and woods of Gomera. Master Bernardo had in his cabin drugs and tinctures, and we breathed now all the salt of Ocean-Sea, and the ship was clean. I talked to Beltran the cook about diet, and I chose Sancho and a man that I liked, one Luis Torres, for nurses. Two others sickened this night, and one the next day, but none afterward. None died; in ten days all were recovered. Other ailments aboard I doctored also. Don Diego de Arana was subject to fits of melancholy with twitchings of the body. I had watched Isaac the Physician cure such things as this, and now I followed instruction. I put my hands upon the patient and I strengthened his will with mine, sending into him desire for health and perception of health. His inner man caught tune. The melancholy left him and did not return. Master Bernardo threw off the fever, sat up and moved about. But he was still weak, and still I tended the others for him.

The *Pinta* had signaled four men ill. But Garcia Fernandez, the Palos physician, was there with Martin Pinzon, and the sick recovered. The *Niña* had no doctor and now she came near to the *Santa Maria* and sent a boat. She had five sick men and would borrow Bernardo Nuñez.

The Admiral spoke with Nuñez, now nearly well. Then the physician made a bundle of drugs and medicaments, said farewell to all and kindly enough to me, and rowed away to the *Niña*. He was a friend of the Pinzons, and above the vanity of the greater ship. The sick upon the *Niña* prospered under him.

But Juan Lepe was taken from the forecastle, and slept where Nuñez had slept, and had his place at the table in the great cabin. He turned from the sailor Juan Lepe to the physician Juan Lepe, becoming "Doctor" and "Señor." The wheel turns and a man's past makes his present.

A few days from Gomera, an hour after sunset, the night was torn by the hugest, flaming, falling star that any of us had ever seen. The mass drove down the lower skirt of the sky, leaving behind it a wake of fire. It plunged into the sea. There is no sailor but knows shooting stars. But this was a hugely great one, and Ocean-Sea very lonely, and to most there our errand a spectral and frightening one. It needed both the Admiral and Fray Ignatio to quell the panic.

The next day a great bird like a crane passed over the *Santa Maria*. It came from Africa, behind us. But it spoke of land, and the sailors gazed wistfully.

This day I entered the great cabin when none was there but the Admiral, and again he sat at table with his charts and his books. He asked of the sick and I answered. Again he sat looking through open door and window at blue water, a great figure of a man with a great head and face and early-silvered hair. "Do you know aught," he asked, "of astrology?"

I answered that I knew a little of the surface of it.

"I have a sense," he said, "that our stars are akin, yours and mine. I felt it the day Granada fell, and I felt it on Cordova road, and again that day below La Rabida when we turned the corner and the bells rang and you stood beside the vineyard wall. Should I not have learned in more than fifty years to know a man? The stars are akin that will endure for vision's sake."

I said, "I believe that, my Admiral."

He sat in silence for a moment, then drew the log between us and turned several pages so that I might see the reckoning. "We have come well," I said. "Yet with so fair a wind, I should have thought—"

He turned the leaves till he rested at one covered with other figures. "Here it is as it truly is, and where we truly are! We have oversailed all that the first show, and so many leagues besides."

"Two records, true and untrue! Why do you do it so?"

"I have told them that after seven hundred leagues we should find land. Add fifty more for our general imperfection. But it may be wider than I think. We may not come even to some fringing island in eight hundred leagues, no, nor in more than that! If it be a thousand, if it be two thousand, on I go! But after the seven hundred is passed, it will be hard to keep them in hand. So, though we are covering more, I let them think we are covering only this."

I could but laugh. Two reckonings! After all, he was not Italian for nothing!

"The master knows," he said, "and also Diego de Arana. But at least one other should know. Two might drown or perish from sickness. I myself might fall sick and die, though I will not believe it!" He paused a moment, then said, looking directly at me, "I need one in whom I can utterly confide. I should have had with me my brother Bartholomew. But he is in England. A man going to seek a Crown jewel for all men should have with him son or brother. Diego de Arana is a kinsman of one whom I love, and he partly believes. But Roderigo Sanchez and the others believe hardly at all. There is Fray Ignatio. He believes, and I confess my sins to him. But he thinks only of penitents, and this matter needs mind, not heart alone. Because of that sense of the stars, I tell you these things."

The next day it came to me that in that Journal which he meant to make like Cæsar's Commentaries, he might put down the change in the *Santa Maria's* physicians and set my name there too often. I watched my chance and finding it, asked that he name me not in that book. His gray eyes rested upon me; he demanded the reason for that. I said that in Spain I was in danger, and that Juan Lepe was not my name. More than that I did not wish to say, and perchance it were wiser for him not to know. But I would not that the powerful should mark me in his Journal or elsewhere!

Usually his eyes were wide and filled with light as though it were sent into them from the vast lands that he continuously saw. But he could be immediate captain and commander of things and of men, and when that was so, the light drew into a point, and he became eagle that sees through the wave the fish. Had he been the seer alone, truly he might have been the seer of what was to be discovered and might have set others upon the path. But he would not have sailed on the *Santa Maria*!

In his many years at sea he must many times have met men who had put to sea out of fear of land. He would have sailed with many whose names, he knew, were not those given them at birth. He must have learned to take reasons for granted and to go on—where he wished to go on. So we gazed at each other.

"I had written down," he said, "that you greatly helped the sick, and upon Bernardo Nuñez's going to the *Niña*, became our physician. But I will write no more of you, and that written will pass in the flood of things to come." After a moment, he ended with deliberation, "I know my star to be a great star, burning long and now with a mounting flame. If yours is in any wise its kin, then there needs must be histories."

CHAPTER XII

It was a strange thing how utterly favoring now was the wind! It blew with a great steady push always from the east, and always we ran before it into the west. Day after day we experienced this warm and steadfast driving; day after day we never shifted sail. The rigging sang a steady song, day and night. The crowned woman, our figurehead, ran, light-footed, over a green and blue plain, and where the plain ended no man might know! "Perhaps it does not end!" said the mariners.

Of the hidalgos aboard I like best Diego de Arana who had cast off his melancholy. He was a man of sense, candid and brave. Roderigo Sanchez sat and moved a dull, good man. Roderigo de Escobedo had courage, but he was factious, would take sides against his shadow if none other were there. Pedro Gutierrez had been a courtier, and had the vices of that life, together with a daredevil recklessness and a kind of wild wit. I had liking and admiration for Fray Ignatio, but careful indeed was I when I spoke with him!

The wind blew unchanging, the stark blue shield of sea, a water-world, must be taken in the whole, for there was no contrasting point in it to catch the eye. Sancho, forward, in a high sweet voice like a jongleur's voice, was singing to the men an endless ballad. Upon the stern deck Escobedo and Gutierrez, having diced themselves to an even wealth or poverty, turned to further examination of the Admiral's ways. Endlessly they made him and his views subject of talk. Roderigo Sanchez listened with a face like an owl, Diego de Arana with some irony about his lips. I came and stood beside the latter.

They were upon the beggary of Christopherus Columbus. "How did the Prior of La Rabida—?"

"I'll tell you, for I heard it. One evening at vesper bell comes our Admiral—no less a man!—to Priory gate with a young boy in his hand. Not Fernando his love-child, but Diego the elder, who was born in Lisbon. All dusty with the road, like any beggar you see, and not much better clad, foot-sore and begging bread for himself and the boy. And because of his white hair, and because he carried himself in that absurd way that makes the undiscerning cry, 'Ah, my lord king in disguise!' the porter must have him in, and by and by comes the prior and stands to talk with him, 'From where?' 'From Cordova.' 'Whither?' 'To Portugal.' 'For why?' 'To speak again with King John!' 'Are you in the habit of speaking with kings?' 'Aye, I am!' 'About what, may I ask?' 'About the finding of India by way of Ocean-Sea, the possession of idolatrous countries and the great wealth thereof, and the taking of Christ to the heathen who else are lost!' "

"Ha, ha! Ha, ha!" This was Escobedo.

"The prior thinks, 'This is an interesting madman.' And being a charitable good man and lacking entertainment that evening, he brings the beggar in to supper and sits by him."

Roderigo Sanchez opened his mouth. "All Andalusia knows Fray Juan Perez is a kind of visionary!"

"Aye, like to like! 'Have you been to our Queen and the King?' 'Aye, I have!' saith the beggar, 'but they are warring with the Moors and will pull Granada down and do not see the greater glory!' "

All laughed at that, and indeed Gutierrez could mimic to perfection. We got, full measure, the beggar's loftiness.

"So the siren sings and the prior leaps to meet her, or tarantula stings him and be dances! 'I am growing mad too,' thinks Fray Juan Perez, and begins presently to tell that last week he dreamed of Prester John. The end is that he and the beggar talk till midnight and the next morning they talk again, and the prior sends for his friends Captain Martin Alonzo Pinzon and the physician Garcia Fernandez. The beggar gains them all!"

"Do you think a beggar can do that?" I said. "Only a giver can do that."

Pedro Gutierrez turned black eyes upon Juan Lepe, whom he resented there on the stern deck. "How could you have learned so much, Doctor, while you were making sail and washing ship?" He was my younger in every way, and I answered equably, "I learned in the same way that the Admiral learned while he begged."

"Touched!" said Diego de Arana. "So that is the way the prior came into the business?"

"He enters with such vigor," said Gutierrez, "that what does he do but write an impassioned letter to the Queen, having long ago, for a time, been her confessor? What he tells her, God knows, but it seems that it changes the world! She answers that for herself she hath grieved for Master Columbus's departure from the court and the realm, and that if he will turn and come to Santa Fé, his propositions shall at last be thoroughly weighed. Letter finds the beggar with his boy honored guest of La Rabida, touching heads with Martin Pinzon over maps and charts and the 'Book of Travels' of Messer Marco Polo. There is great joy! The beggar hath the prior's own mule and his son a jennet, and here we go to Santa Fé! That was last year. Now the boy that whimpered for bread at convent gate is Don Diego Colon, page to Prince Juan, and the Viceroy sails on the *Santa Maria* for the countries he will administer!"

Gutierrez shook the dice in the box. "Oh, Queen Luck, that I have served for so long! Why do you not make me viceroy?"

Said Escobedo, "Viceroy of the continent of water and Admiral of seaweed and fishes!"

Diego de Arana took that up. "We are obliged to find something! No sensible man can think like some of those forward that this goes on forever and we shall sail till the wood rots and sails grow ragged and wind carries away their shreds or they fall into dust!"

"Who knows anything of River-Ocean? We may not find the western shore, if there be such a thing, for a year! By that time storm will sink us ten times over, or plague will take us—"

"There's not needed plague nor storm. Just say, food won't last, and water is already half gone!"

"That's the undeniable truth," quoth Roderigo Sanchez, and looked with a perturbed face at the too-smooth sea.

Smooth blue sea continued, wind continued, pushing like a great, warm hand, east to west. The Admiral spent hours alone in his sleeping cabin. There were men who said that he studied there a great book of magic. He had often a book in his hand, it is true, but Juan Lepe the physician knew what he strove to keep from others, that the gout that at times threatened crippling was upon him and was easier to bear lying down.

Sunset, vesper prayer and *Salve Regina*. As the strains died, there became evident a lingering on the part of the seamen. The master spoke to the Admiral. "They've found out about the needle, sir! Perhaps you'd better hear them and answer them."

Almost every day he heard them and answered them. To make his seamen, however they groaned and grumbled and plotted, yet abide him and his purpose was a day-after-day arising task! Now he said equably, in the tone almost of a father, "What is it today, men?"

The throng worked and put forward a spokesman, who looked from the Admiral to the clear north. "It is the star, sir! The needle no longer points to it! We thought you might explain to us unlearned—What we think is that distance is going to widen and widen! What's to keep needle from swinging right south? Then will we never get home to Palos and our wives and children—never and never and never!"

Said the Admiral, "It will not change further, or if it does a very little further!" In his most decisive, most convincing voice he explained why the needle no longer pointed precisely to the star. The deviation marked and allowed for, it was near enough for practical purposes, and the reasons for the wandering—

I do not know if the wisdom of our descendants will confirm his explanation. It is so often to explain the explanation! But one as well as another might do here. What the *Santa Maria* wanted was reassurance, general and large, stretching from the Canaries to India and Cathay and back again. He knew that, and after no great time spent with compass needle and circularly traveling polar star, he began to talk gold and estate, and the pearls and silk and spices they would surely take for gifts to their family and neighbors, Palos or Huelva or Fishertown!

It was truly the hope that upheld many on a voyage that they chose to think a witches' one. He talked now out of Marco Polo and he clad what that traveler had said in more gorgeous attire. He meant nothing false; his exalted imagination saw it so. He was painter of great pageants, heightening and remodeling, deepening and purifying colors, making humdrum and workaday over to his heart's desire. The Venetian in his book, and other travelers in their books, had related wonders enough. These grew with him, it might be said—and indeed in his lifetime was often said—into wonders without a foot upon earth. But if one took as figures and symbols his gold roofs and platters, temples and gardens, every man a merchant in silks and spices, strange fruit-dropping trees and pearls in carcanets, the Grand Khan and Prester John—who could say that in the long, patient life of Time the Admiral was over-esteeming? The pity of it was that most here could not live in great lengths of time. They wanted riches now, now! And they wanted only one kind of riches; here and now, or at the most in another month, in the hands and laps of Pedro and Fernando and Diego.

Chapter XIII

There grew at times an excited feeling that he was a prophet, and that there were fabulously great things before us. As I doctored some small ill one day in the forecastle, a great fellow named Francisco from Huelva would tell me his dream of the night before. He had already told it, it seemed, to all who would listen, and now again he had considerable audience, crowding at the door. He said that he dreamed he was in Cipango. At first he thought it was heaven, but when he saw golden roofs he knew it must be Cipango, for in heaven where it never rained and there were no nights, we shouldn't need roofs. One interrupted, "We'd need them to keep the flying angels from looking in!"

"It was Cipango," persisted Francisco, "for the Emperor himself came and gave me a rope of pearls. There were five thousand of them, and each would buy a house or a fine horse or a suit of velvet. And the Emperor took me by the hand, and he said, 'Dear Brother—' You might have thought I was a king—and by the mass, I was a king! I felt it right away! And then he took me into a garden, and there were three beautiful women, and one of them would push me to the other, and that one to the third, and that to the first again, as though they were playing ball, and they all laughed, and I laughed. Then there came a great person with five crowns on his head, and all the light blazed up gold and blue, and somebody said, 'It's Prester John'!"

His dream kept a two-days' serenity upon the ship. It came to the ear of the Admiral, who said, " 'In dreams will I instruct thee.'—I have had dreams far statelier than his."

Pedro Gutierrez too began to dream,—fantastic things which he told with an idle gusto. They were of wine and gold and women, though often these were to be guessed through strange, jumbled masks and phantasies. "Those are ill dreams," said the Admiral. "Dream straight and high!" Fray Ignatio, too, said wisely, "It is not always God who cometh in dreams!"

But the images of Gutierrez's dreams seemed to him to be seated in Cathay and India. They bred in him belief that he was coming to happiness by that sea road that glistered before us. He and Roderigo de Escobedo began to talk with assurance of what they should find. Having small knowledge of travelers' tales they made application to the Admiral who, nothing loth, answered them out of Marco Polo, Mandeville and Pedro de Aliaco.

But the ardor of his mind was such that he outwent his authors. Where the Venetian said "gold" the Genoese said "Much gold." Where the one saw powerful peoples with their own customs, courts, armies, temples, ships and trade, the other gave to these an unearthly tinge of splendor. Often as he sat in cabin or on deck, or rising paced to and fro, we who listened to his account, listened to poet and enthusiast speaking of earths to come. Besides books like those of Marco Polo and John Mandeville and the Bishop of Cambrai he had studied philosophers and the ancients and Scripture and the Fathers. He spoke unwaveringly of prophecies, explicit and many, of his voyage, and the rounding out of earth by him, Christopherus Columbus. More than once or twice, in the great cabin, beneath the swinging lantern, he repeated to us such passages, his voice making great poetry of old words. "Averroes saith—Albertus Magnus saith—Aristotle saith—Seneca saith—Saint Augustine saith—Esdras in his fourth book saith—" Salt air sweeping through seemed to fall into a deep, musical beat and rhythm. "After the council at Salamanca when the great churchmen cried Irreligion and even Heresy upon me, I searched all Scripture and drew testimony together. In fifty, yea, in a hundred places it is plain! King David saith—job saith—Moses saith—Thus it reads in Genesis—"

Diego de Arana smote the table with his hand. "I am yours, Señor, to find for the Lord!" Fray Ignatio lifted dark eyes. "I well believe that nothing happens but what is chosen! I will tell you that in my cell at La Rabida I heard a cry, 'Come over, Ignatio the Franciscan!'"

And I, listening, thought, "Not perhaps that ancient spiritual singing of spiritual things! But in truth, yes, it is chosen. Did not the Whole of Me that I can so dimly feel set my foot upon this ship?" And going out on deck before I slept, I looked at the stars and thought that we were like the infant in the womb that knows not how nor where it is carried.

We might be four hundred leagues from Spain. Still the wind drove us, still we hardly shifted canvas, still the sky spread clear, of a vast blue depth, and the blue glass plain of the sea lay beneath. It was too smooth, the wind in our rigging too changeless of tune. At last, all would have had variety spring. There began a veritable hunger for some change, and it was possible to feel a faint horror. *What if this is the horror—to go on forever and ever like this*?

Then one morning when the sun rose, it lit a novel thing. Seaweed or grass or herbage of some sort was afloat about us. Far as the eye might reach it was like a drowned meadow, vari-colored, awash. All that day we watched it. It came toward us from the west; we ran through it from the east. Now it thinned away; now it thickened until it seemed that the sea was strewn with rushes like a castle floor. With oars we caught and brought into ship wreaths of it. All night we sailed in this strange plain. A yellow dawn showed it still on either side the *Santa Maria*, and thicker, with fewer blue sea straits and passes than on yesterday.

The *Pinta* and the *Niña* stood out with a strange, enchanted look, as ships crossing a plain more vast than the plain of Andalusia. Still that floating weed thickened. The crowned woman at our prow pushed swathes of it to either side. Our mariners hung over rail, talking, talking. "What is it—and where will it end? Mayhap presently we cannot plough it!"

I was again and again to admire how for forty years he had stored sea-knowledge. It was not only what those gray eyes had seen, or those rather large, well molded ears had heard, or that powerful and nervous hand had touched. But he knew how to take, right and left, knowledge that others gathered, as he knew that others took and would take what he gathered. He knew that knowledge flows. Now he stood and told that no less a man than Aristotle had recorded such a happening as this. Certain ships of Gades—that is our Cadiz—driven by a great wind far into River-Ocean, met these weeds or others like them, distant parents of these. They were like floating islands forever changing shape, and those old ships sailed among them for a while. They thought they must have broken from sea floor and risen to surface, and currents brought other masses from land. Tunny fish were caught among them.

And that very moment, as the endless possibilities of things would have it, one, leaning on the rail, cried out that there were tunnies. We all looked and saw them in a clear canal between two floating masses. It brought the Admiral credence. "Look you all!" he said, "how most things have been seen before!"

"But Father Aristotle's ship—Was he 'Saint' or 'Father'?"

"He was a heathen—he believed in Mahound."

"No, he lived before Mahound. He was a wise man—"

"But his ships turned back to Cadiz. They were afraid of this stuff—that's the point!"

"They turned back," said the Admiral. "And the splendor and the gold were kept for us."

A thicker carpet of the stuff brushed ship side. One of the boys cried, "Ho, there is a crab!" It sat indeed on a criss-cross of broken reeds, and it seemed to stare at us solemnly. "Do not all see that it came from land, and land to the west?"

"But it is caught here! What if we are caught here too? These weeds may stem us—turn great crab pincers and hold us till we rot!"

"If—and if—and if" cried the Admiral. "For Christ, His sake, laugh at yourselves!"

On, on, we went before that warm and potent wind, so steadfast that there must be controlling it some natural law. Ocean-Sea spread around, with that weed like a marsh at springtide. Then, suddenly, just as the murmuring faction was murmuring again, we cleared all that. Open sea, blue running ocean, endlessly endless!

The too-steady sunshine vanished. There broke a cloudy dawn followed by light rain. It ceased and the sky cleared. But in the north held a mist and a kind of semblance of far-off mountains. Startled, a man cried "Land!" but the next moment showed that it was cloud. Yet all day the mist hung in this quarter. The *Pinta* approached and signaled, and presently over to us put her boat, in it Martin Pinzon. The Admiral met him as he came up over side and would have taken him into great cabin. But, no! Martin Pinzon always spoke out, before everybody! "Señor, there is land yonder, under the north! Should not we change course and see what is there?"

"It is cloud," answered the Admiral. "Though I do not deny that such a haze may be crying, 'Land behind!' "

"Let us sail then north, and see!"

But the Admiral shook his head. "No, Captain! West—west—arrow straight!"

Pinzon appeared about to say, "You are very wrong, and we should see what's behind that arras!" But he checked himself, standing before Admiral and Don and Viceroy, and all those listening faces around. "I still think," he began.

The other took him up, but kept considerate, almost deferring manner. "Yes, if we had time or ships to spare! But now it is, do not stray from the path. Sail straight west!"

"We are five hundred leagues from Palos."

"Less than that, by our reckoning. The further from Palos, the nearer India!"

"We may be passing by our salvation!"

"Our salvation lies in going as we set forth to go." He made his gesture of dismissal of that, and asked after the health of the *Pinta*. The health held, but the stores were growing low. Biscuit enough, but bacon almost out, and not so many measures of beans left. Oil, too, approached bottom of jars. The *Niña* was in the same case.

"Food and water will last," said the Admiral. "We have not come so far without safely going farther."

Martin Alonso Pinzon was the younger man and but captain of the *Pinta*, while the other stood Don and Admiral, appointed by Majesty, responsible only to the Crown. But he had been Master Christopherus the dreamer, who was shabbily dressed, owed money, almost begged. He owed large money now to Martin Pinzon. But for the Pinzons, he could hardly have sailed. He should listen now, take good advice, that was clearly what the captain of the *Pinta* thought!

Undoubtedly Master Christopherus dreamed true to a certain point, but after that was not so followable! As for Cristoforo Colombo, Italian shipmaster, he had, it was true, old sea wisdom. But Martin Pinzon thought Martin Pinzon was as good there!—Captain Martin Alonso said good-by with some haughtiness and went stiffly back over blue sea to the *Pinta*.

The sun descended, the sea grew violet, all we on the *Santa Maria* gathered for vesper prayer and song. Fray Ignatio's robe and back-thrown cowl burned brown against the sea and the sail. One last broad gold shaft lighted the tall Admiral, his thick white hair, his eagle nose, his strong mouth. Diego de Arana was big, alert and soldierly; Roderigo Sanchez had the look of alcalde through half a lifetime. I had seen Roderigo de Escobedo's like in dark streets in France and Italy and Castile, and Pedro Gutierrez wherever was a court. Juan de la Cosa, the master, stood a keen man, thin as a string. Out of the crowd of mariners I pick Sancho and Beltran the cook, Ruiz the pilot, William the Irishman and Arthur the Englishman, and two or three others. And Luis Torres. The latter was a thinker, and a Jew in blood. He carried it in his face, considerably more markedly than I carried my grandmother Judith. But his family had been Christian for a hundred years. Before I left forecastle for stern I had discovered that he was learned. Why he had turned sailor I did not then know, but afterwards found that it was for disappointed love. He knew Arabic and Hebrew, Aristotle and Averroes, and he had a dry curiosity and zest for life that made for him the wonder of this voyage far outweigh the danger.

There was a hymn that Fray Ignatio taught us and that we sang at times, beside the Latin chant. He said that a brother of his convent had written it and set it to music.

Thou that art above us,
Around us, beneath us,
Thou who art within us,
Save us on this sea!
Out of danger,
Teach us how we may
Serve thee acceptably
Teach us how we may
Crown ourselves, crowning Thee!

Beltran the cook's voice was the best, and after him Sancho, and then a sailor with a great bass, William the Irishman. Fray Ignatio sang like a good monk, and Pedro Gutierrez like a troubadour of no great weight. The Admiral sang with a powerful and what had once been a sweet voice. Currents and eddies of sweetness marked it still. All sang and it made together a great and pleasurable sound, rolling over the sea to the *Pinta* and the *Niña*, and so their singing, somewhat less in volume, came to us. All grew dusk, the ships were bat wings sailing low; out sprang the star to which the needle no longer pointed. The great star Venus hung in the west like the lantern of some ghostly air ship, very vast.

Thou that art above us,
Around us, beneath us,
Thou that art within us,
Save us on this sea!

CHAPTER XIV

We were a long, long way from Spain. A flight of birds went over us. They were flying too high for distinguishing, but we did not hold them to be sea birds. We sounded, but the lead touched no bottom. West and west and west, pushed by that wind! Late September, and we had left Palos the third of August.

The wind shifted and became contrary. The sea that for so long had been glassy smooth took on a roughness. A bird that was surely a forest bird beaten to us perched upon a stretched rope and uttered three quick cries. A boy climbed and softly took it from behind. It fluttered in the Admiral's two hands. All came to look. Its plumage was blue, its breast reddish. We wondered, but before we could make it a cage, it strongly strove and was gone. One flash and all the azure took it to itself.

In the night the waves flattened. Rose-dawn showed smooth sea and every sail filled again with that westward journeying wind. Yesterday's roughness and the bird tossed aboard were as a dream.

A day and a day and a day. As much Ocean-Sea as ever, and Asia a lie, and alike at this end and that of the vessel a dull despondency, and Pedro Gutierrez's wit grown ugly. So naked, so lonely, so indifferent spread the Sea of Darkness!

Another day and another and another. When half the ship was at the point of mutiny signs reappeared and thickened.

Birds flew over the ships; one perched beside the Admiral's banner and sang. More than that, a wood dove came upon the deck and ate corn that was strewed for it. "Colombo—Colombo!" quoth the Admiral. "I, too, am 'dove.' '*And he opened a window and sent forth a "dove" to find if there were land!*' "

Almost the whole ship from Jason down took these two birds for portents. Fray Ignatio lifted hands. “The Blessed Francis who knew that birds have souls to save hath sent them!” We passed the drifting branch of a tree. It had green leaves. The sea ran extremely blue and clear, and half the ship thought they smelled frankincense, brought on the winds which now were changeable. At evening rose a great cry of “Land!” and indeed to one side the sinking sun seemed veritable cliffs with a single mountain peak. The Admiral, who knew more of sea and air than any two men upon those ships, cried “Cloud—cloud!” but for a time none believed him. There sprang great commotion, the *Pinta* too signaling. Then before our eyes came a rift in the mountain and the cliffs slipped into the sea.

But now all believed in land ahead. It was as though someone had with laughter tossed them that assurance over the horizon straight before us. Every mariner now was emulous to be the lookout, every man kept eyes on the west. Now sprang clear and real to them the royal promise of ten thousand maravedies pension to him who first sighted Cipango, Cathay or India. The Admiral added a prize of a green velvet doublet.

We had come nigh eight hundred leagues.

In the cabin, upon the table he spread Toscanelli’s map, and beside it a great one like it, of his own making, signed in the corner *Columbus de Terra Rubra*. The depiction was of a circle, and in the right or eastern side showed the coasts of Ireland and England, France, Spain and Portugal, and of Africa that portion of which anything was known. Out in Ocean appeared the islands gained in and since Prince Henry’s day. Their names were written,—Madeira, Canaria, Cape de Verde and Azores. West of these and filling the middle map came Ocean-Sea, an open parchment field save for here a picture of a great fish, and here a siren and here Triton, and here the Island of the Seven Cities and here Saint Brandon’s Isle, and these none knew if they be real or magical! Wide middle map and River-Ocean! The eye quitting that great void approached the left or western side of the circle. And now again began islands great and small with legends written across and around them. The great island was Cipango, and across the extent of it ran in fine lettering. “Marco Polo was here. It is the richest of the eastern lands. The houses are roofed with gold. The people are idolaters. There are spices and pearls, nutmegs, pepper and precious stones. Very much gold so that the common people use it as they wish."

We read, the Admiral seated, we, the great cabin group, standing, bending over the table. After the islands came mainland. "Cathay" ran the writing. "Mangi. Here is the seat of the Great Khan. His city is Cambalu." South of all this ran other drawings and other legends. "Here, opposite Africa, near the equator, are islands called Manillas. They have lodestone, so that no ship with iron can sail to them. Here is Java of all the spices. Here is great India that the ancients knew."

"We are bearing toward Cipango," said the Admiral. "I look first for small outward islands, where perhaps the folk are uncouth and simple, and there is little gold."

And again days passed. When many times upon the *Santa Maria* and as often on the *Pinta* and the *Niña* someone had cried "Land!" and the ships been put in commotion and the land melted into air before our eyes, and another as plausible island or coast formed before us only to vanish, despair seized us again. Witchcraft and sorcery and monstrous ignorance, and fooled to our deaths! "West—west—west!" till the west was hated. The Pinzons thought we should change course. If there were lands we were leaving them in the north where hung the haze. But the Madman or the Black Magician, our Italian Admiral, would not hear good advice! It was Gutierrez's word, under his breath when the Admiral was in earshot, and aloud when he was not. "Our Italian—our Italian! Why did not Italy keep him? And Portugal neither would have him! Castile, the jade, takes him up!"

Then after absence began again the signs. Flocks of birds went by us. I saw him watching, and truly these flights did seem to come from south of west. On the seventh of October he altered course. We sailed southwest. This day there floated by a branch with purple berries, and we saw flying fish. Dolphins played about the ship. The very sea felt warm to the hand, and yet was no oppression, but light and easily breathed air, fragrant and lifting the spirits.

And now we saw floating something like a narrow board or a wide staff. The master ordered the boat lowered; we brought it in and it was given dripping into the Admiral's hand. "It is carved by man," he said. "Look!" Truly it was so, rudely done with bone or flint, but carved by man with something meant for a picture of a beast and a tree.

We sailed west by south this day and the next. No more man-wrought driftage came our way, but other signs multiplied. We saw many birds, the water was strangely warm and clear, when the wind blew toward us it had a scent, a tone, that cried land breeze! Then came by a branch with yellow flowers, and upon one a butterfly. After this none doubted, not Fernando nor any. "Gold flowers — gold flowers—gold, gold!"

This night we lay by so that we should not slip past land in the darkness. When day came there showed haze south and west. A gentle wind sang in our rigging. On board the *Santa Maria*, the *Pinta* and the *Niña* all watched for land. Excitement and restlessness took us all. The Admiral's eyes burned like deep gray seas. I could read in them the images behind. *Prester John and the Release of the Sepulchre. The Grand Khan a tributary Prince. Argosies of gold, silk and spices, sailing steady, sailing fast over a waterway unblocked by Mahound and his soldans. All Europe burning bright, rising a rich Queen. Holy Church with another cubit to her stature. Christopherus Columbus, the Discoverer, the Enricher, the Deliverer! Queen Isabella, and on her cheeks a flush of gratitude; all the Spanish court bowing low. All the friends, the kindred, all so blessed! Sons, brothers; Genoa, and Domenico Colombo clad in velvet, dining with the Doge.*

Dolphins were all about us; once there rose a cry from the mariners that they heard singing over the waves. We held breath and listened, but if they were sirens they ceased their song. But at eve, the sky pale gold, the water a sapphire field, we ourselves sang mightily our *"Salve Regina."*

The Admiral would speak to us. Now all loved him, with golden India rising tomorrow from the sea, with his wisdom proving itself! He had this eve a thrilling voice. God had been good to us; who could say other? This very eve, at Palos, they thought of us. At Santa Maria de la Rabida, chanting vesper hymn, they prayed for us also. In

Cordova the Queen prayed. In Rome, the Holy Father had us in mind. Would we lessen ourselves, disappointing so many, and very God, grieving very Christ? "No! But out of this ship we shall step on this land to come, good men, true men, servants and sons of Christ in His kingdom. This night, in India before us, men sigh, 'We weary of our idols! Why tarrieth true God?' There the learned think, bending over their maps, 'Why doth not someone put forth, bringing all the lands into one garland?' They look to their east whence we come, and they may see in dream tonight these three ships!" His voice rang. "I tell you these Three Ships shall be known forever! Your grandchildren's grandchildren shall say, 'The *Santa Maria*, the *Pinta* and the *Niña*—and one that was our ancestor sailed in this one or in that one, to the glory and gain of the world, wherefore we still make festival of his birthday!' "

At this they stirred, whether from Palos or Huelva or Fishertown. They looked at him now as though indeed he were great mage, or even apostle.

That evening I heard Roderigo de Escobedo at an enumeration. He seemed to have committed to memory some Venice list. "Mastic, aloes, pepper, cloves, mace and cinnamon and nutmeg. Ivory and silk and most fine cloth, diamonds, balasses, rubies, pearls, sapphires, jacinth and emeralds. Silver in bulk and gold common as iron with us. Gold—gold!"

Pedro Gutierrez was speaking. "Gold to carry to Spain and pay my debts, with enough left to go again to court—"

Said Escobedo, "The Admiral saith, 'No fraud nor violence, quarreling nor oppression'!"

Gutierrez answered: "The Admiral also thinks to pay his debts! He may think he will be strict as the Saints, but he will not!"

The Admiral was walking the deck. He stopped beside Juan Lepe who leaned upon the rail and watched a strange, glistering sea. It was that shining stuff we see at times at night in certain weather. But tonight Luis Torres, passing, had said, "Strewn ducats!"

The Admiral and Juan Lepe watched. "Never a sail!" said I. "How strange a thing is that! Great populous countries that trade among themselves, and never a sail on this sea rim!"

He drummed upon the rail. "Do not think I have not thought of that! I looked to meet first a ship or ships. But now I think that truly there may be many outlying islands without ships. Or there may be a war between princes, and all ships drawn in a fleet to north or south. One beats one's brains—and time brings the solution, and we say, 'How simple!' "

Turning his great figure, he mounted to our castle built up from deck, whence he could see great distances. The wind had freshened; we were standing to the west; it was behind us again and it pushed us like a shuttle in a giant's hand. The night was violet dark and warm; then at ten the moon rose. Men would not sleep while the ship sailed. A great event was marching, marching toward us. We thought we caught the music of it; any moment heralds, banners, might flame at end of road. We were watching for the Marriage Procession; we were watching for Kings, for the Pope, for I know not what! But there was certain to be largesse.

I went among the mariners. Sancho met me, a young man whom then and afterwards I greatly liked. "Well, we've had luck, Señor! Saint Noah himself, say I, wasn't any luckier!"

"Yes, we've done well!"

Beltran the cook's great easy voice rolled in. "Fear's your only barnacle, say I!"

Luis Torres said, "When I studied Arabic and the Hebrew, I thought it was for the pleasure of it. They said around me, 'How you waste your time!' But now some about the Grand Khan should know Arabic. I will be of use."

Pedro said, "Well, it has turned out better than any reasonable man could have expected!" and Fernando, "Yes, it has! Of course there may be witches. I've heard it said there are great necromancers in India!"

"Necromancers! That's them that show you a thing and then blow it away—"

I said, "Do you not know that we are the only necromancers?"

"Did you see," asked Sancho, "the glistering in the water? Are we going to lie to after midnight? Saint George! I would like to plunge in and swim!"

On stern deck, Diego de Arana called me to him. "Well, Doctor, how goes it?" He and I rested good friends. I said, "Why, it goes well."

"I was thinking, watching the moon, how little I ever dreamed, being no sea-going man, of such a thing as this. Who knows his fate? A man's a strange matter!"

"He is a ballad," I answered., "One stave leads to another and the story mounts."

"I cannot think what tomorrow may show us!"

"Nor can I! But it will be important. We enter by a narrow strait great widths of the future."

"There will be great changes, doubtless. Our world is growing little. Everybody feels that we must push out! It isn't only Spain, but all kingdoms."

Pedro Gutierrez joined us. "You are a learned man, Doctor! What like are the women of Cipango?"

The moon, past the full yet strong enough to silver this vast shield, rose higher. The sails of the *Pinta* and the *Niña* were curves of pearl, our sails above us pale mountains. The light dimmed our lanterns. Crowned woman at our prow would be bathed in it as she ran across Ocean-Sea. It washed our decks, pricked out our moving men. They cast shadows. The master had served out an extra draught of wine. It was hardly needed. We were all lifted, with visions drumming in our heads. Fray Ignatio stood against the mast, and I knew that he felt a pulpit and was making his sermon. After a time, Diego de Arana and Pedro Gutierrez moving away, I was alone. Mind and heart tranquilized, and into them stepped Isabel, and she and I, hand in hand, walked fields of the west.

The moon shone. The Admiral's voice came from above us where he watched from the castle. "Come up here, one or two of you!" Gutierrez was nearest the ladder. He mounted and I after him, and we stood one on either hand the Admiral. He pointed south of west. "A light!" His voice was an ocean. "It is as it should be. I, Christopherus Columbus, have first seen the Shore of Asia!"

We followed his extended hand. Clear under sail we saw it, dimmed by the moon, but evident, a light as it were of a fire on a beach. Diego de Arana came up also and saw it. It was, we thought, more than a league away, a light that must be on land and made by man. It dwindled, out it went into night and there ran only plain silver. We waited while a man might have swam from us to the *Pinta*, then forth it started again, red star that was no star. Someone below us cried, "Ho, look!" The Admiral raised his voice, it rang over ship. "Aye! I saw it a time ago, have seen it thrice! I, the Admiral, saw first." Men were crowding to the side to look, then it went out as though a wave had crept up and drenched it. We gazed and gazed, but it did not come again.

It might have been not land, but a small boat afire. But that is not probable, and we upon the *Santa Maria* held that to see burning wood on shore, though naught showed of that shore itself, was truly first to view, first of all of us, that land we sought. He did not care for the ten thousand maravedies, but he cared that it should be said that God showed it first to him.

The wind pushed us on with the flat of a great hand. Midnight and after midnight. At the sight of that flame we should have fired our cannon, but for some reason this was not done. Now the silver silence beyond the ship was torn across by the *Pinta's* gun. She fired, then came near us. "Land! Land!" Now we saw it under the moon, just lifting above the sea,—lonely, peaceful, dark.

It was middle night. The *Santa Maria*, the *Pinta* and the *Niña* went another league, then took in sail and came to anchor.

CHAPTER XV

The Admiral set a watch and commanded all beside to sleep. Tomorrow might be work and wakefulness enough! The ship grew silent. With the *Pinta* and the *Niña* it lay under the moon, and all around was silver water.

He did not sleep this night, I am sure. At all times he was a provident and wakeful sea king who knew his ship through and through. His habit was light sleep and not many hours of that. He studied his books at night while others slept. Lying in his bed, with eyes open or eyes shut, he watched form in the darkness lands across sea.

This night so far from Europe passed. The sense of day at hand wrapped us. In the east arose a cool, a stern and indifferent pallor. It changed, it flushed. We carried in the *Santa Maria* a cock and hens. Cock crew.

Christopherus Columbus had Italian love for fit, harmonious noting of vast events. This morning the trumpeter also of the *Santa Maria* waked those who slept. The clear and joyful notes were heard by the *Pinta* and the *Pinta*, too, answered with music. The *Niña* took it from her. Beltran the cook and his helpers gave us a stately breakfast. The Admiral came forth from his cabin in a dress that a prince might have worn, crimson and tawny, and around his throat a golden chain. Far and near rushed into light, for in these lands and seas the dawn makes no tarrying. It is almost night, then with a great clap of light it is day.

We had voyaged, all thought, to Asia over an untrodden way. Every eye turned to land. Not haze, not dissolving cloud, not a magic nothing in the thought, but land, land, solid, palpable, like Palos strand! Had we seen a great port city, had we seen ships crowding harbor, had we seen a citadel on some height, armed and frowning, had we marked temples and palaces and banners afloat in this divine cool wind of morning, many aboard us would have had now no surprise, would have cried, "Of course, I really knew it, though for the fun of it I pretended otherwise!"

But others among us could not expect such as this after the quiet night; no light before us save that one so soon quenched, no stir of boat at all or large or small; an unearthly quiet, a low land still as a sleeping marsh under moon.

The light brightened. The water about us turned a blue that none there had ever seen, so turquoise, so cerulean, so penetrable by the eye! Before us gentle surf broke on a beach bone-white. The beach with little rise met woodland; thick it seemed and of a vivid greenness and fairly covering the island. It was island, masthead told us, who saw blue ribbon going around. Moreover, there were two others, no greater, upon the horizon. Nor, though the woodland seemed thick as pile of velvet, was it desolate isle. We made out in three places light plumes of smoke. Now someone uttered a cry, "Men!"

They were running out of the wood, down upon the white beach. There might be a hundred.

"Naked men! They are dark—They are negroes!"—"Or magicians!"

The Admiral lifted his great voice. "Mariners all! India and Cathay are fringed with islands, as are many parts of Europe. A dozen of you have sailed among the Greek islands. There may be as many here as those. This is a small island and its folk simple. They are not Negroes, but the skin of the Indian is darker than ours, and that of Cipango and Cathay is yellow. As for clothing, in all warm lands the simpler folk wear little. But as for magicians, there may be magicians among them as there are among all peoples, but it is falseness and absurdity to speak of all as magicians! Nonsense and cowardice! The man who cried that goes not ashore today!"

Not Great India before us nor Golden Cipango! But it was land—land—it was solid, there were folk! How long had flowed the sea around us, for this was the twelfth of October, five weeks since Gomera and above two months since Palos had sunk away and we had heard the last faint bell of La Rabida! And there had been strong doubt if ever we should see again a white beach, or a tree, or a kindly fire ashore, or any men but those of our three ships, or ever another woman or a child. But land—land! Here was land and green woods and crowds of strange folk. The mariners laughed, and the tears stood in their eyes and friends embraced. And they grew mightily respectful to the Admiral.

So many were to go ashore in the first boat, and so many in the second. The *Pinta* and the *Niña* were lowering their boats. Our hidalgos aboard, Diego de Arana, Roderigo Sanchez and the rest, had also fine apparel with them—seeing that the Grand Khan would have a court and our Sovereigns must be rightly represented—and this morning they suited themselves only less splendidly than did the Admiral. The great banner of Castile and Leon was ready for carrying. Trumpet, drum and fife should land. Fray Ignatio was ready—oh, ready! His liquid dark eyes had an unearthly look. Gifts were being sorted out. There were aboard rich things, valued in any land of ours, for gifts to the Grand Khan and his ministers, or the Emperor of Cipango and his. For Queens and Empresses and Ladies also. And there was a wondrous missal for Prester John did we find him! But this was evidently a little island afar, and these were naked, savage men. The expedition was provident. It had for all. The Portuguese, our great navigators, had taught what the naked African liked. A basket stood at hand filled with pieces of colored cloth, beads, caps, hawk bells, fishhooks, toys of sorts. For that we might have trouble, four harquebus men and four crossbows were going. The *Santa Maria* carried two cannon. Now at the Admiral's signal, one of these was discharged. It was a voice not heard before in this world. If he wished to produce awe that should accompany him like the ancient pillars of cloud and fire, he had success. When the smoke cleared we saw the wild men prostrate upon the ivory beach as though a scythe had cut them down. They lay like fallen grain, then rose and made haste for the wood. We could thinly hear their shouting.

Christopherus Columbus descended into the boat of the *Santa Maria*, Fray Ignatio after him. Diego de Arana, Roderigo Sanchez, Escobedo, Gutierrez and Juan Lepe the physician followed. Juan de la Cosa stayed with the ship, it not being wise to take away all authority. Our armed men came after and the rowers. We drew off and the small boat filled. Boats of the *Pinta* and the *Niña* joined us. The great banner over us, the Admiral's hand upon its standard, we rowed for Asia.

Nearer and nearer. The water hung about us, plain marvel, not dark blue, but turquoise and clear as air. We could see the strange, bright-hued fish and the white bottom. The air breathed Maytime, and now we thought we could tell the spices. And so ivory-white it was, the long curved beach, and so gayly bright the emerald of the wood! There were many palms with other trees we knew not. It was low, the island, and it shone before us silver and green, and the trees moved gently in a wind more sweet, we thought, than any Andalusian zephyr. Pedro Gutierrez stared. "Paradise—Paradise!"

It was not what we had looked for, but it was good enough. It seemed divine, that morning!

Nearer we drew, nearer. The beach was now bare. We made out the dark, naked folk at edge of the wood, in tree shadows, watching us. Were they strange to us, be sure we were stranger to them!

The azure water, so marvelous, met that sand white like crushed bone, strewn with delicate shells. Never was wind so sweet as that which blew this morning! Green plumes, the palms brushed the sky; there seemed to us fruit trees also, with satin stems and wide-laden boughs. When we looked over shoulder the *Santa Maria*, the *Pinta* and the *Niña* each rode double, mast and hull in sky, mast and hull in mirror sea. Something strange and divine was about us, over us. We wished to laugh, we wished to weep.

Boat head touched clean sand. The oars rested. Christopherus Columbus the Admiral stepped from boat first and alone, all waiting as was right. He took with him the banner of Spain. He walked a few yards, then struck the standard into the sand. There was air enough to open the folds, to make them float and fly. Kneeling, he bowed himself and kissed the earth. We heard his strong voice praying. "*Domine Deus, æterne et omnipotens, sacro tuo verbo cœlum, et terra, et mare, creasti—*"

We also bowed our heads. He rose and cried to Fray Ignatio. The

Franciscan was the next to enter this new world. After him sprang out Diego de Arana and the others. The Pinzons, too, were now leaving their boats. All were at last gathered about the Admiral, between blue water and green wood. Fifty Spaniards, we gathered there, and we heard our fellows left upon the ships cheering us. We kneeled and Fray Ignatio thanked God for us.

We rose, drew long breath and looked about us, then turned to the Admiral with loud praise and gratulation. He was girded with a sword, cross-hilted. Drawing it, he set its point in the sand. Then with one hand upon the cross, and one lifted and wrapped in the banner folds, he, with a great voice, proclaimed Spain's ownership. To the King and Queen of the Spains all lands unchristian and idolatrous that we might find and use and hold, all that were clearly away from the line of the King of Portugal, drawn for him by the Holy Father! In the name of God, in the name of Holy Church, in the name of Isabella, Queen of Castile, and Ferdinand, King of Aragon and their united Power, amen and amen! He motioned to the trumpeter who put trumpet to his lips and blew a blast to the north and the south and the east and the west. At the sound there seemed to come a cry from the fringing wood, a cry of terror.

The island was ours,—if all this could make it ours.

A piece of scarlet cloth spread upon the sand had heaped upon it necklaces of glass and three or four hawk bells with other toys. We placed it there, then stood back. At the Admiral's command the harquebus and crossbow men laid their weapons down, though watchful eye was kept. But no arrow flights had come from the wood, and as far as could be seen some kind of lance, not formidable looking, was their only weapon. Next the Admiral made our fifer to play a merry and peaceful air.

We had noted a clump of trees advanced into the sand and we thought that the bolder men were occupying this. Now a man started out alone, a young man by the looks of him, drawn as he was against the white sand, and a paladin, for he marched to meet alone he knew not what or whom. "Blackamoor!" exclaimed De Arana beside me, but as he came nearer we saw that the dead blackness was paint, laid in a fantastic pattern upon his face and body. Native hue of skin, as we came presently to find in the unpainted, was a pleasing red-brown. He advanced walking daintily and proudly, knowing that his people were watching him. Single Castilian, single Moor, had advanced so, many a time, between camps, or between camp and fortress.

Halting beside the red cloth he stooped and turned over the trinkets. When he straightened himself he had in hand a string of great beads, rose and blue and green. He fingered these, seemed about to put the necklet on, then refrained as too daring. Laying it gently back upon the scarlet he next took up a hawk bell. These bells, as is known, ring very clear and sweet. I was afterwards told that the Portuguese had noted their welcome among the African people. There was no nail's breadth of information that this man Columbus could not use! He had used this, and in a list for just possibly found savage Indians had put down, "good number of hawk bells."

The red man painted black, took up the hawk bell. It chimed as he moved it. He dropped it on the sand and gave back a step, then picked it up and set it tinkling. His face, the way in which he moved, said "Music from heaven!"

The Admiral motioned to Fray Ignatio to move toward him. That good man went gently forward. The youth gave back, but then braced himself, under the eyes of his nation. He stood. The Franciscan put out a gowned arm and a long, lean kindly hand. The youth, naked as the bronze of a god, hesitated, raised his own arm, let it drop upon the other's. Fray Ignatio, speaking mild words, brought him across and to the Admiral. The latter, tallest of us all and greatly framed, lofty of port, dressed with magnificence, silver-haired, standing forth from his officers and men, the banner over him, would be taken by any for Great Captain, chief god of these gods, and certes, at the first they thought that we were gods! The Indian put his hands to his face, shrank like a girl and came slowly to his knees and lower yet until his forehead rested upon the earth. The Admiral lifted him, calling him "son."

Those of his kind watching from the wood now sent forth a considerable deputation. There came to us a dozen naked men, fairly tall, well-shaped, skin of red copper, smeared often with paint in bars and disks and crescents. Their hair was not like the Negro's, the only other naked man our time knew, but was straight, black, somewhat coarse, not bushy but abundant, cut short with the men below the ear. They are a beardless people. Our beards are an amazement to them, as are our clothes. A fiercely quarrelsome folk, a peace-keeping, gentle folk will sound their note very soon. These belonged to the latter kind. Their lances were not our huge knightly ones, nor the light, hard ones of the Moors. They were hardly more than stout canes, the head not iron — they had no iron — but flint or bone shaped by a flint knife. Where the paint was not splashed or patterned over them, their faces could be liked very well. Lips were not over full, the nose slightly beaked, the forehead fairly high, the eyes good. They did not jabber nor move idly but kept measure and a pleasant dignity. They seemed gentle and happy. So were they when we found them.

Their speech sounded of no tongue that we knew. Luis Torres and I alike had knowledge of Arabic. We had no Persian that might be nearer yet, but Arabia being immemorially caravan-knit with India, it was thought that it might be understood. But these bare folk had no notion of it, nor of the Hebrew which Luis tried next. The Latin did not do, the Greek of which I had a little did not do. But there is an old, old language called Gesture. If, wherever there is a common language there is one people, then in end and beginning surely we are one folk around the earth!

We were to be friends with these islanders. "Friends first and last!" believed the Admiral. Indeed, all felt it so, this bright day. If they were not all we had imaged, sailing to them, yet were they men, and unthreatening, novel, very interesting to us with their island and their marvelous blue water. All was heightened by sheer joy of landing, and of finding—finding something! And what we found was not horrible nor deathful, but bright, promising, scented like first fruits.

To them we found we were gods! They moved about us with a kind of ceremony of propitiation. Two youths came with a piece of bark carried like a salver, piled with fruits and with thin cakes of some scraped root. Another brought a parrot, a great green and rose bird that at once talked, though we could not understand his words. Two older men had balls, as large as melons, of some wound stuff that we presently found to be cotton loosely twisted into yarn. The Admiral's eyes glowed. "Now if any bring spices or pepper—" But they did not, nor did they bring gold.

All these things they put down before us, in silence or with words that we thought were petitions, moving not confusedly but with a manner of ritual. The Admiral took a necklace and placed it round the throat of the young man who first had dared, and in his hand put a hawk bell. That was enough for himself to do, who was Viceroy. Three of us finished the distribution. They who had brought presents were given presents. All would have us go with them to their village, just behind the trees. A handful of men we left with the boats and the rest of us crossed sand. Harquebuses and crossbows went with us, but we had no need of them. The island apparently followed peace, and its folk greatly feared to give offense to gods from the sky. Above the ships held a range of pearly clouds, out of which indeed one might make strange lands and forms. The Indians —Christopherus Columbus called them "Indians"—pointed from ships to cloud. They spoke with movements of reverence. "You have come down—you have come down!" We understood them, though their words were not ours.

Now the greenwood rose close at hand. The trees differed, the woven thickness of it, the color and blossom, from any wood at home. A space opened before us, and here was the village of these folk,—round huts thatched with palm leaves, set on no streets, but at choice under trees. Earth around was trodden hard, but the green woods pressed close. Here and there showed garden patches with plants whose names and uses we knew not. Now we came upon women and children. Like the men the women were naked. Well-shaped and comely, with long, black, braided hair, they seemed to us gentle, pleasing and fearless. The children were a crew that any might love.

Time lacks to say all that we did and heard and guessed this day upon this island! It was first love after long weeks at sea, and our cramped ships and all our great uncertainty! If it was not what we had expected, still here it was, tangible land that never had been known, wonderful to us, giving us already rich narrative for Palos and

Huelva and Fishertown, for Cordova and the Queen and King. We were sure now that other land was to be met, so soon as we sailed a reasonable distance to meet it. Under the horizon would be land surely, and surely of an import that this small island lacked, like Paradise though it seemed to us this day! Any who looked at the Admiral saw that he would make no long tarrying here. He named this island San Salvador, but we would not wait in San Salvador.

This day in shifts, all our men were brought ashore, each division having three hours of blessed land. So good was earth under foot, so good were trees, so delectable the fruit, so lovely to move and run and watch every moving, running, walking thing! And these good, red-brown folk, naked it was true, but mannerly after their own fashion, who thought every seaman a god, and the ship boys sons of gods! And we also were good and mannerly, the *Santa Maria*, the *Pinta* and the *Niña*. I look back and I see a strange, a boyish and a happy day.

The sun was westering. We felt the exhaustion of a long holiday with novelties so many that at last the senses did not answer. Perhaps the Indians felt it too. Often and often have I seen great wisdom guide the Admiral. An hour before approaching night might have said "Go!" he took us one and all back to the ships. "*Salve Regina*" was a sound that evening to hear, and afterwards it was to sleep, sleep,—tired as from the Fair at Seville!

CHAPTER XVI

At first, the day before, we had not made out that the Indians had boats. Later, straying here and there, we had seen them drawn upon the shore and covered with boughs of trees. They called them "canoes", made them, large and small, out of trunks of trees, hollowed by fire, and with their stone knives. We had seen one copper knife. Asked about that, they pointed to the south and seemed to say that yonder dwelled men who had all they wished of most things.

From dark the east grew pale, from pallor put on roses. This day no mariner grumbled at the call to awake. Here still lay our Fortunate Isle, our San Salvador; here our ivory beach, our green wood. Up went the little curls of smoke.

We had breakfast. So great was now the deference to him who three days ago had been "madman" and "black magician", "dreaming fool" and "spinner without thread!" Now it was "Admiral", "Excellency", and "What shall we do next?" and "What is your opinion, sir?"

The immediate thing to do proved to be to come forth from cabin and mark the beach thronging with thrice the number of yesterday, and the canoes putting off to us. We counted eight. Only one was a long craft, holding twenty men; the others came in cockle boats, with one or two or three. Not only canoes, but they came swimming, men and boys, all a dark grace in the cerulean, lucid sea. They were so fearless—for we came from heaven and would not harm them. We were going to make them rich; we were going to "save" them.

A score perhaps were helped aboard the *Santa Maria*. The *Pinta*, the *Niña*, had others. They were like children, touching, staring, excitedly talking and gesturing among themselves, or gazing in a kind of fixed awe, asking of the least sailor with all reverence, bowing themselves before the Admiral, the over-god. The Admiral moved richly dressed, rapt and benignant, yet sparing a part of himself to keep all order, measure, rightness on the ship, and another part to find out with keen pains, "What of other lands? What of folk who must be your superiors?"

They had brought offerings. Half a dozen parrots were perched around, very gorgeously colored, loquacious in a speech we did not know. We had stacks of the large round thin cakes baked on stones which afterwards we called cassava, and great gourds, "calabashes" filled with fruit, and balls of cotton in a rude thread. We gave beads, bits of cloth, little purses, and the small bells that caused extravagant delight. But ever the Admiral looked for signs of gold, for he must find for princes and nobles and merchants gold or silver, or precious stones or spice, or all together. If he found them not, half his fortunes fell; a half-wind only would henceforth fill his sails.

And at last came in a canoe with three a young Indian who wore in his ear a knob of gold. Roderigo Sanchez saw this first and brought him to the Admiral. The latter, taking up an armlet of green glass and a hawk bell, touched the gold in the ear. "Do you trade?" Glad enough was the Indian to trade. It lay in the Admiral's palm, a piece of gold as great as a filbert.

Juan Lepe watched him make inquisition, Diego de Arana, Sanchez and Escobedo at his elbow. He did it to admiration, with look, gesture and tone ably translating his words. "Gold — gold?" The Indian said, or we put down in this wise what he said, "Harac."

Was there more harac on the island? We would give heavenly things for harac. The Indian was doubtful; he thought proudly that he had the only harac. "Where did he get it?" He indicated the south.

"Little island like this one?"

"No. Great land. Harac there in many ears. Much harac."

So we understood him. "Cipango!" breathed the Admiral. "Or neighbor to Cipango, increasingly rich and civilized as we go."

He took a case of small boxes, each box filled with merchandise of spice which he desired. Cinnamon, nutmeg, pepper, saffron, cloves and others. He made the islander smell and taste.

"Had they aught like these?"

The Indian seemed to say they had not, but would like to have. He looked about for something with which to trade, a parrot, or heap of cakes, or ball of cotton. I thought that it was the box of boxes that he extremely wished, but the Admiral thought it was the spicery, and that he must have known them wherever he got the gold. "Were they found yonder?"

The Admiral stretched arm out over blue sea and the Indian followed his gesture. He shot out his own arm, "South—southwest—west," nodded the Admiral. "Many islands, or the mainland. Gates open before us!"

"Had the Indian been to these lands?" No, it seemed, but one had come in a boat, wearing this knob of gold, and he had told them. Was he living? No, he was not living. What kind of a person was he? Such as us? Emphatically no. Not such as us! Much, we gathered, as was the Indian himself. "Pearls have come from Queen's neck to Queen's neck," quoth the Admiral, "by a thousand rude hands and twisting ways!"

There was one woman among the visitors to the *Santa Maria*, a young woman, naked, freely moving and smiling. Eyes dwelled on her, eyes followed her. She was with an Indian who might be brother or husband. The Admiral gave her a worked, Moorish scarf. She tied it about her head, and the bright ends fell down beside her long, black, braided hair. None touched her, but they were woman-starved, and they looked at her hungrily. She had beauty in her way, and a kind of innocence both frank and shy. She was like a doe in the green forest, come silently upon at dawn.

Fed full of marvel at last, these Indians left us. But no sooner had they reached land and told of great kindness on the part of the inhabitants of heaven than other canoes and other swimmers put forth. This might go on all day, so we checked it by ourselves going ashore.

This day we filled our water casks and took aboard much fruit and all the cakes that they brought us. Moreover we explored the island, finding two villages of a piece with the first, and in the middle land a fair pool of water.

This day like yesterday was blissful wine.

All blessed Christopherus Columbus. No man now but, for a while, did his bidding with an open heart.

In the morning we sailed away, not without plentiful promises of return. When we put up our white sails they cried out and pointed to the cloud sierra. No! We would not go back to heaven—or if we did so we would come again, loving so our gentle friends upon earth! We sailed, and in all our after wanderings we never came back to this island. And never again, I think, while Columbus voyaged, did there come to us just the bright, exquisite thrill of that first land after long doubt and no land. San Salvador—Holy Saviour Island!

CHAPTER XVII

We were in a throng of islands. We might drop all for a little while, then from masthead "Land ho!" None were great islands, many far smaller than San Salvador. At night we lay to, not knowing currents and shoals; then broke the day and we flung out sail.

We had with us upon the *Santa Maria* three San Salvador men. They had come willingly, two young, fearless men, and one old man with a wrinkled, wise, interested face. Assiduous to gain their tongue and impart our own, the Admiral, beside his own effort, told off for especial teachers and scholars Luis Torres and Juan Lepe. We did gain knowledge, but as yet everything was imperfect, without fine shading, and subject to all miscomprehension. But like the rest of us, the Admiral guessed in accordance with his wishes and his previous belief.

All these islands lay flat or almost flat upon the sea. All showed ivory beach, vivid wood, surrounding water, transparent and heavenly blue, inhabited by magically colored fish. When we dropped anchor, took boat and landed, it was to find the same astonished folk, naked, harmless, holding us for gods, bringing all they had, eager for our toys which were to them king's treasures and holy relics. Every island the Admiral named; he gave them goodly names! Over and over the Indians pointed south and west. We understood great lands, clothed men, much gold. But when we next came to anchor, like small island, like men, women and children. We traded for a few more knobs of gold, but they were few.

Toscanelli's map and the Admiral's map lay on cabin table. "Islands in the Sea of Chin—Polo and Mandeville alike say thousands

—all grades then of advance. Beyond any manner of doubt, persevering west or west by south, we shall come to main Asia." So long as he ruled, there would be perseverance!

At Santa Maria de la Concepcion a solitary large canoe crowded with Indians was rowing toward us. One of the San Salvador young men aboard us fancied some slight, experienced some fear, or may even,—who knows?—have wearied of the gods. Springing upon the rail he threw himself into sea and made off with great strokes toward the canoe. Pedro behind him shouted "Escape!" There was a rush to the side to observe. Fernando bawled, "Come back! or we'll let fly an arrow."

He swam, the dark, naked fellow, like a fish. Reaching the canoe, the Indians there took him in; he seemed to have a tale to tell, they all broke into talk, the canoe went round, they rowed fast back to land. The *Niña*, lying near us, had her boat filling to go ashore. Her men had seen the leap overboard and the swimmer. Now they put after, rowing hard for the canoe, that having the start came first to beach. The Indians sprang out, the San Salvador man with them. Leaving canoe, they ran across sand into wood. The *Niña's* men took the canoe and brought it to the *Santa Maria*. In it were balls of cotton and calabashes filled with fruit and a chattering parrot. It was the first thing of this kind that had happened, and the Admiral's face was wrathful. He had a simple, kindly heart, and though he could be vexed or irritated, he rarely broke into furious anger. But first and last he desired peaceful absorption, if by any means that were possible, of these countries. We absorbing them, they absorbing us; both the gainers! And he had warm feeling of romance-love for all this that he was finding. He saw all his enterprise milk-white, rose-bright. And his pride was touched that the Indian who had seemed contented had not truly been so, and that the *Niña*'s men had disobeyed strict commands for friendliness. He would restore that content if possible, and he would have no more unordered chasing of canoes. The *Niña*'s men got anger and rebuke, Captain Cristoforo Colombo mounting up in the Admiral.

He would let nothing in the canoe be touched. Instead he had placed aboard a pot of honey and a flask of wine and three pieces of cloth, then with a strong shove it was sent landward, and the tide making in, it came to shore. We saw two venture from the wood and draw it up on beach.

In a little while came around a point of shore a canoe with one Indian who made toward us, using his oar very dexterously, and when he entered our shadow holding up cotton and fruit. It was to be seen that he had had no communication with the men of the large canoe.

The Admiral himself called out encouragingly and snatching the first small thing at hand held it up. The Indian scrambled on board. He stood, as fine a piece of bronze as any might see, before the Genoese, as great a figure as might be found in all Italy—all Spain—all Europe.

The elder touched the younger, the white man the red man, as a king, a father, might have touched a prince, a son. He himself took the youth over our ship, showing him this, showing him that, had the music play for him, brought him to Fray Ignatio who talked of Christ, pointing oft to heaven. (To my thinking this action, often repeated, was one of the things that for so long made them certain we had come from the skies.) In the cabin he gave the Indian a cup of wine and a biscuit dipped in honey. He gave him a silken cap with a tassel and himself put round his throat one of our best strings of beads, and into his hand not one but three of the much-coveted hawk bells. He was kinder than rain after drought. First and last, he could well lend himself to the policy of kindness, for it was not lending. Kindness was his nature.

In an hour this Indian, returned to his canoe, was rowing toward shore with a swelling heart and a determined loyalty. He touched the island, and we could trust him to be missionary, preaching with all fervor of heaven and the gods.

Ay, me!

Whatever the other's defection, he more than covered it, the return of the canoe aiding. Santa Maria de la Concepcion became again friendly. But the Admiral that evening gave emphatic instruction to Martin and Vicente Pinzon and all the gathered Spaniards. Just here, I think, began the rift between him and many. Many would have by prompt taking, as they take in war. Were not all these heathen and given? But he would have another way round, though often he compromised with war; never wanting war but forced by his time and his companions. Sometimes, in the future, forced by the people we came among, but far oftener forced by greed and lust and violence of our own. Alas, again! Alas, again and again!

After Santa Maria de la Concepcion, Fernandina, and after Fernandina the most beautiful of islands, Isabella, where we lay three days. People upon this island seemed to us more civilized than the Salvador folk. The cotton was woven, loin cloths were worn, they had greater variety of calabashes, the huts were larger, the villages more regular. They slept in "hamacs" which are stout and wide cotton nets slung between posts, two or three feet above earth. Light, space-giving, easy of removal, these beds greatly took our fancy.

Here we sought determinedly for spice-giving trees and medicinal herbs and roots. It was not a spicery such as Europe depended upon, but still certain things seemed valuable! We gathered here and gathered there what might be taken to Spain. There grew an emulation to find. The Admiral offered prizes for such and such a commodity come upon.

We sailed from Isabella and after three days came to Cuba.

CHAPTER XVIII

Cuba! At first he called it Juana, but we came afterwards still to use the Indian name. Cuba! We saw it after three days, and it was little enough like Isabella, Fernandina, Concepcion, San Salvador and the islets the Admiral called Isles de Arena. It covered all our south, no level, shining thing that masthead could see around, but a mighty coast line, mountainous, with headlands and bays and river mouths. Now after long years, I who outlive the Admiral, know it for an island, but how could he or I or any know that in November fourteen hundred and ninety-two? He never believed it an island.

He stood on deck watching. "Cuba—Cuba! Have you not read of Cublai Khan? The sounds chime!"

"Cublai Khan. He lives in Quinsai."

"Ay. His splendid, capital city. Buildings all wonderful, and gardens like Mahound's paradise!"

"But if it is Cipango?"

"Ay. It may be Cipango. We have no angel here to tell us which. I would one would fly down and take us by the hand! Being men, we must make guesses."

Beautiful to us, splendid to us, was this coast of Cuba! We sailed by headlands and deep, narrow-necked bays, river mouths and hanging forests and bold cliffs. We sailed west and still headland followed headland, and still the lookout cried, "It stretched forever like the main!"

We came to a river where ships might ride. Sounding, we found deep water, entered river mouth and dropped anchor, then went ashore in the boats. Palms and their water doubles, and in the grove a small abandoned village. We had seen the people flee before us, and they were no more nor other kind of people than had showed in Concepcion or Fernandina. Yet were they a little wealthier. We found parrots on their perches, and two dogs, small and wolf-like that never barked. In one hut lay a harpoon tipped with bone, and a net for fishing. In another we found a wrought block of wood which Fray Ignatio pronounced their idol.

We went back to our ships, and leaving river, sailed on in a bright blue sea. The next day we doubled a cape and found a great haven, but silent and sailless, with no maritime city thronging the shore. What was this world, so huge, so sparely, rudely peopled?

We came to anchor close under shore in this haven. Again the marvelous water, but now it laved a bold and great country! We landed. Canoes fastened in a row, another village, most of the folk decamped, but a few brave men and women tarrying to find out something about heaven and its inmates. With toys again and pacific gestures we wiled them to us.

There was upon the *Santa Maria* a young Indian who had chosen to come with us from Fernandina. He had courage and intelligence, was willing to receive instruction and baptism from Fray Ignatio, and first and last followed the Admiral with devotion. The latter had him christened Diego Colon. We taught him Spanish as fast and soundly as we might, and used him as interpreter. The tongue of his island was not just the tongue of Cuba, but near enough to serve. All these Indians have a gift of oratory and dote to speak at length, with firm voice and great gestures. Now we set Diego Colon to his narration. We of Castile had so much of the tongue by now that we could in some wise follow.

Forth it poured! We were gods come from heaven. Yonder stood the chief god that the others obeyed. He was very great, strong, good, wise, kind, giving beautiful gifts! We were all kind—no one was going to be hurt. We made magic with harac—which we called "gold." In heaven was not enough harac. So important is it to the best magic that a chief god has come to earth to seek it. We also liked cotton and things to eat, especially cassava cakes, and we liked a very few parrots. But it was gold that in chief we wanted. The man who brought the gods gold might go home with gifts so beautiful that there was never anything seen like them! Especially is there something that the gods call "bells" that ring and sound in your hand when you dance! Gold—do you know where to find it? Another thing! They desire to find a god who dropped out of the sky a long time ago, and has now a people and a great, marvelous village. Thinking he might be here, they have dived down to our land, for they dive in the sky as we dive in water! The name of the god they hunt is Grand Khan or Cublai Khan, and his village is Quinsai. Have you heard of him? They are very anxious to find him. The chief god with white hair and wonderful clothes—It is what they call clothes; under it they are as you and me, only the color is different—the chief god will give many bells to any folk who can show him the way to Quinsai. Gold and Quinsai where lives the god Grand Khan."

As might have been expected, this brought tidings. "Cubanacan! Cubanacan!" Whatever that might mean, they said it with assurance, pointing inland. Diego Colon interrupted their further speech. "There is a river. Go up it three days and come to great village. Cacique there wearing clothes. All men there have gold!"

Pedro Gutierrez spoke. "They'll promise anything for a hawk bell!"

"What do they understand and what do they not understand? What do they say and what do they not say?" That was Martin Pinzon. "Between them all we are fooled!"

The Admiral, who was gazing inland after the dark pointing finger, turned and spoke. "At the root of all things sit Patience and Make Trial!

"Well, I know," answered Pinzon, "that if these ships be not careened and mended we shall have trouble! Weather changes. There will be storm!"

He was right as to ships and weather, and the Admiral knew it and said as much. I never saw him grudge recognition to Martin Pinzon. It has been said that he did, but I never saw it.

That night, on board the *Santa Maria* there was held a great council. At last it was settled that we should rest here a week and overhaul the ships, and that while that was doing, there should be sent two or three with Indian guides to find, if might be, this river and this town. And there were chosen, and given a week to go and come, Juan Lepe, Luis Torres and a seaman Roderigo Jerez, with Diego Colon, the Fernandina youth. Likewise there would go two Indians of this village, blithe enough to show their country to the gods and the gods to their country.

The next day being Sunday, Fray Ignatio preached a sermon to the Indians. He assumed, and at this time I think the Admiral assumed, that these folk had no religion. That was a mistake. I doubt if on earth can be found a people without religion.

Men and women they watched and listened, still, attentive, knowing that it had somehow to do with heaven. After sermon and after we had prayed and sung, we fashioned and set up a great cross upon cliff brow. Again the Indians watched and seemed to have some notion of what we did.

The remainder of the day we rested, and on Monday early Roderigo Jerez, Luis Torres and Juan Lepe with Diego Colon and two Cuba men made departure, We had a pack of presents and a letter from the Admiral. For we might meet some administrator or commandant or other, from Quinsai or Zaiton or we knew not where. This was the first of many—ah, so many—expeditions, separations from main body and return, or not return, as the case might be!

CHAPTER XIX

Splendid and endless forest! We white men often saw no path, but the red-brown men saw it. It ran level, it climbed, it descended; then began the three again. It was lost, it was found. They said, "Here path!" But we had to serpent through thickets, or make way on edge of dizzy crag, or find footing through morass. We came to great stretches of reeds and yielding grass, giving with every step into water. It was to toil through this under hot sun, with stinging clouds of insects. But when they were left behind we might step into a grove of the gods, such firmness, such pleasantness, such shady going or happy resting under trees that dropped fruit.

We met no great forest beasts. There seemed to be none in this part of Asia. And yet Luis and I had read of great beasts. Dogs of no considerable size were the largest four-footed things we had come upon from San Salvador to Cuba. There were what they called *utias*, like a rabbit, much used for food, and twice we had seen an animal the size of a fox hanging from a bough by its tail.

If the beasts were few the birds were many. To see the parrots great and small and gorgeously colored, to see those small, small birds like tossed jewels that never sang but hummed like a bee, to hear a gray bird sing clear and loud and sweet every strain that sang other birds, was to see and hear most joyous things. Lizards were innumerable; at edge of a marsh we met with tortoises; once we passed coiled around a tree a great serpent. It looked at us with beady eyes, but the Indians said it would not harm a man. A thousand, thousand butterflies spread their painted fans.

The trees! so huge of girth and height and wherever was room so spreading, so rich of grain, so full, I knew, of strange virtues! We found one that I thought was cinnamon, and broke twigs and bark and put in our great pouch for the Admiral. Only time might tell the wealth of this green multitude. I thought, "Here is gold, if we would wait for it!" Fruit trees sprang by our path. We had with us some provision of biscuit and dried meat, and we never lacked golden or purple delectable orbs. We found the palm that bears the great nut, giving alike meat and milk.

By now Luis Torres and I had no little of Diego Colon's tongue and he had Spanish enough to understand the simplest statements and orders. Ferdandina tongue was not quite Cuba tongue, but it was like enough to furnish sea room. We asked this, we asked that. No! No one had ever come to the end of their country. When one town was left behind, at last you came to another town. One by one, were they bigger, better towns? They seemed to say that they were, but here was always, I thought, doubtful understanding. But no one had ever walked around their country—they seemed to laugh at the notion—land that way, always land! On the other hand, there was sea yonder—like sea here. They pointed south. Not so far there! "It must be," said Luis, "that Cuba is narrow, though without end westwardly. A great point or tongue of Asia?"

The Cubans were strong young men and not unintelligent. "Chiefs?" Yes, they had chiefs, they called them *caciques*. Some of them were fighters, they and their people. Not fighters like Caribs! Whereupon the speaker rose—we were resting under a tree—and facing south, used for gesture a strong shudder and a movement as if to flee.

South—south—always they pointed south! We were going south—inland. Would we come to Caribs? But no. Caribs seemed not to be in Cuba, but beyond sea, in islands.

Luis and I made progress in language and knowledge. Roderigo Jerez, a simple man, slept or tried the many kinds of fruit, or teased the slender, green-flame lizards.

We slept this night high on the mountainside, on soft grass near a fall of water. The Indians showed no fear of attack from man or beast. They could make fire in a most ingenious fashion, setting stick against larger stick and turning the first with such skill, vigor and persistence that presently arose heat, a spark, fire. But they seemed to need or wish no watch fire. They lay, naked and careless, innocent —fearless, as though the whole land were their castle. Luis tried to find out how they felt about dangers. We pieced together. "None here! And the Great Lizard takes care!" That was the Cuban. Diego Colon said, "The Great Turtle takes care!"

Luis Torres laughed. "Fray Ignatio should hear that!"

"It is on the road," I said and went to sleep.

The second day's going proved less difficult than the first. Less difficult means difficult enough! And as yet we had met no one nor anything that remotely favored golden-roofed Cipango, or famous, rich Quinsai, or Zaiton of the marble bridges. Jerez climbed a tall tree and coming down reported forest and mountain, and naught else. Our companions watched with interest his climbing. "Do you go up trees in heaven?"

This morning we had bathed in a pool below the little waterfall. Diego Colon by now was used to us so, but the Cuba men displayed excitement. They had not yet in mind separated us from our clothes. Now we were separated and were found in all our members like them, only the color differing. Color and the short beards of Luis Torres and Juan Lepe. They wished to touch and examine our clothes lying upon the bank, but here Diego Colon interfered. They were full of magic. Something terrible might happen! When Luis and I came forth from water and dried ourselves with handfuls of the warm grass, they asked: "Do they do so in heaven?" The stronger, more intelligent of the two, added, "It is not so different!"

I said to Luis as we took path after breakfast, "It is borne in upon me that only from ourselves, Admiral to ship boy, can we keep up this heaven ballad! Clothes, beads and hawk bells, cannon, harquebus, trumpet and banner, ship and sails, royal letters and blessing of the Pope — nothing will do it long unless we do it ourselves!"

"Agreed!" quoth Luis. "But gods and angels are beginning to slip and slide, back there by the ships! We have the less temptation here."

He began to speak of a sailor and a brown girl upon whom he had stumbled in a close wood a little way from shore. She thought Tomaso Pasamonte was a god wooing her and was half-frightened, half-fain. "And two hours later I saw Don Pedro Gutierrez—"

"Ay," said Juan Lepe. "The same story! The oldest that is!" And as at the word our savages, who had been talking together, now at the next resting place put forward their boldest, who with great reverence asked if there were women in heaven.

Through most of this day we struggled with a difficult if fantastically beautiful country. Where rock outcropped and in the sands of bright rapid streams we looked for signs of that gold, so stressed as though it were the only salvation! But the rocks were silent, and though in the bed of a shrunken streamlet we found some glistening particles and scraping them carefully together got a small spoonful to wrap in cloth and bestow in our pouch of treasures, still were we not sure that it was wholly gold. It might be. We worked for an hour for just this pinch.

Since yesterday morning our path had been perfectly solitary. Then suddenly, when we were, we thought, six leagues at least from the ships, the way turning and entering a small green dell, we came upon three Indians seated resting, their backs to palm trees. We halted, they raised their eyes. They stared, they rose in amazement at the sight of those gods, Roderigo Jerez, Luis Torres and Juan Lepe. They stood like statues with great eyes and parted lips. For us, coming silently upon them, we had too our moment of astonishment.

They were three copper men, naked, fairly tall and well to look at. But each had between his lips what seemed a brown stick, burning at the far end, dropping a light ash and sending up a thin cloud of odorous smoke. These burning sticks they dropped as they rose. They had seemed so silent, so contented, so happy, sitting there with backs to trees, a firebrand in each mouth, I felt a love for them! Luis thought the lighted sticks some rite of their religion, but after a while when we came to examine them, we found them not true stick, but some large, thickish brown leaf tightly twisted and pressed together and having a pungent, not unpleasing odor. We crumbled one in our hands and tasted it. The taste was also pungent, strange, but one might grow to like it. They called the stick tobacco, and said they always used it thus with fire, drinking in the smoke and puffing it out again as they showed us through the nostrils. We thought it a great curiosity, and so it was!

But to them we were unearthly beings. The men from the sea told of us, then as it were introduced Diego Colon, who spoke proudly with appropriate gesture, loving always his part of herald Mercury —or rather of herald Mercury's herald—not assuming to be god himself, but cherishing the divine efflux and the importance it rayed upon him!

The three Indians quivered with a sense of the great adventure! Their town was yonder. They themselves had been on the path to such and such a place, but now would they turn and go with us, and when we went again to the sea they, if it were permitted, would accompany us and view for themselves our amazing canoes! All this to our companion. They backed with great deference from us.

We went with these Indians to their town, evidently the town which we sought. And indeed it was larger, fitter, a more ordered community than any we had met this side Ocean-Sea, though far, far from travelers' tales of Orient cities! It was set under trees, palm trees and others, by the side of a clear river. The huts were larger than those by the sea, and set not at random but in rows with a great trodden square in the middle. From town to river where they fished and where, under overhanging palms, we found many Canoes, ran a way wider than a path, much like a narrow road. But there were no wheeled vehicles nor draught animals. We were to find that in all these lands they on occasion carried their caciques or the sick or hurt in litters or palanquins borne on men's shoulders. But for carrying, grinding, drawing, they knew naught of the wheel. It seemed strange that any part of Asia should not know!

In this town we found the cacique, and with him a *butio* or priest. Once, too, I thought, our king and church were undeveloped like these. We were looking in these lands upon the bud which elsewhere we knew in the flower. That to Juan Lepe seemed the difference between them and us.

The people swarmed out upon us. When the first admiration was somewhat over, when Diego Colon and the two seaside men and the

Cubans of the burning sticks had made explanation, we were swept with them into their public square and to a hut much larger than common where we found a stately Indian, the cacique, and an ancient wrinkled man, the *butio*. These met us with their own assumption of something like godship. They had no lack of manner, and Luis and I had the Castilian to draw upon. Then came presents and Diego Colon interpreting. But as for the Admiral's letter, though I showed it, it was not understood.

It was gazed upon and touched, considered a heavenly rarity like the hawk bells we gave them, but not read nor tried to be read. The writing upon it was the natural veining of some most strange leaf that grew in heaven, or it was the pattern miraculously woven by a miraculous workman with thread miraculously finer than their cotton! It was strange that they should have no notion at all—not even their chieftains and priests—of writing! Any part of Asia, however withdrawn, surely should have tradition there, if not practice!

In this hut or lodge, doored but not windowed, we found a kind of table and seats fashioned from blocks of some dark wood rudely carved and polished. The cacique would have us seated, sat himself beside us, the *butio* at his hand.

There seemed no especial warrior class. We noted that, it being one of the things it was ever in order to note. No particular band of fighting men stood about that block of polished wood, that was essentially throne or chair of state. The village owned slender, bone or flint-headed lances, but these rested idly in corners. Upon occasion all or any might use them, but there was no evidence that those occasions came often. There was no body of troops, nor armor, no shields, no crossbows, no swords. They had knives, rudely made of some hard stone, but it seemed that they were made for hunting and felling and dividing. No clothing hid from us any frame. The cacique had about his middle a girdle of wrought cotton with worked ends and some of the women wore as slight a dress, but that was all. They were formed well, all of them, lithe and slender, not lacking either in sinew and muscle, but it was sinew and muscle of the free, graceful, wild world, not brawn of bowman and pikeman and swordman and knight with his heavy lance. In something they might be like the Moor when one saw him naked, but the Moor, too, was perfected in arms, and so they were not like.

We did not know as yet if ever there were winter in this land. It seemed perpetual, serene and perfect summer. Behind these huts ran small gardens wherein were set melons and a large pepper of which we grew fond, and a nourishing root, and other plants. But the soil was rich, rich, and they loosened and furrowed it with a sharpened stick. There were no great forest beasts to set them sternly hunting. What then could give them toil? Not gathering the always falling fruit; not cutting from the trees and drying the calabashes, great and small, that they used for all manner of receptacle; not drawing out with a line of some stouter fiber than cotton and with a hook of bone or thorn the painted fish from their crystal water! To fell trees for canoes, to hollow the canoe, was labor, as was the building of their huts, but divided among so many it became light labor. In those days we saw no Indian figure bowed with toil, and when it came it was not the Indian who imposed it.

But they swam, they rowed their canoes, they hunted in their not arduous fashion, they roved afar in their country at peace, and they danced. That last was their fair, their games, their tourney, their pilgrimage, their processions to church, their attendance at mass, their expression of anything else that they felt altogether and at once! It was like children's play, renewed forever, and forever with zest. But they did not treat it as play. We had been showed dances in Concepcion and Isabella, but here in Cuba, in this inland town, Jerez and Luis and I were given to see a great and formal dance, arranged all in honor of us, gods descended for our own reasons to mix with men! They danced in the square, but first they made us a feast with *hutias* and cassava and fish and fruit and a drink not unlike mead, exhilarating but not bestowing drunkenness. Grapes were all over these lands, purple clusters hanging high and low, but they knew not wine.

Men and women danced, now in separate bands, now mingled together. Decorum was kept. We afterwards knew that it had been a religious dance. They had war dances, hunting dances, dances at the planting of their corn, ghost dances and others. This now was a thing to watch, like a beautiful masque. They were very graceful, very supple; they had their own dignity.

We learned much in the three days we spent in this town. Men and women for instance! That nakedness of the body, that free and public mingling, going about work and adventure and play together, worked, thought Juan Lepe no harm. Later on in this vast adventure of a new world, some of our churchmen were given to asserting that they lived like animals, though the animals also are there slandered! The women were free and complaisant; there were many children about. But matings, I thought, occurred only of free and mutual desire, and not more frequently than in other countries. The women were not without modesty, nor the men without a pale chivalry. At first I thought constraint or rule did not enter in, but after a talk with their priest through Diego Colon, I gathered that there prevailed tribe and kinship restraints. Later we were to find that a great network of "thou shalt" and "thou shalt not" ran through their total society, wherever or to what members it might extend. Common good, or what was supposed to be common good, was the master here as it is everywhere! The women worked the gardens, the men hunted; both men and women fished. Women might be caciques. There were women caciques, they said, farther on in their land. And it seemed to us that name and family were counted from the mother's side.

The Admiral had solemnly laid it upon us to discover the polity of this new world. If they held fief from fief, then at last we must come through however many overlords to the seigneur of them all, Grand Khan or Emperor.

We applied ourselves to cacique and butio, but we found no Grand Seigneur. There were other caciques. When the Caribs descended, they banded together. They had dimly, we thought, the idea of a war-lord. But it ended there, when the war ended. Tribute: He found they had no idea of tribute. Cotton grew everywhere! Cotton, cassava, calabashes, all things! When they visited a cacique they took him gifts, and at parting he gave them gifts. That was all.

Gold? They knew of it. When they found a bit they kept it for ornament. The cacique possessed a piece the size of a ducat, suspended by a string of cotton. It had been given to him by a cacique who lived on the great water. Perhaps he took it from the Caribs. But it was in the mountains, too. He indicated the heights beyond. Sometimes they scraped it from sand under the stream. He seemed indifferent to it. But Diego Colon, coming in, said that it was much prized in heaven, being used for high magic, and that we would give heavenly gifts for it. Resulted from that the production in an hour of every shining flake and grain and button piece the village owned. We carried from this place to the Admiral a small gourd filled with gold. But it was not greatly plentiful; that was evident to any thinking man! But we had so many who were not thinking men. And the Admiral had to appease with his reports gold-thirsty great folk in Spain.

We spent three days in this village and they were days for gods and Indians of happy wonder and learning. They would have us describe heaven. Luis and I told them of Europe. We pointed to the east. They said that they knew that heaven rested there upon the great water. The town of the sun was over there. Had we seen the sun's town? Was it beside us in heaven, in "Europe"? The sun went down under the mountains, and there he found a river and his canoe. He rowed all night until he came to his town. Then he ate cassava cakes and rested, while the green and gold and red Lizard [These were "Lizard" folk. They had a Lizard painted on a great post by the cacique's house.] went ahead to say that he was coming. Then he rose, right out of the great water, and there was day again! But we must know about the sun's town; we, the gods!

Luis and I could have stayed long while and disentangled this place and loved the doing it.

But it was to return to the Admiral and the waiting ships.

The three tobacco men would go with us to see wonders, so we returned nine in number along the path. Before we set out we saw that a storm threatened. All six Indians were loth to depart until it was over, and the cacique would have kept us. But Luis and I did not know how long the bad weather might hold and we must get to the ships. It was Jerez who told them boastfully that gods did not fear storms,—specimen of that Spanish folly of ours that worked harm and harm again!

We traveled until afternoon agreeably enough, then with great swiftness the clouds climbed and thickened. Sun went out, air grew dark. The Indians behind us on the path, that was so narrow that we must tread one after the other, spoke among themselves, then Diego Colon pushed through marvelously huge, rich fern to Luis and me. "They say, 'will not the gods tell the clouds to go away?'" But doubt like a gnome sat in the youth's eye. We had had bad weather off Isabella, and the gods had had to wait for the sun like others. By now Diego Colon had seen many and strange miracles, but he had likewise found limitations, quite numerous and decisive limitations! He thought that here was one, and I explained to him that he thought correctly. Europeans could do many things but this was not among them. Luis and I watched him tell the Cubans that he, Diego Colon, had never said that we three were among the highest gods. Even the great, white-headed, chief god yonder in the winged canoe was said to be less than some other gods in heaven which we called Europe, and over all was a High God who could do everything, scatter clouds, stop thunder or send thunder, everything! Had we brought our butio with us he might perhaps have made great magic and helped things. As it was, we must take luck. That seeming rational to the Indians, we proceeded, our glory something diminished, but still sufficient.

The storm climbed and thickened and evidently was to become a fury. Wind began to whistle, trees to bend, lightnings to play, thunder to sound. It grew. We stood in blazing light, thunder almost burst our ears, a tree was riven a bow-shot away. Great warm rain began to fall. We could hardly stand against the wind. We were going under mountainside with a splashing stream below us. Diego Colon shouted, as he must to get above wind and thunder. "Hurry! hurry! They know place." All began to run. After a battle to make way at all, we came to a slope of loose, small stones and vine and fern. This we climbed, passed behind a jagged mass of rock, and found a cavern. A flash lit it for us, then another and another. At mouth it might be twenty feet across, was deep and narrowed like a funnel. Panting, we threw ourselves on the cave floor.

The storm prevailed through the rest of this day and far into the night. *"Hurricane!"* said the Cubans. "Not great one, little one!" But we from Spain thought it a great enough hurricane. The rain fell as though it would make another flood and in much less than forty days. We must be silent, for wind and thunder allowed no other choice. Streams of rain came into the cavern, but we found ledges curtained by rock. We ate cassava cake and drank from a runlet of water. The storm made almost night, then actual night arrived. We curled ourselves up, hugging ourselves for warmth, and went to sleep.

The third day from the town we came to the sea and the ships. All seemed well. Our companions had felt the storm, had tales to tell of wrenched anchors and the *Pinta's* boat beat almost to pieces, uprooted trees, wind, lightning, thunder and rain. But they cut short their recital, wishing to know what we had found.

Luis and I made report to the Admiral. He sat under a huge tree and around gathered the Pinzons, Fray Ignatio, Diego de Arana, Roderigo Sanchez and others. We related; they questioned, we answered; there was discussion; the Admiral summed up.

But later I spoke to him alone. We were now on ship, making ready for sailing. We would go eastward, around this point of Asia, since from what all said it must be point, and see what was upon the other side. "They all gesture south! They say 'Babeque—Babeque! Bohio!' "

I asked him, "Why is it that these Indians here seem glad for us to go?"

He sighed impatiently, drawing one hand through the other, with him a recurring gesture. "It is the women! Certain of our men—" I saw him look at Gutierrez who passed.

"Tomaso Passamonte, too," I said.

"Yes. And others. It is the old woe! Now they have only to kill a man!"

He arraigned short-sightedness. I said, "But still we are from heaven?"

"Still. But some of the gods—just five or six, say—have fearful ways!" He laughed, sorrowfully and angrily. "And you think there is little gold, and that we are very far from clothed and lettered Asia?"

"So far," I answered, "that I see not why we call these brown, naked folk Indians."

"What else would you call them?"

"I do not know that."

"Why, then, let us still call them Indians." He drummed upon the rail before him, then broke out, "Christ! I think we do esteem hard, present, hand-held gold too much!"

"I say yes to that!"

He said, "We should hold to the joy of Discovery and great use hereafter—mounting use!"

"Aye."

"Here is virgin land, vast and beautiful, with a clime like heaven, and room for a hundred colonies such as Greece and Rome sent out! Here is a docile, unwarlike people ready to be industrious servitors and peasants, for which we do give them salvation of their souls! It is all Spain's, the banner is planted, the names given! We are too impatient! We cannot have it between dawn and sunset! But look into the future—there is wealth beyond counting! No great amount of gold, but enough to show that there is gold."

I followed the working of his mind. It was to smile somewhat sorrowfully, seeing his great difficulties. He was the born Discoverer mightily loving Discovery, and watching the Beloved in her life through time. But he had to serve Prince Have-it-now, in the city Greed. I said, "Señor, do not put too much splendor in your journal for the King and Queen and the Spanish merchants and the Church and all the chivalry that the ended war releases! Or, if you prophesy, mark it prophecy. It is a great trouble in the world that men do not know when one day is talked of or when is meant great ranges of days! Otherwise you will have all thirsty Spain sailing for Ophir and Golden Chersonesus, wealth immediate, gilding Midas where he stands! If they find disappointment they will not think of the future; they will smite you!"

I knew that he was writing in that book too ardently, and that he was even now composing letters to great persons to be dispatched from what Spanish port he should first enter, coming back east from west, over Ocean-Sea, from Asia!

But he had long, long followed his own advice, stood by his own course. The doing so had so served him that it was natural he should have confidence. Now he said only, "I do the best I can! I have little sea room. One Scylla and Charybdis? Nay, a whole brood of them!"

I could agree to that. I saw it coming up the ways that they would give him less and less sea room. He went on, "Merchandise has to be made attractive! The cook dresses the dish, the girl puts flowers in her hair. . . .Yet, in the end the wares are mighty beyond description! The dish is for Pope and King—the girl is a bride for a paladin!"

Again he was right afar and over the great span. But they would not see in Spain, or not many would see, that the whole span must be taken. But I was not one to chide him, seeing that I, too, saw afar, and they would not see with me either in Spain.

CHAPTER XX

We sailed for two days east by south. But the weather that had been perfection for long and long again from Palos, now was changed. Dead winds delayed us, the sea ridged, clouds blotted out the blue. We held on. There was a great cape which we called Cape Cuba. Off this a storm met us. We lived it out and made into one of those bottle harbors of which, first and last, we were to find God knows how many in Cuba!

The Admiral named it Puerto del Principe, and we raised on shore here a very great cross. We had done this on every considerable island since San Salvador and now twice on this coast. There were behind us seven or eight crosses. The banner planted was the sign of the Sovereignty of Spain, the cross the sign of Holy Church, Sovereign over sovereigns, who gave these lands to Spain, as she gave Africa and the islands to Portugal. We came to a great number of islets, rivers of clear blue sea between. The ships lay to and we took boat and went among these. The King's Gardens, the Admiral called them, and the calm sea between them and mainland the Sea of Our Lady. They were thickly wooded, and we thought we found cinnamon, aloes and mastic. Two lovely days we had in this wilderness of isles and channels where was no man nor woman at all, then again we went east and south, the land trending that way. Very distant, out of eastern waste, rose what seemed a large island. The Admiral said that we should go discover, and we changed course toward it, but in three hours' time met furious weather. The sea rose, clouds like night closed us in. Night came on without a star and a contrary wind blew always. When the dawn broke sullenly we were beaten back to Cuba, and a great promontory against which truly we might have been dashed stood to our north and shut out coast of yesterday. Here we hung a day and night, and then the wind lulling and the sea running not so high, we made again for that island which might be Babeque. We had Indians aboard, but the sea and the whipping and groaning of our masts and rigging and sails and the pitching of the ship terrified them, and terror made them dull. They sat with knees drawn up and head buried in arms and shivered, and knew not Babeque from anything else.

Christopherus Columbus could be very obstinate. Wishing strongly to gain that island, through all this day he had us strive toward it. But the wind was directly ahead and strong as ten giants. The master and others made representations, and at last he nodded his gray head and ordered the *Santa Maria* put about and the *Pinta* and the *Niña* signaled. The *Niña* harkened and turned, but the *Pinta*. at some distance seemed deaf and blind. Night fell while still we signaled. We were now for Cuba, and the wind directly behind us, but yet as long as we could see, the *Pinta* chose not to turn. We set lights for signals, but her light fell farther and farther astern. She was a swifter sailer than we; there was no reason for that increasing distance. We lay to, the *Niña* beside us. Before long we wholly lost the *Pinta*'s light. Night passed. When morning broke Captain Martin Alonso Pinzon and the *Pinta* were gone.

The sea, though rough, was not too perilous, and never a signal of distress had been seen nor heard.

"Lost? Is the *Pinta* lost?"

"Lost! No!—But, yes. Willfully lost!"

It was Roderigo Sanchez who knew not much of the sea who asked, and the Admiral answered. But having spoken it that once, he closed his strong lips and coming down from deck said he would have breakfast. All that day was guessing and talk enough upon the *Santa Maria*; silent or slurred talk at last, for toward noon the Admiral gave sharp order that the *Pinta* should be left out of conversation. Captain Martin Pinzon was an able seaman. Perhaps something (he reminded us of the rudder before the Canaries) had gone wrong. Captain Pinzon may have thought the island was the nearer land, or he may have returned to Cuba, but more to the north than were we.

He looked for the *Pinta*. again in a reasonable time. In the meantime let it alone!

So soon as the sea allowed, Vicente Pinzon came in his boat to the *Santa Maria*, but he seemed as perplexed as we. He did not know his brother's mind. But Martin Pinzon forever and always was a good sea captain and a Castilian of his word, knowing what was proper observance to his Admiral. If he did this or that, it would be for good reasons. So Vicente, and the Admiral was cordial with him, and saw him over rail and down side with cheerful words. He was cheerful all that day in his speech, cheerful and suave and prophesying good in many directions. But I knew the trouble behind that front.

In some ways the *Pinta* was the best of our ships. Martin Pinzon was a bold and ready man, and those aboard with him devoted to his fortunes. He did not lack opinions of his own, and often they countered the Admiral's. He was ambitious, and the Admiral's rights were so vast and inclusive that there seemed not much room to make name and fame. Much the same with riches! What Martin Pinzon had loaned would come back to him beyond doubt, back with high interest and a good deal more. But still it would seem to him that room was needed. In his mind he had said perhaps many times to the Admiral, "Do not claim too much soil! Do not forget that other trees want to grow!"

Martin Pinzon might have put back to Spain, but who knew the man would not think that likely. Far more probable that he might be doing discovery of his own. Perhaps he would rejoin us later with some splendid thing to his credit, claim that Spain could not deny!

Cuba coast rose high and near. It is a shore of the fairest harbors! We made one of these into which emptied a little river. He named haven and river Saint Catherine. In the bed of this stream, when we went ashore, we found no little gold. He took in his hand grains and flakes and one or two pieces large as beans. It was royal monopoly, gold, and every man under strict command—to bring to the Admiral all that was found. Seamen and companions gathered around him, Admiral, Viceroy and Governor, King Crœsus to be, a tenth of all gold and spoil filling his purse! And they, too, surely some way they would be largely paid! The dream hovered, then descended upon us, as many a time it descended. Great riches and happiness and all clothed in silk, and every man as he would be and not as he was, a dim magnificence and a sense of trumpets in the air, acclaiming us! I remember that day that we all felt this mystic power and wealth, the Admiral and all of us. For a short time, there by Saint Catherine's River, we were brought into harmony. Then it broke and each little self went its way again. But for that while eighty men had felt as though we were a country and more than a country. The gold in the Admiral's hand might have been gold of consciousness.

After this day for days we sailed along Cuba strand, seeing many a fair haven and entering two or three. There were villages, and those dusk, naked folk to whom by now we were well used, running to beach or cliff brow, making signs, seeming to cry, "Heaven come down, heaven, heaven and the gods!" The notion of a sail had never come to them, though with their cotton they might have made them. They were slow to learn that the wind pushed us, acting like a thousand tireless rowers. We were thrillingly new to them and altogether magical. To any seeing eye a ship under full sail is a beautiful, stately, thrilling thing! To these red men there was a perilous joy in the vision. If to us in the ships there hung in this voyage something mystic, hidden, full of possibility, inch by inch to unroll, throbbing all with the future which is the supernatural, be sure these, too, who were found and discovered, moved in a cloud of mystery torn by strange lightnings!

Sometimes we came into haven, dropped anchor and lowered sails, whereupon those on the shore again cried out. When we took our boats and went to land we met always the same reception, found much the same village, carried on much the same conversations. Little by little we collected gold. By now, within the Admiral's chest, in canvas bags, rested not a little treasure for Queen Isabella and King Ferdinand. And though it was forbidden, I knew that many of our seamen hid gold. All told we found enough to whet appetite. But still the Indians said south, and Babeque and Bohio!

At last we had sailed to the very eastern end of Cuba and turned it as we might turn the heel of Italy. A great spur that ran into the ocean the Admiral dubbed Alpha and Omega, and we planted a cross.

It fell to me here to save the Admiral's life.

We had upon the *Santa Maria* a man named Felipe who seemed a simple, God-fearing soul, very attentive to Fray Ignatio and all the offices of religion. He was rather a silent fellow and a slow, poor worker, often in trouble with boatswain and master. He said odd things and sometimes wept for his soul, and the forecastle laughed at him. This man became in a night mad.

It was middle night. The *Santa Maria* swung at anchor and the whole world seemed a just-breathing stillness. There was the watch, but all else slept. The watch, looking at Cuba and the moon on the water, did not observe Felipe when he crept from forecastle with a long, sharp two-edged knife such as they sell in Toledo.

Juan Lepe woke from first sleep and could not recover it. He found Bernardo Nuñez's small, small cabin stifling, and at last he got up, put on garments, and slipped forth and through great cabin to outer air. He might have found the Admiral there before him, for he slept little and was about the ship at all hours, but tonight he did sleep.

I spoke to the watch, then set myself down at break of stern to breathe the splendor of the night. The moon bathed Alpha and Omega, and the two ships, the *Niña* and the *Santa Maria*. It washed the *Pinta* but we saw it not, not knowing where rode the *Pinta* and Martin Alonzo Pinzon. So bright, so pleasureable, was the night!

An hour passed. My body was cooled and refreshed, my spirit quiet. Rising, I entered great cabin on my way to bed and sleep. I felt that the cabin was not empty, and then, there being moonlight enough, I saw the figure by the Admiral's door. "Who is it?" I demanded, but the unbolted door gave to the man's push, and he disappeared. I knew it was not the Admiral and I followed at a bound. The cabin had a window and the moonbeams came in. They showed Felipe and his knife and the great Genoese asleep. The madman laughed and crooned, then lifted that Toledo dagger and lunged downward with a sinewy arm. But I was upon him. The blow fell, but a foot wide of mark. There was a struggle, a shout. The Admiral, opening eyes, sprang from bed.

He was a powerful man, and I, too, had strength, but Felipe

fought and struggled like a desert lion. He kept crying, “I am the King! I will send him to discover Heaven! I will send him to join the prophets!” At last we had him down and bound him. By now the noise had brought the watch and others. A dozen men came crowding in, in the moonlight. We took the madman away and kept him fast, and Juan Lepe tried to cure him but could not. In three days he died and we buried him at sea. And Fernando, creeping to me, asked, “Señor, don’t you feel at times that there is madness over all this ship and this voyage and *him*—the Admiral, I mean?”

I answered him that it was a pity there were so few madmen, and that Felipe must have been quite sane.

“Then what do you think was the matter with Felipe, Señor?”

I said, “Did it ever occur to you, Fernando, that you had too much courage and saw too far?” At which he looked frightened, and said that at times he had felt those symptoms.

CHAPTER XXI

Martin Pinzon did not return to us. That tall, blond sea captain was gone we knew not where. The *Santa Maria* and the *Niña* sailed south along the foot of Cuba. But now rose out of ocean on our southeast quarter a great island with fair mountain shapes. We asked our Indians—we had five aboard beside Diego Colon—what it was. "Bohio! Bohio!" But when we came there, its own inhabitants called it Hayti and Quisquaya.

The Admiral paced our deck, small as a turret chamber, his hands behind him, his mind upon some great chart drawn within, not without. At last, having decided, he called Juan de la Cosa. "We will go to Bohio."

So it was done whereby much was done, the Woman with the distaff spinning fast, fast!

As this island lifted out of ocean, we who had said of Cuba, "It is the fairest!" now said, "No, this is the fairest!" It was most beautiful, with mountains and forests and vales and plains and rivers.

The twelfth day of December we came to anchor in a harbor which the Admiral named Concepcion.

On this shore the Indians fled from us. We found a village, but quite deserted. Not a woman, not a man, not a child! Only three or four of those silent dogs, and a great red and green parrot that screamed but said nothing. There was something in this day, I know not what, but it made itself felt. The Admiral, kneeling, kissed the soil, and he named the island Hispaniola, and we planted a cross.

For long we had been beaten about, and all aboard the ships were well willing to leave them for a little. We had a dozen sick and they craved the shore and the fruit trees. Our Indians, too, longed.

So we anchored, and mariners and all adventurers rested from the sea. A few at a time, the villagers returned, and fearfully enough at first. But we had harmed nothing, and what greatness and gentleness was in us we showed it here. Presently all thought they were at home with us, and that heaven bred the finest folk!

Our people of Hispaniola, subjects now, since the planting of the flag, were taller, handsomer, we thought, than the Cubans, and more advanced in the arts. Their houses were neat and good, and their gardens weeded and well-stocked. The men wore loin cloths, the women a wide cotton girdle or little skirt. We found three or four copper knives, but again they said that they came from the south. As in Spain "west—west" had been his word, so now the Admiral brooded upon south.

These folk had a very little gold, but they seemed to say that theirs was a simple and poor village, and that we should find more of all things farther on. So we left Concepcion, the cross upon the rock showing a long way through the pure air.

For two days we coasted, and at the end of this time we came to a harbor of great beauty and back from it ran a vale like Paradise, so richly sweet it was! Christopherus Columbus was quick to find beauty and loved it when found. Often and often have I seen his face turn that of a child or a youth, filled with wonder. I have seen him kiss a flower, lay a caress upon stem of tree, yearn toward palm tops against the blue. He was well read in the old poets, and he himself was a poet though he wrote no line of verse.

We entered here and came to anchor and the sails rattled down. "Hispaniola—Hispaniola, and we will call this harbor St. Thomas! He was the Apostle to India. And now we are his younger brothers come after long folding away. Were we more—did we have a fleet—we might set a city here and, it being Christmas, call it La Navidad!" Out came the canoes to us, out the swimmers, dark and graceful figures cleaving the utter blue. Someone passing that way overland, hurrying with news, had told these villages how peaceful, noble, benevolent, beneficent we were.

The canoes were heaped with fruit and cassava bread, and they had cotton, not in balls, but woven in pieces. And these Indians had about neck or in ear some bits of gold. These they changed cheerfully, taking and valuing what trifle was given. "Gold. Where do you get your gold? Do you know of Cipango or Cathay or India? Have ever you heard of Zaiton, or of Quinsai and Cublai Khan?" They gave us answers which we could not fully understand, and gestured inland and a little to the east. "Cibao! Cibao!" They seemed to say that there was all the gold there that a reasonable mortal might desire. "Cibao?—Cipango?" said the Admiral. "They might be the same."

"Like Cuba and Cublai Khan," thought Juan Lepe.

Around a point of shore darted a long canoe with many rowers. Other canoes gave way for it, and the Indians already upon the *Santa Maria* exclaimed that it was the boat of the cacique, though not the cacique but his brother sat in it. Guacanagari was the cacique. His town was yonder! They pointed to a misty headland beyond St. Thomas's bay.

The Indian from the great canoe came aboard, a handsome fellow, and he brought presents not like any we had seen. There was a width of cotton embroidered thick with bits of gleaming shell and bone, but what was most welcome was a huge wooden mask with eyes and tongue of gold. Fray Ignatio crossed himself. "The devil they worship,—poor lost sheep!" The third gift was a considerable piece of that mixed and imperfect gold which afterwards we called guanin. And would we go to visit the cacique whose town was not so far yonder?

It was Christmas Eve. We sailed with a small, small wind for the cacique's village, out from harbor of St. Thomas, around a headland and along a low, bright green shore. So low and fitful was the wind that we moved like two great snails. Better to have left the ships and gone, so many of us, in our boats with oars, canoes convoying us! The distance was not great, but distance is as the power of going. "I remember," quoth the Admiral, "a calm, going from the Levant to Crete, and our water cask broken and not a mouthful for a soul aboard! That was a long, long two days while the one shore went no further and the other came no nearer. And going once to Porto Santo with my wife she fell ill and moaned for the land, and we were held as by the sea bottom, and I thought she would die who might be saved if she could have the land. And I remember going down the African coast with Santanem—"

Diego de Arana said, "You have had a full life, Señor!"

He was cousin, I had been told, to that Dona Beatrix whom the Admiral cherished, mother of his youngest son, Fernando. The Admiral had affection for him, and Diego de Arana lived and died, a good, loyal man. "A full outward life," he went on, "and I dare swear, a full inward one!"

"That is God's truth!" said the Admiral. "You may well say that, Señor! Inside I have lived with all who have lived, and discovered with all who have discovered!"

I remember as a dream this last day upon the *Santa Maria*. Beltran the cook had scalded his arm. I dressed it each day, and dressing it now, half a dozen idling by, watching the operation, I heard again a kind of talk that I had heard before. Partly because I had shipped as Juan Lepe an Andalusian sailor and had had my forecastle days, and partly because men rarely fear to speak to a physician, and partly because in the great whole there existed liking between them and me, they talked and discussed freely enough what any other from the other end of ship could have come at only by formal questioning. Now many of the seamen wanted to know when we were returning to Palos, and another number said that they would just as soon never return, or at least not for a good while! But they did not wish to spend that good while upon the ship. It was a good land, and the heathen also good. The heathen might all be going to burn in hell, unless Fray Ignatio could get them baptized in time, and so numerous were they that seemed hardly possible! Almost all might have to go to hell. But in the meantime, here on earth, they had their uses, and one could even grow fond of them—certainly fond of the women. The heathen were eager to work for us, catch us coneys, bring us gold, put hammocks for us between trees and say "Sleep, Señor, sleep!" Here even Tomaso Passamonte was "Señor" and "Don." And as for the women—only the skin is dark—they were warm-hearted! Gold and women and never any cold nor hunger nor toil! The heathen to toil for you—and they could be taught to make wine, with all these grapes dangling everywhere? Heathen could do the gathering and pressing, and also the gold hunting in rocks and streams. Spain would furnish the mind and the habit of command. It were well to stay and cultivate Hispaniola! The Admiral and those who wanted to might take home the ships. Of course, the Admiral would come again, and with him ships and many men. No one wanted, of course, never to see again Castile and Palos and his family! But to stay in Hispaniola a while and rest and grow rich,—that was what they wanted. And no one could justly call them idle! If they found out all about the land and where were the gold and the spices, was there not use in that, just as much use as wandering forever on the *Santa Maria*?

Mother earth was kind, kind, here, and she didn't have a rod like mother country and Mother Church! They did not say this last, but it was what they meant.

"You don't see the rod, that is all," said Juan Lepe.

But there had eventually to be colonies, and I knew that the Admiral was revolving in his head the leaving in this new world certain of our men, seed corn as it were, organs also to gather knowledge against his speedy return with power of ships and men. For surely Spain would be grateful,—surely, surely! But he was not ready yet to set sail for Spain. He meant to discover more, discover further, come if by any means he could to the actual wealth of great, main India; come perhaps to Zaiton, where are more merchants than in all the rest of the world, and a hundred master ships laden with pepper enter every year; or to Quinsai of the marble bridges. No, he was not ready to turn prow to Spain, and he was not likely to bleed himself of men, now or for many days to come. All these who would lie in hammocks ashore must wait awhile, and even when they made their colony, that is not the way that colonies live and grow.

Beltran said, "Some of you would like to do a little good, and some are for a sow's life!"

It was Christmas Eve, and we had our vespers, and we thought of the day at home in Castile and in Italy. Dusk drew down. Behind us was the deep, secure water of St. Thomas, his harbor. The Admiral had us sound and the lead showed no great depth, whereupon we stood a little out to avoid shoal or bar.

For some nights the Admiral had been wakeful, suffering, as Juan Lepe knew, with that gout which at times troubled him like a very demon. But this night he slept. Juan de la Cosa set the watch. The helmsman was Sancho Ruiz than whom none was better, save only that he would take a risk when he pleased. All others slept. The day had been long, so warm, still and idle, with the wooded shore stealing so slowly by.

Early in the night Sancho Ruiz was taken with a great cramp and a swimming of the head. He called to one of the watch to come take the helm for a little, but none answered; called again and a ship boy sleeping near, uncurled himself, stretched, and came to hand. "It's all safe, and the Admiral sleeping and the master sleeping and the watch also!" said the boy. Pedro Acevedo it was, a well-enough meaning young wretch.

Sancho Ruiz put helm in his hand. "Keep her so, while I lie down here for a little. My head is moving faster than the *Santa Maria*!"

He lay down, and the swimming made him close his eyes, and closed eyes and the disappearance of his pain, and pleasant resting on deck caused him to sleep. Pedro Acevedo held the wheel and looked at the moon. Then the wind chose to change, blowing still very lightly but bearing us now toward shore, and Pedro never noticing this grow larger. He was looking at the moon, he afterwards said with tears, and thinking of Christ born in Bethlehem.

The shore came nearer and nearer. Sancho Ruiz slept. Pedro now heard a sound that he knew well enough. Coming back to here and now, he looked and saw breakers upon a long sand bar. The making tide was at half, and that and the changed wind carried us toward the lines of foam. The boy cried, "Steersman! Steersman!" Ruiz sat up, holding his head in his hands. "Such a roaring in my ears!" But "Breakers! Breakers!" cried the boy. "Take the helm!"

Ruiz sprang to it, but as he touched it the *Santa Maria* grounded. The shock woke most on board, the immediate outcry and running feet the rest.

The harm was done, and no good now in recriminations! It was never, I bear witness, habit of Christopherus Columbus.

The *Santa Maria* listed heavily, the sea pounding against her, driving her more and more upon the sand. But order arrived with the Admiral. The master grew his lieutenant, the mariners his obedient ones. Back he was at thirty, with a shipwreck who had seen many and knew how to toil with hands and with head. Moreover, the great genius of the man shone in darkness. He could encourage; he could bring coolness.

We tried to warp her off, but it was not to be done. We cut away mast to lighten her, but more and more she grew fast to the bank, the waves striking all her side, pushing her over. Seams had opened, water was coming in. The *Niña* a mile away took our signal and came nearer, lay to, and sent her boat.

The *Santa Maria*, it was seen, was dying. Nothing more was to be done. Her mariners could only cling to her like bees to comb. We got the two boats clear and there was the boat of the *Niña*. Missioned by the Admiral, Juan Lepe got somehow into cabin, together with Sancho and Luis Torres, and we collected maps and charts, log, journal, box with royal letters and the small bags of gold, and the Admiral's personal belongings, putting all into a great sack and caring for it, until upon the *Niña* we gave it into his hand. Above us rang the cry, "All off!"

From Christopherus Columbus to Pedro Acevedo all left the *Santa Maria* and were received by the *Niña*. Crowded, crowded was the *Niña*! Down voyaged the moon, up came with freshness the rose-chapleted dawn. A wreck lay the *Santa Maria*, painted against the east, about her a low thunder of breakers. Where was the *Pinta* no man knew! Perhaps halfway back to Spain or perhaps wrecked and drowned like the flagship. The *Niña*, a small, small ship and none too seaworthy, carried all of Europe and Discovery.

CHAPTER XXII

In the small, small cabin of the *Niña,* Christopherus Columbus sat for a time with his head bowed in his arms, then rose and made up a mission to go to the cacique Guacanagari and, relating our misfortune, request aid and shelter until we had determined upon our course. There went Diego de Arana and Pedro Gutierrez with Luis Torres and one or two more, and they took Diego Colon and the two St. Thomas Indians. It was now full light, the shore and mountains green as emerald, the water its old unearthly blue.

The *Niña* swung at anchor just under the land and the now receding tide uncovered more and more those sands where the *Santa Maria* lay huddled and dying. The Admiral gazed, and the tears ran down his face. He was so great that he never thought to hide just emotion. He spoke as though to himself. "Many sins have I, many, many! But thou wilt not, O God, cast me utterly away because of them! I will not doubt Thee, nor my calling!"

There was little space about him. The *Niña* seemed to quiver, packed and dark with men. His deep voice went on, and they could hear him, but he did not seem to know that they were there. "As though upon a raft, here a thousand leagues in Ocean-Sea! Yet wilt Thou care for thy Good News. I will come to Spain, and I will tell it. Chosen, and almost by very name pointed out in Thy Book! The first Christian shore that I touch I will walk barefoot and in my shirt at the head of twelve to the first shrine. And, O my Lord, never more will I forget that that tomb in which thou didst rest, still, still is held by the infidel!" He beat his breast. "*Mea culpa! mea culpa!*"

His voice sank, he looked at the sky, then with a turn of the wrist at the wheel he put that by and became again the vigilant Admiral of a fleet of one. "She will hold together yet a while! When the tide is out, we can get to her and empty her. Take all ashore that can be carried or floated and may be of use. Up and down—down and up!"

The inhabitants of Hispaniola were now about us in canoes or swimming. They seemed to cry out in distress and sympathy, gazing at the *Santa Maria* as though it were a god dying there. Their own canoes were living things to them as is any ship to a mariner, and by analogy our great canoe was a Being dying, more of a Being than theirs, because it had wings and could open and fold them. And then back came our boat with Diego de Arana and the others, and they had with them that same brother of the cacique who had come to us in St. Thomas Harbor. And had we been wrecked off Palos, not Palos could have showed more concern or been more ready to help than were these men.

We had three boats and the Indian canoes and hands enough, white and copper-hued. Now at low tide, we could approach and enter the *Santa Maria*. A great breach had been made and water was deep in her hold, but we could get at much of casks and chests, and could take away sails and cordage, even her two cannon. Eventually, as she broke up, we might float away to shore much of her timber. When I looked from the wreck to the little *Niña*, I could see, limned as it were in air, the Viceroy's first colony, set in Hispaniola, beside Guacanagari's town. All Christmas day we toiled and the Indians at our side. We found them ready, not without skill, gay and biddable.

Toward sunset came Guacanagari. All the little shore was strewn and heaped with our matters. And here I will say that no Indian stole that day though he might have stolen, and though our possessions seemed to him great wonders and treasure beyond estimation. What was brought from the *Santa Maria* lay in heaps and our men came and went. The most of our force was ashore or in the boats; only so many on the *Niña*. The Admiral, just returned to the ship, stretched himself upon the bench in her small cabin. Powerful was his frame and constitution, and powerfully tried all his life with a thousand strains and buffetings! It seemed still to hold; he looked a muscular, sinewy, strong and ruddy man. But there were signs that a careful eye might find. He lay upon the bench in the cabin and I, who was his physician, brought him wine and biscuit and made him eat and drink who, I knew, had not touched food since the evening before; after which I told him to close eyes and go away to Genoa and boyhood. He shut them, and I sitting near brought my will as best I could to the quieting of all heavy and sorrowful waves.

But then the cacique came. So small was the *Niña* that we could hear well enough the word of his arrival. The Admiral opened his eyes and sat stiffly up. He groaned and took his head into his hands, then dropped these and with a shake of his shoulders resumed command. So many and grievous a sea had dashed over him and retreated and he had stood! What he said now was, "The tide of the spirit goes out; the tide comes back in. Let it come back a spring tide!"

Guacanagari entered. This cacique, whose fortunes now began to be intertwined with ours, had his likeness, so far as went state and custom, to that Cuban chieftain whom Luis Torres and I had visited. But this was an easier, less strongly fibred person, a big, amiable, indolent man with some quality of a great dog who, accepting you and becoming your friend, may never be estranged. He was brave after his fashion, gifted enough in simple things. In Europe he would have been an. easy, well-liked prince or duke of no great territory. He kept a simple state, wore some slight apparel of cotton and a golden necklet. He brought gifts and an unfeigned sympathy for that death upon the sand bar.

He and the Admiral sat and talked together. "Gods from heaven?" —"Christian men and from Europe," and we could not make him, at this time, understand that that was not the same thing. We began to comprehend that "heaven" was a word of many levels, and that they ascribed to it everything that they chose to consider good and that was manifestly out of the range of their experience.

In his turn the Admiral was ready for all that Guacanagari could tell him. "Gold?" His eyes were upon the Indian's necklet. Removing it, the cacique laid it in the god's hand. All Indians now understood that we made high magic with gold, getting out of it virtues beyond their comprehension. In return the Admiral gave him a small brazen gong and hammer. "Where did they get the gold?" Again like the

Cuban chief this cacique waved his hand to the mountains. "Cibao!" and then turning he too pointed to the south. "Much gold there," said Diego Colon. "Inland, in the mountains," quoth the Admiral, "and evidently, in very great quantity, in some land to the south! This is not Cipango, but I think that Cipango lies to the south." He asked who ruled Hayti that we called Hispaniola. We understood that there were a number of caciques, but that for a day's journey every way it was Guacanagari's country.

"A cacique who ruled them all?" No, there was no such thing.

"Had ships like ours and clothed men ever before come to them?"

No, never! But then he seemed to say that there was undoubtedly a tradition. Gods had come, and would come again, and when they did so great things would follow! But no cacique nor priest nor any knew when the gods had come.

The Admiral made some question of Caribs. Again there was gesture southward, though it seemed to us that something was said of folk within this great island who were at least like Caribs. And where was the most gold and the greatest other wealth that they knew of? Again south, though this time we thought it rather south by west. The Admiral sighed, and spoke of Cuba. Yes, Guacanagari knew of Cuba. Had it end far yonder to the westward, or no end? Had any one ever come to its end? The cacique thought not, or knew not and assumed deliberation. Luis and I agreed that we had not met among these Indians any true notion of a continent. To them Hayti was vast, Cuba was vast, the lands of the Caribs, wherever they were, were vast, and vast whatever other islands there might be. To them this was the *Œcumene*, the inhabited and inhabitable world, Europe —Asia—Africa? Their faces stayed blank. Were these divisions of heaven?

Guacanagari would entertain and succor us. This canoe—oh, the huge marvel!—was too crowded! Yonder lay his town. All the houses that we might want were ours, all the hammocks, all the food. And he would feast the gods. That had been preparing since yesterday, A feast with dancing. He hoped the great cacique and his people from far nearer heaven than was Guacanagari would live as long as might be in his town. Guarico was his town. A big, easy, amiable, likeable man, he sat in nakedness only not utter, save for that much like a big hidalgo offering sympathy and shelter to some fire-ousted or foe-ousted prince! As for the part of prince it was not hard for the Admiral to play it. He was one naturally.

He thanked the cacique to whom, I could see, he had taken liking. Seven houses would be enough. Tonight some of us would sleep upon the beach beside the heaped goods. Tomorrow we would visit Guacanapri. The big, lazy, peaceable man expressed his pleasure, then with a wide and dignified gesture dismissing all that, asked to be shown marvels.

CHAPTER XXIII

Guacanagari's town was much perhaps as was Goth town, Frank town, Saxon town, Latin town, a sufficient time ago. As for clothed and unclothed, that may be to some degree a matter of cold or warm weather. We had not seen that ever it was cold in this land.

Guacanagari feasted us with great dignity and earnestness, for he and his people held it a momentous thing our coming here, our being here. Utias we had and iguana, fish, cassava bread, potato, many a delicious fruit, and that mild drink that they made. And we had calabashes, trenchers and fingers, stone knives with which certain officers of the feast decorously divided the meat, small gourds for cups, water for cleansing, napkins of broad leaves. It was a great and comely feast. But before the feast, as in Cuba, the dance.

I should say that three hundred young men and maidens danced. They advanced, they retreated, they cowered, they pressed forward. They made supplication, arms to heaven or forehead to ground, they received, they were grateful, they circled fast in ease of mind, they hungered again and were filled again, they flowed together, they made a great square, chanting proudly!

Fray Ignatio beside me glowered, so far as so good a man could glower. But Juan Lepe said, "It is doubt and difficulty, approach, reconciliation, holy triumph! They are acting out long pilgrimages and arrivals at sacred cities and hopes for greater cities. It is much the same as in Seville or Rome!" Whereupon he looked at me in astonishment, and Jayme de Marchena said to Juan Lepe, "Hold thy tongue!"

Dance and the feast over, it became the Admiral's turn. He was set not to seem dejected, not to give any Spaniard nor any Indian reason to say, "This Genoese—or this god—does not sustain misfortune!" But he sat calm, pleased with all; brotherly, fatherly, by that big, easy, contented cacique. Now he would furnish the entertainment! Among us we had one Diego Minas, a huge man and as mighty a bowman as any in Flanders or England. Him the Admiral now put forward with his great crossbow and long arrows. A stir ran around. "Carib! Carib!" We made out that those mysterious Caribs had bows and arrows, though not great ones like this. Guacanagari employed gestures and words that Luis Torres and I strove to understand. We gathered that several times in the memory of man the Caribs had come in many canoes, warred dreadfully, killed and taken away. More than that, somewhere in Hayti or Quisquaya or Hispaniola were certain people who knew the weapon. "Caonabo!" He repeated the name with respect and disliking. "Caonabo, Caonabo!" Perhaps the Caribs had made a settlement.

Diego fastened a leaf upon the bark of a tree and from a great distance transfixed it with an arrow, then in succession sent four others against the trunk, making precisely the form of a cross. The Indians cried, "Hai! Hai!" But when the four harquebus men set up their iron rests, fixed the harquebuses, and firing cut leaves and twigs from the same tree, there was a louder crying. And when there was dragged forth, charged with powder and fired, one of the lombards taken from the *Santa Maria*, wider yet sprang the commotion. Pedro Gutierrez and a young cavalier from the *Niña* deigned to show lance play, and Vicente Pinzon who had served against the Moors took a great sword and with it carved calabashes and severed green boughs. The sword was very marvelous to them. We might have danced for them for Spain knows how to dance, or we might have sung for them, for our mariners sing at sea. But these were not the superior things we wished to show them.

Guacanagari, big and easy and gentle, said, "Live here, you who are so great and good! We will take you into the people. We shall be brothers." We understood them that the great white heron was their guardian spirit and would be ours. I said, "They do not think of it as just those stalking, stilly standing birds! It is a name for something hovering, brooding, caring for them."

The Viceroy spoke with energy. "Tell them of Father, Son and Holy Ghost!"

Fray Ignatio stood and spoke, gentle and plain. Diego Colon made what headway he could. Guacanagari listened, attentive. The Franciscan had a certainty that presently he might begin to baptize. His face glowed. I heard him say to the Admiral, "If it be possible, Señor, leave me here when you return to Spain! I will convert this chief and all his people—by the time you come again there shall be a church!"

"Let me ponder it yet a while," answered the other.

He was thoughtful when he went back to the *Niña*. Vicente Pinzon, too, was anxious for light. "This ship is crowded to sinking! If we meet wretched weather, or if sickness break out, returning, we shall be in bad case!" Roderigo Sanchez also had his word. "Is it not very important, Señor, that we should get the tidings to the Sovereigns? And we have now just this one small ship, and so far to go, and all manner of dangers!"

"Aye, it is important!" said the Admiral. "Let me think it out, Señor."

He had not slept at all, thought Juan Lepe, when next morning he came among us. But be looked resolved, hardy to accomplish. He had his plan, and he gave it to us in his deep voice that always thrilled with much beside the momentary utterance. We would build a fort here on shore, hard by this village, felling wood for it and using also the timbers of the *Santa Maria*. We would mount there her two guns and provide an arsenal with powder, shot, harquebuses and bows. Build a fort and call it La Navidad, because of Christmas day when was the wreck. It should have a garrison of certainly thirty men, a man for each year of Our Lord's life when He began his mission. So many placed in Hispaniola would much lighten the *Niña*, which indeed must be lightened in order with safety to recross Ocean-Sea. For yes, we would go back to Palos! Go, and come again with many and better ships, with hidalgos and missionary priests, and very many men! In the meantime so many should stay at La Navidad.

"In less than a year—much less, I promise it—I the Admiral will be here again at La Navidad, when will come happy greeting between brothers in the greatest service of our own or many ages! Sea and land, God will keep us so long as we are His!"

All loved Christopherus Columbus that day. None was to be forced to stay at La Navidad. It was easy to gain thirty; in the end there tarried thirty-eight.

The building of the fort became a pleasurable enterprise. We broke up with singing the *Santa Maria*, and with her bones built the walls. Guacanagari and his people helped. All was hurried. The Admiral and Viceroy, now that his mind was made up, would depart as soon as might be.

We built La Navidad where it might view the sea, upon a hillside above a brown river sliding out to ocean. Beyond the stream, in the groves, a quarter-league away, stood the hundred huts of Guarico. We built a tower and storehouse and wall of wood and we digged around all some kind of moat, and mounted three lombards. All that we could lift from the *Santa Maria* and what the *Niña* could spare us of arms, conveniences and food went into our arsenal and storehouse. We had a bubbling spring within the enclosure. When all was done the tower of La Navidad, though an infant beside towers of Europe, might suffice for the first here of its brood. It was done in a week from that shipwreck.

Who was to be left at La Navidad? Leave was given to volunteer and the mariners' list was soon made up, good men and not so good. From the stern there volunteered Pedro Gutierrez and Roderigo de Escobedo. The Admiral did not block their wish, but he gave the command not to Escobedo who wished it, but to Diego de Arana whom he named to stay, having persuaded him who would rather have returned with the *Niña*. But he could trust Diego de Arana, and, with reason, he was not sure of those other hidalgos. De Arana stayed and fulfilled his trust, and died a brave man. Fray Ignatio would stay. "Bring me back, Señor, a goodly bell for the church of La Navidad! A bell and a font."

Juan Lepe would stay. There needed a physician. But also Jayme de Marchena would stay. He thought it out. Six months had not abolished the Holy Office nor converted to gentleness Don Pedro nor the Dominican.

But the Admiral had assigned me to return with the *Niña*. I told him in the evening between the sunset and the moonrise what was the difficulty. He was a man profoundly religious, and also a docile son of the Church. But I knew him, and I knew that he would find reasons in the Bible for not giving me up. The deep man, the whole man, was not in the grasp of bishop or inquisitor or papal bull.

He agreed. "Aye, it is wiser! I count two months to Spain, seeing that we may not have so favorable a voyage. Three or maybe four there, for our welcome at court, and for the gathering a fleet—easy now to gather for all will flock to it, and masters and owners cry, 'Take my ship—and mine!' Two months again to recross. Look for me it may be in July, it may be in August, it may be in September!"

The Viceroy spoke to us, gathered by our fort, under the banner of Castile, with behind us on hill brow a cross gleaming. Again, all that we had done for the world and might further do! Again, we returning on the *Niña* or we remaining at La Navidad were as crusaders, knights of the Order of the Purpose of God! "Cherish good—oh, men of the sea and the land, cherish good! Who betrays here betrays almost as Judas! The Purpose of God is Strength with Wisdom and Charity which only can make joy! Therefore be ye here at La Navidad strong, wise and charitable!"

He said more, and he gave many an explicit direction, but that was the gist of all. Strength, wisdom and charity.

Likewise he spoke to the Indians and they listened and promised and meant good. An affection had sprung between Guacanagari and Christopherus Columbus. So different they looked! and yet in the breast of each dwelled much guilelessness and the ability to wonder and revere. The Viceroy saw in this big, docile ruler of Guarico however far that might extend, one who would presently be baptized and become a Christian chief, man of the Viceroy of Hispaniola, as the latter was man of the Sovereigns of Spain. All his people would follow Guacanagari. He saw Christendom here in the west, and a great feudal society, acknowledging Castile for overlord, and Alexander the Sixth as its spiritual ruler.

Guacanagari may have seen friends in the gods, and especially in this their cacique, who with others that they would bring, would be drawn into Guarico and made one and whole with the people of the heron. But he never saw Guacanagari displanted—never saw Europe armed and warlike, hungry and thirsty.

The *Niña* and La Navidad bade with tears each the other farewell. It was the second of January, fourteen hundred and ninety-three. We had mass under the palm trees, by the cross, above the fort. Fray Ignatio blessed the going, blessed the staying. We embraced, we loved one another, we parted. The *Niña* was so small a ship, even there just before us on the blue water! So soon, so soon, the wind blowing from the land, she was smaller yet, smaller, smaller, a cock boat, a chip, gone!

Thirty-eight white men watched her from the hill above the fort, and of the thirty-eight Juan Lepe was the only one who saw the Admiral come again.

CHAPTER XXIV

The butio of this town had been absent for some reason in the great wood those days of the shipwreck and the building of La Navidad. Now he was again here, and I consorted with him and chiefly from him learned their language. The Admiral had taken Diego Colon to Spain, and to Spain was gone too Luis Torres, swearing that he would come again. To Spain was gone Sancho, but Beltran the cook stayed with us. Pedro and Fernando also.

Time passed. With the ending of January the heat increased. The butio knew all manner of simples; he was doctor and priest together. He had a very simple magic. He himself did not expect it to reach the Great Spirit, but it might affect the innumerable *zemes* or under and under-under spirits. These barbarians, using other words for them, had letter-notion of gnome, sylph, undine and salamander. All things lived and took offense or became propitious. Effort consisted in making them propitious. If the effort was too great one of them killed you. Then you went to the shadowy caves. There was a paradise, too, beautiful and easy. But the Great Spirit could not be hurt and had no wish to hurt any one else, whether *zemes* or men. To live with the Great Spirit, that was really the Heron wish, though the little herons could not always see it.

This butio—Guarin his name—was a young man with eyes that could burn and voice that fell naturally into a chant. He took me into the forest with him to look for a very rare tree. When it was found I watched him gather plants from beneath it and scrape bits off its bark into a small calabash. I understood that it was good for fever, and later I borrowed from him and found that he had grounds for what he said.

La Navidad and Guarico neighbored each other. The Indians came freely to the fort, but Diego de Arana made a good *alcayde* and he would not have mere crowding within our wooden wall. Half of our thirty-eight, permitted at a time to wander, could not crowd Guarico. But in himself each Spaniard seemed a giant. At first a good giant, profoundly interesting. But I was to see pleased interest become a painful interest.

Women. The first complaint arose about the gods or the giants and women. Guacanagari came to La Navidad with Guarin and several old men his councilors. Diego de Arana received them and there was talk under the great tree within our gate. Then all the garrison was drawn up, and in the presence of the cacique Arana gave rebuke and command, and the two that had done the outrage had prison for a week. It was our first plain showing in this world that heaven-people or Europeans could differ among themselves as to right and wrong, could quarrel, upbraid and punish. But here was evidently good and bad. And what might be the proportion? As days went by the question gathered in this people's bosom.

It was not that their women stood aloof from our men. Many did not so in the least! But it was to be free will and actual fondness, and in measure. But there were those among us who, finding in lonely places, took by force. These became hated.

Diego de Arana was to collect the gold that was a royal monopoly. Trading for gold for one's self was forbidden. Assuredly taking it by force—assuredly all robbery of that or anything else—was forbidden. But there came a robbery, and since it was resisted, murder followed. This was a league from Guarico and from La Navidad. The slain Indian's companion escaping, told.

This time Diego de Arana went to Guarico and Guacanagari. He took with him a rich present, and he showed how the guilty men were punished. "You do not slay them?" asked Guacanagari. Arana shook his head. He thought we were too few in this land to be ridding of life the violent and lustful. But the Indians seemed to think that he said that he could not. They still doubted, I think, our mortality. As yet they had seen no mighty stranger bleed or die.

Arana would have kept his garrison within the walls. But indeed it was not healthful for them there, and at the very word of confinement faction rose. There were now two parties in La Navidad, the Commandant's party and Escobedo's party.

The heat increased. It was now March. An illness fell among us. I took Guarin into counsel and gave in water the bitter inner bark of that tree shredded and beaten fine. Those who shook with cold and burned with fever recovered.

Fray Ignatio was among those who sickened. He left after some days his hammock, but his strength did not come back to him. Yet, staff in hand, he went almost daily to Guarico. Then, like that! Fray Ignatio died. He died—his heart stopped—on the path between Guarico and La Navidad. He had been preaching, and then, Guarin told me, he put his hand to his side, and said, "I will go home!" He started up the path, but at the big tree he dropped. Men and women ran to him, but the butio was dead.

We buried Fray Ignatio beneath the cross on the hilltop. The Indians watched, and now they knew that we could die.

The heat increased.

At first Diego de Arana sent out at intervals exploring parties. We were to learn, at least, Guacanagari's country. But the heat was great, and so many of those left at La Navidad only idle and sensual. They would push on to a village—we found in Guacanagari's country many hamlets, but no other town like Guarico—and there they would stop, with new women, new talk, and the endless plenty to eat and sleep in the shade. When, at their own sweet will, they returned to La Navidad, the difficulties had been too great. They could not get to the high mountains where might or might not be the mines. But what they did was to spread over the country scandalous news of scandalous gods.

At last Arana sorted out those who could be trusted at least to strive for knowledge and self-control and sent these. But that weakened him at La Navidad, draining him of pure blood and leaving the infected, and by mid-April he ceased any effort at exploration. It must wait until the Admiral returned, and he began to be hungry indeed for that return.

Escobedo and Pedro Gutierrez were not hungry for it—not yet.

These two became the head and front of ill, encouraging every insubordinate, infuriating all who suffered penalties, teaching insolence, self-will and license. They drew their own feather to them, promising evil knows what freedom for rapine.

All the silver weather, golden weather, diamond weather since we had left Gomera in the Canaries—how many ages since!—now was changed. We had thought it would last always, but now we entered the long season of great heat and daily rain. At first we thought these rains momentary, but day after day, week after week, with stifling heat, the clouds gathered, broke, and came mighty rain that at last ceased to be refreshing, became only wearying and hateful. It did not cool us; we lived in a sultry gloom. And the garrison of La Navidad became very quarrelsome. La Navidad showed the Indians Europeans cursing one another, giving blows, only held back by those around from rushing at each other, stabbing and cutting. Finally they saw Tomaso Passamonte kill one Jacamo. Diego de Arana hung Tomaso Passamonte. But what were the Indians to think? Not what they thought when first we came from the winged canoes to their beaches.

The last of April fell the second sickness and it was far worse than the first. Eleven men died, and we buried them. When it passed we were twenty-five Spaniards in Hispaniola, and we liked not the Indians as well as we had done, and they liked not us. Oh, the pity—pity—pity, the pity and the blame!

Guacanagari came to visit the commandant, none with him but the butio Guarin, and desiring to speak with Arana out of the company. They talked beneath the big tree, that being the most comfortable and commodious council chamber. Don Diego was imperfect yet in the tongue of Guarico, and he called Juan Lepe to help him out.

It was a story of Caonabo, cacique of Maguana that ran into the great mountains of Cibao, that cacique of whom we had already heard as being like Caribs. Caonabo had sent quite secretly two of his brothers to Guacanagari. He had heard ill of the strangers and thought they were demons, not gods! He advised the cacique of Guarico to surprise them while they slept and slay them. It was in his experience that all who ate and slept could be slain. If his brother

Guacanagari needed help in the adventure, Caonabo would give it. He would even come in person.

Diego de Arana said, "What did you answer, O Cacique."

Guacanagari spoke at some length of our Great Cacique and his longing that he might return. Everything had gone well while he was here! "He will return," said Arana. "And he has your word."

Guacanagari stated that he meant to keep his word. He had returned answer to Caonabo that there had been misfortunes but that the mighty strangers were truly mighty, and almost wholly beneficent. At any rate, he was not prepared to slay them, did not wish to slay them.

Arana spoke vigorously, pointing out to the cacique all the kindliness that had attended our first intercourse. The unhappinesses of February, March and April he attributed to real demons, not to our own fiend but to small powers at large, maleficent and alarmed, heathen powers in short, jealous of the introduction of the Holy Catholic religion. Guacanagari seemed to understand about these powers. He looked relieved. But Guarin who was with him regarded the sea and I saw his lip curl.

The commandant wished to know if there were any danger of Caonabo, alone, descending upon us from the mountains. But no! Maguana and Guarico were friends. They had not always been so, but now they were friends. De Arana looked doubtfully, and I saw him determine to keep watch and ward and to hold the men within or near to fort. But Guacanagari sat serene. He repeated that there were always preliminaries before wars, and that for a long time there had only been peace between Guarico and Maguana. "Caonabo is Carib," said the young copper priest. The cacique answered, "Carib long ago. Not now."

At sunset, the rain ceasing for a little, the earth smoking, the west a low, vaporous yellow, the swollen river sounding, Diego de Arana had summoned by the drum every man in La Navidad. He stood beneath our banner and put his hand upon the staff and spoke earnestly to those gathered before him, in their duty and out of their duty. He told of Caonabo, and of his own sense that Guacanagari was too confident. He told of Guacanagari's fidelity to the Admiral, and he appealed to every Christian there to be at least as faithful. We were few and far from Spain, and we had perhaps more than we could conceive in trust. "Far from Spain, but no farther than we will from the blessed saints and the true Christ. Let us put less distance there, being few in this land and in danger!"

He knew that he had a dozen with him, and looked straight at Escobedo.

The latter said, "Live in the open and die there, if need be! To live in this rat hole, breathing plague, is dying already! Caonabo is a fable! These people! Spaniards have but to lift voice and they flee!"

He received from his following acquiescent sound. Spoke Pedro Gutierrez. "Guacanagari wishes to bottle us here; that is the whole of it. Why play his game? I never saw a safer land! Only La Navidad is not safe!"

Those two had half and perhaps more than half of the garrison. Arana cried, "Don Roderigo de Escobedo and Don Pedro Gutierrez, you serve the Queen ill!"

"You, Señor," answered Gutierrez, "serve my Lady Idle Fear and my Lord Incapacity!"

Whereupon Arana put him in arrest and he lay that night in prison. The cloud was black over La Navidad.

CHAPTER XXV

It did not lighten. Escobedo waited two days, then in the dark night, corrupting the watch, broke gaol for Pedro Gutierrez and with him and nine men quitted La Navidad. Beltran the cook it was who heard and procured a great smoking torch, and sent out against them a voice like a bull of Bashan's. Arana sprang up, and the rest of us who slept. They were eleven men, armed and alert. There were shouts, blows, a clutching and a throwing off, a detaining and repelling. In the east showed long ghost fingers, the rain held away. They were at the gate when we ran upon them; they burst it open and went forth, leaving one of their own number dead, and two of them who stayed with Arana desperately hurt. We followed them down the path, through the wood, but they had the start. They did not go to Guarico, but they seized the boat of the *Santa Maria* which the Admiral had left with us and went up the river. We heard the dash of their oars, then the rain came down, with a weeping of every cloud.

The dead man they left behind was Fernando. I had seen Pedro in the gate, going forth.

Fourteen men, two of whom were ill and two wounded, stayed at La Navidad. Arana said with passion, "Honest men and a garrison at one! There is some gain!"

That could not be denied. Gain here, but how about it yonder?

It was May. And now the rain fell in a great copious flood, huge-dropped and warm, and now it was restrained for a little, and there shone a sun confused and fierce. Earth and forest dripped and streamed and smoked. We were Andalusians, but the heat drained us. But we held, we fourteen men. Arana did well at La Navidad. We all did what we could to live like true not false Castilians, true not false Christians. And I name Beltran the cook as hero and mighty encourager of hearts.

We went back and forth between La Navidad and Guarico, for though the Admiral had left us a store of food we got from them fruit and maize and cassava. They were all friendly again, for the fourteen withheld themselves from excess. Nor did we quarrel among ourselves and show them European weakness.

Guacanagari remained a big, easy, somewhat slothful, friendly barbarian, a child in much, but brave enough when roused and not without common sense. He had an itch for marvels, loved to hear tales of our world that for all one could say remained to them witchcraft and cloudland, world above their world! What could they, who had no great beasts, make of tales of horsemen? What could their huts know of palace and tower and cathedral, their swimmers of stone bridges, their canoes of a thousand ships greater far than the *Santa Maria* and the *Niña*? What could Guarico know of Seville? In some slight wise they practiced barter, but huge markets and fairs to which traveled from all quarters and afar merchants and buyers went with the tales of horsemen. And so with a thousand things! We were the waving oak talking to the acorn.

But there were among this folk two or three ready for knowledge. Guarin was a learning soul. He foregathered with the physician Juan Lepe, and many a talk they had, like a master and pupil, in some corner of La Navidad, or under a palm-thatched roof, or, when the rain held, by river or sounding sea. He had mind and moral sense, though not the European mind at best, nor the European moral sense at highest. But he was well begun. And he had beauty of form and countenance and an eager, deep eye. Juan Lepe loved him.

It was June. Guacanagari came to La Navidad, and his brown face was as serious as a tragedy. "Caonabo?" asked Diego de Arana.

A fortnight before this the cacique, at Arana's desire, had sent three Indians in a canoe up the river, the object news if possible of that ten who had departed in that direction. Now the Indians were back. They had gone a long way until the high mountains were just before them, and there they heard news from the last folk who might be called Guarico and the first folk who might be called Maguana. The mighty strangers had gone on up into the mountains and Caonabo had put them to death.

"To death!"

It appeared that they had seized women and had beaten men whom they thought had gold which they would not give. They were madmen, Escobedo and Gutierrez and all with them!

Guacanagari said that Caonabo had invited them to a feast. It was spread in three houses, and they were divided so, and around each Spaniard was put a ring of Indians. They were eating and drinking. Caonabo entered the first house, and his coming made the signal. Escobedo and Pedro Gutierrez were in this house. They raised a shout, "Undone, Spaniards!" But though they were heard in the other houses—these houses being nothing more than booths—it was to no use. There followed struggle and massacre; finally Gutierrez and Escobedo and eight men lay dead. But certain Indians were also killed and among them a son of Caonabo.

It was July. We began to long toward the Admiral's return. A man among us went melancholy mad, watching the sea, threatening the rain when it came down and hid the sea, and the Admiral might go by! At last he threw himself into ocean and was drowned. Another man was bitten by a serpent, and we could not save him. We were twelve Spaniards in La Navidad. We rested friends with Guarico, though now they held us to be nothing more than demigods. And indeed by now we were ragged!

Then, in a night, it came. Guacanagari again appeared. It had reached him from up the river that Caonabo was making pact with the cacique of Marien and that the two meant to proceed against us. Standing, he spoke at length and eloquently. If he rested our friend, it might end in his having for foes Maguana and Marien. There had been long peace, and Guarico did not desire war. Moreover, Caonabo said that it was idle to dread Caribs and let in the mighty strangers! He said that all pale men, afraid of themselves so that they covered themselves up, were filled with evil *zemes* and were worse than a thousand Caribs! But Caonabo was a mocker and a hard-of-heart! Different was Guacanagari. He told us how different. It all ended in great hope that Caonabo would think better of it.

We kept watch and ward. Yet we could not be utterly cooped within La Navidad. Errands must be done, food be gathered. More than that, to seem to Guarico frightened, to cry that we must keep day and night behind wall with cannon trained, notwithstanding that Caonabo might be asleep in the mountains of Cibao, would be but to mine our own fame, we who, for all that had passed, still seemed to this folk mighty, each of us a host in himself! And as nothing came out of the forest, and no more messengers of danger, they themselves had ceased to fear, being like children in this wise. And we, too, at last; for now it was late August, and the weather was better, and surely, surely, any day we might see a white point rise from blue ocean,—a white point and another and another, like stars after long clouded night skies!

So we watched the sea. And also there was a man to watch the forest. But we did not conceive that the dragon would come forth in the daytime, nor that he could come at any time without our hearing afar the dragging of his body and the whistling of his breath.

It was halfway between sunrise and noon. Five of us were in the village, seven at La Navidad. The five were there for melons and fruit and cassava and tobacco which we bought with beads and fishhooks and bits of bright cloth. Three of the seven at La Navidad were out of gate, down at the river, washing their clothes. Diego Minas, the archer, on top of wall, watched the forest. Walking below, Beltran the cook was singing in his big voice a Moorish song that they made much of year before last in Seville. I had a book of Messer Petrarca's poems. It had been Gutierrez's, who left it behind when he broke forth to the mountains.

Beltran's voice suddenly ceased. Diego the archer above him on wall had cried down, "Hush, will you, a moment!" Diego de Arana came up. "What is it?"

"I thought," said the archer, "that I heard a strange shouting from toward village. Hark ye! There!"

We heard it, a confused sound. "Call in the men from the river!" Arana ordered.

Diego Minas sent his voice down the slope. The three below by the river also heard the commotion, distant as Guarico. They were standing up, their eyes turned that way. Just behind them hung the forest out of which slid, dark and smooth, the narrow river.

Out of the forest came an arrow and struck to the heart Gabriel Baraona. Followed it a wild prolonged cry of many voices, peculiar and curdling to the blood, and fifty—a hundred—a host of naked men painted black with white and red and yellow markings. Guarico did not use bow and arrow, but a Carib cacique knew them, and had so many, and also lances flint or bone-headed, and clubs with stones wedged in them and stone knives. Gabriel Baraona fell, whether dead or not we could not tell. Juan Morcillo and Gonzalo Fernandez sent a scream for aid up to La Navidad. Now they were hidden as some small thing by furious bees. Diego de Arana rushed for his sword. "Down and cut them out!"

Diego Minas fired the big lombard, but for fear of hurting our three men sent wide the ball. We looked for terror always from the flame, the smoke and great noise, and so there was terror here for a moment and a bearing back in which Juan and Gonzalo got loose and made a little way up path. But a barbarian was here who could not long be terrified. Caonabo sent half his horde against Guarico, but himself had come to La Navidad. That painted army rallied and overtook the fleeing men.

Shouting, making his swung sword dazzle in light, Diego de Arana raced down path, and Diego Minas and Beltran the cook and Juan Lepe with him. Many a time since then, in this island, have I seen half a dozen Christians with their arms and the superstitious terror that surrounded them put to flight twenty times their number. But this was early, and the spirit of these naked men not broken, and Caonabo faced us. It was he himself who, when three or four had been wounded by Arana, suddenly rushed upon the commandant. With his stone-headed club he struck the sword away, and he plunged his knife into Arana's breast. He died, a brave man who had done his best at La Navidad.

Juan Morcillo and Gonzalo Fernandez and Diego Minas were slain. I saw a lifted club and swerved, but too late.

Blackness and neither care nor delight. Then, far off, a little beating of surf on shore, very far and nothing to do with anything.

Then a clue of pain that it seemed I must follow or that must follow me, and at first it was a little thin thread, but then a cable and all my care was to thin it again. It passed into an ache and throb that filled my being like the rain clouds the sky. Then suddenly there were yet heavy clouds but the sky around and behind. I opened my eyes and sat up, but found that my arms were bound to my sides.

"We aren't dead, and that's some comfort, Doctor, as the cock said to the other cock in the market pannier!" It was Beltran the cook who spoke and he was bound like me. Around us lay the five dead. A score of Indians warded us, mighty strangers in bonds, and we heard the rest up at the fort where they were searching and pillaging.

Guarico, and the men there?

We found that out when at last they were done with La Navidad and they and we were put on the march. We came to where had been Guarico, and truly for long we had smelled the burning of it, as we had heard the crying and shouting. It was all down, the frail houses. I made out in the loud talking that followed the blending of Caonabo's bands what had been done and not done. Guacanagari, wounded, was fled after fighting a while, he and his brother and the butio and all the people. But the mighty strangers found in the village, were dead. They had run down to the sea, but Caonabo's men had caught them, and after hard work killed them. Juan Lepe and Beltran, passing, saw the five bodies.

I do not think that Caonabo had less than a thousand with him. He had come in force, and the whole as silent as a bat or moth. We were to learn over and over again that "Indians" could do that, travel very silently, creatures of the forest who took by surprise. Well, Guarico was destroyed, and Guacanagari and Guarin fled, and in all Hispaniola were only two Spaniards, and we saw no sail upon the sea, no sail at all!

CHAPTER XXVI

We turned from the sea. Thick forest came between us and it. We were going with Caonabo to the mountains. Beltran and I thought that it had been in question whether he should kill us at once, or hold us in life until we had been shown as trophies in Maguana, and that the pride and vanity of the latter course prevailed. After two days in this ruined place, during which we saw no Guarico Indian, we departed. The raid was over. All their war is by raid. They carried everything from the fort save the fort itself and the two lombards. In the narrow paths that are this world's roads, one man must walk after another, and their column seems endless where it winds and is lost and appears again. Beltran and I were no longer bound. Nor were we treated unkindly, starved nor hurt in any way. All that waited until we should reach Caonabo's town.

Caonabo was a most handsome barbarian, strong and fierce and intelligent, more fierce, more intelligent than Guacanagari. All had been painted, but the heat of the lowland and their great exertion had made the coloring run and mix most unseemly. When they left Guarico they plunged into the river and washed the whole away, coming out clear red-brown, shining and better to look upon. Caonabo washed, but then he would renew his marking with the paint which he carried with him in a little calabash.

A pool, still and reflecting as any polished shield, made his mirror. He painted in a terrific pattern what seemed meant for lightning and serpent. It was armor and plume and banner to him. I thought of our own devices, comforting or discomforting kinships! He had black, lustrous hair, no beard—they pluck out all body hair save the head thatch—high features, a studied look of settled and cold fierceness. Such was this Carib in Hispaniola.

Presently they put a watch and the rest all lay down and slept, Beltran beside me. The day had been clear, and now a great moon made silver, silver, the land around. It shone upon the Spanish sailor and upon the Carib chief and all the naked Manguana men. I thought of Europe, and of how all this or its like had been going on hundred years by hundred years, while perished Rome and quickened our kingdoms, while Charlemagne governed, while the Church rose until she towered and covered like the sky, while we went crusades and pilgrimages, while Venice and Genoa and Lisbon rose and flourished, while letters went on and we studied Aristotle, while question arose, and wider knowledge. At last Juan Lepe, too, went to sleep.

Next day we traveled among and over mountains. Our path, so narrow, climbed by rock and tree. Now it overhung deep, tree-crammed vales, now it bore through just-parted cliffs. Beltran and Juan Lepe had need for all their strength of body. The worst was that that old tremor and weakness of one leg and side, left after some sea fight, which had made Beltran the cook from Beltran the mariner, came back. I saw his step begin to drag. This increased. An hour later, the path going over tree roots knotted like serpents, he stumbled and fell. He picked himself up. "Hard to keep deck in this gale!"

When he went down there had been an exclamation from those Indians nearest us. "Aiya!" It was their word for rotten, no good, spoiled, disappointing, crippled or diseased, for a misformed child or an old man or woman arrived at helplessness. Such, I had learned from Guarin, they almost invariably killed. It was why, from the first, we hardly saw dwarfed or humped or crippled among them.

We had to cross a torrent upon a tree that falling had made from side to side a rounded bridge. Again that old hurt betrayed him. He slipped, would have fallen into the torrent below, but that I, turning, caught him and the Indian behind us helped. We managed across. "My ship," said Beltran, "is going to pieces on the rocks."

The path became ladder steep. Now Beltran delayed all, for it was a lame man climbing. I helped him all I could.

The sun was near its setting. We were aloft in these mountains. Green heads still rose over us, but we were aloft, far above the sea.

And now we were going through a ravine or pass where the walking was better. Here, too, a wind reached us and it was cooler. Cool eve of the heights drew on. We came to a bubbling well of coldest water and drank to our great refreshment. Veritable pine trees, which we never saw in the lowlands, towered above and sang. The path was easier, but hardly, hardly, could Beltran drag himself along it. His arm was over my shoulder.

Out of the dark pass we came upon a table almost bare of trees and covered with a fine soft grass. The mountains of Cibao, five leagues—maybe more—away, hung in emerald purple and gold under the sinking sun. The highest rocky peaks rose pale gold. Below us and between those mountains on which we stood and the golden mountains of Cibao, spread that plain, so beautiful, so wide and long, so fertile and smiling and vast, that afterwards was called the Royal Plain! East and west one might not see the end; south only the golden mountains stopped it. And rivers shone, one great river and many lesser streams. And we saw afar many plumes of smoke from many villages, and we made out maize fields, for the plain was populous. *Vega Real!* So lovely was it in that bright eve! The very pain of the day made it lovelier.

The high grassy space ran upon one side to sheer precipice, dropping clear two hundred feet. But there was camping ground enough—and the sun almost touched the far, violet earth.

The Indians threw themselves down. When they had supper they would eat it, when they had it not they would wait for breakfast. But Caonabo with twenty young men came to us. He said something, and my arms were caught from behind and held. He faced Beltran seated against a pine. "Aiya!" he said. His voice was deep and harsh, and be made a gesture of repugnance. There was a powerfully made Indian beside him, and I saw the last gleam of the sun strike the long, sharp, stone knife. "Kill!" said the cacique.

A dozen flung themselves upon Beltran, but there was no need, for he sat quite still with a steady face. He had time to cry to Juan Lepe, who cried to him, "That's what I say! Good cheer and courage and meet again!"

He had no long suffering. The knife was driven quickly to his heart. They drew the shell to the edge of the precipice and dropped it over.

It was early night, it was middle night, it was late night. They had set no watch, for where and what was the danger here on this mountain top?

One side went down in a precipice, one sloping less steeply we had climbed from the pine trees and the well, one of a like descent we would take tomorrow down to the plain, but the fourth was mountain head hanging above us and thick wood,—dark, entangled, pathless. And it chanced or it was that Juan Lepe lay upon the side toward the peak, close to forest. The Indians had no thought to guard me. We lay down under the moon, and that bronze host slept, naked beautiful statues, in every attitude of rest.

The moon shone until there was silver day. Juan Lepe was not sleeping.

There was no wind, but he watched a branch move. It looked like a man's arm, then it moved farther and was a full man,—an Indian, noiseless, out clear in the moon, from the wood. I knew him. It was the priest Guarin, priest and physician, for they are the same here. Palm against earth, I half rose. He nodded, made a sign to rise wholly and come. I did so. I stood and saw under the moon no waking face nor upspringing form. I stepped across an Indian, another, a third. Then was clear space, the wood, Guarin. There was no sound save only the constant sound of this forest by night when a million million insects waken.

He took my hand and drew me into the brake and wilderness. There was no path. I followed him over I know not what of twined root and thick ancient soil, a powder and flake that gave under foot, to a hidden, rocky shelf that broke and came again and broke and came again. Now we were a hundred feet above that camp and going over mountain brow, going to the north again. Gone were Caonabo and his Indians; gone the view of the plain and the mountains of Cibao. Again we met low cliff, long stony ledges sunk in the forest, invisible from below. I began to see that they would not know how to follow. Caonabo might know well the mountains of Cibao, but this sierra that was straight behind Guarico, Guarico knew. It is a blessed habit of their priests to go wandering in the forest, making their medicine, learning the country, discovering, using certain haunts for meditation. Sometimes they are gone from their villages for days and weeks. None indeed of these wild peoples fear reasonable solitude. Out of all which comes the fact that Guarin knew this mountain. We were not far, as flies the bird, from the burned town of Guarico, from the sea without sail, from the ruined La Navidad. When the dawn broke we saw ocean.

He took me straight to a cavern, such another as that in which Jerez and Luis Torres and I had harbored in Cuba. But this had fine sand for floor, and a row of calabashes, and wood laid for fire.

Here Juan Lepe dropped, for all his head was swimming with weariness. The sun was up, the place glistered. Guarin showed how it was hidden. "I found it when I was a boy, and none but Guarin hath ever come here until you come, Juan Lepe!" He had no fear, it was evident, of Caonabo's coming. "They will think your idol helped you away. If they look for you, it will be in the cloud. They will say, 'See that dark mark moving round edge of cloud mountain! That is he!' " I asked him, "Where are Guacanagari and the rest?"

"Guacanagari had an arrow through his thigh and a deep cut upon the head. He was bleeding and in a swoon. His brother and the Guarico men and I with them took him, and the women took the children, and we went away, save a few that were killed, upon the path that we used when in my father's time, the Caribs came in canoes. After a while we will go down to Guacanagari. But now rest!"

He looked at me, and then from a little trickling spring he took water in a calabash no larger than an orange and from another vessel a white dust which he stirred into it, and made me drink. I did not know what it was, but I went to sleep.

But that sleep did not refresh. It was filled with heavy and dreadful dreams, and I woke with an aching head and a burning skin. Juan Lepe who had nursed the sick down there in La Navidad knew feebly what it was. He saw in a mist the naked priest, his friend and rescuer, seated upon the sandy floor regarding him with a wrinkled brow and compressed lips, and then he sank into fever visions uncouth and dreadful, or mirage-pleasing with a mirage-ecstasy.

Juan Lepe did not die, but he lay ill and like to die for two months. It was deep in October, that day at dawn when I came quietly, evenly, to myself again, and lay most weak, but with seeing eyes. At first I thought I was alone in the cavern, but then I saw Guarin where he lay asleep.

That day I strengthened, and the next day and the next. But I had lain long at the very feet of death, and full strength was a tortoise in returning. So good to Juan Lepe was Guarin!

Now he was with me, and now he went away to that village where was Guacanagari. He had done this from the first coming here, nursing me, then going down through the forest to see that all was well with his wounded cacique and the folk whose butio he was. They knew his ways and did not try to keep him when he would return to the mountain, to "make medicine." So none knew of the cavern or that there was one Spaniard left alive in all Hayti.

I strengthened. At last I could draw myself out of cave and lie, in the now so pleasant weather, upon the ledge before it. All the vast heat and moisture was gone by; now again was weather of last year when we found San Salvador.

I could see ocean. No sail, and were he returning, surely it should have been before this! He might never return.

When Guarin was away I sat or lay or moved about a small demesne and still prospered. There were clean rock, the water, the marvelous forest. He brought cassava cake, fruit, fish from the sea. He brought me for entertainment a talking parrot, and there lived in a seam of the rock a beautiful lizard with whom I made friends. The air was balm, balm! A steady soft wind made cataract sound in the forest. Sunrise, noon, sunset, midnight, were great glories.

It was November; it was mid-November and after. Now I was strong and wandered in the forest, though never far from that cliff and cavern. It was settled between us that in five days I should go down with Guarin to Guacanagari. He proposed that I should be taken formally into the tribe. They had a ceremony of adoption, and after that Juan Lepe would be Guarico. He would live with and teach the Guaricos, becoming butio — he and Guarin butios together. I pondered it. If the Admiral came not again it was the one thing to do.

I remember the very odor and exquisite touch of the morning. Guarin was away. I had to myself cave and ledge and little waterfall and great trees that now I was telling one from another. I had parrot and lizard and spoke now to the one and now to the other. I remember the butterflies and the humming birds.

I looked out to sea and saw a sail!

It was afar, a white point. I leaned against the rock for I was suddenly weak who the moment before had felt strong. The white point swelled. It would be a goodly large ship. Over blue rim slipped another flake. A little off I saw a third, then a fourth. Juan Lepe rubbed his eyes. Before there came no more he had counted seventeen sail. They grew; they were so beauteous. Toward the harbor sailed a fleet. Now I made out the flagship.

O Life, thou wondrous goddess of happenings!

An hour I sat on cliff edge and watched. They were making in, the lovely white swans. When they were fairly near, when in little time the foremost would bring to, down sail and drop anchor, Juan Lepe, gathering his belongings together, bidding the lizard farewell and taking the parrot with him on shoulder, left cavern and cliff and took Guarin's path down through the forest.

Halfway to level land he met Guarin coming up; the two met beneath a tree huge and spreading, curtained with a vine, starred with flowers. "He has come!" cried the Indian. "They have come!" In his voice was marveling, awe, perturbation.

The sun in the sky shone, and in the bay hung that wonder of return, the many ships for the *Niña*. Juan Lepe and Guarin went on down through wood to a narrow silver beach, out upon which had cast itself an Indian village.

Guacanagari was not here. He waited within his house for the Admiral. But his brother, and others of Guarico, saw me and there rose a clamor and excitement that for the moment took them from the ships. Guarin explained and Juan Lepe explained, but still this miraculous day dyed also for them my presence here. I had been slain, and had come to life to greet the Great Cacique! It grew to a legend. I met it so, long afterwards in Hispaniola.

CHAPTER XXVII

One by one were incoming, were folding wings, were anchoring, Spanish ships. Three were larger each than the *Santa Maria* and the *Pinta* together; the others caravels of varying size. Seventeen in all, a fleet, crowded with men, having cannon and banners and music. Europe was coming with strength into Asia! The Indians on the beach were moved as by an unresting wind. They had terror, they had delight, and some a mere stupidity of staring. The greatest ship, the first to anchor, carried the banner of Castile and Leon, and the Admiral's banner. Now a boat put off from her, boats also from the two ships next in grandeur.

As they came over the blue wave Juan Lepe stepped down sand to water edge. Not here, but somewhat to the west, before La Navidad would one look for this anchoring. He thought rightly that the Admiral came here from La Navidad, where he found only ruin, but also some straying Indian who could give news. So it was, for presently in the foremost boat I made out two Guarico men. They had told of Caonabo and of Guacanagari's fortunes, and of every Spaniard dead of that illness or slain by Caonabo. They would put Juan Lepe among these last, but here was Juan Lepe, one only left of that thirty-eight.

The boat approached. I saw the bared head, higher than any other, the white hair, the blue-gray eyes, the strong nose and lips, the whole majestic air of the man, as of a great one chosen. Master Christopherus—Don Cristoval—*el Almirante!* One of the rowers, and that was Sancho with whom I had walked on the Fishertown road, first saw me and gave a startled cry. All in the boat turned head. I heard the Admiral's voice, "Aye, it is! It is!"

Boat touched sand, there was landing. All sprang out. The Admiral took me in his arms. "You alone—one only?"

I answered, "One only. The most died in their duty."

He released me. "Señors, this is Señor Juan Lepe, that good physician whom we left. Now tell—tell all—before we go among this folk!"

By water edge I told, thirty men of Spain around me. A woeful story, I made it short. These men listened, and when it was done fell a silence. Christopherus Columbus broke it. "The wave sucks under and throws out again, but we sail the sea, have sailed it and will sail it!—Now were these Indians false or fair?"

I could tell how fair they had been—could praise Guarico and Guacanagari and Guarin. He listened with great satisfaction. "I would lay my head for that Indian!"

Talk with him could not be prolonged, for we were in a scene of the greatest business and commotion. When I sought for Guarin he was gone. Nor was Guacanagari yet at hand. I looked at the swarming ships and ship boats, and the coming and coming upon the beach of more and more clothed men, and at the tall green palms and the feathered mountains. This host, it seemed to me, was not so artlessly amazed as had been we of the *Santa Maria*, the *Pinta* and the *Niña*, when first we came to lands so strange to Europe. Presently I made out that they had seen others of these islands and shores. Coming from Spain they had sailed more southerly than we had done before them. They had made a great dip and had come north-by-west to Hispaniola. I heard names of islands given by the Admiral, Dominica, Marigalante, Guadaloupe, *Santa Maria* la Antigua, San Juan. They had anchored by these, set foot upon them, even fought with people who were Caribs, Caribals or Cannibals. They had a dozen Caribs, men and women, prisoners upon the *Marigalante* that was the Admiral's ship.

This group about Juan Lepe, survivor of La Navidad, talked like seasoned finders and takers. For the most part they were young men and hidalgos, fighters against the Moors, released by the final conquest of those paynims, out now for further wild adventure and for gold with which to return, wealthy and still young, to Spanish country, Spanish cities, Spanish women! They had the virtue and the vice of their sort, courage, miraculous generosities and as miraculous weaknesses. Gold, valor, comradeship—and eyes resting apprais-ingly upon young Guarico women there upon the silver beach with Guarico men.

I heard one cry "Master Juan Lepe!" and turning found Luis Torres. We embraced, we were so glad each to see the other. My hi-dalgos were gone, but before I could question Luis or he me, there bore down upon us, coming together like birds, half a dozen friars. "We bring twelve—number of the Apostles!" said Luis. "Monks and priests. Father Bernardo Buil is their head. The Holy Father hath appointed him Vicar here. You won't find him a Fray Ignatio!"

A bull-necked, dark-browed, choleric looking man addressed me. His Benedictine dress became him ill. He should have been a Captain of Free Lances in whatever brisk war was waging. He said, "The survivor, Juan Lepe?—We stopped at your La Navidad and found ruin and emptiness. There must have been ill management—gross!"

"They are all dead," I answered. "None of us manage the towers so very well!"

He regarded me more attentively. "The physician, Juan Lepe. Where did you study?"

"In Poitiers and in Paris, Father."

"You have," he said, "the height and sinew and something of the eye and voice of a disappeared heretic, Jayme de Marchena, who slipped the Dominicans. I saw him once from a doorway. But that the Prior of La Rabida himself told me that he had accurate knowledge that the man had gone with the Jews to Fez, I could almost think—But of course it is not possible, and now I see the differences."

I answered him with some indifferent word, and we came to the Haytiens, and how many had Fray Ignatio made Christian? "I knew him," said the Benedictine. "A good man, but weak, weak!"

Juan Lepe asked of the Indians the Admiral had taken to Spain. "But six reached us alive. We instructed them and baptized them. A great event—the Grand Cardinal and the King and the Queen attend-ing! Three died during the summer, but blessedly, being the first of all their people in all time to enter heaven. A great salvation!"

He looked at the forest and mountains, the sands, the Guaricos, as at a city he was besieging.

"Ha!" said Father Buil, and with his missionaries moved up the beach.

Luis and I began to talk. "No need to tell me that Spain gave you welcome!" '

"The royalest ever! First we came to Lisbon, driven in by storm, and had it there from King John, and then to Palos which, so to speak, went mad! Then through Spain to Barcelona, where was the court, and all the bells in every town ringing and every door and window crowded, and here is the Færy Prince on a white charger, his Indians behind him and gold and parrots and his sailors! Processions and processions—alcalde and alcayde and don and friar and priest, and let us stop at the church and kneel before high altar, and vow again in seven years to free the Sepulchre! He hath walked and ridden, waked and slept, in a great, high vision! Most men have visions but he can sustain vision."

"Aye, he can!"

"So at last into Barcelona, where grandees meet us, and so on to the court, and music as though the world had turned music! And the King and Queen and great welcome, and, 'Sit beside us, Don Cristoval Colon!' and 'Tell and tell again', and 'Praise we Most High God!' "

"It is something for which to praise! Ends of the earth beginning to meet."

"Aye! So we write that very night to the Pope to be confirmed that the glory and profit under God are to Castile and Aragon. But the Queen thought most of the heathen brought to Christ. And the Admiral thinks of his sons and his brothers and his old father, and of the Holy Sepulchre and of the Prophecies, and he has the joy of the runner who touches the goal!—I would you could have seen the royalty with which he was treated—not one day nor week but a whole summer long—the flocking, the bowing and capping, the 'Do me the honor—', the 'I have a small petition.' Nothing conquers like conquering!"

"He had long patience."

"Aye. Well, he is at height now. But he has got with him the old disastrous seeds. Fifteen hundred men, and among them quite a plenty like Gutierrez and Escobedo! But there are good men, too, and a great lot of romantical daredevils. No pressing this time! We might have brought five thousand could the ships have held them. 'Come to the Indies and make your fortune!'—'Aye, that is my desire!' "

I said, "I am looking now at a romantical daredevil whom I have seen before, though I am sure that he never noticed me."

"Don Alonso de Ojeda? He is feather in cap, and sometimes cap, and even at stress head within the cap! Without moving you've beckoned him."

There approached a young man of whom I knew something, having had him pointed out by Enrique de Cerda in Santa Fé. I had before that heard his name and somewhat of his exploits. In our day, over all Spain, one might find or hear of cavaliers of this brand. War with the Moor had lasted somewhat longer than the old famed war with Troy. It had modeled youth; young men were old soldiers. When there came up a sprite like this one he drank war like wine. A slight young man, taut as a rope in a gale, with dark eyes and red lips and a swift, decisive step, up he came.

"Oh, you are the man who lived out of all your fort? How did you manage it?"

"I had a friend among these friendly Indians who rescued me."

"Yes! It is excellent warfare to have friends. You have seen no knight nor men-at-arms, nor heard of such?"

"Not under those names."

"How far do you think we may be from true houses and cities, castles, fortresses?"

"I haven't the least idea. By the looks of it, pretty far."

"It seems to me that you speak truth," he answered. "Well, it isn't what we looked for, but it's something! Room yet to dare!" Off he went, half Mercury, half Mars, and a sprig of youth to draw the eyes.

"Was there nothing ever heard," I asked Luis, "of the *Pinta* and Martin Pinzon?"

"He is dead."

"You saw the wreck?"

"No, not that way, though true it is that he wrecked himself! I forget that you know nothing. We met the *Pinta* last January, not a day from here, with Monte Cristi there yet in sight. When he came aboard and sat in the great cabin I do not know what he said, except that it was of separation by that storm, and the feeling that two parties discovering would thereby discover the more, and the better serve their Majesties. The Admiral made no quarrel with him. He had some gold and some news of coasts that we had not seen. And he did not seem to think it necessary to seem penitent or anything but just naturally Martin Pinzon. So on we sailed together, he on the *Pinta* and the Admiral on the *Niña*. But that was a rough voyage home over Ocean-Sea! Had we had such weather coming, might have been mutiny and throat-cutting and putting back, Cathay and India being of no aid to dead men! Six times at least we thought we were drowned, and made vows, kneeling all together and the Admiral praying for us, Fray Ignatio not being there. Then came clear, but beyond Canaries a three days', three nights' weather that truly drove us apart, the *Pinta* and the *Niña*. We lost each other in the darkness and never found again. We were beaten into the Tagus, the *Pinta* on to Bayonne. Then, mid-March, we came to Palos, landed and the wonder began. And in three days who should come limping in but the *Pinta*? But she missed the triumph, and Martin Pinzon was sick, and there was some coldness shown. He went ashore to his own house, and his illness growing worse he died there. Well, he had qualities."

"Aye," I answered, with a vision of the big, bluff, golden-haired man.

"Vicente Pinzon is here; his ship the *Cordera* yonder. What's the stir now? The Admiral will go to see Guacanagari?"

That, it seemed, was what it was, and presently came word that Juan Lepe should go with him. A body of cavaliers sumptuously clad, some even wearing shining corselet, greaves and helm, was forming about him who was himself in a magnificent dress. Besides these were fifty of the plainer sort, and there lacked not crossbow, lance and arquebus. And there were banners and music. We were going like an army to be brotherly with Guacanagari. Father Buil was going also, and his twelve gowned men. "Who," I asked Luis, "is the man beside the Admiral? He seems his kin."

"He is. It is his brother, Don Diego. He is a good man, able, too, though not able like the Admiral. They say the other brother, Bartholomew, who is in England or in France, is almost as able. How dizzily turns the wheel for some of us! Yesterday plain Diego and Bartholomew, a would-be churchman and a shipmaster and chartmaker! Now Don Diego—Don Bartholomew! And the two sons watching us off from Cadiz! Pages both of them to the Prince, and pictures to look at! 'Father!' and 'Noble father! and 'Forget not your health, who are our Dependance!' "

Waiting for all to start, I yet regarded that huge dazzle upon the beach, so many landed, so many coming from the ships, the ships themselves so great a drift of sea birds! As for those dark folk—what should they think of all these breakers-in from heaven? It seemed to me today that despite their friendliness shown us here from the first, despite the miracle and the fed eye and ear and the excitement, they knew afar a pale Consternation.

At last, to drum and trumpet, we passed from shining beach into green forest. I found myself for a moment beside Diego Colon—not the Admiral's brother, but the young Indian so named. Now he was Christian and clothed, and truly the Haitiens stared at him hardly less than at the Admiral. I greeted him and he me. He tried to speak in Castilian but it was very hard for him, and in a moment we slipped into Indian.

I asked him, "How did you like Spain?"

He looked at me with a remote and childlike eye and began to speak of houses and roads and horses and oxen.

A message came from the Admiral at head of column. I went to him. Men looked at me as I passed them. I was ragged now, grizzle-bearded and wan, and they seemed to say, "Is it so this strange land does them? But those first ones were few and we are many, and it does not lie in our fortune! Gold lies in ours, and return in splendor and happiness." But some had more thoughtful eyes and truer sense of wonder.

We found Guacanagari in a new, large, very clean house, and found him lying in a great hammock with his leg bound with cotton web, around him wives and chief men. He sat up to greet the Admiral and with a noble and affecting air poured forth speech and laid his hand upon his hidden hurt.

Now I knew, because Guarin had told me so, that that wound was healed. It had given trouble—the Caribs poisoned their darts—but now it was well. But they are simpler minded than we, this folk, and I read Guacanagari that he must impress the returning gods with his fidelity. He had proved it, and while Juan Lepe was by he did not need this mummery, but he had thought that he might need. So, a big man evidently healthful, he sighed and winced and half closed his eyes as though half-dying still in that old contest when he had stood by the people from the sky.

I interpreted his speech, the Admiral already understanding, but not the surrounding cavaliers. It was a high speech or high assurance that he had done his highest best.

"Do I not believe that, Guacanagari?" said the Admiral, and thinking of Diego de Arana and Fray Ignatio and others and of the good hope of La Navidad, tears came into his eyes.

He sat upon the most honorable block of wood which was brought him and talked to Guacanagari. Then at his gesture one brought his presents, a mirror, a rich belt, a knife, a pair of castanets. Guacanagari, it seemed, since the sighting of the ships, had made collection on his part. He gave enough gold to make lustful many an eye looking upon that scene.

The women brought food and set before the Spaniards in the house. I found Guarin and presently we came to be standing without the entrance—they had no doors; sometimes they had curtains of cotton—looking upon that strange gathering in the little middle square of the town. So many Spaniards in the palm shadows, and the women feeding them, and Alonso de Ojeda's hand upon the arm of a slender brown girl with a wreath of flowers around her head. Father Buil was within with the Admiral, truculently and suspiciously regarding the idolater who now had left the hammock and seemed as well of a wound as any there! But here without were eight or ten friars, gathered together under a palm tree, making refection and talking among themselves. One devout brother, sitting apart and fasting, told his beads.

Said Guarin, "I have been watching him. He is talking to his *zeme*. — They are all butios?"

"Yes. Most of them are good men."

"What is going to happen here to all my people? Something is over against me and my people, I feel it! Even the cacique has fear."

"It is the dark Ignorance and the light Ignorance, the clothed Ignorance and the naked Ignorance. I feel it too, what you feel. But I feel, O Guarin, that the inner and true Man will not and cannot take hurt!"

He said, "Do they come for good?"

I answered, "There is much good in their coming. Seen from the mountain brow, enormous good, I think. In the long run I am fain to think that all have their market here, you no less than I, Guacanagari no less than the Admiral."

"I do not know that," he said. "It seems to me the sunny day is dark."

I said, "In the main all things work together, and in the end is honey."

Out they came from palm-roofed house, the Admiral of the Ocean-Sea and Viceroy of what Indies he could find for Spain and Spain could take, and the Indian king or grandee or princeling. Perceiving that what he did was appreciated for what it was, Guacanagari had recovered his lameness. The cotton was no longer about his thigh; he moved straight and lightly,—a big, easy Indian.

It was now well on in the afternoon, but he would go with the Mighty Stranger, the Great Cacique his friend, to see the ships and all the wonders. His was a childlike craving for pure novelty and marvel.

So we went, all of us, back through vast woodland to cerulean water. Water was deep, the *Marigalante* rode close in, and about and beyond her the *Santa Clara*, the *Cordera*, the *San Juan*, the *Juana*, another *Niña*, the *Beatrix* and many another fair name. They were beautiful, the ships on the gay water and about them the boats and the red men's canoes.

We went to the *Marigalante*, I with the Admiral. Dancing across in the boat there spoke to me Don Diego Colon, born Giacomo

Colombo, and I found him a sober, able man, with a churchly inclination. Here rose the Marigalante, and now we were upon it, and it was a greater ship than the *Santa Maria*, a goodly ship, with goodly gear aboard and goodly Spaniards. Jayme de Marchena felt the tug of blood, of home-coming into his country.

CHAPTER XXVIII

Finding young Sancho upon the *Marigalante*, I kept him beside me for information's sake.

He, too, had his stories. And he asked me how Pedro and Fernando died.

In this ship were two sets of captives, animals brought from Spain and Indians from those fiercer islands to the south. The *Monsalvat* that was a freight ship had many animals, said Sancho, cattle and swine and sheep and goats and cocks and hens, and thirty horses. But upon the *Marigalante*, well-penned, the Admiral had a stallion and two mares, a young bull and a couple of heifers, and two dogs—bloodhounds. The Caribs were yonder, five men in all.

He took me to see them. They were tall, strong, sullen and desperate in aspect, hardier, fiercer than Indians of these northward lands. But they were Indians, and their guttural speech could be made out, at least in substance. They asked with a high, contemptuous look when we meant to slay and eat them.

"They eat men's flesh, every Caribal of them! We saw horrid things in Guadaloupe!"

Away from these men sat or stood seven women. "They were captives," said Sancho. "Caribs had ravished them from other islands and they fled in Guadaloupe to us."

These women, too, seemed more strongly fibred, courageous, high of head than the Hayti women. There was among them one to whom the others gave deference, a chieftainess, strong and warlike in mien, not smoothly young nor after their notions beautiful, but with an air of sagacity and pride. A ship boy stood with us. "That is Catalina," he said. "Ho, Catalina!"

The woman looked at him with disdain and what she said was, "Young fool with fool-gods!"

"They came to us for refuge," said Sancho. "We think they are Amazons. There was an island where they fought us like men—great bow-women! Don Alonso de Ojeda first called this one Catalina, so now we all call her Catalina. At first they liked us, but now that they are safe away from Caribs—all but these five and they can't hurt them—they sit and pine! I call it ungrateful, Catalina!"

We moved away. There came from the great cabin where they had wine and fine sweet cakes the Admiral and Guacanagari, with them Don Diego and three or four cavaliers. Guarin was not with the cacique, upon the *Marigalante*. He would not come. I had a vision of him, in the forest seated motionless, communing with the deepest self he could reach, seeking light with the other light-seekers.

Christopherus Columbus beckoned me and I went the round of the ship with him and others and his guest, this far-away son of Great India. So, presently, he was taken to view the horses and the cattle. Whoever hath seen lions brought to a court for show hath seen some shrinking from too-close and heard timorous asking if the bars be really strong. And the old, wild beasts at Rome for the games. If one came by chance upon them in a narrow quarter there might be terror. And the bull that we goad to madness for a game in Spain—were barriers down would come a-scrambling! This cacique had never seen an animal larger than a fox or a dog, Yet he stood with steadiness, though his glance shot here and there. The stallion was restless and fiery-eyed; the bull sent forth a bellow. "Why do they come? What will they do here? Will you put them in the forest? The people will be afraid to wander!"

He looked away to sky and sea and shore. "It grows toward night," he said. "I will go back to my town."

The Admiral said, "I would first show you the Caribs," and took him where they were bound. The Haytien regarded them, but the Caribs were as contemptuously silent as might have been Alonso de Ojeda in like circumstances. Only as Guacanagari turned away, one spoke in a fierce, monotonous voice. "You also, Haytien, one moon!"

"You lie! Only Caribs!" Guacanagari said back.

The cacique stood before the woman whom they called Catalina. She broke into speech. It was cacique to cacique. She was from Boriquen — she would return in a canoe if she were free! Better drown than live with the utterly un-understandable—only that they ate and drank and laid hold of women whether these would or would not, and were understandable that far! Gods! At first she thought them gods; now she doubted. They were magicians. If she were free — if she were free — if she were free! Home — Boriquen! If not that, at least her own color and the understandable!"

Guacanagari stood and listened. She spoke so fast—the Admiral never became quite perfect in Indian tongues, and few upon the *Marigalante* were so at this time. Juan Lepe understood. But just as he was thinking that in duty bound he must say to the Admiral, "She is undermining reputation. Best move away!" Guacanagari made a violent gesture as though he would break a spell. "Where could they come from with all that they have except from heaven? Who can plan against gods? It is sin to think of it! *El Almirante* will make you happy, Boriquen woman!"

We left the women. But Guacanagari himself was not happy, as he had been that Christmas-tide when first the gods came, when the *Santa Maria* was wrecked and he gave us hospitality.

The Admiral did not see that he was unhappy. The Admiral saw always a vast main good, and he thought it pearl and gold in every fiber. As yet, he saw no rotted string, no snarl to be untangled. It was his weakness, and maybe, too, his strength.

The sunset hung over this roadstead and the shore. The mountains glowed in it, the nearer wood fell dark, the beach showed milky white, a knot of palms upon a horn of land caught full gold and shone as though they were in heaven. Over upon the *Cordera* they were singing. The long cacique-canoe shot out from the shadow of the *Marigalante*.

Sun dipped, night cupped hands over the world. The long day of excitement was over. Mariners slept, adventurers gentle and simple, the twelve friars and Father Buil. Seventeen ships, nigh fifteen hundred men of Europe, swinging with the tide before the land we were to make Spanish.

The watch raised a cry. Springing from his bed Juan Lepe came on deck to find there confusion, and under the moon in the clear water, swimming forms, swimming from us in a kind of desperate haste and strength. There was shouting to man the boat. One jostling against me cried that they were the captive Indians. They had broken bonds, lifted hatch, knocked down the watch, leapt over side. Another shouted. No, the Caribs were safe. These were the women—

The women—seven forms might be made out—were not far from land. I felt tingling across to me their hope and fear. Out of ship shadow shot after them our boat. Strongly rowed, it seemed to gain, but they made speed strongly, strongly. The boat got into trouble with the shallows. The swimmers now stood and ran, now were racers; in a moment they would touch the dry, the shining beach. Out of boat sprang men running after them, running across low white lines of foam. The women, that strong woman cacique ahead, left water, raced across sand toward forest. Two men were gaining, they caught at the least swift woman. The dark, naked form broke from them, leaped like a hurt deer and running at speed passed with all into the ebony band that was forest.

Alonso de Ojeda burst into a great laugh. "Well done, Catalina!"

The Admiral's place could ever be told by his head over all. Moreover his warm, lifted, powerfully pulsing nature was capable of making around him a sphere that tingled and drew. One not so much saw him as felt him, here, there. Now I stood beside him where he leaned over rail. "Gone," he said. "They are gone!" He drew a deep breath. I can swear that he, too, felt an inner joy that they had escaped clutching.

But in the morning he sent ashore a large party under his brother, Don Diego. We received another surprise. No Indians on the beach, none in the forest, and when they came to the village, only houses, a few parrots and the gardens, dewy fresh under the sun's first streaming. No Indians there, nor man nor woman nor child, not Guacanagari, not Guarin, not Catalina and her crew—none! They were gone, and we knew not where, Quisquaya being a huge country, and the paths yet hidden from us or of doubtful treading. But the heaped mountains rose before us, and Juan Lepe at least could feel assured that they were gone there. They vanished and for long we heard nothing of them, not of Guacanagari, nor of Guarin who had saved Juan Lepe, not of Catalina, nor any.

This neighborhood, La Navidad and the shipwreck of the *Santa Maria*, burned Guarico and now this empty village, perpetual reminder that in some part our Indian subjects liked us not so well as formerly and could not be made Christian with a breath, grew no longer to our choice. Something of melancholy overhung for the Admiral this part of Hispaniola. He was seeking a site for a city, but now he liked it not here. The seventeen ships put on sail and, a stately flight of birds greater than herons, pursued their way, easterly now, along the coast of Hispaniola.

Between thirty and forty leagues from the ruin of La Navidad opened to us a fair, large harbor where two rivers entered the sea. There was a great forest and bright protruding rock, and across the south the mountains. When we landed and explored we found a small Indian village that had only vaguely heard that gods had descended. Forty leagues across these forests is a long way. They had heard a rumor that the cacique of Guarico liked the mighty strangers and Caonabo liked them not, but as yet knew little more. The harbor, the land, the two rivers pleased us. "Here we will build," quoth the Viceroy, "a city named Isabella."

CHAPTER XXIX

Christmastide, a year from the sinking of the *Santa Maria*, came to nigh two thousand Christian men dwelling in some manner of houses by a river in a land that, so short time before, had never heard the word "Christmas." Now, in Spain and elsewhere, men and women, hearing Christmas bells, might wonder, "What are they doing—are they also going to mass—those adventurers across the Sea of Darkness? Have they converted the Indies? Are they moving happily in the golden, spicy lands? Great marvel! Christ now is born there as here!"

Juan Lepe chanced to be walking in the cool of the evening with Don Francisco de Las Casas, a sensible, strong man, not unread in the philosophers. He spoke to me of his son, a young man whom he loved, who would sooner or later come out to him to Hispaniola, if he, the elder, stayed here. So soon as this we had begun to speak thus, "Come out to Hispaniola." "Come out to Isabella in Hispaniola." What a strong wind is life, leaping from continent to continent and crying, "Home wherever I can breathe and move!" This young man was Bartolomé, then at Salamanca, at the University. Bartolomé de Las Casas, whom Juan Lepe should live to know and work with. But this evening I heard the father talk, as any father of any promising son.

With us, too, was Don Juan Ponce de Leon, who had a story out of Mandeville of a well by the city of Polombe in Prester John's country. If you drank of the well, though you were dying you would never more have sickness, and though you were white-bearded you would come young again!

The palms waved above Isabella that was building behind the

camp by the river. It was beginning, it was planned out; the stone church, the stone house of the Viceroy were already breast-high. A Spanish city building, and the bells of Europe ringing.

Out sprang the noise of a brawl. There was that in the Admiral that would have when it could outward no less than inward magnificence. He could go like a Spartan or Diogenes the Cynic, but when the chance came—magnificence! With him from Spain traveled a Viceroy's household. He had no less than thirty personal servants and retainers. Hidalgos here at Isabella had also servants, but no one more than two or three. It was among these folk that first arose our amazing jealousies and envies. Now and again the masters must take part. Not the Viceroy who in such matters went very stately, but certain of our gentlemen. Loud and angry voices rose under the palms, under a sky of pale gold.

Sent for, I found the Admiral lying on his bed, not yet in his stone house but in a rich and large pavilion brought out especially for the Viceroy and now pitched upon the river bank, under palms. I came to him past numbers out of that thirty. Idle here; they certainly were idle here! With him I found a secretary, but when he could he preferred always to write his own letters, in his small, clear, strong hand, and now he was doing this, propped in bed, in his brow a knot of pain. He wrote many letters. Long afterwards I heard that it had become a saying in Spain, "Write of your matters as often as Christopherus Columbus!"

I sat waiting for him to finish and he saw my eyes upon yet unfolded pages strewing the table taken from the *Marigalante* and set here beside him. "Read if you like," he said. "The ships set sail day after tomorrow."

I took and read in part his letter to a learned man with whom, once or twice, Jayme de Marchena had talked. It was a long letter in which the Admiral, thinker to thinker, set forth his second voyage and now his city building, and at last certain things for the mind not only of Spain but of France and Italy and England and Germany. "All lands and all men whom so far we have come to," wrote the Admiral, "are heathen and idolaters. In the providence of God all such are given unto Christendom. Christendom must take possession through the acts of Christian princes, under the sanction of Holy Church, allowed by the Pope who is Christ our King's Viceroy. Seeming hardship bringeth great gain! Millions of souls converted, are baptized. Every infant feeleth the saving water. Souls that were lost now are found. Christ beameth on them! To that, what is it that the earthly King of a country be changed?"

His quill traveled on over paper. Another sheet came into my hand. I read it, then sat pondering. He sighed with pain, pushed all aside and presently bade the secretary forth. When the man was gone he told me of an agony behind his eyes that now stabbed and now laid him in a drowsiness. I did what I could for him then waited until the access was over. It passed, and he took again his pen.

I said, "You advise that there be made a market for Carib slaves, balancing thus the negroes the Portuguese are bringing in, and providing a fund for our needs—"

He said, "They are eaters of men's flesh, intractable and abominable, not like the gentler people we find hereabouts! It is certain that before long, fleet after fleet coming, our two thousand here growing into many thousands, more cities than Isabella arising, commerce and life as in Europe beginning—Well, these fiercer, Caribal islands will be overrun, taken for Spain! What better to do with their people? I do not wish to slay them and eat them!"

"Slaves—"

"How many Moors in Castile and Arragon, slaves and none the worse for it, being baptized, being kindly enough entreated! And now the Portuguese bring Negroes, and are they the worse off, being taken from a deep damnation? Long ago, I have read, the English were taken to Rome and sold in the market place, and the blessed Gregory, seeing them, cried, 'Christ shall be preached in their nation!' Whereupon he sent Augustine and all England was saved. Look you, this world is rude and worketh rudely! But it climbs in the teeth of its imperfections!"

"I do not doubt that," I said. "When it wills to climb."

"I do but lay it before the Sovereigns," he answered. "I do not know what they will think of it there. But truly I know not what else to do with these Asiatics when they withstand us! And even in slavery they must gain from Christians! What matters masters when they find the True Master?"

Juan Lepe brooded still while the pen scratched and scratched across the page. The noise ceased. I looked up to see if he were in pain again, and met gray-blue eyes as longing as a child's. "What I would," he said, "is that the Lord would give to me forever to sail a great ship, and to find, forever to find! The sea is wider than the land, and it sends its waves upon all lands. Not Viceroy, but the Navigator, the Finder—"

Juan Lepe also thought that there streamed his Genius. Here he was able, but there played the Fire. But he, like many another, had bound himself. Don Cristoval Colon—Viceroy—and eighths and tenths!

CHAPTER XXX

Twelve of our ships went home to Spain. February wheeled by. March was here, and every day the sun sent us more heat. The Indians around us still were friendly—women and all. From the first there was straying in the woods with Indian women. Doubtless now, in the San Salvador islands, in Cuba and in Hispaniola, among those Guaricos fled from us to the mountains, would be infants born of Spanish fathers. Juan Lepe contemplated that filling in the sea between Asia and Europe with the very blood.

Sickness broke out. It was not such as that first sickness at La Navidad, but here were many more to lie ill. Besides Juan Lepe, we now possessed three physicians. They were skillful, they labored hard, we all labored. Men died of the malady, but no great number. But now among the idle of mind and soul and the factious arose the eternal murmur. Not heaven but hell, these new lands! Not wealth and happy ease, but poverty and miserable toil! Not forever new spectacle and greedy wonder, but tiresome river, forest and sea, tiresome blue heaven, tiresome delving and building, tiresome rules, restrictions, commandments, yeas and nays! Parties arose, two main parties, and within each lesser differings.

The Viceroy stiffly withstood the party that was not his, and upon some slur and insolence took from a man his office. Followed a week of glassy smoothness. Then suddenly, by chance, was discovered the plot of Bernal Diaz de Pisa—the first of many Spanish conspiracies. It involved several hundred men and was no less a thing than the seizure in the dark night of the ships and the setting sail for Spain, there to wreck the fame of Christopherus Columbus and if possible obtain the sending out of some prince over him, who would beam kindly on all hidalgos and never put them to vulgar work. A letter was found in Bernal Diaz's hand, and if therein any ill was left unsaid of the Admiral and Viceroy, I know not what it might be! The "Italian", the "Lowborn", the "madly arrogant and ambitious", the "cruel" and "violent", the "tyrant" acted. Bernal Diaz was made and kept prisoner on Vicente Pinzon's ship. Of his following one out of ten lay in prison for a month. Of the seamen concerned three were flogged and all had their pay estopped.

One might say that Isabella was builded. Columbus himself stood and moved in better health. Now he would go discovering on dry land, to Alonso de Ojeda's glee, glee indeed of many. The mountains of Cibao, where might be the gold,—and gold must be had!

And we might find Caonabo, and what peoples were behind our own mountains, and perhaps come upon Guacanagari. We went, four hundred men and more, an army with banners. We wished to impress, and we took any and all things that might help in that wise. Drum and trumpet beat and sang. Father Buil was not with us. But three of his missionaries accompanied us, and they carried a great crucifix. There were twenty horses, and terrible were these to this land as the elephants of the Persians to the Greeks. And much we marveled that Cuba and Hayti had no memory nor idea of elephants. A throng of Indians would go with us, and in much they carried our supplies. It was first seen clearly at this time, I think, the uses that might be drawn from our heathen subjects. Alonso de Ojeda, Juan Ponce de Leon and Pedro Margarite rode with the Admiral. Others followed on black and bay and white horses. Juan Lepe marched with the footmen. He was glad to find Luis Torres.

Before setting out we went to mass in the new church. Candles burned, incense rose in clouds, the friars chanted, the bell rang, we took the wafer, the priest lifted the chalice.

The sun rose, the trumpets rang, we were gone. South, before us, the mountain line was broken by a deep notch. That would be our pass, afar, and set high, filled with an intense, a burning sapphire. We had Indian guides.

Day, evening, camp and night. Dawn, trumpets, breakfast and good understanding and jollity. After breakfast the march, and where was any road up the heights? And being none we would make one and did, our hidalgos toiling with the least. By eve we were in the high pass, level ground under our feet, above us magnificent trees. We called it the Pass of the Hidalgos. We threw ourselves down and slept. At sunrise we pushed on, and presently saw what Juan Lepe once before had seen, the vast southward-lying plain and the golden mountains of Cibao.

There rose a cry, it was so beautiful! The Admiral named it Vega Real, the Royal Plain.

Sweating, panting, we came at last down that most difficult descent into rolling forest and then to a small bright stream, beside it garden patches and fifty huts. The inhabitants fled madly, we heard their frightened shouts and the screaming of children. Thereafter we tried to keep in advance a small body of Indians, so that they might tell that the gods were coming, but that they would not injure.

Acclivity and declivity fell away. We were fully in an enormous, fertile and populous plain.

The horses and the horsemen! At first they thought that these were one. When some cowering group was surrounded and kept from breaking away, when Alonso de Ojeda or another leaped from steed to earth, from earth again to steed, they moaned with astonishment and some relief. But the horses, the horses—never to have seen any great four-footed things, and now these that were proud and pawed the earth and neighed and — De Ojeda's black horse — reared, curvetted, bounded, appeared to threaten! The eyes, the mane, the great teeth!—There grew a legend that they were fed upon men's flesh, red men's flesh!

How many red men were in Quisquaya I do not know. In some regions they dwelled thickly, in others were few folk. In this wide, long, laughing plain dwelled many, in clean towns sunk among trees good to look at and dropping fruit; by river or smaller stream, with plantings of maize, batata, cassava, jucca, maguey, and I know not what beside. If the stream was a considerable one, canoes. They had parrots; they had the small silent dogs. In some places we saw clay pots and bowls. They wove their cotton, though not very skillfully. They crushed their maize in hand mills. We found caciques and butios, and heard of their main cacique, Gwarionex. But he did not come to meet us; they said he had gone on a visit to Caonabo in Cibao. They brought us food and took our gifts in exchange; they harangued us in answer to our harangues; they made dances for us. The children thronged around, fearless now and curious. The women were kind. Old men and women together, and sometimes more women than men, sat in a council ring about some venerable tree.

There was no quarrel and no oppression upon this adventure. I look back and I see that single journey in Hispaniola a flower and pattern of what might be.

They gave us what gold they had—freely—and we gave in return things that they prized. But always they said Cibao for gold.

We rode and marched afoot, with many halts and turns aside, five leagues across plain. A large river barred our way,—the Yaqui they called it. Here we spent two days in a village a bowshot from the water. We searched for gold, we sent from Indian to Indian rumor that it was the highest magic, god-magic that of all things in the world we most desired and took it from their hands, yet still we paid for it in goods for which they lusted, and we neither forced nor threatened force.

And though we were four hundred, yet there might be in the Royal Plain forty thousand, and their hue and their economy was yet prince in the land, and the Spaniard a visitor. And there commanded the four hundred a humane man, with something of the guilelessness of the child.

We crossed the Yaqui in canoes and upon rafts. White, brown and black, the horses swam the stream. Again nigh impenetrable forest, again villages, again clear singing and running waters. But ever the mountains came closer. At last we entered hilly country and the streams pushed with rapidity, flowing to the Yaqui, flowing to the sea. Now we began to find gold. It glistened in the river sands. Sometimes we found nuts of it, washed from the rocks far above. There came upon us the gold fever. Mines—we must open mines! Fermin Cedo, our essayer, would have it that it was not Ophir, but at that time he was hardly believed. The Admiral wrote a letter about these golden mines.

An Indian brought him a piece of amber; another, a lump of blue stone. We found jasper, we were sure of copper.

We came to a natural rampart, wide at top, steeply descending on three sides, set in a loop of a little clear river named Yanique. "Ho!" cried Alonso de Ojeda. "Here is the cradle for the babe! Round tower, walls, barbican yonder, and Mother Nature has dug the moat!" He sent his voice across to the Viceroy. "A fort, Señor, a fort!"

Council was held by the Yanique. A fort,—a luckier than La Navidad! Men left here to collect gold, establish a road, keep communication with Isabella which in turn should forward supplies and men. The returning fleet might bring two thousand—nay, five thousand men! It would certainly bring asses and mules as well as horses. We should have burden-bearers. Moreover, a company of Indians might be trained to come and go as carriers. Train them, set some sort of penalty for malfeasance.

"They should be taught to mine for us," said Pedro Margarite. "Pay them? Of course—of course! But do not pay them too much. Do not we protect them from Caribs and save their souls to boot? Take it as tribute!" It was the first time the word was said, in Spanish, here.

We built a fort much after the model of La Navidad and named it St. Thomas. When after days it was done, and commandant must be chosen, the Viceroy's choice fell upon Pedro Margarite. And that was great pity. But he could not know Margarite then as afterwards he came to know him. Fifty-six men he left with Margarite, and the rest of us marched home across the Vega and the northern mountains to Isabella.

Sickness. Quarrels. Idleness, vanity, dissensions and accusations. Heat, more sickness, wild quarrels.

Tidings from Margarite at St. Thomas. The Indians would no longer bring food. Caonabo was threatening from the higher mountains. The Viceroy wrote to Margarite. Compel the Indians to bring food, but as it were to compel them gently!

Quarrels — quarrels at Isabella. Two main parties and all the lesser ones. Disease and scarcity. Fray Geronimo arrived from St.

Thomas. He had stories. The Viceroy grew dark red, his eyes lightened. Yet he believed that what was told pertained to men of Margarite, not to that cavalier himself. He wrote to Margarite—I do not know what. But presently a plan arose in his mind and was announced. Don Alonso de Ojeda was to command St. Thomas. Don Pedro Margarite should have a moving force of several hundred Castilians, mainly for exploration, but at need for other things. Going here and there about the country, it might impress upon Caonabo that the Spaniard though gentle by nature, was dangerous when aroused.

Alonso de Ojeda, three hundred men behind him, went forth on his black horse, to trumpet and drum, very gay and ready to go. In a week he sent into Isabella six Indians in chains. These had set upon three of Margarite's men coming with a letter to the Viceroy and had robbed them, though without doing them bodily injury. Alonso de Ojeda had cut off their ears and sent them all in heavily chained. The Viceroy condemned them to be beheaded, but when they were on their knees before the block reprieved them, one by one. He kept them chained for a time for all visiting Indians to see, then formally pardoned them and let them go.

Matters quieted. Sickness again sank, a flood retiring, leaving pools. Alonso de Ojeda and Pedro Margarite reported peace in Hispaniola. The Admiral came forth from his house one day and said quietly to this one and that one that now he meant again to take up Discovery.

He gave authority in Isabella to Don Diego, and made him a council where sat Father Buil, Caravajal, Coronel and Juan de Luxan. Then out of five ships we took the *Cordera*, the *Santa Clara* and the *San Juan*, and we set sail on April the twenty-fourth.

CHAPTER XXXI

The island, we learned, was named Jamaica. The Admiral called it Santiago, but it also rests Jamaica. Of all these lands, outside of the low, small islands to which we came first, Cuba seemed to us the peaceable land. Jamaica gave us almost Carib welcome. Its folk had the largest canoes, the sharpest, toughest lances. Perhaps they had heard from some bold sea rover that we had come, but that we were not wholly gods!

Our crossbow men shot amongst them. The arrows failed to halt them, but when we sent a bloodhound the dog did our work. It was to them what griffon or fire-breathing dragon might be to a Seville throng. When the creature sprang among them they uttered a great cry and fled. Jamaica is most beautiful.

For not a few days we visited, sailing and anchoring, lifting again and stopping again. Once the people were pacified, they gave us kindly enough welcome, trading and wondering. We slipped by bold coasts and headlands which we must double, mountains above us. They ran by inland paths, saving distance, telling village after village. When we made harbor, here was the thronged beach. Some of these people wore a slight dress of woven grass and palm leaves, and they used crowns of bright feathers. We got from them in some quantity golden ornaments. But south for gold, south—south, they always pointed south!

The *Cordera*, the *Santa Clara* and the *San Juan* set sail out of the Harbor of Good Weather, in Santiago or Jamaica. A day and a night of pleasant sailing, then we saw the great Cuba coast rise blue in the distance. The weather wheeled.

There was first a marvelous green hush, while clouds formed out of nothing. We heard a moaning sound and we did not know its quarter. The sea turned dead man's color. Then burst the wind. It was more than wind; it seemed the movement of a world upon us. Bare of all sails, we labored. We were driven, one from the other. The mariners fell to praying.

A strange light was around us, as though the tempest itself made a light. By it I marked the Admiral, upright where he could best command the whole. He had lashed himself there, for the ship tossed excessively. His great figure stood; his white, blowing hair, in that strange light, made for him a nimbus. It was strange, how the light seemed to seize that and his brow and his gray-blue eyes. Below the eyes his lips moved. He was shouting encouragement, but only the intention could be heard. The intention was heard. He looked what he was, something more than a bold man and a brave sea captain, and there streamed from him comfort. It touched his mariners; it came among them like tongues of flame.

Darkness increased. We were now among lightnings like javelins and loud thunder. Then fell the rain, in torrents, in drops large as plums. It was as though another ocean was descending upon us.

It lasted and we endured. After long while came lessening in that weight of rain, and then cessation. Suddenly the tempest was over. There shone a star—three stars and on topmast and bowsprit Saint Elmo's lights.

Our mariners shouted, "Safe—safe! Saint Elmo!"

Suddenly, over all the sky, were stars shining. The Admiral raised his great voice. "Sing, all of us! 'Stella Maris—Sancta Maria!' "

With the morning the *Santa Clara* and the *San Juan*, beaten about, some injury done, but alive! And the coast of Cuba, nearer, nearer, tall and blue—and at last very tall and green and gold.

Off Cuba and still off Cuba, the southern coast now, as against the northern that once we tried for a while. Sail and come to land, stay a bit, and shake out sails once more!

Wherever we tarried we found peaceable if vastly excited Indians. But still naked, but still unwise as to gold and spices, traders and markets. Cambalu, Quinsai and Zaiton of the marble bridges!

" 'Somewhere,' saith Messer Marco, 'in part the country is savage, filled with mountains, and here come few strangers, for the king will not have them, in order that his treasures and certain matters of his kingdom come not into the world's knowledge.' And again he saith, 'The folk here are naked.'—What wonder then," said the Admiral, "that we find these things! Yea, I feel surprised at the incessancy, but I check myself and think, how vast is Asia, and what variousness must needs be!"

But we moved in a cloud of differences, and while on the one hand this world was growing familiar, on the other the sense increased. "How vast indeed must be Asia, if all this and yet we come not—and now it is going on two years—to any clear hint of other than this!"

He himself, the Admiral, began to feel this strangeness. Or rather, he had long felt it and fought the feeling, but now strongly it came creeping over.

We were among the hugest number of small islands. Starboard loomed, until it was lost in the farness, that coast that we were following, but the three ships were in a half-land, half-water world. We wandered in this labyrinth, keeping with difficulty our way, so crooked and narrow the channels, so many the sandbars. From deck it minded me of that sea of weed we met in the first passage.

Waves of fragrance struck us. "Ha!" cried the Admiral. "Can you not smell cinnamon, spikenard, nutmeg, cloves and galingal?" His faith was so strong that we did smell. From one of these islands, the *Cordera* lying at anchor and a boat going ashore, we took a number of pigeons. So unafraid were these birds that our men approached them easily and beat them down with a pike. We had them for supper, and when their crops were opened, the cook found and brought to the Admiral a number of brown seeds. The Admiral dropped them into clear water, then smelled and tasted. "Cloves? Are they not cloves?" He gave to Juan de la Cosa and to me who also tasted and thought they might be cloves. But we did not find their tree, and we saw no signs of ever a merchant of Cathay or Mangi or Ind.

Christopherus Columbus leaned upon the rail of the *Cordera*. In this islet world we lay at anchor for the night. "Do you know what it is," he asked, "to have a word color the whole day long?" He glanced around, but none was very near. "My Word today is *magic*. I'd not give it to any but you, and I drop my voice in saying it. I'll sail on through magic and against magic, for I have Help from Above! But I'll not lay a fearsome word among those who are not so accorded! All say India hath high magic, and the Grand Khan takes from that country his astrologers and sorcerers. I have read that at Shandu, if there be long raining, they will mount a tower by the palace and wave it back, so that the falling rain makes but a pleasant wall around the king's fair garden that itself rests in sunshine. Also that without touching them they cause the golden flagons to fill with red wine and to move through air, with no hand upon them, to the king's table. That was long ago. We have had no news of them of late. They may do now more marvelous, vaster things."

"And the moral?"

"I said, 'They do them there.' Perhaps this is there."

"I take you!" I said and half-laughed. "We may be in Cathay all this while, under the golden roofs, with the bells strung from the eaves. Yonder line of cranes standing in the shallow water, watching us, may, God wot, be tall magicians in white linen and scarlet silk!"

He crossed himself. The cranes had lifted themselves and flown away. "If they heard—"

"Are you in earnest?"

He put his hands over his eyes. "Sometimes I think it may be fact, sometimes not! Sorcery is a fact, and who knows how far it may go? At times my brain is like to crack, I have so cudgeled it!"

That he cudgeled it was true, and though his brain never cracked and to the end was the best brain in a hundred, yet from this time forth I began to mark in him an unearthliness.

These islands we named the Queen's Gardens, and escaping from them came again to clean coast. On we went for two days, and this part of Cuba had many villages, at sea edge or a little from the water, and all men and women were friendly and brought us gifts.

I remember a moonlight night. All were aboard the *Cordera*, the *Santa Clara* and the *San Juan*, for we meant to sail at dawn. We had left a village yet dancing and feasting. The night was a miracle of silver. Again I stood beside Christopherus Columbus; from land streamed their singing and their thin, drumming and clashing music. At hand it is rather harsh than sweet, but distance sweetened it.

"What will be here in the future—if there are not already here, after your notion, great cities and bridges and shipping, and only our eyes holden and our hands and steps made harmless? Or nearly harmless, for we have slain some Indians!"

He had made a gesture of deprecation. "Ah, that, I hardly doubt, was my fancy! But in the future I see them, your cities!"

"Do you see them, from San Salvador onward and everywhere, —Spanish cities?"

"Necessarily—seeing that the Holy Father hath given the whole of the land to Spain." He looked at the moon that was so huge and bright, and listened to the savage music. "If we go far enough—walking afar—who knoweth what we shall find?" He stood almost motionless. "I do not know. It is in God's hands!"

"Do you see," I asked, "a great statue of yourself?"

"Yes, I see that."

The moon shone so brightly it was marvel. Land breeze brought perfume from the enormous forest. "It is too fair to sleep!" said the Admiral. "I will sit here and think."

He slept little at any time. His days were filled with action. Never was any who had more business to attend to! Yet he was of those to whom solitude is as air,—imperiously a necessity. Into it he plunged through every crack and cranny among events. He knew how to use the space in which swim events. But beside this he must make for himself wide holdings, and when he could not get them by day he took from night.

We came again to a multitude of islets like to the Queen's Gardens. And these were set in a strange churned and curdled sea, as white as milk. Making through it as best we might, we passed from that silverness and broken land into a great bay or gulf, so deep that we might hardly find bottom, and here we anchored close to a long point of Cuba covered thick with palms.

We went ashore for water and fruit. Solitary—neither man nor woman! We found tracks upon the sand that some among us would have it were made by griffons. One of our men had the thought that he might procure some large bird for the Admiral's table. Taking a crossbow he passed alone through the palms into the deeper wood. He was gone an hour, and when he returned it was in haste, with a chalk face and great eyes. I was seated in the boat with the master of the *Cordera* and heard his tale. He had found what he thought a natural aisle of the forest and had stolen down it, looking keenly for pigeon or larger bird. A tree with drooping branches stood across the aisle, he said. He went around the trunk, which was a great one, and it was as though he had turned into the nave of the cathedral. There was space, but trees like pillars on either side, and at the end three great trees covered to the tops with vine and purple grapes. And here he saw before him, under the greatest tree, a man in a long white gown like a White Friar. The sight halted him, turned him, he averred, to stone. Two more men in white dresses but shorter than that of the first, came from among the trees and he saw behind these a number in like clothing. He could not tell, now he thought of it, if they were carrying lances or palms. We had looked so long for clothed folk that it was the white clothes he thought of. The same with their faces—he could not tell about them—he thought they were fair. Suddenly, it seemed, Pan had fallen upon him and put him forth in terror. He had turned and raced through the forest, here to the sea. He did not think the white-clad men had seen him.

We took him to the Admiral who listened, then brought his hands together. "Hath it not—I ask you—sound of Prester John?"

With the dawn he had men ashore, and there he went himself, with him Juan de la Cosa and Juan Lepe. The crossbowman—it was Felipe Garcia—showed the way. We found indeed the forest aisle and nave, and the three trees and the purple grapes, a vast vine with heavy clusters, but we found no men and no sign of men.

The Admiral was not discouraged. "If he truly saw then, and I believe he did, then are they somewhere—"

We beat all the neighborhood. Solitary, solitary! He divided the most determined of us—so many from each ship—into two bands and sent in two directions. We were to search, if necessary, through ten leagues. We went, but returned empty of news of clothed men. We found desolate forest, and behind that a vast, matted, low growth, impenetrable and extending far away. At last we determined that Felipe Garcia had seen white cranes. Unless it were magic—

We sailed on and we sailed on. The *Cordera*, the *Santa Clara* and the *San Juan* were in bad case, hurt in that storm between Jamaica and Cuba, and wayworn since in those sandy seas, among those myriad islets. Our seamen and our shipmasters now loudly wished return to Isabella. He pushed us farther on and farther on, and still we did not come to anything beyond those things we had already reached, nor did we come either to any end of Cuba. And what was going on in Hispaniola—in Isabella? We had sailed in April and now it was July.

It became evident to him at last that he must turn. The Viceroy and the Admiral warred in him, had long warred and would war. Better for him had he never insisted upon viceroyship! Then, single-minded, he might have discovered to the end of his days.

We turned, the *Cordera*, the *Santa Clara* and the *San Juan*, and still he believed that the long, long coast of Cuba was the coast of the Asia main. He saw it as a monster cape or prolongation, sprouting into Ocean-Sea as sprouts Italy into Mediterranean. Back—back—the way we had come, entering again that white sea, entangled again among a thousand islets!

At last we came again to that Cape of the Cross to which we had escaped in the Jamaica tempest. One thing he would yet do in this voyage and that was to go roundabout homeward by Jamaica and find out further things of that great and fair island. We left Cuba that still we thought was the main. Santiago or Jamaica rose before us, dark blue mountains out of the dark blue sea. For one month we coasted this island, for always the weather beat us back when we would quit it, setting our sails for Hispaniola.

We came to Hayti upon the southern side, and because of some misreckoning failed of knowing that it was Hayti, until an Indian in a canoe below us, called loudly "El Almirante!" And yet Isabella was the thickness of the island from us, and the weather becoming foul, we beat about for long days, struggling eastward and pushed back, and again parting upon a stormy night one ship from the others. The *Cordera* anchored by a tall, rocky islet and rode out the storm. Here, when it was calm, we went ashore, but found no man, only an unreckonable number of pigeons. The Admiral lay on clean, warm sand and rested with his eyes shut. I was glad we were nigh to Isabella and his house there, for I did not think him well. He sat up, embracing his great knees and then looking at the sea and the *Cordera*. "I have been thinking, Doctor."

"For your health, my Admiral, I wish you could rest a while from thinking!"

"We were upon the south side of Mangi. I am assured of that! Could I, this time, have sailed on—Now I see it!"

He dropped his hands from his knees and turned full toward me. I saw that lying thus for an hour he had gathered strength and now was passed, as he was wont to pass after quiet, into a high degree of vision, accompanied by forth-going energy. "Now I see, and as soon as I may, I will do! Beyond Mangi, Champa. Beyond Champa, the coast trending southward, India of the Ganges and the Golden Chersonese. Land of Gold—Land of Gold!—are they not forever pointing southward? But it is not of gold—or wholly gold—that now I think! *Aurea Chersonesus* maketh a vast peninsula, greater maybe than Italy, Greece and Spain taken together. But I will round it, and I will come to the mouth of Ganges! Then again, I read, we go southward! There is the Kingdom of Maabar where Saint Thomas is buried, and the Kingdom of Monsul where the diamonds are found. Then we come to the Island of Zeilan, where is the Tomb of our Father Adam. Here are sapphires, amethysts, topaz, garnet and rubies. There is a ruby here beyond price, large as a man's two fists and a well of red fire. But what I should think most of would be to stand where Adam laid him down. Now from the Island of Zeilan I sail across the India sea. And I go still south, three hundred leagues, and I find the great island of Madagascar whose people are Saracens and there is the rukh-bird that can lift an elephant, and they cut the red sandal there and find ambergris. Then lifteth Zanzibar whose women are monsters and where the market is in elephant teeth. And so I come at last to the extremity of Africa which Bartholomew Diaz found—my brother, Don Bartholomew being with him—and named Good Hope. So I round Good Hope, and I come home by Cape Bojador which I myself have seen. I will pass Fez and Ercilla and the straits and Cadiz. I will enter the River Sagres at Palos, for there was where I first put forth. The bells of La Rabida will ring, for a thing is done that was never done before, and that will not cease to resound! I shall have sailed around the earth. Christopherus Columbus. Ten ships. Ten chances of there being one in which I may come home!"

"There have been worse dreams!" said Juan Lepe.

"I warrant you! But I am not dreaming."

He rose and stood with arms outstretched, crosswise.

" 'Nought is hid,' saith Scripture, 'but shall be found!' Here is Earth. Do you not think that one day we shall go all about it? Aye, freely, freely! With zest and joy, discovering that it is a loved home. For every road some man or men broke the clods!"

They hailed us from the *Cordera*. One had seen from topmast the *Santa Clara*. Still we sailed by the south coast of Hispaniola. We knew now that it was not Cipango. But it was a great island, nonetheless, and one day might be as Cipango. Beata, Soana, Mona were the little islands that we found. We sailed between them and our great island, and at last we came to the corner and turned northward, and again after days to another corner and sailed west once more, with hopes now of Isabella. It was the first week in September.

In a great red dawn, Roderigo, the Admiral's servant, roused Juan Lepe. "Come—come—come, Doctor!"

I sprang from my bed and followed him. Christopherus Columbus lay in a deep swoon. Round he came from that and said, "Roderigo, tell them that I am perfectly well, but wish to see no one!" From that, he came to recognize me. "Doctor, I am tired. God and Our Lady only know how tired I am!"

His eyes shut, his head sank deep into the bed. He said not another word, that day nor the next nor the next. Roderigo and I forced him to swallow a little food and wine, and once he rose and made as if to go on deck. But we laid him down again and he sank into movelessness and a sleep of all the faculties. Juan de la Cosa took care of the *Cordera*. So we sighted Isabella and in the harbor four caravels that had not been there when we had sailed in April.

Chapter XXXII

Two men came into the cabin, Don Diego Colon, left in charge of Hispaniola, and with him a tall, powerful, high-featured man, gray of eye and black and silver of hair and short beard. As he stood beside the bed, one saw that he must be kinsman to the man who lay upon it. "O Bartholomew! And is this the end?" cried Don Diego, and I knew that the stranger was that brother, Bartholomew, for whom the Admiral longed.

These three brothers! One lay like a figure upon a tomb save for the breathing that stirred his silver hair. One, Don Diego, tall, too, and strong, but all of a gentle, quiet mien sank on his knees and seemed to pray. One, Don Bartholomew, stood like rock or pine, but he slowly made the sign of the cross, and I saw his gray eyes fill. It seemed to me that the Admiral's eyelids flickered. "Speak to him again," I said. "Take his hand."

Bartholomew Columbus, kneeling in the *Cordera's* cabin, put his arm about his great brother. That is what he called him:

"Christopher, my great brother, it is Bartholomew! Don't you know me? Don't you remember? I must go to England, you said, to see King Henry. To tell him what you could do—what you have done, my great brother! Don't you remember? I went, but I was poor like you who are now Viceroy of the Indies—and I was shipwrecked besides and lost the little that we had scraped—do you remember?—and must live like you by making maps and charts, and it was long before I saw King Henry!—Christopher, my great brother! He lies like death!"

I said, "He is returning, but he is yet a long way off. Keep on speaking."

"But King Henry said at last, 'Go bring us that brother of yours, and we think it may be done!' And he gave me gold. So I would come back to Spain for you, and I reached Paris, and it was the summer of 1493. Christopher, my great brother, don't you hear me? For it was at Paris that I heard, and it came like a flood of glory, fallen in one moment from Heaven! I heard, 'Christopherus Columbus! He has found the Indies for King Ferdinand and Queen Isabella!'—Don't you hear, Christopher? All the world admiring—all the world saying, 'Nothing will ever go just the same way again!' You have done the greatest thing, my great brother! Doctor, is he dying?"

"He will not die," I said. "You are cordial to him, though he hears you yet from leagues and leagues away. Go on!"

"Christopher, from Paris I got slowly, slowly, so slowly I thought it!—to Seville. But I was not poor. They gave me gold, the French King gave it, their nobles, their bishops. I walked in that glory; it flooded me from you! All your people, Christopher, your sons and your brothers and our old father. You build us again, you are our castle and great ship and Admiral! When I came to Barcelona, how they praised you! When I came to Toledo, how they praised you! When I came to Seville, how they praised you! But at Seville I learned that I was too late, and you were gone upon your second voyage. Then I went to Valladolid and the Queen and the King were there, and they said, 'He has just sailed, Don Bartholomew, from Cadiz with sixteen ships—your great brother who hath crossed Ocean-Sea and bound to us Asia!'—But, sweet Jesu, what entertainment they gave me, all because I had lain in our old wooden cradle at Genoa a couple of years or so after you!—Genoa!—They say Genoa *aches* because she did not send you. Christopher, do you remember the old rock by the sea—and you begged colors from Messer Ludovico and painted upon it a ship and we called it the Great Doge—"

The Admiral's eyes opened slowly like a gray dawn; he moved ever so slightly in the bed, and his lips parted. "Brother," he whispered.

We got him from the *Cordera* to Hispaniola shore, and so in a litter to his own house in Isabella. All our town was gathered to see him carried there. He began to improve. The second day he said to

Don Bartholomew, "You shall be my lieutenant and deputy. Adelantado—I name you Adelantado."

Don Bartholomew said bluntly, "Is not that hard upon Diego?"

"No, no, Bartholomew!" answered Don Diego, who was present. "If it were question of a prior of Franciscans, now! But Christopher knows and I know that I took this stormy world but for lack of any other in blood to serve him. Our Lady knows that I never held myself to be the man for the place! Be Adelantado and never think of me!"

The Admiral upon his bed spoke. "We have always worked together, we Colombos. When it is done for the whole there is no jealousy among the parts. I love Diego, and I think he did well, constraining his nature to it, here among the selfish, the dangerous and factious! And others know that he did well. I love him and praise him. But Bartholomew, thou art the man for this!"

Accordingly, the next noontide, trumpets, and a proclamation made before the great cross in the middle of our town. The Viceroy's new-come brother had every lieutenant power.

I do not know if he ever disappointed or abused it. He became great helper to his great brother.

These three! They were a lesson in what brothers might be, one to the other, making as it were a threefold being. Power was in this family, power of frame and constitution, with vital spirit in abundance; power of will, power of mind, and a good power of heart. Their will was good toward mankind.

They had floods to surmount and many a howling tempest to outendure. By and large they did well with life,—very well. There was alloy, base metal of course, even in the greatest of the three. They were still men. But they were such men as Nature might put forward among her goodly fruit.

The Viceroy lay still in his bed, for each time he would rise came faintness and old fatigue. The Adelantado acted.

There was storm in Hispaniola, storm of human passions. I found Luis Torres, and he put me within leg-stride of the present.

Margarite! It seemed to begin with Don Pedro Margarite.

He and his men had early made choice between the rich, the fruitful, easy Vega and the mountains they were to pierce for gold and hunt over for a fierce mountain chief. In the Vega they established themselves. The Indians brought them "tribute", and they exacted over-tribute, and reviled and slew when it pleased them, and they took the Indian women, and if it pleased them they burned a village. "Sorry tale," said Luis. "Old, sorry tale!"

Indians came to Isabella and with fierce gesture and eyes that cast lances talked to Don Diego. Don Diego sent a stern letter to Don Pedro Margarite. Don Pedro answered that he was doing soldier's duty, as the Sovereigns would understand when it came before them. Don Diego sent again, summoning him upon his allegiance to Isabella. He chose for a month no answer to that at all, and the breezes still brought from the Vega cries of anger, wails of sorrow. Then he appeared suddenly in Isabella.

Don Diego would have arrested him and laid him in prison to await the Admiral's return. But with suddenness, that was of truth no suddenness, Margarite had with him three out of four of our hidalgos, and more than that, our Apostolic Vicar of the Indies! Don Diego must bend aside, speak him fair, remonstrate, not command. The Viceroy of the Indies and Admiral of Ocean-Sea? Dead probably!—and what were these Colombos? Italian wool-combers! But here stood hidalgos of Spain!—"Old story," said Luis Torres. "Many times, many places, man being one in imperfection."

A choppy sea had followed Margarite's return. Up and down, to and fro, and one day it might seem Margarite was in control, and the next, Don Diego, but with Margarite's wave racing up behind. Then appeared three ships with men and supplies and Don Bartholomew! Margarite saw Don Diego strengthened. He was bold enough, Margarite! on a dark night, at eve, there were so many ships before Isabella but when morn broke they were fewer by two. Margarite and the Apostolic Vicar and a hundred disaffected were departed the Indies! "Have they gotten to Spain? And what do they say? God, He knoweth!—There have been great men and they have been stung to death."

"Ay, ay, the old story!" I said, and would learn about the pacification of the Indians.

"Why, they are not pacified," answered Luis. "Worse follows

worse. Pedro Margarite left two bands in the Vega, and from all I hear they turned devils. It looked like peace itself, didn't it, this great, fair, new land, when first we stepped upon it, and raised the banner and then the cross? It's that no longer. They're up, the Indians, Caonabo and three main caciques, and all the lesser ones under these. In short, we are at war," ended Luis. "Alonso de Ojeda at the moment is the Cid. He maneuvers now in the Vega."

I looked around. We were sitting under palm trees, by the mud wall of our town. Beyond the forest waved in the wind, and soft white clouds sailed over it in a sky of essential sapphire. "There's an aspect here of peace!"

"That is because Guacanagari, from his new town, holds his people still. For that Indian the scent of godship has not yet departed! He sees the Admiral always as a silver-haired hero bringing warmth and light. He is like a dog for fidelity!—But I saw three Indians from outside his country curse him in the name of all the other tribes, with a kind of magical ceremony. Is he right, or is he wrong, Juan Lepe? Or is he neither the one nor the other, but Something moves him from above?"

"Have you never seen again the butio, Guarin?"

"No."

We sat and looked at the rich forest, and at that strange, rude, small town called Isabella, and at the blue harbor with the ships, and the blue, blue sea beyond. Over us—what is over us? Something seemed to come from it, stealing down the stair to us!

The fourth day after his return, Don Francisco de Las Casas, Don Juan Ponce de Leon, and others told to the Viceroy, lying upon his bed in his house, much what Luis Torres told Juan Lepe. "Sirs," he said, when they had done, "here is my brother, Don Bartholomew, who will take order. He is as myself. For Christopherus Columbus, he is ill, and must be ill awhile."

The sixth day came Guacanagari, and sat in the room and talked sorrowfully. Caonabo, Gwarionex, Behechio, Cotubanama, said, "Were these or were these not gods, yet would they fight!"

The Admiral said, "The Future is the god. But there are burrs on his skirt!"

Guacanagari at last would depart. He stood beside the bed and the silver-haired great cacique from heaven. The Admiral put forth a lean, knotted, powerful hand and laid it on the brown, slim, untoiled hand. "I wish peace," he said. "My brother Bartholomew and I will do what we can do to gain it. Good peace, true peace!"

Without the room, I asked the cacique about Guarin. He was gone, he said, to the mountains. He would not stay with Guacanagari, and he would not go to Caonabo or Gwarionex. "All old things and ways are broken," said Guacanagari. "All our life is broken. I do not know what we have done. The women sit and weep. And I, too, sometimes I weep!"

The seventh day came in Alonso de Ojeda from St. Thomas.

The Viceroy and the Adelantado and Ojeda talked alone together in the Viceroy's house. But next day was held a great council, all our principal men attending. There it was determined to capture, if possible, Caonabo, withdrawing him so from the confederacy. The confederacy might then go to pieces. In the meantime use every effort to detach from it Gwarionex who after Guacanagari was our nearest great cacique. Send a well-guarded, placating embassy to him and to Cotubanama. Try kindness, kindness everywhere, kind words and good deeds!—And build another fort called Fort Concepcion.

Take Caonabo! That was a task for Alonso de Ojeda! He did it. Five days after the council, the Viceroy being now recovered and bringing strength to work that needed strength, the Adelantado vigorously helping, Isabella in a good mood, the immediate forest all a gold and green peacefulness, Don Alonso vanished, and with him fourteen picked men, all mounted.

For six weeks it was as though he had dropped into the sea, or risen into the blue sky above eyesight.

Then on a Sunday he and his fourteen rode into town. We had a great church bell and it was ringing, loudly, sonorously. He rode in and at once there arose a shout, "Don Alonso de Ojeda!" All his horsemen rode with him, and rode also one who was not Castilian. On a gray steed a bare, bronze figure—Caonabo!

The church bell swung, the church bell rang. Riding beneath the squat tower, all our people pouring forth from our poor houses upon the returned and his captive, the latter had eyes, it seemed to me, but for that bell. A curious, sardonic look of recognition, appraisal, relinquishment, sat in the Indian's face. From wrist to wrist of Caonabo went a bright, short chain. The sun glittered upon the bracelets and the links. I do not know—there was for a moment—something in the sound of the bell, something in the gleam of the manacles, that sent out faint pity and horror and choking laughter.

All to the Viceroy's house, and Don Alonso sitting with Christopherus Columbus, and Caonabo brought to stand before them. Indians make much of indifferent behavior, taunting calm, when taken. It is a point of honor, meeting death so, even when, as often befalls, their death is a slow and hard one. Among themselves, in their wars, it is either death or quick adoption into the victor's tribe. They have no gaols nor herds of slaves. Caonabo expected death. He stood, a strong, contemptuous figure. But the Viceroy meant to send him to Spain—trophy and show, and to be made, if it could be, Christian.

CHAPTER XXXIII

It did not end the war. For a fortnight we thought that it had done so. Then came loud tidings. Caonabo's wife, Anacaona, had put on the lioness. With her was Caonabo's brother Manicoatex and her own brother Behechio, cacique of Xaragua. There was a new confederacy, Gwarionex again was with it. Only Guacanagari remained. Don Alonso marched, and the Adelantado marched.

At dawn one morning, four sails. We all poured forth to watch them grow bigger and yet bigger. Four ships from Cadiz, Antonio de Torres commanding, and with him colonists of the right kind, mechanics and husbandmen.

Many proposals, much of order, came with Torres. The Admiral had gracious letters from the Queen, letters somewhat cooler from King Ferdinand, a dry, dry letter from Fonseca. Moreover Torres brought a general letter to all colonists in Hispaniola. The moral of which was, Trust and Obey the Viceroy of the Indies, the Admiral of the Ocean-Sea!

"Excellent good!" said Luis Torres. "Don Pedro Margarite and the Apostolic Vicar had not reached Cadiz when Don Antonio sailed!"

The Admiral talked with me that night. Gout again crippled him. He lay helpless, now and then in much pain. "I should go home with Antonio de Torres, but I cannot!"

"You are not very fit to go."

"I do not mean my body. My will could drag that on ship. But I cannot leave Hispaniola while goes on formal war. But see you, Doctor, what a great thing their Majesties plan for, and what courtesy and respect they show me! See how the Queen writes!"

I knew that it was balm and wine to him, how she wrote. The

matter in question was nothing more or less than an amicable great meeting between the two sovereigns and the King of Portugal, the wisest subjects of both attending. A line was to be drawn from top to bottom of Ocean-Sea, and Portugal might discover to the east of it, and Spain to the west! The Holy Father would confirm, and so the mighty spoil be justly divided. Every great geographer should come into counsel. The greatest of them all, the Discoverer, surely so! The Queen urged the Admiral's presence.

But he could not go. Sense of duty to his Viceroyship held him as with chains. Then Bartholomew? But Bartholomew was greatly needed for the war. He sent Don Diego, a gentle, able man who longed for a cloister and a few hundred monks, fatherly, admirably, to rule.

Antonio de Torres stayed a few weeks in Hispaniola. The Viceroy and Admiral would have his letter in the royal hands. Torres took that and took gold and strange plants, and also six hundred Indian captives to be sold for slaves.

War went on in Hispaniola, but not for long. We had horses and bloodhounds and men in armor, trained in the long Moorish strife. There was a battle in the Vega that ended as it must end.

Behechio and Anacaona fled to the high mountains. Manicoatex and Gwarionex sued for peace. It was granted, but a great tribute was imposed. Now all Hayti must gather gold for Spain.

Now began, a little today and a little tomorrow, long woe for Hayti! It was the general way of our Age. But our Age sinned.

The year wheeled to October. Juan Aguado came with four caravels to Isabella, and he brought letters of a different tenor from those that Torres brought. We heard in them the voice of Margarite and the Apostolic Vicar. But now the Admiral was well again, the Indians defeated, Hispaniola basking in what we blithely called peace. Aguado came to examine and interrogate. He had his letters. "Cavaliers, esquires and others, you are to give Don Juan Aguado faith and credit. He is with you on our part to look into—"

Aguado looked with a hostile eye toward Viceroy and Adelantado. Where was a malcontent he came secretly if might be, if not openly, to Aguado. Whoever had a grudge came; whoever thought he had true injury. Every one who disliked Italians, fire-new nobles, sea captains dubbed Admirals and Viceroys came. Every one who had been restrained from greed, lust and violence came. Those who held an honest doubt as to someone policy, or act, questioned, found their mere doubt become in Aguado's mind damning certainty. And so many good Spaniards dead in war, and so many of pestilence, and such thinness, melancholy, poverty in Isabella!

And where was the gold? And was this rich Asia of the spices, the elephants, the beautiful thin cloths and the jewels? The friends of Christopherus Columbus had their say also, but suddenly there arose all the enemies.

"When he sails home, I will sail with him!" said the Admiral, "My name is hurt, the truth is wounded!"

In the third week of Aguado's visit, arose out of far ocean and rushed upon us one of those immense tempests that we call here "hurricane". Not a few had we seen since 1492, but none so great, so terrible as this one. Eight ships rode in the harbor and six were sunk. Aguado's four caravels and two others. Many seamen drowned; some got ashore half-dead.

"How will I get away? I must to Spain!" cried Aguado. The Admiral said, "There is the *Niña*."

The *Niña* must be made seaworthy, and in the end we built a smaller ship still which we called the *Santa Cruz*. Aguado waited, fretting. Christopherus Columbus kept toward him a great, calm courtesy.

It was at this moment that Don Bartholomew found, through Miguel Diaz, the mines of Hayna, that was a great river in a very rich country. The Adelantado brought to Isabella ore in baskets. Pablo Belvis, our new essayer, pronounced it true and most rich. Brought in smaller measures were golden grains, knobs as large as filberts, golden collars and arm rings from the Indians of Bonao where flowed the Hayna.

"Ophir!" said the Admiral. "Mayhap it is Ophir! Then have we passed somewhere the Gulf of Persia and Trapoban!"

With that gold he sailed, he and Aguado and two small crowded ships. With him he carried Caonabo. It was early March in 1496.

But Juan Lepe stayed in Hispaniola, greatly commended by the Admiral to the Adelantado. A man might attach himself to the younger as well as the elder of these brothers. Don Bartholomew had great qualities. But he hardly dreamed as did Christopherus Columbus. I loved the latter most for that—for his dreams.

Days and days and days! We sought for gold in the Hayna country and found a fair amount. And all Hayti now, each Indian cacique and his country, must gather for us. *Must*, not may. We built the fortress of San Cristoval, and at last, to be nearer the gold than was Isabella, the Adelantado founded the city of San Domingo, at the mouth of the Ozema, in the Xaragua country. Spaniards in Hispaniola now lived, so many in Isabella, so many in San Domingo, and garrisons in the forts of St. Thomas, Concepcion, and San Cristoval.

Weeks—months. July, and Pedro Alonzo Nino with three caravels filled with strong new men and with provisions. How always we welcomed these incoming ships and the throng they brought that stood and listened and thought at first, after the sea tossing and crowding, that they were come to heaven! And Pedro Nino had left Cadiz in June, three days after the arrival there of the *Niña* and the *Santa Cruz*. "June! They had then a long voyage!"—"Long enough! They looked like skeletons! If the Admiral's hair could get whiter, it was whiter."

He had letters for the Adelantado from the great brother, having waited in Cadiz while they were written.

Juan Lepe had likewise a letter. "I was in the *Niña*, Don Juan de Aguado in the Santa Cruz. We met at once head winds that continued. At first I made east, but at last of necessity somewhat to the southward. We saw Marigalante again and Guadaloupe, and making for this last, anchored and went ashore, for the great relief of all, and for water and provision. Here we met Amazons, wearing plumes and handling mightily their bows and arrows. After them came a host of men. Our cannon and arquebuses put them to flight but three of our sailors were wounded. Certain prisoners we took and bound upon the ships. In the village that we entered we found honey and wax. They are Cannibals; they eat men. After four days we set sail, but met again tempest and head winds, checking us so that for weeks we but crept and crawled over ocean. At last we must give small doles of bread and water. There grew famine, sickness and misery. I and all may endure these when great things are about. But they blame me. O God, who wills that the Unknown become the Known, I betake myself to Thy court! Famine increased. There are those, but I will not name them, who cried that we must kill the Indians with us and eat them that we might live. I stood and said, 'Let the Cannibals stand with the Cannibals!' But no man budged. I will not weary thee, best doctor, with our woes! At last St. Vincent rose out of sea, and we presently came to Cadiz. Many died upon the voyage, and among them Caonabo. In the harbor here we find Pedro Alonzo Nino who will bear my letters.

"In Cadiz I discover both friends and not friends. The sovereigns are at Burgos, and thither I travel. My fortunes are at ebb, yet will the flood come again!"

Time passed. Hispaniola heard again from him and again. When ships put forth from Cadiz—and now ships passed with sufficient regularity between Spain in Europe and Spanish Land across Ocean-Sea—he wrote by them. He believed in the letter. God only knows how many he wrote in his lifetime! It was ease to him to tell out, to dream visibly, to argue his case on fair paper. And those who came in the ships had stories about him—El Almirante!

Were his fortunes at ebb, or were they still in flood? There might be more views here than one. Some put in that he was done for, others clamored that he was yet mounting.

But he wrote to the Adelantado and also to Juan Lepe that he sat between good and bad at court. The Queen was ever the great head of the good. We knew from him that Pedro Margarite and Father Buil and Juan Aguado altered nothing there. But elsewhere now there were warm winds, and now biting cold. And warm and cold, he could not get the winds that should fill his sails. He begged for ships—eight he named—that he might now find for the sovereigns main Asia—not touch here and there upon Cuba shore, but find the Deep All. But forever promised, he was forever kept from the ships! True it was that the sovereigns and the world beside were busy folk! There were Royal Marriages and Naples to be reconquered for its king.

We heard of confirmations of all his dignities and his tithes of wealth. He was offered to be made Marquess, but that he would not have. "The Admiral" was a better title. But he sued for and obtained entail upon his sons and their sons forever of his nobility and his great Estate in the West. "Thus," he wrote, "have I made your fortunes, sons and brothers! But truly not without you and your love and strengthening could I have made aught! A brother indeed for my left hand and my right hand, and to beckon me on, two dear sons!"

CHAPTER XXXIV

Two years! It was March, 1496, when he sailed in the *Niña*. It was the summer of 1498 when Juan Lepe was sent as physician with two ships put forth from San Domingo by the Adelantado upon a rumor that the Portuguese had trespassed, landing from a great carrack upon Guadaloupe. Five days from Hispaniola we met a hurricane that carried us out of all reckoning. When stillness came again we were far south. No islands were in sight; there was only the sea vast and blue. There seemed to breathe from it a strangeness. We were away and away, said our pilots, from the curve, like a bent bow, of the Indian islands. A day and a night we hung in a dead calm. Dawn broke. "Sail, ho! Sail, ho!"

We thought that it might be the Portuguese and made preparation. Three ships lifted over the blue rim. There was now a light wind; it brought them nearer, they being better sailers than the *Santa Cruz* and the *Santa Clara*. We saw the banner. "Castile!" and a lesser one. "El Almirante!"

Now we were close together. The masters hailed, "What ships?" — "From Hispaniola!" —"From Cadiz. The Admiral with us! Come aboard, your commander!"

That was Luis Mendez, and in the boat with him went Juan Lepe. The ships were the *Esperanza*, the *San Sebastian* and the *San Martin*, the first fairly large and well decked, the others small. They who looked overside and shouted welcome seemed a medley of gentle and simple, mariners, husbandmen, fighting men and hidalgos.

The Admiral! His hair was milk-white, his tall, broad frame gaunt as a January wolf. Two years had written in his face two years' experience — fully written, for he was sensitive to every wind of experience. "Excellency!"—"Juan Lepe, I am as glad of you as of a brother!—And what do you do, Señors, here?"

Luis Mendez related. "I think it false news about the Portuguese," said the Admiral and gave reasons why. "Then shall we keep with you, sir?"

"No, since you are sent out by my brother and must give him account. Have you water to spare? We will take that from you. I am bound still south. I will find out what is there!"

Further talk disclosed that he had left Spain with six ships, but at the Canaries had parted his fleet in two, sending three under Alonzo de Caravajal upon the straight course to Hispaniola, and himself with three sailing first to the Green Cape islands, and thence southwest into an unknown sea.

So desolate, wide and blue it looked when the next day we parted,—two ships northward, three southward! But Juan Lepe stayed with the *Esperanza* and the Admiral. As long since, between the *Santa Maria* and the *Pinta*, there had been exchange of physicians, so now again was exchange between the *Santa Cruz* and the *Esperanza*.

Days of blue sea. The *Esperanza* carried a somewhat frank and friendly crew of mariners and adventurers. Now he would sail south, he said, until he was under the Equator.

Days of stark blue ocean. Then out of the sea to the south rose a point of land, becoming presently three points, as it were three peaks. The Admiral stared. I saw the enthusiasm rise in his face. "Did I not write and say to the Sovereigns and to Rome that in the Name of the Holy Trinity, I would now again seek out and find? There! Look you! It is a sign! Trinidad—we will name it Trinidad."

The next morning we came to Trinidad, and the palms trooped to the water edge, and we saw sparkling streams, and from the heights above the sea curls of smoke from hidden huts. We coasted, seeking anchorage, and at last came into a clear, small harbor, and landing, filled our water casks. We knew the country was inhabited for we saw the smokes, but no canoes came about us, and though we met with footprints upon the sand the men who made them never returned. We weighed anchor and sailed on along the southern coast, and now to the south of us, across not many leagues of blue water, we made out a low shore. Its ends were lost in haze, but we esteemed it an island, and he named it Holy Island. It was not island, as now we know; but we did not know it then. How dreamlike is all our finding, and how halfway only to great truths! Cuba we thought was the continent, and the shore that was continent, we called "island."

Now we came to a long southward running tongue of Trinidad. Point Arenal, he named it. A corresponding tongue of that low Holy Island reached out toward it, and between the two flowed an azure strait. Here, off Point Arenal, the three ships rested at anchor, and now there came to us from Holy Island a big canoe, filled with Indians. As they came near the *Esperanza* we saw that they were somewhat lighter in hue than those Indians to whom we were used. Moreover they wore bright-colored loin cloths, and twists of white or colored cotton about their heads, like slight turbans, and they carried not only bows and arrows to which we were used, but round bucklers to which we were not used. They looked at us in amazement, but they were ready for war.

We invited them with every gesture of amity, holding out glass beads and hawk bells, but they would not come close to us. As they hung upon the blue water out of the shadow of the ship, the Admiral would have our musicians begin loudly to play. But when the drums began, the fife and the castanets, the canoe started, quivered, the paddlers dipped, it raced back to that shore whence it came, that shore that we thought island.

"Lighter than Haytiens!" exclaimed the Admiral. "I have thought that as we neared the Equator we should find them black!"

Afterwards he expanded upon this. "Jayme Ferrer thinks as I think, that the nearer we come to the Equator the more precious grow all things, the more gold, the more diamonds, rubies and emeralds, the more prodigal and delicious the spices! The people are burnt black, but they grow gentler and more wise, and under the line they are makers of white magic. I have not told you, Juan Lepe, but I hold that now we begin to come to where our Mother Earth herself climbs, and climbs auspiciously!"

"That we come to great mountains?"

"No, not that, though there may be great mountains. But I have thought it out, and now I hold that the earth is not an orb, but is shaped, as it were, like a pear. It would take an hour to give you all the reasons that decide me! But I hold that from hereabouts it mounts fairer and fairer, until under the line, about where would be the stem of the pear, we come to the ancient Earthly Paradise, the old Garden of Eden!"

I looked to the southward. Certainly there is nowhere where there is not something!

He gazed over the truly azure and beauteous sea, and the air blew soft and cool upon our foreheads, and the fragrance which came to us from land seemed new. "Would you not look for the halcyons? Trinidad! Holy Island! We approach, I hold, the Holy Mountain of the World. And hark to me, Juan Lepe, make vow that if it be permitted I will found there an abbey from whence shall arise perpetual orison for the souls of our first parents!"

We found that night that the ships swung, caught in a current issuing from the strait before us. In the morning we made sail and prepared to pass through this narrow way between the two lands, seeing open water beyond. We succeeded by great skill and with Providence over us, for we met as it were an under wall of water ridged atop with strong waves. The ships were tossed as by a tempest, yet was the air serene, the sky blue. We came hardly through and afterwards called that strait Mouth of the Serpent. Now we were in a great bay or gulf, and still the sea shook us and drove us. Calm above, around, but underneath an agitation of waters, strong currents and boilings. Among our mariners many took fright. "What is it? Are there witches? We are in a cauldron!"

Christopherus Columbus himself took the helm of the *Esperanza*. Many a man in these times chose to doubt what kind of Viceroy he made, but no man who ever sailed with him but at last said, "Child of Neptune, and the greatest seaman we have!"

We outrode danger and came under land to a quiet anchorage, the *San Sebastian* and the *San Martin* following us as the chickens the hen. Still before us we saw that current ridge the sea. The Admiral stood gazing upon the southward shore that hung in a dazzling haze.

Now we thought water, now we thought land. He called to a ship boy and the lad presently brought him a pannikin of water dipped from the sea. The Admiral tasted. "Fresh! It is almost fresh!"

He stood with a kindling face. "A river runs into sea from this land! Surely the mightiest that may be, rushing forth like a dragon and fighting all the salt water! So great a river could not come from an island, no, not if it were twice as large as Hispaniola! Such a river comes downward with force hundreds of leagues and gathers children to itself as it comes. It is not an island yonder; it is a great main!"

We called the gulf where we were the Gulf of the Whale. Trinidad stood on the one hand, the unknown continent on the other. After rest in milky water, we set sail to cross the width of the Whale, and found glass-green and shaken water, but never so piled and dangerous as at the Mouth of the Serpent. So we came to that land that must be—we knew not what! It hung low, in gold sunlight. We saw no mountains, but it was covered with the mightiest forest.

Anchoring in smooth water, we took out boats and went ashore, and we raised a cross. "As in Adam we all die, so in Christ we be alive!" said the Admiral, and then, "What grandeur is in this forest!"

In truth we found trees that we had not found in our islands, and of an unbelievable height and girth. Upon the boughs sat parrots, and we were used to them, but we were not used to monkeys which now appeared, to our mariners' delight. We met footprints of some great animal, and presently, being beside a stream, we made out upon a mud bank those crocodiles that the Indians call "cayman." And never have I seen so many and such splendid butterflies. All this forest seemed to us of a vastness, as the rivers were vast. There rang in our ears "New! New!"

And at last came an Indian canoe—two—three, filled with light-hued, hardly more than tawny, folk, with cloth of cotton about their middles and twisted around their heads, with bows and arrows and those new bucklers. But seeing that we did not wish to fight, they did not wish to fight either; and there was all the old amaze.

Gods—gods—gods! We sought the Earthly Paradise, and they thought we came therefrom.

Paria. We made out that they called their country Paria.

They had in their canoes a bread like cassava, but more delicate, we thought, and in calabashes almost a true wine. We gave them toys, and as they always pointed westward and seemed to signify that there was *the* land, we returned after two hours to the ships and set ourselves to follow the coast. Two or three of this people would go with the gods.

We came to that river mouth that troubled all this sea. What shall I say but that it was itself a sea, a green sea, a fresh sea? We crossed it with long labor. The men of Paria made us understand that their season of rain was lately over, and that ever after that was more river. Whence did it come? They spoke at length and, Christopherus Columbus was certain, of some heavenly country.

The dawn came up sweet and red. The country before us had hills and we made out clearings in the monster forest, and now the blue water was thronged with canoes. We anchored; they shot out to us fearlessly. The Jamaica canoe is larger and better than the Haytien, but those of this land surpass the Jamaican. They are long and wide and have in the middle a light cabin. The rowers chant as they lift and dip their broad oars. If we were gods to them, yet they seemed gay and fearless of the gods. I thought with the Admiral that they must have tradition or rumor, of folk higher upon the mount of enlightenment than themselves. Perhaps now and again there was contact. At any rate, we did not meet here the stupefaction and the prostrations of our first islands. We had again no common tongue, but they proved masters of gesture. Gold was upon them, and that in some amount, and what was extraordinary, often enough in well-wrought shapes of ornament. A seaman brought to the Admiral a golden frog, well-made, pierced for a red cotton string, worn so about a copper-colored neck. He had traded for it three hawk bells. The Admiral's face glowed. "It has been wrought by those who know how to work in metals! Tubal-cain!"

Moreover, now we found pearls. There came to us singing a great canoe and in it a plumed cacique with his wife and daughters. All wore twists of pearls around throat and arms. They gave them freely for red, blue and green beads, which to them were indeed rubies, sapphires and emeralds. Whence came the pearls? It seemed from the coast beyond and without this gulf. Whence the gold? It seemed from high mountains far behind the country of Paria. It was dangerous in the extreme to go there! "Because of the light which repels all darkness!" said the Admiral. "When we go there, it must be gently and humbly like shriven men."

It was August. He knew that Don Bartholomew in Hispaniola craved his return. The three ships, too, were weatherworn, with seams that threatened gaping. And as for our adventurers and the husbandmen and craftsmen, they were most weary of the sea. The mariners were used to it, the Admiral had lover's passion for it, but not they! Here before us, truly, loomed a promising great land, but it was not our port; our port was San Domingo! There, there in Hispaniola, were old Castilians in plenty to greet and show. There were the mines that were actually working, gold to pick up, and Indians trained to bring it to you! There, for the enterprising and the lucky, were gifts of land, to each his *repartimentio!* There was companionship, there was fortune, there was ease! Others were getting, while we rode before a land we were too few to occupy. They went in company to the Admiral. We had discovered. Now let us go onto Hispaniola! The ships—our health.

When it came to health it was he who had most to endure.

The gout possessed him often. His brow knotted with pain; his voice, by nature measured and deep, a rolling music, became sharp and dry. He moved with difficulty, now and then must stay in bed, or if on deck in a great chair which we lashed to the mast. But now a trouble seized his eyes. They gave him great pain; at times he could barely see. Bathe them with a soothing medicine, rest them. But when had he rested them, straining over the ocean since he was a boy? He was a man greatly patient under adversity, whether of the body or of the body's circumstance, but this trouble with the eyes shook him. "If I become blind—and all that's yet to do and find! Blessed Mother of God, let not that happen to me!"

I thought that he should go to Hispaniola, where in the Adelantado's house in San Domingo he might submit to bandaging, light and sea shut out.

At last, "Well, well, we will turn! But first we must leave this gulf and try it out for some distance westward!"

We left this water by a way as narrow as the entering strait, as narrow and presenting the like rough confusion of waters, wall against wall. We called it the Mouth of the Dragon. Mouth of the Dragon, Mouth of the Serpent, and between them the Gulf of the Whale or of Paria. Now was open sea, and south of us ran still that coast that he would have mount to the Equator and to that old, first Garden Land where all things yet were fair and precious! "I cannot stay now, but I will come again! I will find the mighty last things!" His eyes gave him great pain. He covered them, then dropped his hands and looked, then must again cover.

A strange thing! We were borne westward ever upon a vast current of the sea, taking us day and night, so that though the winds were light we went as though every sail was wholly filled.

Christopherus Columbus talked of these rivers in ocean. "A day will come when they will be correctly marked. Aye, in the maps of our descendants! Then ships will say, 'Now here is the river so and so,' as today the horseman says, 'Here is the Tagus, or the Guadalquiver!' "

Another thing he said was that to his mind all the islands that we had found in six years, from San Salvador to Cubagua, had once been joined together. Land from this shore to Cuba and beyond. So the peoples were scattered.

He talked to us much upon this voyage of the great earth and the shape of it, and its destinies; of the stars, the needle, the Great Circle and the lesser ones, and the Ocean. He had our time's learning, gained through God knows how many nights of book by candle! And he had a mind that took eagle flights with spread of eagle wings, and in many ways he had the eagle's eye.

It was not Cipango and Cathay that now he talked of, but of this great land-mass before us which he would have rise to Equator and all Wonder. And he talked also of some water passage, some strait lying to the westward, by which we might sail between lands and islands to the further Indian Ocean, and so across to the Sea of Araby, and then around Africa by Good Hope and then northward,

northward, to Spain, coming into Cadiz with banners, having sailed around the world!

He talked, and all the time his pain ate him, and he must cover eyes to keep the sword-light out.

In middle August we turned northward from our New Land, and a fortnight later we came to San Domingo, that Christopherus Columbus had never seen, though to us in Hispaniola it was an old town, having been builded above two years.

The Viceroy and the Adelantado clasped hands, embraced; tears ran down their bronzed cheeks.

Not later than a day after our anchoring, the ships being unladed, all San Domingo coming and going, trumpets blew and gathered all to our open place before the Viceroy's house. Proclamation—Viceregal Proclamation! First, thanks to God for safe return, and second, hearty approval of the Adelantado, all his Acts and Measures.

There were two parties in San Domingo, and one now echoed in a shout approval of the Adelantado, and the other made here a dead silence, and here a counter-murmur. I heard a man say, "Fool praises fool! Villain brother upholding villain brother!"

Now I do not think the Adelantado's every act was wise, nor the Viceroy's either, for that matter. But they were far, far, those brothers, from fool and villain!

The Proclamation arrived at long thunders against Francisco Roldan his sedition. Here again the place divided as before. Roldan, I had it from Luis Torres, was in Xaragua, safe and arrogant, harking on Indian war, undermining everywhere. Our line of forts held for the Adelantado, but the two or three hundred Spaniards left in Isabella were openly Roldan's men. The Viceroy, through the voice of Miguel the Herald, recited, denounced and warned, then left Francisco Roldan and with suddenness made statement that within a few days five ships would sail for Spain, and that all Spaniards whomsoever, who for reasons whatsoever desired Home, had his consent to go! Consent, Free Passage, and No Questioning!

Whereat the place buzzed loudly, and one saw that many would go.

Many did go upon the ships that sailed not in a few days but a few weeks. Some went for good reasons, but many for ill. Juan Lepe heard afar and ahead of time the great tide of talk when they should arrive in Spain! And though many went who wished the Admiral ill, many stayed, and forever Roldan made for him more enemies, open or secret.

He sent, it is true, upon those ships friends to plead his cause. Don Francisco de Las Casas went to Spain and others went. And he sent letters. Juan Lepe, much in his house, tending him who needed the physician Long-Rest and Ease-of-Mind, heard these letters read. There was one to the Sovereigns in which he related with simple eloquence that discovery to the South, and his assurance that he had touched the foot of the Mount of all the World. With this letter he sent a hundred pearls, the golden frog and other gold. Again he took paper and wrote of the attitude of all things in Hispaniola, of Roldan and evil men, of the Adelantado's vigilance, justice and mercy, of natural difficulties and the need to wait on time, of the Indians. He begged that there be sent him ample supplies and good men, and withal friars for the Indian salvation, and some learned, wise and able lawyer and judge, much needed to give the law upon a thousand complaints brought by childish and factious men. And if the Sovereigns saw fit to send out some just and lofty mind to take evidence from all as to their servant Christopherus Columbus's deeds and public acts and care of their Majesties' New Lands and all the souls therein, such a one would be welcomed by their Graces' true servant.

So he himself asked for a commissioner—but he never thought of such a one as Francisco de Bobadilla!

So the ships sailed. Time passed.

CHAPTER XXXV

Up and down went the great Roldan scission. Up and down went Indian revolt, repression, fresh revolt, fresh repression. On flowed time. Ships came in, one bearing Don Diego; ships went out. Time passed. Alonso de Ojeda, who by now was no more than half his friend, returned to Spain and there proposed to the Sovereigns a voyage of his own to that Southern Continent that never had the Admiral chance to return to! The Sovereigns now were giving such consent to this one and to that one, breaking their pact with Christopherus Columbus. In our world it was now impossible that that pact should be letter-kept, but the Genoese did not see it so. Ojeda sailed from Cadiz for Paria with four ships and a concourse of adventurers. With him went the pilot Juan de la Cosa, and a geographer of Florence, Messer Amerigo Vespucci.

It came to us in Hispaniola that Ojeda was gone. Now I saw the Admiral's heart begin to break. Yet Ojeda in his voyage did not find the Earthly Paradise, only went along that coast as we had done, gathered pearls, and returned.

Time passed. Other wild and restless adventurers beside Roldan broke into insurrections less than Roldan's. The Viceroy hanged Moxica and seven with him, and threw into prison Guevara and Requelme. Roldan, having had his long fling—too powerful still to hang or to chain in someone of our forts—Roldan wrote and received permission, and came to San Domingo, and was reconciled.

Suddenly, after long time of turmoil, wild adventure and uncertainty, peace descended. Over all Hispaniola the Indians submitted. Henceforth they were our subjects; let us say our victims and our slaves! Quarrels between Castilians died over night. Miraculously the sky cleared. Miraculously, or perhaps because of long, patient steering through storm. For three months we lived with an appearance of blossoming and prospering. It seemed that it might become a peaceful, even a happy island.

The Viceroy grew younger, the Adelantado grew younger, and Don Diego, and with them those who held by them through thick and thin. The Admiral began to talk Discovery. It was two years since there, far to the south, we had passed in by the Mouth of the Serpent, and out by the Mouth of the Dragon.

The Viceroy, inspecting the now quiet Vega, rode to an Indian village, near Concepcion. He had twenty behind him, well-armed, but arms were not needed. The people came about him with an eagerness, a docility. They told their stories. He sat his horse and listened with a benignant face. Certain harshnesses in times and amounts of their tribute he redressed. Forever, when personal appeal came to him, he proved magnanimous, often tender, fatherly and brotherly. At a distance he could be severe. But when I think of the cruelties and high-handedness of others here, the Adelantado and the Viceroy shine mildly.

We rode back to Concepcion. I remember the jewel-like air that day, the flowers, the trees, the sky. Palms rustled above us, the brilliant small lizards darted around silver trunks. "The fairest day!" quoth the Admiral. "Ease at heart! I feel ease at heart."

This night, as I sat beside him, wiling him to sleep, for he always had trouble sleeping—a most wakeful man!—he talked to me about the Queen. Toward this great woman he ever showed veneration, piety, and knightly regard. Of all in Spain she it was who best understood and shared that religious part in him that breathed upward, inspired, longed and strained toward worlds truly not on the earthly map. She, like him—or so took leave to think Juan Lepe—received at times too docilely word of authority, or that which they reckoned to be authority. Princes of the Church could bring her to go against her purer thought. The world as it is, dinging ever, "So important is wealth—so important is herald-nobility—so important is father-care in these respects for sons!" could make him take a tortuous and complicated way, could make him bow and cap, could make him rule with an ear for world's advice when he should have had only his book and his ship and his dream and a cheering cry "Onward!" Or so thinks Juan Lepe. But Juan Lepe and all wait on full light.

He talked of her great nature, and her goodness to him. Of how she understood when the King would not. Of how she would never listen to his enemies, or at the worst not listen long.

He turned upon his bed in the warm Indian night. I asked him if I should read to him but he said, not yet. He had talked since the days of his first seeking with many a great lord, aye, and great lady. But the Queen was the one of them all who understood best how to trust a man! Differences in mind arose within us all, and few could find the firm soul behind all that! She could, and she was great because she could. He loved to talk with her. Her face lighted when he came in. When others were by she said "Don Cristoval", or "El Almirante", but with himself alone she still said "Master Christopherus" as in the old days.

At last he said, "Now, let us read." Each time he came from Spain to Hispaniola he brought books. And when ships came in there would be a packet for him. I read to him now from an old poet, printed in Venice. He listened, then at last he slept. I put out the candle, stepped softly forth past Gonsalvo his servant, lying without door.

An hour after dawn a small cavalcade appeared before the fort. At first we thought it was the Adelantado from Xaragua. But no! it was Alonzo de Carvajal with news and a letter from San Domingo, and in the very statement ran a thrilling something that said, "Hark, now! I am Fortune that turns the wheel."

Carvajal said, "Señor, I have news and a letter for your ear and eye alone!"

"From my brother at San Domingo?"

"Aye, and from another," said Carvajal. "Two ships have come in." With that the Admiral and he went into Commandant's house.

The men at Concepcion made Carvajal's men welcome. "And what is it?" "And what is it?" They had their orders evidently, but much wine leaked out of the cask. If one wished the Viceroy and his brothers ill, it was found to be heady wine; if the other way round, it seemed thin, chilly and bitter. Here at Concepcion were Admiral's friends.

After an hour he came again among us, behind him Carvajal.

Now, this man, Christopherus Columbus, always appeared most highly and nobly Man, most everlasting and universal, in great personal trouble and danger. It was, I hold, because nothing was to him smally personal, but always pertained to great masses, to worlds and to ages.

Now, looking at him, I knew that trouble and danger had arrived. He said very little. If I remember, it was, "My friends, the Sovereigns whom we trust and obey, have sent a Commissioner, Don Francisco de Bobadilla, whom we must go meet. We ride from Concepcion at once to Bonao."

We rode, his company and Carvajal's company.

Don Francisco de Bobadilla! Jayme de Marchena had some association here. It disentangled itself, came at last clear. A Commander of the Order of Calatrava—about the King in some capacity—able and honest, men said. Able and honest, Jayme de Marchena had heard said, but also a passionate man, and a vindictive, and with vanity enough for a legion of peacocks.

We came to Bonao and rested here. I had a word that night from the Admiral. "Doctor, Doctor, a man must outlook storm! He grew man by that."

I asked if I might know what was the matter.

He answered, "I do not know myself. Don Diego says that great powers have been granted Don Francisco de Bobadilla. I have not seen those powers. But he has demanded in the name of the Sovereigns our prisoners, our ships and towns and forts, and has cited us to appear before him and answer charges—of I know not what! I well think it is a voice without true mind or power behind it—I go to San Domingo, but not just at his citation!"

Later, in the moonlight, one of our men told me that which a man of Carvajal had told him. All the Admiral's enemies, and none ever said they were few, had this fire-new commissioner's ear! A friend could not get within hail. Just or unjust, every complaint came and squatted in a ring around him. Maybe some were just—such as soldiers not being able to get their pay, for instance. There was never but one who lived without spot or blemish. But of course we knew that the old Admiral wasn't really a tyrant, cruel and a fool! Of course not. Carvajal's man was prepared to fight any man of his own class who would say that to his face! He'd fight, too, for the Adelantado. Don Francisco de Bobadilla had no sooner landed than he began to talk and act as though they were all villains. Don Diego—whom it was laughable to call a villain—and all. He went to mass at once—Don Francisco de Bobadilla—and when it was over and all were out and all San Domingo there in the square, he had his letters loudly read. True enough! He is Governor, and everybody else must obey him! *Even the Admiral!*

At dawn Juan Lepe walked and thought. And then he saw coming the Franciscan, Juan de Trasiena and Francisco Velasquez the Treasurer. That which Juan de Trasiena and Francisco Velasquez brought were attested copies of the royal letters.

I saw them. "Wherefore we have named Don Francisco de Bobadilla Governor of these islands and of the main land, and we command you, cavaliers and all persons whatever, to give him that obedience which you do owe to us." And to him, the new Governor: "Whomsoever you find guilty, arrest their persons and take over their goods." And, "If you find it to our service that any cavaliers or other persons who are at present in these islands should leave them, and that they should come and present themselves before us, you may command it in our names and oblige it." And, "Whomsoever you thus command, we hereby order that immediately they obey as though it were ourselves." "And if thus and thus is found to be the case, the said Admiral of the Ocean-Sea shall give into your hands, ships, fortresses, arms, houses and treasure, and he shall himself be obedient to your command."

The Admiral said, "If it be found thus and thus! But how shall he find it, seeing that it is not so?"

We rode to San Domingo, but not many rode. He would not have many. "No show of force, no gaud of office!"

He rode unarmored, on his gray horse. The banner that was always borne with him—"Yea, carry it still, until he demands it!"

We were a bare dozen, but when we entered San Domingo one might think that Don Francisco de Bobadilla feared an army, for he had all his soldiers drawn up to greet us! The rest of the population were in coigns, gazing. We saw friends—Juan Ponce de Leon and others—but they were helpless. For all the people in it, the place seemed to me dead quiet, hot, sunny, dead quiet.

The Admiral rode to the square. Here was his house, and the royal banner over it. He dismounted and spoke to men before the door. "Tell Don Francisco de Bobadilla that Don Cristoval Colon is here."

There came an officer with a sword, behind him a dozen men. "Señor, in the name of the Sovereigns, I arrest you!"

Christopherus Columbus gazed upon him. "For what, Señor?"

The other, an arrogant, ill-tempered man, answered loudly so that all around could hear, "For ill-service to our lord the King and Queen, and to their subjects here in the Indies, and to God!"

"God knows, you hurt the truth!" said the Admiral. "Where is my brother, Don Diego?"

"Laid by the heels in the Santa Catarina," answered the graceless man; then to one of the soldiers, "Take the banner from behind him and rest it against the wall."

The Admiral said, "I would see Don Francisco de Bobadilla."

"That is as he desires and when he desires," the other replied. "Close around him, men!"

The fortress of San Domingo is a gloomy place. They prisoned him here, and they put irons upon him. I saw that done. One or two of his immediate following, and I his physician might enter with him.

He stood in the dismal place where one ray of light came down from a high, small, grated window, and he looked at the chains which they brought. He asked, "Who will put them on?"

He looked at the chains and at the soldier who brought them. "Put them on, man!" he said. "What! Once thou didst nail God's foot to a cross! As for me, I will remember that One who saved all, and be patient."

They chained him and left him there in the dark.

I saw him the next day, entering with his gaoler. Had he slept?

"Yes."

"How did he find himself?"

"How does my body find itself? Why, no worse than usual, nowadays that I am getting old! My body has been unhappier a thousand times in storm and fight, and thirst and famine."

"Then mind and soul?" I asked.

"They are well. There is nothing left for them but to feel well. I am in the hand of God."

I did what service for him I could. He thanked me. "You've been ever as tender as a woman. A brave man besides! I hope you'll be by me, Juan Lepe, when I die."

"When you die, Señor, there will die a great servant of the world."

I spoke so because I knew the cordial that he wanted.

His eyes brightened, strength came into his voice. "Do you know aught of my brother the Adelantado?"

"No. He may be on his way from Xaragua. What would you wish him to do, sir?"

"Come quietly to San Domingo as I came. This Governor is but a violent, petty shape! But I have sworn to obey the Queen and the King of the Spains. I and mine to obey."

I asked him if he believed that the Sovereigns knew this outrage. I could believe it hardly of King Ferdinand, not at all of the Queen.

Again I felt that this was cordial to him. I had spoken out of my conviction, and he knew it. "No," he said. "I do not believe it. I will never believe it of the Queen! Look you! I have thought it out in the night. The night is good for thinking out. You would not believe how many enemies I have in Spain. Margarite and Father Buil are but two of a crowd. Fonseca, who should give me all aid, gives me all hindrance. I have throngs of foes; men who envy me; men who thought I might give them the golden sun, and I could not; hidalgos who hold that God made them to enjoy, standing on other men's shoulders, eating the grapes and throwing down the empty skins, and I made them to labor like the others; and not in Heaven or Hell will they forgive me! And others—and others. They have turned the King a little their way. I knew that, before I went to find that great new land where are pearls, that slopes upward by littles to the Height of the

World and the Earthly Paradise. Turned the King, but not the Queen. But now I make it they have worked upon her. I make it that she does not know the character of Don Francisco de Bobadilla. I make it that, holding him to be far wiser than he is, she with the King gave him great power as commissioner. I make it that they gave him letters of authority, and a last letter, superseding the Viceroy, naming him Governor whom all must obey. I make it that he was only to use this if after long examination it was found by a wise, just man that I had done after my enemies' hopes. I make it that here across Ocean-Sea, far, far from Spain, he chose not to wait. He clucked to him all the disaffected and flew with a strong beak at the eyes of my friends." He moved his arms and his chains clanked. "I make it that this severity is Don Francisco de Bobadilla's, not King Ferdinand's, not—oh, more than not—the good Queen's!"

Juan Lepe thought that he had made out the probabilities, probably the certainties.

"If I may win to Spain!" he ended. "It all hinges on that! If I may see the Sovereigns—if I may see the good Queen! I hope to God he will soon chain me in a ship and send me!"

Had he seen Don Francisco de Bobadilla?

No, he had not seen Don Francisco de Bobadilla. He thought that on the whole that Hidalgo and Commander of Calatrava was afraid.

Outside of the fortress that afternoon Juan Lepe kept company with one who had come with the fire-new Governor, a grim, quiet fellow named Pedro Lopez. He and Luis Torres had been neighbors in Spain; it was Luis who brought us together. I gave him some wine in Doctor Juan Lepe's small room and he told readily the charges against the Viceroy that Bobadilla, seizing, made into a sheaf.

Already I knew what they were. I had heard them. One or two had, I thought, faint justification, but the mass, no! Personal avarice, personal greed, paynim luxury, arrogance, cruelty, deceit—it made one sorrowfully laugh who knew the man! Here again clamored the old charge of upstartness. A low-born Italian, son of a wool-comber, vindictive toward the hidalgo, of Spain! But there were new charges. Three men deposed that he neglected Indian salvation. And I heard for the first time that so soon as he found the Grand Khan he meant to give over to that Oriental all the islands and the main, and so betray the Sovereigns and Christ and every Spaniard in these parts!

The Adelantado arrived in San Domingo. He came with only a score or two of men, who could have raised many more. Don Francisco de Bobadilla saw to it that he had word from his great brother, and that word was "Obedience." The Adelantado gave his sword to Don Francisco. The latter loaded the first with chains and put him aboard a caravel in the harbor. He asked to be imprisoned with his brother; but why ask any magnanimity from an unmagnanimous soul?

Out in the open now were all the old insurgents. Guevara and Requelme bowed to the earth when the Governor passed, and Roldan sat with him at wine.

CHAPTER XXXVI

The caravel tossed in a heavy storm. Some of her mariners were old in these waters, but others, coming out with Bobadilla, had little knowledge of our breadths of Ocean-Sea. They had met naught like this rain, this shaken air, these thunders and lightnings. There rose a cry that the ship would split. All was because they had chained the Admiral!

Don Alonso de Villejo, the Captain taking Christopherus Columbus to Spain, called to him Juan Lepe. "Witness you, Doctor, I would have taken away the irons so soon as we were out of harbor! I would have done it on my own responsibility. But he would not have it!"

"Yes, I witness. In chains in Hispaniola, he will come to Spain in chains."

"If the ship goes down every man must save himself. He must be free. I have sent for the smith. Come you with me!"

We went to that dusky cabin in the ship where he was prisoned. "It is a great storm, and we are in danger, Señor!" said Villejo. "I will take away these irons so that if—"

The Admiral's silver hair gleamed in the dusk. He moved and his gyves struck together. "Villejo!" he said, "if I lie tonight on the floor of Ocean-Sea, I will lie there in these chains! When the sea gives up its dead, I will rise in them!"

"I could force you, Señor," said Villejo.

The other answered, "Try it, and God will make your hands like a babe's!"

Villejo and the smith did not try it. There was something around him like an invisible guard. I knew the feel of it, and that it was his will emerged at height.

"Remember then, Señor, that I would have done it for you!" Villejo touched the door. The Admiral's voice then came after. "My brother, Don Bartholomew, he who was responsible to me and only through me to the Sovereigns, free him, Villejo, and you have all my thanks!"

We went to take the gyves from Don Bartholomew. It would have been comfort to these brothers to be together in prison—but that the Governor of Hispaniola straitly forbade. When Villejo had explained what he would do, the Adelantado asked then, "What of the Admiral?"

"I wish to take them from him also. But he is obstinate in his pride and will not!"

"He will go as he is to the Queen and Spain and the world," said Juan Lepe.

"That is enough for me," answered the Adelantado. "I do not go down tonight a freed body while he goes down a chained. Farewell, Señor! I think I hear your sailors calling."

Villejo hesitated. "Let them have their will, Señor," said Juan Lepe. "Their will is as good as ours."

Don Bartholomew turned to me. "How fares my brother, Doctor? Is he ill?"

"He is better. Because he was ill I was let to come with him. But now he is better."

"Give him my enduring love and constancy," said the Adelantado. "Good night, Villejo!" and turned upon his side with a rattling of his chain.

Returning to the Admiral, Juan Lepe sat beside him through the night. The tempest continuing, there were moments when we thought, It may be the end of this life! We thought to hear the cry "She sinks!" and the rush of feet.

At times when there fell lulls we talked. He was calmly cheerful.

"It seems to me that the storm lessens. I have been penning in my mind, lying here, a letter to one who will show it to the Queen. Writing so, I can say with greater freedom that which should be said."

"What do you say?"

He told me with energy. His letter related past events in Hispaniola and the arrival of Bobadilla and all that took place thereupon. He had an eloquence of the pen as of speech, and what he said to Dona Juana de la Torre moved. A high simplicity was his in such moment, an opening of the heart, such as only children and the very great attain. He told his wrongs, and he prayed for just judgment, "not as a ruler of an ordered land where obtain old, known, long-followed laws, and where indeed disorder might cry 'Weakness and ill-doing!' But I should be judged rather as a general sent to bring under government an enemy people, numerous, heathen, living in a most difficult, unknown and pathless country. And to do this I had many good men, it is true, but also a host that was not good, but was factious, turbulent, sensual and idle. Yet have I brought these strange lands and naked peoples under the Sovereigns, giving them the lordship of a new world. What say my accusers? They say that I have taken great honors and wealth and nobility for myself and my house. Even they say, O my friend! that from the vast old-and-new and fairest land that I have lately found, I took and kept the pearls that those natives brought me, not rendering them to the Sovereigns. God judge me, it is not so! Spain becometh vastly rich, and the head of the world, and her Sovereigns, lest they should scant their own nobility, give nobility, place and wage to him who brought them Lordship here. It is all! And out of my gain am I not pledged to gather an army and set it forth to gain the Sepulchre? Have I fallen, now and again, in all these years in my Government, into some error? How should I not do so, being human? But never hath an error been meant, never have I wished but to deal honestly and mercifully with all, with Spaniards and with Indians, to serve well the Sovereigns and to advance the Cross. I call the saints to witness! All the way has been difficult, thorns of nature's and my enemies' planting, but God knoweth, I have trodden it steadily. I have given much to the Sovereigns, how much it is future days brighter than these will show! I have been true servant to them. If now, writing in chains, upon the caravel *Santa, Marta*, I cry to them for justice, it is because I do not fear justice!"

He ceased to speak, then presently, "I would that all might see the light that I see over the future!—Thou seest it, Juan Lepe."

"Aye, I see light over the future."

By littles the storm fell. Before dawn we could say, "We shall outlive it!" He slept for an hour then waked. "I was dreaming of the Holy Land—but do you know, Juan Lepe, it was seated here in the lands we found!"

"Seated here and everywhere," I said. "As soon as we see it so and make it so."

"Aye, I know that the sea is holy, and so should be all the land! The prophet sees it so—"

The dawn came faintly in upon us. All was quieter, the footing overhead steady, not hasting, frightened. Light strengthened. A boy brought him breakfast. He ate with appetite. "You are better," I said, "and younger."

"It is a strange thing," he answered, "but so it had been from my boyhood. Is the danger close and drear, is the ship upon the reef, then someone pours for me wine! Someone, do I say? I know Who!"

I began to speak of the Adelantado. "Aye, there he is the same! 'Peril—darkness? Well, let's meet it!' We are alike, we three brothers, alike and different. Diego serves God best in a monastery, and I serve best in a ship with a book and a map to be followed and bettered. Bartholomew serves best where he has been, Adelantado and Alcayde. He is powerful there, with judgment and action. But he is a sea master too, and he makes a good map. I thank God who gave us good parents, and to us all three mind and a firm will! The inheritance passes to my sons. You have not seen them? They are youths of promise! A family that is able and at one, loving and aiding each other, honoring its past and providing for its future, becomes, I tell you, an Oak that cannot be felled—an Ark that rides the waters!"

As he moved, his chains made again their dull noise. "Do they greatly gall you?"

"Yes, they gall! Flesh and spirit. But I shall wear them until the Queen saith, 'Away with them!' But ever after I shall keep them by me! They shall hang in my house where forever men shall see them! In my son's house after me, and in his son's!"

Alonso de Villejo visited him. "The tempest is over, Señor. I take it for good augury in your affair!"

Juan Lepe upon the deck found beside him a man whom he knew. "What d'ye think? At the worst, in the middle night, there came to Don Alonso and the master the old seamen and would have him freed so that he might save us! They said that they had seen his double upon the stern, looking at the sea and waving his arm. Then it vanished! They wanted the whole man, they wanted the Admiral! The master roared at them and sent them back, but if it had come to the worst—I don't know!"

Cadiz—the *Santa Marta* came to Cadiz. Before us had arrived Bobadilla's ships, one, two and three. What he found to say through his messengers of the Admiral and Viceroy was in the hands and eyes and ears of all. He said at the height of his voice, across the ocean from Hispaniola, violent and villainous things.

Cadiz—Spain. We crowded to look.. Down plunged anchor, down rattled sails, around us came the boats. The Admiral and the Adelantado rested in chains. The corregidor of Cadiz took them both thus ashore and to a house where they were kept, until the Sovereigns should say, "Bring them before us!"

Juan Lepe the physician was let to go in the boat with him. Juan Lepe—Jayme de Marchena. It was eight years since I had quitted Spain. I was older by that, grizzled, bearded and so bronzed by the Indies that I needed no Moorish stain. I trusted God that Don Pedro and the Holy Office had no longer claws for me.

Cadiz, and all the people out, pointing and staring. I remembered what I had been told of the return from his first voyage, and the second voyage. Then had been bells and trumpets, flowers, banners, grandees drawing him among them, shouts and shouts of welcome!

He walked in gyves, he and the Adelantado, to the house of his detention. Once only a single voice was raised in a shout, "El Almirante!" We came to the house, not a prison, though a prison for him. In a good enough room the corregidor sought to have the chains removed. The Admiral would not, keeping back with voice and eye the men who wished to part them from him. When the Sovereigns knew, and when the Sovereigns sent—then, but not before!

Seven days in this house. Then word from the Sovereigns, and it was here indignant, and here comforting. The best was the Queen's word; I do not know if it was so wholly King Ferdinand's. There were letters to the alcalde and corregidor. Release the Admiral of the Ocean-Sea! Don Francisco de Bobadilla had grossly misunderstood! Soothe the Admiral's hurt. Show him trust and gratitude in Cadiz that was become through him a greater city! Fulfill his needs and further him upon the way to Granada. Put in his purse two thousand ducats. But the letter that counted most to Christopherus Columbus was one to himself from the Queen.

Juan Lepe found him with it in his hand. From the wrist yet hung the chain. Tears were running down his cheeks. "You see—you see!" he said. "I thank thee, Christ, who taketh care of us all!"

They came and took away his chains. But he claimed them from the corregidor and kept them to his death. Came hidalgos of Cadiz and entreated him away from this house to a better one. Outside the street was thronged. "The Admiral! The Admiral! Who gave to Spain the Indies!"

Don Bartholomew was by him, freed like him. And there too moved a slender young man who had come from Granada with the Queen's letter, Don Fernando, his eldest son. A light seemed all around them. Juan Lepe thought, "Surely they who serve large purposes are cared for. Even though they should die in prison, yet are they cared for!"

CHAPTER XXXVII

Upon the sand beyond Palos, Juan Lepe lay. The Admiral was with the court in Granada, but his physician, craving holiday, had borne a letter to Juan Perez, the Prior of Santa Maria de la Rabid. I thought the Admiral would go again seafaring, and that I would go with him. Up at La Rabida, Fray Juan Perez was kind. I had a cell, I could come and go; he did not tell Palos that here was the Admiral's physician, who knew the Indies from the first taking and could relate wonders. I lived obscure, but in Prior's room, by a light fire, for it was November, he himself endlessly questioned and listened.

Ocean before me, ocean, ocean! Lying here, those years ago, I had seen the ocean only. Now, far, far, I saw land, saw San Salvador, Cuba that might be the main, Hayti, Jamaica, San Juan, Guadaloupe, Trinidad, Paria that again seemed main. Vast islands and a world of small islands, vast mainlands. Then no sail was seen on far Ocean-Sea; now out there might be ships going from Cadiz, coming, returning from San Domingo. Eight years, and so the world was changed!

I thought, "In fifty years—in a hundred years—in two hundred? What is coming up the long road?"

Ocean murmured, the tide was coming in. Juan Lepe waited till the sands had narrowed, till the gray wave foamed under his hand. Then he rose and walked slowly to La Rabida.

After compline, talk; Fray Juan Perez, the good man, comfortable in his great chair before the fire. He had hungered always, I thought, for adventure and marvel. Here it happened—? And here it then happened—?

Tonight we fell to talk of the Pinzons—Martin who was dead, and Vicente who now was on Ocean-Sea, on a voyage of his own—and of others who had sailed, and what they found and where they were. We were at ease about the Admiral. We had had letters.

He was in Granada, dressed again in crimson and gold, towering again with his silver head, honored and praised. When first he came into the Queen's presence she had trembled a little and turned pale, and there was water in her eyes. "Master Christopherus, forgive us! Whereupon," said the letter, "I wept with her."

Apparently all honors were back; he moved Admiral and Viceroy. His brothers, his sons, all his house walked in a spring sun. He had been shown the letters from Bobadilla, and he who was not lengthy in speech had spoken an hour upon them. His word rang gold; Christ gave it, he said, that his truth was believed. Don Francisco de Bobadilla would quit Hispaniola—though not in chains.

Fray Juan Perez stirred the fire. Upon the table stood a flask of wine and a dish of figs. We were comfortable in La Rabida.

Days passed, weeks passed, time passed. Word from the Admiral, word of the Admiral, came not infrequently to white La Rabida. He himself, in his own person, stood in bright favor, the Queen treasuring him, loving to talk with him, the Court following her, the King at worst only a cool friend. But his affairs of office, Fray Juan Perez and I gathered, sitting solicitous at La Rabida, were not in so fair a posture. He and his household did not lack. Monies were paid him, though not in full his tithe of all gains from his finding. What never shook was his title of The Admiral. But they seemed, the Sovereigns, or at least King Ferdinand, to look through "Viceroy" as though it were a shade. And in Hispaniola, though charged, reproved, threatened, still stayed Bobadilla in the guise of Governor!

"They cannot leave him there," I said. "If the Colombos are not men for the place, what then is Bobadilla?"

Fray Juan Perez stirred the fire. "King Ferdinand, I say it only to you and in a whisper, has not a little of the King of the Foxes! Not, till he has made up his mind, doth he wish there a perfect man. When he has made it up, he will cast about—"

"I do not think he has any better than the Adelantado!"

" 'Those brothers are one. Leave him out!' saith the King. I will read you his mind! 'Master Christopherus Columbus hath had too much from the beginning. Nor is he necessary as he was. When the breach is made, any may take the fortress! I will leave him and give him what I must but no more!' He will send at last another than Bobadilla, but not again, if he can help it, the old Viceroy! Of course there is the Queen, but she has many sorrows these days, and fails, they say, in health."

"It may be," said Juan Lepe slowly. "I myself were content for him to rest The Admiral only. But his mind is yet a hawk towering over land and sea and claiming both for prize. He mingles the earthly and the heavenly."

"It is true," said Fray Juan Perez, "that age comes upon him. And true, too, that King Ferdinand may say, 'Whatever it was at first, this world in the West becomes far too vast a matter for one man and the old, first, simple ways!' "

"You have it there," I answered, and we covered the embers and went to bed in La Rabida.

Winter passed. It was seen that the Admiral could not sail this week nor the next.

Juan Lepe, bearded, brown as a Moor, older than in the year Granada fell, crossed with quietness much of Castile and came on a spring evening to the castle of Don Enrique de Cerda. Again *"Juan Lepe from the hermitage in the oak wood."*

Seven days. I would not stay longer, but in that time the ancient trees waved green again.

Don Enrique had been recently to Granada. "King Ferdinand will change all matters in the West! Your islands shall have Governors, as many as necessary. They shall refer themselves to a High Governor at San Domingo, who in his turn shall closely listen to a Council here."

"Will the High Governor be Don Cristoval Colon?"

"No. I hear that he himself agrees to a suspension of his viceroyalty for two years, seeing well that in Hispaniola is naught but faction, everything torn into 'Friends of the Genoese' and 'Not friends!'. Perhaps he sees that he cannot help himself and that he less parts with dignity by acceding. I do not know. There is talk of Don Nicholas de Ovanda, Commander of Lares. Your man will not, I think, be sent before a steady wind for Viceroy again—never again. If he presses too persistently, there can always be found one or more who will stand and cry, 'He did intend, O King—he doth intend—to make himself King of the Indies!' And King Ferdinand will say he does not believe, but it is manifest that that thought must first die from men's minds. The Queen fails fast. She has not the voice and the hand in all matters that once was so."

"He is one who dies for loyalties," I said. "He reverences all simply the crowns of Castile and Leon. For his own sake I am not truly so anxious to have him Viceroy again! They will give him ships and let him discover until he dies?"

"Ah, I don't think there is any doubt about that!" he answered.

We talked somewhat of that great modern world, evident now over the horizon, bearing upon us like a tall, full-rigged ship. All things were changing, changing fast. We talked of commerce and inventions, and of letters and of arts, of religion and the soul of man. Out of the soil were pushing everywhere plants that the old called heretical.

Seven days. We were, as we shall be forever, friends.

But Juan Lepe would go back to La Rabida. He was, for this turn of life, man of the Admiral of the Ocean-Sea. So we said farewell, Enrique de Cerda and Jayme de Marchena.

Three leagues Seville side of Cordova I came at eve to a good inn known to me of old. Riding into its court I found two travelers entering just before me, one a well-formed hidalgo still at prime, and the other a young man evidently his son. The elder who had just dismounted turned and I recognized Don Francisco de Las Casas. At the same instant he saw me. "Ha, Friend! Ha, Doctor!"

We took our supper together in a wide, low room, looking out upon the road. Don Francisco and Juan Lepe talked and the young man listened. Juan Lepe talked but his eyes truly were for this young man. It was not that he was of a striking aspect and better than handsome, though he was all that—but I do not know—it was the future in his countenance! His father addressed him as Bartolomé. Once he said, "When my son was at the University at Salamanca," and again, "My son will go out with Don Nicholas de Ovando." Juan Lepe, sitting in a brown study, roused at that. "If you go, Señor, you will find good memories around the name of Las Casas."

The young man said, "I will strive in no way to darken them, Señor."

He might be a year or two the younger side of thirty. The father, it was evident, had great pride in him, and presently having sent him on some errand—sending him, I thought, in order to be able to speak of him—told me that he was very learned, a licentiate, having mastered law, theology and philosophy. He himself would not return to Hispaniola, but Bartolomé wished to go. He sighed, "I do not know. Something makes me consent," and went on to enlist Doctor Juan Lepe's care if in the island ever arose any chance to aid—

The son returned. There was something—Juan Lepe knew it—something in the future. Later, Don Francisco having gone to bed, the young man and I talked. I liked him extraordinarily. I was not far from twice his age, as little man counts age. But he had soul and mind, and while these count age it is not in the short, earthly way. He asked me about the Indians, and again and again we came back to that, pacing up and down in the moonlight before the Spanish inn.

The next morning parting. They were going to Cordova, I to the sea.

The doves flew over the cloister of La Rabida. The bells rang; in the small white church sang the brothers, then paced to their cells or away to their work among the vines. Prior had a garden, small, with a tree in each corner, with a stone bench in the sun and a stone bench in the shade, and the doves walked here all day long. And here I found the Adelantado with Fray Juan Perez.

The Admiral was well?

Aye, well, and next month would come to Seville. A new Voyage.

We sat under the grape arbor and he told me much, the Prior listening for the second time. The doves cooed and whirred and walked in the sun and shadow. According to Don Bartholomew, half in his pack was dark and half was light.

Ovando? We heard again of all that. He was going out, Don Nicholas de Ovando, with a great fleet.

The Adelantado possessed a deal of plain, strong sense. "I do not think that Cristoforo will ever rule again in Hispaniola! King Ferdinand has his own measure and goes about to apply it. The Queen flinches now from decisions. Well, what of it? After all, we were bred to the sea, I have a notion that his son Diego—an able youth—may yet be Viceroy. He has established his family, if so be he does not bring down the structure by obstinating overmuch! He sees that, the Admiral, and nods his head and steps aside. As for native pride and its hurt he salves that with great enterprises. It is his way. Drought? Frost? Out of both he rises, green and hopeful as grass in May!"

"What of the Voyage?" asked Juan Lepe.

"That's the enterprise that will go through. Now that Portugal and Vasco da Gama are actually in at the door, it behooves us—more and more it behooves us," said Bartolomeo Colombo, "to find India of All the Wealth! Spain no less than Portugal wants the gold and diamonds, the drugs and spices, the fine, thin, painted cloths, the carved ivory and silver and amber. 'Land, land, so much land!' says King Ferdinand. 'But wealth? It is all out-go! Even your Crusade were a beggarly Crusade!' "

"Ha! That hurt him!" quoth Fray Juan Perez.

"Says the King. 'Pedro Alonso Nino has made for us the most profitable voyage of any who have sailed from Cadiz.' 'From Cadiz, but not from Palos,' answers the Admiral."

"Ha! Easy 'tis when he has shown the way!" said Fray Juan Perez.

Don Bartholomew drew with the Prior's stick in the sand at our feet. "He conceives it thus. Here to the north is Cuba, stretching westward how far no man knoweth. Here to the south is Paria that he found—no matter what Ojeda and Nino and Cabral have done since!—stretching westward how far no man knoweth, and between is a great sea holding Jamaica and we do not know what other islands. Cuba and Paria curving south and north and between them where they shall come closest surely a strait into the sea of Rich India!"

He drew Cuba and Paria approaching each the other until there was space between like the space from the horn of Spain to the horn of Africa. "Rich India—now, now, now—gold on the wharves, canoes of pearls, not cotton and cassava, is what we want in Spain! So the

King says, 'Very good, you shall have the ships,' and the Queen, 'Christ have you in his keeping, Master Christopherus!' So we go. All his future hangs, he knows, on finding Rich India."

"How soon do we go?"

"As soon as he can get the ships and the men and the supplies. He wants only three or four and not great ones. Great ships for war-ships and storeships, but little ships for discovery!"

"Aye, I hear him!" said Fray Juan Perez. "September—October."

But it was not until March that we sailed on his last voyage.

CHAPTER XXXVIII

The ships were the *Consolacion*, the *Margarita*, the *Juana* and the *San Sebastian*, all caravels and small ones, the *Consolacion* the largest and the flagship. The *Margarita*, that was the Adelantado's ship, sailed badly. There was something as wrong with her as had been with the *Pinta* when we started from Palos in '92.

The men all told, crews and officers and adventurers, were less than two hundred.

Pedro de Terreros, Bartholomew Fiesco, Diego Tristan, Francisco de Porras were the captains of the caravels Juan Sanchez and Pedro Ledesma the chief pilots. Bartholomew Fiesco of the *Consolacion* was a Genoese and wholly devoted to the greater Genoese. We had for notary Diego Mendez. There were good men upon this voyage, and very bold men.

The youth Fernando Colon sailed with his father. He was now fourteen, Don Fernando, slim, intelligent, obedient and loving always to the Admiral.

Days of bright weather, days and days of that marvelous favorable wind that blows over Ocean-Sea. The twenty-fifth of May the Canaries sank behind us. On and on, all the sails steady.

We were not first for Hispaniola. All must be strange, this voyage! Jamaica, not San Domingo, was our star. Rest there a moment, take food and water, then forth and away. West again, west by south. He was straitly forbidden to drop anchor in any water of Hispaniola. "For why?" said they. "Because the very sight of his ships will tear asunder again that which Don Nicholas de Ovando is healing!"

The *Margarita*, that was next to the *Consolacion* in greatness, sailed so infirmly that mercy 'twas the seas were smooth. It was true accident. She had been known at Palos, Cadiz and San Lucar for good ship. But at Ercilla where we must stop on the Sovereigns' business, a storm had beaten her upon the shore where she got a great wound in her side. That was staunched, but all her frame was wrenched and she never did well thereafter. In mid-June we came to an island of the Caribs which they called Mantineo. Here we rested the better part of a week, keeping good guard against the Caribs, then sailed, and now north by west, along a vast curve, within a world of islands. They are great, they are small, they are of the extremest beauty! San Martin, Dominica, Guadaloupe, San Juan—the Boriquen whence had come, long ago, that Catalina whom Guacanagari aided—and untouched at, or under the horizon, many another that the Admiral had named; *Santa Maria* la Antigua, Santa Cruz, Santa Ursula, Montserrat, Eleven Thousand Virgins, Marigalante and all beside. What a world! Plato his Atlantis. How truly old we are God only knows!

The *Margarita* sailed most badly. At San Juan that is the neighbor great island to Hispaniola, council, two councils, one following the other. Then said the Admiral, "We are to find the Strait that shall at last carry us to clothed Asia of all the echoes, and to find we have but four small ships and one of them evidently doomed. And in that one sails my brother. What is the Sovereigns' command? 'Touch not on your outward way at Hispaniola!' What is in their mind here? 'Hale and faring well, you have no need.'—But if we are not hale and faring well by a fourth of our enterprise? They never meant it to a drowning man, or one whose water cask was empty! Being Christian, no! We will put into San Domingo and ask of Don Nicholas de Ovando a ship in place of the *Margarita*."

Whereat all cheered. We were gathered under palms, upon a fair point of land in San Juan le Bautista. Next day we weighed anchor, and in picture San Domingo rose before us.

He felt no doubt of decent welcome, of getting his ship. Fifteen sail had gone out with Ovando. Turn the cases around, and he would have given Ovando welcome, he would give him a good ship. How much more then Christopherus Columbus! The enterprise was common in that all stood to profit. It was royal errand, world service! So he thought and sailed in some tranquillity of mind for San Domingo.

But the Adelantado said in my ear. "There will be a vast to-do! Maybe I'll sail the *Margarita* to the end." He was the prophet!

It was late June. Hispaniola rose, faint, faint, upon the horizon. All crowded to look. There, there before us dwelled countrymen, fellow mariners, fellow adventurers forth from the Old into the New! It was haven; it was Spain in the West; it was Our Colony.

The Admiral gazed, and I saw the salt tears blind his eyes. His son was beside him. He put his hand upon the youth's shoulder. "Fernando, there it is—I found and named it Hispaniola!"

The weather hung perilously still, the sea glass. It was so clear above, below, around, that we seemed to see by added light, and yet there was no more sunlight. All the air had thinned, it seemed, away. Every sail fell slack. Colors were slightly altered. The Admiral said, "There is coming a great storm."

The boy Fernando laughed. "Why, father!"

"Stillness before the leap," said the Admiral. "Quiet at home because the legions have gone to muster."

It was hard to think it, but too often had it been proved that he was in the secret of water and air. Now Bartholomew Fiesco the Genoese said. "Aye, aye! They say on the ships at Genoa that when it came to weather, even when you were a youngster, you were fair necromancer!"

The sky rested blue, but the sea became green oil. That night there were all around us fields of phosphorescence. About midnight these vanished; it was very black for all the stars, and we seemed to hear a sighing as from a giant leagues away. This passed, and the morning broke, silent and tranquil, azure sky and azure sea, and not so sharply clear as yesterday. The great calm wind again pushed us.

Hispaniola! Hispaniola! Her mountains and her palms before us.

We coasted to the river Hayna and the Spanish city of San Domingo. Three hours from sunset down in harbor plunged our anchors, down rattled our sails.

The *Consolacion's* long boat danced by her side. The Admiral would send to land but one boat, and in it for envoy Pedro de Terreros, a well-speaking man and known to Don Nicholas de Ovando. Terreros was envoy, but with him the Admiral sent Juan Lepe, who through the years in Hispaniola had tried to heal the sick, no matter what their faction. The Admiral stayed upon the *Consolacion*, the Adelantado upon the *Margarita*.

The harbor was filled with ships. We counted eighteen. We guessed that they were preparing for sailing, the little boats so came and went between. And our entry had caused excitement. Ship and small boat hailed us, but to them we did not answer. Then came toward us from the shore a long boat with the flag of Spain and in it an official.

Our wharf! Juan Lepe had left it something more than a year and a half ago. San Domingo was grown, many Spaniards having sailed for the west in that time. I saw strangers and strangers, though of Spanish blood. Walking with the officer and his people to the Governor's house gave time for observation and swift thought. Throng was forming. One had early cried from out it, "That's the doctor, Juan Lepe! 'Tis the Admiral out there!" That it was the Admiral seemed to spread. San Domingo buzzed like the air about a hive the first spring day. Farther on, out pushed a known voice. "Welcome, welcome, Doctor!" I looked, and that was Sancho. Luis Torres was in Spain. I had seen him in Cadiz. The crowd was thickening—men came running—there was cry and query. Suddenly rose a cheer. "The Admiral and the Adelantado in their little ships!" At once came a counter-shout. "The Genoese! The Traitors!"

I saw—I saw that there was some wisdom in King Ferdinand!

The Governor's house that used to be the Viceroy's house. State—state! They had cried out upon the Genoese's keeping it—but Don Nicholas de Ovando kept more. While we waited in the antechamber I saw, out of window and the tail of my eye, files of soldiery go by. Ovando would not have riot and disturbance if twenty Admirals hung in the offing! He kept us waiting. He would be cool and distant and impregnable behind the royal word. Juan Lepe saw plainly that that lavish and magnanimous person aboard the *Consolacion* would not meet here his twin. The Adelantado must still, I thought, sail the *Margarita*. And yet, looking at all things, that exchange of ships should have been made. A Spaniard, wheresoever found, should have cried "Aye!" to it.

The Governor's officer who still kept by us was not averse to talk. All those preparing ships in the harbor? Why, they were the returning fleet that brought Don Nicholas in. Sailing tomorrow—hence the hubbub on land and water. They had a lading now! He gazed a moment at us, and as we seemed sober folk, saw no reason why we should not have the public news. Forth it came like water out of bottle. Bobadilla was returning. "A prisoner?" "Why, hardly that! Roldan, too." "A prisoner?" "Why, not precisely so." Many of the old régime—Bobadilla's régime—were returning and Roldan men likewise. Invited to go, in fact, though with no other harsh treatment. One of the ships would be packed with Indian rebels, Gwarionex among them. Chained, all these. The notable thing about the fleet, after all that, was the gold that was going! A treasure fleet! Bobadilla *had* gathered gold for the crown. He was taking, they said, a sultan's ransom. He had one piece that weighed, they said, five thousand castellanos. Roldan too had gold. And the Governor was sending no man knew how much. More than that—" He looked at us, then, being a kindly soul, quoth, "Why shouldn't the Admiral know? Alonso de Carvajal has put on board the *Santa Clara* for the Admiral's agent in Cadiz five thousand pieces—fully due, as the Governor had allowed."

Door was opened. "His Excellency the Governor will see you now."

Why tarry over a short story? Don Nicholas de Ovando pleaded smoothly the Sovereign's most strict command which *in any* to disobey were plain malfeasance! As he spoke he looked dreamily toward blue harbor and the *Consolacion*. And as to a ship! Every ship, except two or three, old and crippled and in the hands of the menders, no whit better it was certain than the *Margarita*, was laded and on the point of sailing. Literally he had none, absolutely not one! He understood that Jamaica was expressly named to the Admiral for resting and overhauling. Careen the *Margarita* there and rectify the wrong—which he trusted was not great. If ships had been idle and plentiful—but he could not splinter any from the fleet that was sailing tomorrow. He was sorry—and trusted that the Admiral was in health?

Terreros said, "His ship is worse off than you think, Excellency. He has great things to do, confided into his hands by the Sovereigns who treasure him who found all. Here is emergency. May we carry to him invitation to enter San Domingo for an hour and himself present his case?"

But no—but no—but no! Thrice that!

The Governor rose. Audience was over.

For the rest he was courteous—asked of the voyage—and of the Admiral's notion of the Strait. "A great man!" he said. "A Thinker, a Seer." He sent him messages of courtesy three-piled. And so we parted.

This was the Governor of whom one said long afterwards,

"He was a good governor for white men, but not for Indians."

As life and destiny would have it, in the place without the Governor's house I met him who was to say it. Terreros and I with the same escort were for the water side, the *Consolacion's* long boat. The crowd kept with us, but His Excellency's soldiers held it orderly. Yet there were shouts and messages for the Admiral, and for this one and that one aboard our ships. Then came a young man, said a word to the officer with us, and put out his hand to mine. It was that Bartolomé de Las Casas with whom I had walked the white road, under moon, before the inn between Seville and Cordova.

CHAPTER XXXIX

The Admiral took it with some Italian words under breath. Then he wheeled and left the cabin. A minute later I heard the master from the *Consolacion* hail the *Margarita* that lay close by. "*Margarita*, ahoy! Orders! Clap on sail and follow!" The trumpet cried to the Juana and the *San Sebastian*, "Make ready and follow!"

Our mariners ran to make sail. But the long boat waited for some final word that they said was going ashore. Terreros would take it. We were so close that we saw the yet watching crowd, wharf and water side, and the sun glinting upon Ovando's order-keeping soldiery. The Admiral called me to him. I read the letter to the Governor, Terreros would deliver to our old officer, probably waiting on the wharf to see us quite away. The letter—there was naught in it but the sincerest, gravest warning that a hurricane was at hand. A great one; he knew the signs. It might strike this shore late tomorrow or the next day or the next. Wherefore he begged his Excellency the Governor to tarry the fleet's sailing. Let it wait at least three days and see if his words came not true! Else there would be scattering of ships and destruction—and he rested his Excellency's servant. *El Almirante*.

Terreros went, delivered that letter, and returned to the *Juana*. And our sails were made and our anchors lifted, and it was sunset and clear and smooth, and every palm frond of San Domingo showed. Eighteen ships in harbor, and fifteen, they said, going to Spain, and around and upon them all bustle of preparation. One saw in fancy Bobadilla and Roldan and Gwarionex and the much gold, including that piece of virgin ore weighing five thousand castellanos. Fifteen ships preparing for Spain, and San Domingo, of which the Adelantado had laid first stone, and a strange, green, sunset sky. And the *Consolacion*, the *Margarita*, the Juana and the *San Sebastian* away to the west, to the sound of music, for the Admiral cried to our musicians, "Play, play in God's name!"

Night passed. Morning broke. So light was the wind that the shore went by slowly. There gathered an impatience. "If we must to Jamaica, what use in following every curve of Hispaniola that is forbid us?" At noon the wind almost wholly failed, then after three hours of this rose with a pouncing suddenness to a good breeze. We rounded a point thronged with palms. Before us a similar point, and between the two that bent gently each to the other, slept a deep and narrow bight. "Enter here," said the Admiral.

We anchored. There was again a strange sunset, green and gold in the lower west, but above an arc of clouds dressed in saffron and red. And now we could hear, though from very far off, a deep and low murmur, and whether it was the forest or the sea or both we did not know. But now all the old mariners said there would be storm, and we were glad of the little bay between the protecting horns. The Admiral named it Bay of Comfort. The *Consolacion Margarita*, *Juana*, *San Sebastian*, lay under bare masts, deep within the bight.

The next day, an hour before noon, arrived that king hurricane.

They are known now, these storms of Europe's west and Asia's east. Take all our Mediterranean storms and heap them into one!

Through the day our anchors held in our Bay of Comfort, and we blessed our Admiral. But at eve the *Margarita*, the *Juana* and the *San Sebastian* lost bottom, feared breaking against the rocky shore and stood out for sea room. The *Consolacion* stayed fast, and at dawn was woe to see nothing at all of the three. In the howling tempest and the quarter light we knew not if they were sunk or saved.

With the second evening the hurricane sank; at dawn the seas, though running high, no longer pushed against us like white-maned horses of Death. We waited till noon, then the sea being less mountainous, quitted the Bay of Comfort and went to look for the three ships.

The *Juana* and the *San Sebastian* we presently sighted and rejoiced thereat. But the *Margarita*! We saw her nowhere, and the

Admiral's face grew gray. His son Fernando pressed close to him. "My uncle is a bold man, and they say the second seaman in the world! Let's hope and hope—and hope!"

"Why, aye!" said the Admiral. "I'm a good scholar in hope. I told them in San Domingo the ship was not seaworthy. What cared they for that? They were willing that all of my name should drown! God judge between us!"

The *Juana* came close and shouted that at eve they had seen the Adelantado in great trouble, close to shore. Then came down the night and once or twice they thought they made out a light but they were not sure.

In this West the weather after a hurricane is weather of heaven. We coasted in a high sea, but with safety under a sky one sapphire, and with a right wind,—and suddenly, rounding a palmy headland, we saw the *Margarita* riding safe in a little bay like the Bay of Comfort. The Admiral fell upon his knees.

The *Margarita* was safe indeed but was so crazed a ship! The *San Sebastian*, too, was in bad case. Hispaniola truly, but some leagues from San Domingo, and a small, desert, lonely bay! We rested here because rest we must, and mended our ships. Days—three days—a week. The Admiral and the Adelantado kept our people close to the ships. There was no Indian village, but a party sent to gather fruit found two Indians biding, watching from a thicket. These, brought to the Admiral, proved to be from a village between us and San Domingo. They had been in that town after the hurricane. It had uprooted the great tree before the Governor's house and thrown down a part of the church.

"Had the fleet sailed?"

Yes, it seemed. The day before the storm. But these men knew nothing of its fortunes. He kept the Indians with us until we sailed, so as not to spread news of where we were, then gave them presents and let them go.

But on the day we set to sail we did not sail, for along the coast and into our bay came a small caravel, going with men to our fort in Xaragua. The captain — Ruy Lopez it was — met us as a wonder, San Domingo having held that the hurricane must have sunk us, the sea swallowed us up. He anchored, took his boat and came to the Admiral upon the *Consolacion*.

"Señor, I am glad to see you living!"

"Yes, I live, Señor. Are you well in San Domingo?"

"Well in body, but sick at heart because of the fleet."

"Because of the fleet?"

"The fleet, Señor, was a day away when the hurricane burst. Half the ships were split, lost, sunken! The others, broken, returned to us. One only went on to Spain. The gold ships are lost. Only, they say, the gold that pertains to you, goes on safely on that one to Cadiz. Gwarionex the Indian is drowned, and Bobadilla and Roldan are drowned."

CHAPTER XL

The Indians called it Guanaja, but the Admiral, the Isle of Pines. It was far, far, from Hispaniola, far, far, from Jamaica, over a wide and stormy sea, reached after many days of horrible weather. Guanaja, small, lofty, covered with rich trees among which stood in numbers the pines we loved because they talked of home. To the south, far off, across leagues of water, we made out land. Mainland it seemed to us, stretching across the south, losing itself in the eastern haze. The weather suddenly became blissful. We had sweet rest in Guanaja.

A few Indians lived upon this small island, like, yet in some ways unlike all those we knew. But they were rude and simple and they talked always of gods *to the west.* We had rested a week when there came a true wonder to us *from the west.*

That was a canoe, of the mightiest length we had yet seen, long as a tall tree, eight feet wide, no less, with twenty-five rowing Indians —tall, light bronze men—with cotton cloth about their loins. Middle of this canoe was built a hut or arbor, thatched with palm. Under this sat a splendid barbarian, tall and strong, with a crown of feathers and a short skirt and mantle of cotton. Beside him sat two women wrapped in cotton mantles, and at their feet two boys and a young maid. All these people wore golden ornaments about their necks.

It was in a kind of amaze that we watched this dragon among canoes draw near to and pass the ships and to the shore where we had built a hut for the Admiral and the Adelantado and the youth Fernando, and to shelter the rest of us a manner of long booth. It seemed that it was upon a considerable voyage, and wanting water, put in here. The Guanaja Indians cried, "Yucatan! Yucatan!"

The Admiral stepped down to meet these strangers. His face glowed. Here at last was difference beyond the difference of the Paria folk!

We found that they were armed, — the newcomers. Strangely made swords of wood and flint, lances, light bucklers and *hatchets of true copper*. They were strong and fearless, and they seemed to say, "Here before us is great wonder, but wonder does not subdue our minds!"

Their language had, it is true, the flow and clink of Indian tongues, yet was greatly different. We had work to understand. But they were past masters of gesture.

The Admiral sent for presents. Again, these did not ravish, though the cacique and his family and the rowers regarded with interest such strange matters. But they seemed to say, "You yourselves and your fantastic high canoes made, it is evident, of many trees, are the wonder!"

But we, the Spaniards, searching now through ten years—long as the War of Troy—for Asia in which that Troy and all wealth beside had been placed, thought that at last we had come upon traces. In that canoe were many articles of copper, well enough wrought; a great copper bell, a mortar and pestle, hatchets and knives. Moreover in Yucatan were potters! In place of the eternal calabash here were jars and bowls of baked clay, well-made, well-shaped, marked with strange painted figures. They had pieces of cotton cloth, well-woven and great as a sail. Surely, with this stuff, before long the notion of a sail would arise in these minds! We saw cotton mantles and other articles of dress, both white and gayly dyed or figured. Clothing was not to them the brute amaze we had found it with our eastern Indians. Matters enough, strange to our experience, were being carried in that great canoe. We found they had a bread, not cassava, but made from maize, and a drink much like English ale, and also a food called cacao.

Gold! All of them wore gold, disks of it, hanging upon their breasts. The cacique had a thin band of gold across his forehead; together with a fillet of cotton it held the bright feathers of his head dress.

They traded the gold—all except the coronal and a sunlike plate upon the breast of the cacique—willingly enough.

Whence? Whence?

It seemed from Yucatan, on some embassy to another coast or island. Yucatan. West—west! And beyond Yucatan richer still; oh, great riches, gold and clothing and—we thought it from their contemptuous signs toward our booths and their fingers drawn in the air—true houses and temples.

Farther on — farther on — farther west! Forever that haunting, deluding cry—the cry that had deluded since Guanahani that we called San Salvador. Now many of our adventurers and mariners caught fire from that cacique's wide gestures. The Adelantado no less. "Cristoforo, it looks satisfaction at last!" And the young Fernando,—"Father, let us sail west!"

The Admiral was trying to come at that Strait. Earnestly, through Juan Lepe and through a Jamaican that we had with us, he strove to give and take light. Yucatan? Was there sea beyond Yucatan? Did sea like a river cut Yucatan? Might a canoe—might canoes like ours—go by it from this sea to that sea?

But nothing did we get save that Yucatan was a great country with sea here and sea there. "A point of the main like Cuba!" said the Admiral. Behind it, to the north of it, it seemed to us, the greater country where were the gold, the rich clothing, the temples. But we made out that Yucatan from sea to sea was many days' march. And as for the country beyond it, that went on, they thought, forever. They called this country Anahuac and they meant the same that years afterward Hernando Cortes found. But we did not know this. We did not know that strange people and their great treasure.

The Admiral looked out to sea. "I have cried, 'West—west—west!' through a-many years! Yucatan! But I make out no sea-passage thence into Vasco da Gama's India! And I am sworn to the Queen and King Ferdinand this time to find it. So it's south, it's south, brother and son!"

So, our casks being full, our fruit gathered, the sky clear and the wind fair, we left the west to others and sailed to find the strait in the south. When we raised our sails that dragon canoe cried out and marveled. But the cacique with the coronal asked intelligent questions. The Admiral showed him the way of it, mast and spar and sail cloth, and how we made the wind our rower. He listened, and at the last he gave Christopherus Columbus for that instruction the gold disk from his breast. I do not know—Yucatan might have gone on from that and itself developed true ship. If it had long enough time! But Europe was at its doors.

The canoe kept with us for a little, then shouted to see the fair breeze fill our sails and carry us from them.

It was mid-August. We came to a low-lying land with hills behind. Here we touched and found Indians, though none such as Yucatan seemed to breed. It was Sunday and under great trees we had mass, having with us the Franciscan Pedro of Valencia. From this place we coasted three days, when again we landed. Here the Indians were of a savage aspect, painted with black and white and yellow and uttering loud cries. We thought that they were eaters of men's flesh. Likewise they had a custom of wearing earrings of great weight, some of copper, some of that mixed gold we called guanin. So heavy were these ornaments that they pulled the ear down to mid-throat. The Admiral named this place the Coast of the Ear.

On we sailed, and on, never out of sight of land to starboard. Day by day, along a coast that now as a whole bent eastward. And yet no strait—no way through into the sea into which poured the Ganges.

CHAPTER XLI

The weather plagued us. The rains were cataracts, the lightning blinding, the thunder loud enough to wake the dead. Day after day, until this weather grew to seem a veritable Will, a Demon with a grudge against us.

The *Margarita* sailed no better; she sailed worse. The Admiral considered abandoning her, taking the Adelantado upon the *Consolacion* and dividing his crew among the three ships. But the Adelantado's pride and obstinacy and seamanship were against that. "I'll sail her, because San Domingo thinks I can!"

Stormy days and nights, and the Admiral watching. "The *Margarita*! Ho, look out! Do you see the *Margarita*?"

In the midst of foul weather came foully back the gout that crippled him. I would have had him stay in his bed. "I cannot! How do you think I can?" In the end he had us build him some kind of shelter upon deck, fastening there a bench and laying a pallet upon this. Here, propped against the wood, covered with cloaks, he still watched the sea and how went our ship and the other ships.

Day after day and day after day! Creeping eastward along a bad shore, in the teeth of the demon. The seas, the winds, the enormous rain wore us out. Men grew large-eyed. If we slept came a shriek and wakened us. We would put to land, but the wind turned and thrust us out again, or we found no harbor. We seemed to be fixed in one place while time rushed by us.

Forecastle began to say, "It is enchantment!" Presently stern echoed it. The boy Fernando brought it to his father. "Alonso de Zamorra and Bernardo the Apothecary say that demons and witches are against us."

"The Prince of the Power of the Air!" said the Admiral. "It may be, child! Paynimry against Christianity. We had a touch of the same quality once off Cuba. But is it, or is it not, Christian men shall win! And send me Bartholomew Fiesco. Such talk is injury. It bores men's courage worse than the *teredo* a ship's bottom!"

We thought the foul weather would never cease, and our toil would never cease—then lo! at the point of despair the sky cleared with a great clap of light, the coast turned sharply, sheerly south—he named the great cape, Cape Gracias a Dios—and we ran freely, West again.

Coming in three days to a wide river mouth, in we turned. The shore was grown with reeds that would do for giants' staffs. On mud banks we saw the crocodile, "cayman" they call it. Again the sky hung a low, gray roof; a thin wind whistled, but for all that it was deathly hot. Seeing no men, we sent two boats with Diego Mendez up the stream. They were not gone a half league, when, watching from the *Consolacion* we marked a strange and horrid thing. There came without wind a swelling of the sea. Our ships tossed as in tempest, and there entered the river a wall of sea water. Meeting the outward passing current, there ensued a fury with whirlpools. It caught the boats. Diego Mendez saved his, but the other was seized, tossed and engulfed. Eight men drowned.

The thing sank as it had come. The River of Disaster, we named it, and left this strip of coast that was to us gloomy and portentous. *"Wizardry! It's not to be lucky, this voyage."* It was now late September.

Next day, we anchored, it being most clear and beautiful. We lay beside a verdurous islet, between it and a green shore. Here were all our fruits, and we thought we smelled cinnamon and clove. Across, upon the main, stood a small village. *Cariari* the Indians there called themselves. They had some gold, but not to touch that canoe from Yucatan. Likewise they owned a few cotton mantles, with jars of baked clay, and we saw a copper hatchet. But they did not themselves make these things. They had drifted to them, we thought, from a people far more skilled.

The Admiral cried, "When and when and when shall we come to this people?"

I answered, "I tell you what is in my mind, and I have got it, I think, from your inmost mind, out of which you will not let it come forth because you have had a great theory and think you must stand to it. But what if this that you have underneath is a greater one? What if the world truly is larger than Alfraganus or the ancients thought? What if all this that we have found since the first island and that means only beginnings of what is to be found; what if it is not Asia at all? What if it is a land mass, great as Europe or greater, that no one knew anything of? What if over by the sunset there is Ocean-Sea again, true ocean and as many leagues to Asia as to Spain? What if they cannot lead us to Quinsai, Cambaluc or Zaiton, or to the Ganges' mouth, or Aurea Chersonesus, because they never heard of them, and they have no ships to pass again an Ocean-Sea? What if it is all New, and all the maps have to be redrawn?"

He looked at me as I spoke, steadily and earnestly. What Juan Lepe said was not the first entry into his mind of something like that. But he was held by that great mass of him that was bound by the thinking of the Venerable. He was free far and far beyond most, but to certain things he clung like a limpet. "The Earthly Paradise!" he said, and he looked toward that Paria that we thought ran across our south. "When our first parents left the Earthly Paradise, they and their sons and daughters and all the peoples to come wandered by foot into Chaldea and Arabia. So it could not be!" His blue-gray eyes under that great brow and shock of white hair regarded the south.

This færy island — the Garden he called it — and the Cariari who came to us from the main. One day they saw one of us take out pen and inkhorn and write down their answers to our many questions. Behind us lay the blue sea, before us the deep groves of the islet; between us and the rich shade stood gathered a score of these Indians. They looked at the one seated on the sand, industriously making black marks upon a white sheet. The Indian speaking stopped short and put up an arm in an attitude of defense; another minute and they had all backed from us into the wood. We saw only excited, huddled eyes. Then one started forth, advancing over the sand, and he had a small gourd filled with some powder which he threw before him. He scattered it ceremonially between us and himself and his fellows, a slow, measured rite with muttered words and now and then a sharp, rising note.

Cried Juan Sanchez the pilot, "What's he doing?"

Juan Lepe answered before he thought, "He thinks the notary yonder is a magician and the pen his wand. Something is being done to them! Counter-magic."

"Then they are enchanters!" cried Alonso de Zamorro.

Our great cluster gave back. "Fix an arrow and shoot him down!" That was Diego de Porras.

The Adelantado turned sharply. "Do no such thing! There may be spells, but the worst spell here would be a battle!" We let fly no arrow, but the belief persisted that here was seen veritably at work the necromancy that all along they had guessed.

A party crossed to the main with the Adelantado and pushed a league into as tall and thick and shadowy a forest as ever we met in all our wanderings. Here we found no village, but came suddenly, right in the wood, upon a very great thatched hut, and in it, upon a stone, lay in state a dead cacique. He seemed long dead, but the body had not corrupted; it was saved by some knowledge such as had the Egyptians. A crown of feathers rested upon the head and gold was about the neck. Around the place stood posts and slabs of a dark wood and these were cut and painted with I do not know what of beast and bird and monstrous idol forms. We stared. The place was shadowy and very silent. At last with an oath said Francisco de Porras, "Take the gold!" But the Adelantado cried, "No!" and going out of the hut that was almost a house we left the dead cacique and his crown and mantle and golden breastplate. Two wooden figures at the door grinned upon us. We saw now what seemed a light brown powder strewed around and across the threshold. One of our men, stooping, took up a pinch then dropped it hastily. "It is the same they threw against us!"

"Wizardry! We'll find harm from them yet!" That song crept in now at every turn.

We sailed from the Garden south by east along the endless coast that no strait broke. At first fair weather ran with us. But the *Margarita* was so lame! And all our other ships wrenched and worm-pierced. And the Admiral was growing old before our eyes. Not his mind or his soul but his frame.

He bettered, left his bed and walked the deck. And then we came to the coast we called the Golden Coast, and his hope spread great wings again, and if our mariners talked of magic it was for a time glistening white.

Gold, gold! A deep bay, thronged at the mouth with islets so green and fair, they were marvel to us who were sated with islands great and small. We entered under overhanging trees, and out at once to us shot twenty canoes. The Indians within wore gold in amount and purity far beyond anything in ten years. Oh, our ships could scarce contain their triumph! The Admiral looked a dreamer who comes to the bliss center in his dream. Gold was ever to him symbol and mystery. He did not look upon it as a buyer of strife and envy, idleness and soft luxury; but as a buyer of crusades, ships and ships, discoveries and discoveries, and Christ to enter heathendom.

Gold! Discs of great size, half-moons, crescent moons, pierced for a cotton string. Small golden beasts and birds, poorly carved but golden. They traded freely; we gathered gold. And there was more and more, they said, at Veragua, wherever that might be, and south and east it seemed to be.

Veragua! We would go there. Again we hoisted sail and in our ships, now all unseaworthy, crept again in a bad wind along the coast of gold,—Costa Rico. At last we saw many smokes from the land. That would be a large Indian village. We beat toward it, found a river mouth and entered. But Veragua must have heard of us from a swift land traveler. When a boat from each ship would approach the land—it was in the afternoon, the sun westering fast—a sudden burst of a most melancholy and awful din came from the forest growing close to water side.

One of our men cried "Wizards!" The Admiral spoke from the stern of the long boat. "And what if they be wizards? We may answer, 'We are Christians!' "

The furious din continued but now we were nearer. "Besides," he said, "those are great shells and drums."

Our rowers held off. Out of the forest on to the narrow beach started several hundred shell-blowing, drum-beating barbarians, marvelously feathered and painted and with bows and arrows and wooden swords.

An arrow stuck in the side of our boat, others fell short. The Admiral rose, tall, broad-shouldered, though lean as winter where there is winter, with hair as white as milk. He held in his hand a string of green beads and another of hawk bells which he made to ring, but he did not depend more upon them than upon what he held within him of powerful and pacific. He sent his voice, which he could make deep as a drum and reaching as one of those great shells. "Friends—friends! Bringing Christ!"

An arrow sang past him. His son would have drawn him down, but, "No—no!" and "Friends—friends! Bringing Christ!"

And whether they thought that "Christ" was the beads and the bell, or whether the bowman in him did send over good will and make it to enter their hearts, or whether it was somewhat of both, they did suddenly grow friendly. Whereupon we landed.

Gold! We took much gold from this place. One of our men, touched by the sun, sat and babbled. "Oh, the faithful golden coast! Oh, the gold that is to come! Great golden ships sailing across blue sea! A hundred—no, a thousand—what do I say? A million Indians with baskets long and wide on their backs and the baskets filled with gold! The baskets are so great and the gold so heavy that the Indians are bowed down till they go on all fours. Gold,—a mountain of pure gold and every Spaniard in Spain and a few Italians—golden kings—" When we had all we could get, up sail and on!

Sail on and on along the golden coast of Veragua! Come to a river and land, for all that again we heard drums and those great shells strongly blown. Make peace and trade. And here again was gold, gold, gold. We were now assured that the main was far richer than any island. Turbulent hope,—that was the chief lading now of the four ships. Gold! Gold! Golden moon disks and golden rude figures. We found a lump of gold wrought like a maize ear.

What was beyond that, by itself under trees, we found an ancient, broken, true wall, stone and lime. The stones were great ones, set truly, with care. The wall was old; the remainder of house, if house or temple there had been, broken from it. Now the forest overran all. We did not know when or by whom it was built, and we found no more like it. But here was true masonry. All of us said that the world of the main was not the world of the islands.

Ciguarre. These Indians declared it was Ciguarre we should seek. Now that we were in Veragua—seek Ciguarre.

So we sailed beyond Veragua hunting the strait which we must pass through to Ganges and Ind of old history.

Chapter XLII

Puerto Bello!

Beautiful truly, and a harbor where might ride a navy.

But no gold; and now came back very evilly the evil weather. Seven days a blast rocked us. We strained eyes to see if the *Margarita* yet lived. The *San Sebastian* likewise was in trouble. No break for seven days. It was those enchanters of Cariari—magic asleep for a while but now awake!

Storm. And two ships nigh to foundering. When wind sank and blue came back, we left Puerto Bello and turned again south by east, but now with crazy, crazy ships, weather-wrenched and worm-eaten, *teredo* pierced. They looked old, so old, with their whipped and darkened sails.

And when we dropped anchor in some bight there was no gold, but all night we heard that harsh blowing of shells and the beating of drums.

Francisco and Diego de Porras, Alonso de Zamorra, Pedro de Villetoro, Bernardo the Apothecary and others, the most upon the *Consolacion*, others on the *Margarita* and the *Juana*, now began to brew mutiny.

We sailed on, and upon this forlorn coast we met no more gold. Our ships grew so worn that now at any threat in the sky we must look and look quickly for harborage, be it good or indifferent bad. To many of us the coast now took on a wicked look. It was deep in November.

No gold. These Indians—how vast anyhow was India?—were hostile, not friendly. Our ships were dying, manifestly. If they sank under us and we drowned, the King and Queen—if the Queen still lived—never would come to know that Christopherus Columbus had found Veragua thrice more golden even than Paria! Found Veragua, met men of Yucatan; and heard of Ciguarre.

At last not only the mutinous but steadfast men cried, "If there is a strait it is too far with these ships!"

For a time he was obstinate. *It must be found,—it must be found!* But one night there fell all but loss of the Margarita. When next he slept he had a dream. "The good Queen came to me and she had in her hand a picture of five stout ships. Out of her lips came a singing voice. 'Master Christopherus, Master Christopherus, these wait for you, riding in Cadiz harbor! But now will you slay your son and your brother and all your men?' Then she said, 'The strait is hidden for a while,' and went."

That day we turned. "We will go back to Veragua and lade with gold, and then we'll sail to Jamaica and to Hispaniola where this time we shall be welcome! Then to Spain where the Queen will give me a stronger fleet."

Our ships hailed the turning. Even the Adelantado, even Diego Mendez and Juan Sanchez and Bartholomew Fiesco who were of the boldest drew long breath as of men respited from death.

Not so many have known and lived to tell of such weather as now we met and in it rolled from wave to wave through a long month.

Would we put to land we were beaten back. We had never seen such waves, and at times they glowed with cold fire. The sea with the wind twisted, danced and shouted. We were deaf with thunder and blind with lightning. When the rain descended, it was as though an upper ocean were coming down. A little surcease, then return of the tempest, like return of Polyphemus. Men died from drowning, and, I think, from pure fright. One day the clouds drove down, the sea whirled up. There was made a huge water column, a moving column that fast grew larger. Crying out, our sailors flung themselves upon their knees. It passed us with a mighty sound, and we were not engulfed.

The Admiral said, "God tries us, but he will not destroy us utterly!"

The boy Fernando, in a moment's wild terror who was ordinarily courageous as any, clung to him. "O my son! I would that you were in La Rabida, safe beside Fray Juan Perez! My son and my brother Bartholomew!"

Now came to us all scarcity of food and a misery of sickness. Now two thirds would have mutinied had we not been going back—but we were going back—creeping, crawling back as the tempest would allow us.

Christmas! We remembered our first Christmas in this world, by Guarico in Hispaniola, when the *Santa Maria* sank. Again we found a harbor, and we lay there between dead and alive, until early January. We sailed and on Epiphany Day entered a river that we knew to be in golden Veragua. The Admiral called it the Bethlehem.

Gold again, gold! Not on the Bethlehem, but on the river of Veragua, not far away, to which the Admiral sent the Adelantado and two long boats filled with our stoutest men. They brought back gold, gold, gold!

The cacique of these parts was Quibian, a barbarian whom at the last, not the first, we concluded to be true brother of Caonabo.

With threescore of our strongest, the Adelantado pushed again up the river of Veragua, too rough and shallow for our ships. He visited Quibian; he traded for gold; he was taken far inland and from a hill observed a country of the noblest, vale and mountain and Indian smokes. The mountains, the Indians said, were packed with gold. He brought back much gold, Indians bearing it for him in deep baskets that they made.

Quibian paid us a visit, looked sullenly around, and left us. Not in the least was he Guacanagari! But neither, quite yet, did he turn into Caonabo.

The Admiral sat pondering, his hands before him between his knees, his gray-blue eyes looking further than the far mountains. Later, on the shore, he and the Adelantado walked up and down under palm trees. The crews watched them, knowing they were planning.

What they planned came forth the next day, and it was nothing short of a colony, a settlement upon the banks of the river Bethlehem. Christopherus Columbus spoke—tall, powerful, gaunt, white-headed, gray-eyed, trusted because he himself so trusted, suasive, filled with the power of his vision. His frame was growing old, but he himself stayed young. His voice never grew old, nor the gray-blue light from his eyes. Here was gold at last, and Veragua manifestly richer than all Hispaniola; aye, richer than Paria! Behind Veragua ran Ciguarre that was fabulously rich, that was indeed India sloping to Ganges. The Indians were friendly enough for all their drum-beating and shell-blowing. Quibian's first frowning aspect had been but aspect. A scarlet cloak and a sack full of toys had made all right. There was rest on land, with fruit and maize as we saw. Build a fort—leave a ship—divide our force. A half would rest here, first settlers of a golden country with all first settlers' advantage. Half sail with Christopherus Columbus back to Spain—straight to Spain—for supplies and men. He would return, he swore it, with all speed. A ship should be left, and beyond the ship, the Adelantado. It was for volunteers for the fortress and city of Veragua!

In the end eighty men said "We will stay." We began to build. How long since we had built La Navidad!

The River Bethlehem, that had been full when we entered, now was half empty of its waters. The *Consolacion*, the *Juana*, and the *San Sebastian* that were to depart for Spain could not pass. The Admiral hung, fitted to go, but waiting perforce for rains that should lift the ships so they might pass the bar.

Again Juan Lepe was to stay—so surely would the staying need a physician.

"It is March," said the Admiral. "God aiding, I and Fernando shall be back in October at latest."

These Indians seemed to us to have Carib markings. Yet they all professed amity and continuously brought in gold. We began to build by the fort a storehouse for much gold.

Suddenly we found—Diego Mendez, bold enough and a great wanderer, doing the finding—that Quibian's village up the river of Veragua contained many too, many young men and men in their prime, and that by day and night these continued to pour in. It had —Diego Mendez thought—much the aspect of a camp whose general steadily received re-enforcement.

Next day came to the Admiral an Indian who betrayed his people. Quibian never meant to have in Veragua a swarm of white caciques! When he had about him every young man, he was coming, coming, coming through the woods!

The Admiral sent the Adelantado. That strong man chose four-score Spaniards, armed them and departed. By boat and through thick forest he reached Quibian's village, descended upon it like a hurricane and seized Quibian, much as long ago—long, long ago it seemed to us—Alonso de Ojeda had seized Caonabo.

Juan Sanchez the pilot held Quibian in the long boat while the Adelantado still wrought upon the land. Juan Sanchez was strong and wary, and watchful; so they swore were all the Spaniards in the boat. Yet when night was fallen that Indian, bound as he was, broke with a shout from them all and leaped from boat into black river.

They thought he perished, seeing him no more for all their moving about and bringing the boat to the land. Juan Sanchez was certain he sank, bound as he was. With other captives and with a great mass of golden ornaments, came back to the ships the Adelantado. The Indian camp was broken, dispersed.

The rains began to fall. The river swelled; the fort and store place and other houses were builded.

The eighty who were to stay and the something under that number who were to go prepared to say farewell. We went to mass under three palm trees, before our fort on the river Bethlehem. That over, those who were to go went aboard the three ships, and the sails were made, and they began to sing as they passed down the Bethlehem. The *Margarita* and we watched their going.

They went a league, and then another—we thought they were wholly gone. But out of the river, though the skies were clear, again rushed against them an enemy wind. They lay at anchor in river mouth, waiting on propitiousness. But we, up the river, thought they were gone. That night, before dawn, Quibian attacked us.

We had several killed, and the Adelantado was hurt in the breast, and many others had their wounds. But we thundered with our cannon and we loosed two bloodhounds and we charged. For a time the brown, naked foe fought desperately, but at last he broke. Far streamed five hundred fleeing particles into the gloomy, the deep, the matted forest. Up the river came a long boat, and we found it to hold Diego Tristan and eight men sent by the Admiral with a forgotten word for the Adelantado. Much we rejoiced that the ships were not clean gone!

Diego Tristan took our news. The Adelantado—his hurt was slight—wrote again to the Admiral. Again we said farewell to Diego Tristan. The long boat passed a turn in the Bethlehem; out of our sight. Once we thought we heard a faint and distant shouting, but there was no telling. But in five hours there staggered into fort Juan de Noya who alone lived of that boatful, set upon by Quibian. Diego Tristan dead, and seven men.

All that night we heard in the wood those throbbing Indian drums and wild-blowing shells.

They were Caribs, now we were sure, and Quibian lived and preached a holy war. Though we had driven them off, we heard them mustering again. If we could not get food—perhaps not water?

Sixty of ours came to the Adelantado. In truth, all might have come, for massacre, slow or swift, was certain if we stayed in Veragua. I read that the Adelantado, who was never accused of cowardice or fickleness, was himself determined. The settlement below the golden mines of golden Veragua must wait a little.

We took our wounded and with the Adelantado, turned Mars in these three days, came down to the Bethlehem, to a pebbly shore from which the water had shrunken. Here at least was our ship with us, and the river that bore to the sea. Here, for the weather was ferocious and Quibian howling around us, we built what shelter we might. Here in much misery we waited days for the long and wild storm to cease. We hoped the Admiral was yet at the mouth of the Bethlehem, but could not do more than hope.

Then came through every peril that might be Pedro Ledesma, from the ships. They waited! Break through—come down!

The *Margarita* could never pass the bar that now the falling water left exposed. We made rafts, we dismantled her and took what we could; we left her in Veragua for Quibian to walk her deck and sail her if he might. Through danger in multitude, with our rafts and two boats, with the loss of six men, we went down the Bethlehem. Some of ours wept when they saw the ships, and the Admiral wept when he and the Adelantado met.

Away from Veragua!

Is it only the Spaniards who suffer, and for what at the last, not at the first, did Quibian fight? In that strong raid when we thought Quibian perished had been taken captive brothers and kinsmen of that cacique. These were prisoned upon the *Juana*, to be taken to Spain, shown, made Christian, perhaps sold, perhaps—who knows? —returned to their land, but never to freedom.

While the *Juana* tossed where Bethlehem met the sea, these Indians broke in the night time up through hatchway and made for the side to throw themselves over. But the watch gave a great cry and sprang upon them, and other Spaniards came instantly. All but two were retaken. These two, wrenching themselves free, sprang away into rough water and dark night, and it is most likely that they drowned, being a mile from shore. But the others were thrust back and down under hatch which then was chained so that they might not again lift it. But in the morning when the captain of the *Juana* went to look, all, all were dead, having hanged themselves.

CHAPTER XLIII

We left one of our ships in the Bethlehem and we lost another upon this disastrous coast before we got clear for Jamaica.

We were sea specters. We had saved our men from the *San Sebastian* as from the *Margarita*. Now all were upon the *Consolacion* and the *Juana*. Fifty fewer were we than when we had sailed from Cadiz, yet the two ships crept over-full. And they were like creatures overcome with eld. Beaten, crazed, falling apart.

On the Eve of Saint John we came to Jamaica.

The ships were riddled by the *teredo*. We could not keep afloat to go to Hispaniola. At Santa Gloria we ran them in quiet water side by side upon the sand. They partly filled, they settled down, only forecastle and stern above the blue mirror. We built shelters upon them and bridged the space between. The ocean wanderers were turned into a fort.

Jamaica, we thanked all the saints, was a friendly land. They brought us cassava and fruit, these Indians; they swarmed about us in their canoes. The gods in trouble, yet still the gods!

We were forty leagues from Hispaniola, and we had no ship!

Again there volunteered Diego Mendez. We ourselves had now but one Christian boat. But there existed canoes a-plenty. Chose one, with six Indians to row! Leave Diego Mendez with one other Spaniard of his choice to cross the sea between us and Hispaniola, get to San Domingo, rouse all Christian men, even Don Nicholas de Ovanda, procure a large ship or two smaller ones, return with rescue!

We sent off Diego Mendez with strong farewells and blessings. The vast blue sea and air withdrew and covered from sight the canoe.

A week—two weeks. Grew out of the azure a single canoe, and approached.

"Diego Mendez—Diego Mendez!"

It was he alone, with a tale to tell of storm and putting ashore and capture after battle by Jamaicans no longer friendly, and of escape alone. But he would go again if so be he might have with him Bartholomew Fiesco. They went, with heavily paid Indians to row the staunchest canoe we could find. This time the Adelantado with twenty kept them company along the shore to end of the island, where the canoe shot forth into clear sea, and the blue curtain came down between the stranded and the going for help. The Adelantado returned to us, and we waited. The weeks crept by.

Great heat and sickness, and the Indians no longer prompt to bring us supplies. Sooner or later, each of these dark peoples found a Quibian or Caonabo.

The most of us determined that Diego Mendez and Fiesco and their canoe were lost. Hispaniola knew nothing of us—nothing, nothing! Suddenly the two Porras brothers led a mad mutiny. "Leave these rotting ships—seize the canoes we need—all of us row or swim to Hispaniola!"

There were fifty who thought thus. The Admiral withstood them with strong words, with the reasoning of a master seaman, and the counsel now—his white and long hair, and eld upon him—of Jacob or Isaac or Abraham. But they would not, and they would not, and at last they departed from us, taking—but the Admiral gave them freely—the dozen canoes that we had purchased, crowding into these, rowing away with cries from that sea fortress, melancholy indeed, in the blinding light.

They vanished. The next day fair, the next a mad storm. Two weeks, and news came of them. They were not nigh to Hispaniola; wrecked, they lost five men, but got, the rest of them, to land, where they now roved from village to village. Another week, and the Indians who came to us and whom we kept friendly, related with passionate and eloquent word and gesture evils that that band was working. Pedro Margarite—Roldan—over and over again!

After much of up and down those mutineers came back to us.

They could not do without us; they could not get to Hispaniola in Indian canoes. The Admiral received them fatherly.

No sail—no sail. Long months and no sail. Surely Diego Mendez and Bartholomew Fiesco were drowned! Hispaniola, if it thought of us at all, might think us now by Ganges. Or as lost at sea.

Christopherus Columbus dreamed again, or had a vision again. "I was hopeless. I wept alone on a desert shore. My name had faded, and all that I had done was broken into sand and swept away. I repined, and cried, 'Why is it thus?' Then came a ship not like ours, and One stepped from it in light and thunder. 'O man of little faith, I will cover thy eyes of today!' He covered them, and I *saw*. And now, Juan Lepe, I care not! We will all come Home, whether or no the wave covers us here."

To mariners and adventurers he said at no time any word of despair. He said, "A ship will come! For if—which the saints forfend —Bartholomew Fiesco and Diego Mendez have not reached San Domingo, yet come at last will some craft to Jamaica! From our island or from Spain. How many times since '92 has there been touching here? Of need now it will be oftener and oftener!"

But still many pined with hope deferred. And then, out of the blue, arose first Diego de Escobar's small ship, and later the two good ships sent by Don Nicholas de Ovando.

The Admiral of the Ocean-Sea lodged in the Governor's house in San Domingo. Who so courteous as Don Nicholas, saving only Don Cristoval?

Juan Lepe found certain ones and his own eyes to tell him of island fortunes. Here was Sancho, a bearded man, and yet looked out the youth who had walked from Fishertown to Palos strand. "Oh, aye! San Domingo's growing! It's to be as great as Seville, with cathedral and fortress and palace. White men build fast, though not so fast as the Lord!"

"The Governor?"

"Oh, he makes things spin! He's hard on the Indians—but then they've surely given us trouble!"

He told of new forts and projected towns and an increasing

stream of ships, from Spain to Spain again. "We're here to stay—as long as there's a rock of gold or anything that can be turned into gold! The old bad times are over—and that old, first simple joy, too, Doctor!—Maybe we'll all ship for Ciguarre."

But no. The colony now was firm, with thousands of Spaniards where once had stood fivescore. Luis Torres sat with me and he told me of Indian war,—of Anacaona hanged and Cotubanama hanged, of eighty caciques burned or hanged, of *peace* at last. Now the Indians worked the mines, and scraped the sands of every stream, and likewise planted cotton and maize for the conquerors. They were gathered in *repartimentios, encomiendas*, parceled out, so many to every Spaniard with power. The old word "gods" had gone out of use. "Master" was now the plain and accurate term.

The Governor was a shrewd, political, strong man,—not without his generosities to white men. But no dreamer! He put down faction, but there was now less faction to put down. All had been united in mastering the Indian, and now with peace the getting of wealth was regularized. He had absolutely the ear of King Ferdinand, and help from Spain whenever he called for it. Yes, he was fairly liked by the generality. And had I noticed the growth in cowls and processions? Mother Church was moving in.

The next day I met again Bartolomé de Las Casas. September now—and a ship from Spain, bringing the news that the Queen was ill. There was another who was ill, and that was the Admiral of the Ocean-Sea:

"I must go—and we quarrel here, this Governor-in-my-place and I—I must go, rest at La Rabida with you, Doctor, and Fray Juan Perez to help me. Then I must go to court and see the Queen."

The Adelantado said, "Both you and the Queen will get well. What, brother, your voyages are just begun! But let us sail now for Spain. I think well of that."

And the son Fernando, Yes, yes, let us go home, father, and see Diego!

CHAPTER XLIV

It was Seville, and an inn there, and the Admiral of the Ocean-Sea laid in a fair enough room. His gout manacled him, and another sickness crept upon him, but he could think, talk and write, and at times, for serenity and a breath of pleasure, read. He was ever a reader.

About him, all day long, came people. They called themselves friends, and many were friends. But some used that holy word for a robber-mask. Others were the idlest wonder-seekers, never finding wonder within, always rushing for it without. His heart, for all his much experience, or perhaps because of that, was a simple heart. He took them for what they said they were, for friends, and he talked of the Indies and all his voyages past and to come, for he would yet find Ciguarre and retake the Sepulchre.

He had not much money. All his affairs were tangled. Yet he rested Admiral of the Ocean-Sea, and in name, at least, Viceroy of the Indies. He was much concerned over his mariners and others who had returned with him to Spain. All their pay was in arrears. He wrote begging letters for them, and with his sons forever in his mind, for himself. Don Diego, Don Fernando, they were pleasant, able youths.

Fray Juan Perez came to Seville. He was worldly comfort, but ghostly comfort too. The Admiral talked of Ciguarre and Jerusalem, but also now of the New Jerusalem and the World-to-come.

Late in November, at Medina del Campo Santo died the Queen!

He told me a dream or a vision that day. There was, he said, a fair, tranquil shore, back of a fair, blue haven, and his wife and his mother, long dead, walked there in talk. Back of the shore rose, he said, a city with wonderful strong walls and towers and a perpetual sweet ringing of church bells. It seemed to climb to one great palace and church, set about with orchards, with many doves. The whole mounted like Monsalvat. The city seemed to be ready for someone. They were hanging out tapestries and weaving garlands and he heard musicians. Everywhere shone a light of gladness. He returned to the seashore, and walking with his wife and mother, asked them about the city. They said that it was the Queen's City. Then, he said, he seemed to hear trumpets, and far on the horizon made out a sail. Then city and shore and all were gone, and it was dark, starry night, and he was in the Azores, alone, with a staff in his hand that he had drawn from the sea.

It was Fray Juan Perez who brought him news of her death. "Queen Isabella," he quietly said, and turned to the wall and lay there praying.

One day there came to see him Amerigo Vespucci, who sailing with Ojeda, knew Paria. They talked of that Vastness to the south. The Venetian thought it might be a continent wholly unknown alike to the ancients and the moderns. "Known," answered the Genoese, "in the far, far past! But unknown, I grant, for so long that it has become again new. All a New World."

"How should we map it?" said the other. "Faith of God! I should like to see the maps a hundred years from now!"

He had something to say of Sebastian Cabot who was finding northward for King Henry of England. But laying a fine small hand upon the Admiral's mighty one, he called him "*magister et dominus*, Christopherus Columbus."

Winter wore away. With the spring he seemed to be better in health. He left his bed. But the physician, Juan Lepe, believed that ports and havens, new lands, and service of an order above this order were even now coloring and thrilling within.

When all spring was singing high, the Admiral, having had a letter from the king, said he would go to court. His sons would have had him travel in a litter, but he waved that away. The Adelantado procured him a mule, and with his sons and brother and a small train beside he started, the King being at Segovia. He had a hardly scraped together purse of gold, and all his matters seemed dejected. Yet his family riding with him rode as nobles of Spain, and his son, Don Diego, should one day become Governor of Hispaniola. Earthly speaking, for all his feeling "All is vain!" he had made his family. Unlike many families so made, this one was grateful.

On the road to Segovia, stayings, restings and meetings were cordial enough to him, for here flocked the people to see the Discoverer. If they heard his voice they were happy; if some bolder one had a moment's speech with him that fortunate went off with the air of, "My children's children shall know of this!" There returned in this springtide travel sunniness, halcyon weather, bright winds of praise. The last health of the present body was his upon this journey. Health and strength harked back. All noted it. Jayme de Marchena held it for the leap of the flame before sinking, before leaving the frame of this world. But his sons and Don Bartholomew cried, "Why, father, why, brother, you will outlive us yet!"

He rode firmly; he looked about with bright, blue-gray eyes; his voice had the old, powerful thrill. It was happiness to him when the simple came crowding, or when in some halt he talked with two or three or with a solitary. The New Lands and the Vast Change, and it would affect all our life, this way, that way and the other way.

But when we came to Segovia, the King was dead, not alive, to Christopherus Columbus. Not dead to the Indies, no! But dead to their old discoverer. We had chilly weather, miserable, and all the buds of promise went back. Or rather there were promises, cold smiles, but even he, the Genoese, saw at last that these buds were *simulacra*, never meant to bloom.

The Queen was gone. The Court wore the King's color. Then the King went to Laredo to meet his daughter Juana, who was now Queen of Castile. With him went all of importance. Segovia became a dull and somewhat hostile water where rode at last anchor the ship of the Admiral.

CHAPTER XLV

Don Fernando met me at the door. "He is wandering—he thinks he is in Cordova with my mother." He came from that and said he would get up and go to mass. Persuaded to lie quiet, he talked of his will, drawn before his third voyage, and said that he would have it read to him, and make a codicil.

This will. It ran at length through preamble and body.

"In the name of the most Holy Trinity who revealed it to me that I could sail westward across Ocean-Sea,—

"As it pleased God, in the year one thousand, four hundred and ninety-two, I discovered the Continent of the Indies and many islands. I returned to Cadiz to their Majesties who allowed my going a second voyage, and in this God gave me victory over the island of Hispaniola, which covers six hundred leagues, and I conquered it and made it tributary; and I discovered many islands dwelled in by Caribals or eaters of men's flesh, and also Jamaica which I named Santiago, and three hundred and thirty leagues of Continent from south to west—"

He recited his rights, dignities, tithes, emoluments,—"whereto I have the sacred word of the Sovereigns." Then came the heirship. All upon Don Diego and the heirs of his body, with lavish provision for the younger son, "having great qualities and most dear to me," and for the brothers, but more especially the Adelantado. Followed gifts to friends and companions, and then far-flung benefactions.

Son and son's son must give, year following year, a tenth of revenue from the Indies to the help of needy men.

"In the city of Genoa in Italy is to be maintained a man and his wife of the line of our family of which he is to be the root in that city, from whence all good may derive unto her, for I was born there and came from thence."

The taking of the Sepulchre. Into the Bank of Saint George in Genoa, "that noble and potent city" was to be put what moneys could be saved and collected for the purpose, "and one day God will bring the purpose about."

His heirs must support the Crown of Spain, "seeing that these Sovereigns, next to God, are responsible for my achieving the property, though true it is that I came into this country to invite them to the enterprise, and that a long while passed before they allowed me to execute it, but this should not surprise us as it was an undertaking of which all the world was ignorant and no one had any faith in it." And if schism arose in Christendom, his heirs must to their uttermost support His Holiness the Pope, and give all and die, if need be, defending the Church of God. And, where it was possible and not contrary to the service and the claims of the Sovereigns of Spain, "let them give aid and service to that noble city of Genoa from which we all spring."

Such and such moneys, accruing, were to be applied to making fit marriages for the daughters of the line.

And let Don Diego his son build in the island of Hispaniola a church and call it Santa Maria de la Concepcion, a church and a hospital and a chapel where masses might be said for the good of the soul of Christopherus Columbus. "Doubtless God will be pleased to give us revenue enough for this and all purposes." And let them maintain in the island of Hispaniola four good teachers of theology to convert to the One Faith the inhabitants of the Indies, "to which end no expense should be thought too considerable."

Many other things he provided for. He cared for that Dona Beatrix who had given him Fernando. Where he had met kindness, there he gave as best he might. Among other small bequests was a silver mark to a poor Jew who had done him service, who lived at the gate of the Ghetto in Lisbon. He gave to many, and closed his will and signed it with his signet letters and below these, EL ALMIRANTE.

After this there came a second leap of the flame. Queen Juana was with her husband, King Phillip, in Laredo,—Queen of Castile as had been the good Queen her mother. The Admiral, utterly revering the Queen who was gone, wrote to the daughter Queen a stately letter of high comfort and offer and promise of service. He would have the Adelantado, no less a man, bear this to Laredo. Don Bartholomew spoke aside to Juan Lepe. "If I do as he wished, I do not know if I will see him again."

"I do not know," I answered. "But his heart is set on . . ."

"Then I will go," he said. "And many's the time I have thought, 'I shall never see him again', and still we met."

For several days after this I thought that after all he might recover. Perhaps even sail again on earthly discoveries. Then, in a night, came the unmistakable stroke upon the door.

He sank, and knew now that he was putting off the body. Fray Juan Perez stayed beside him. His sons and his brother Diego waited with reddened eyes. It was full May, and the bland wind strayed in and out of window and fluttered his many papers upon the great table. It was toward evening of Ascension Day. His son Fernando threw himself on the bed, weeping. The Admiral's great hand fell upon the youth's head. He looked to the window and said clearly, "A light—yonder is a light!" and after a moment, "In manus tuas Domine coinmendo spiritum meum."

The sea by Palos and June in Andalusia. Juan Lepe, staying at La Rabida, walked along the sands and saw Life like a mighty, breathing picture. He stood by the sea and the ripples broke at his feet, and he felt and knew the Master of Life, there where feeling and knowing pass into Being.

He walked a mile beside Ocean-Sea, then sat down beneath ridged sand with the wind singing over. It sang, *Where now, Jayme de Marchena—where now—where now*?

I sat still. Spain rose behind me, Spain and Europe. Before me, out of sea, lifted the New Lands. There fell a moment of great calm and quiet. Then, fleeting, like a spirit, passed before me the Indian

Guarin who had saved me after La Navidad. I saw his dark eyes, then he went. Still space without color or line or form, and outside, dreamily, dreamily, the ocean sounding below La Rabida. Then, in the clear field rose Bartolomé de Las Casas. A quiet, singing voice ran through Jayme de Marchena, and he knew that he would return to Hispaniola and link his life with that younger life which apparently had work to do in the Indies.

THE END

Bibliography

The Prisoners of Hope: A Tale of Colonial Virginia (1898) Boston: Houghton Mifflin; as *The Old Dominion*, London: Constable, 1899.

To Have and to Hold (1900) Boston: Houghton Mifflin; as *By Order of the Company*, London: Constable.

Audrey (1902) Boston: Houghton Mifflin; London: Constable.

Sir Mortimer (1904) New York: Harper; London: Constable.

Lewis Rand (1908) Boston: Houghton Mifflin; London: Constable.

The Long Roll (1911) Boston: Houghton Mifflin.

Cease Firing (1912) Boston: Houghton Mifflin; London: Constable.

Hagar (1913) Boston: Houghton Mifflin; London: Constable.

The Witch (1914) Boston: Houghton Mifflin; London: Constable.

The Fortunes of Garin (1915) Boston: Houghton Mifflin; London: Constable.

Foes (1918) New York: Harper; as *The Laird of Glenfernie*, London: Constable, 1919.

Michael Forth (1919) New York: Harper; London: Constable, 1920.

Sweet Rocket (1920) New York: Harper; London: Constable.

Silver Cross (1922) Boston: Little Brown; London: Butterworth.

1492 (1922) Boston: Little Brown; as *Admiral of the Ocean-Sea*, London: Butterworth, 1923.

Croatan (1923) Boston: Little Brown; London: Butterworth, 1924.

The Slave Ship (1924) Boston: Little Brown; London: Butterworth, 1925.

The Great Valley (1926) Boston: Little Brown; London: Butterworth.

The Exile (1927) Boston: Little Brown; London: Butterworth.

Hunting Shirt (1931) Boston: Little Brown; London: Butterworth, 1932.

Miss Delicia Allen (1933) Boston: Little Brown; London: Butterworth.

Drury Randall (1934) Boston: Little Brown; London: Butterworth, 1935.

www.ingramcontent.com/pod-product-compliance
Lightning Source LLC
Chambersburg PA
CBHW030424310726
48979CB00009B/1600/J

9781932490169